I Laughed the Day
I Died

J R McDowell

Published by J R McDowell

Published by J R McDowell

ISBN (10 digit) 0-9551341-0-2

ISBN (13 digit) 978-0-9551341-0-4

A CIP catalogue record for this book is available from the British Library.

Prepared by York Publishing Services Ltd,
64 Hallfield Road, Layerthorpe, York YO31 7ZQ
Website: www.yps-publishing.co.uk

Printed and bound in Great Britain by Cox & Wyman Limited,
Cardiff Road, Reading, Berkshire, RG1 8EX
Email: coxandwyman@cpi-group.co.uk

ACKNOWLEDGEMENTS

The idea for this story would not have come to pass if it hadn't been for two of my colleagues at work, John Krol and Tim Wilding. From a brief conversation between us regarding reincarnation this unexpected ghost story came to life. I can't thank them enough. And thanks John, for all the answers to my questions.

Special thanks are also deserved by my friend, Jana Tomašová, for all the help she has given me …

Ian Coult for being a pain in the neck with his criticism, but he was right …

Mick Hynds for his music which helped me think while driving up and down the Northern Line …

Duncan Beal at York Publishing Services for his help and advice …

My thanks also go to my friends on London Underground for all their encouragement. It was a pleasure to watch them read some of the passages from the book. I especially want to mention Denis (Nobby) Law for being as funny as he is …

And, of course, I thank my family for putting up with me and my absence from their everyday life.

For Frankie

My loving and extremely funny story-telling sister.
If, Frankie, you've returned as a ghost then
I hope you enjoy the finished article.

CHAPTER ONE

I am beside myself, laughing my head off.

It was all I'd ever dreamt of, while I was alive. Now, I can go anywhere and everywhere, and do everything I want to, and nobody can stop me enjoying myself. To say I am over the moon is an understatement.

I'd been pronounced, officially, dead about twenty minutes ago. The reason it took so long to clear my thoughts is that I'd, actually, died four times on the operating table before the surgeons gave up on me. In a way, I'm sorry to see myself go ... and in such tragic circumstances.

I've had a gay life of sorts, but now I know that I'll have an even gayer one. I don't really believe in reincarnation, and I don't suppose being a ghost counts, but if there is such a thing, then it was more than likely that I'd return as a cat, a dog, or, better still, a fly on the wall. But I'd always had this great desire to be a ghost and, quite often, I'd go to bed with this on my mind.

I'm in heaven. Just think ... doors will be no barrier to me, walls will have no meaning, and I can flit from one bedroom to the next, from house to house and city to city. I might, even, contemplate living in higher circles for a while – at their cocktail parties, or with the horsey set. I hear that they get up to a trick or two. I wouldn't fancy visiting places like prisons – I believe they're a bit rough. Ooh! I don't know, though.

I'd only been talking about people dying, a few days ago. This guy said that if I ever came back from the dead and had the choice, then I'd want to be a ghost, and it's so uncanny ... I'm here, and I'm going to enjoy my new found ghostliness.

I was neither young nor old, but I wouldn't have wanted to stay alive, anyway, after the accident I was involved in. You see, my body is in a terrible state. There's a bloody awful mess in my groin where my best feature once existed. Well, I'd like to think so.

I'd been driving along one of the quiet, country, Newmarket roads in my Mini with my friend Evelyn sitting beside me. No, that's not strictly true, because Evelyn's face was in my lap, giving me the thrill of a lifetime ... and the car was still moving. At the critical moment, I couldn't control my excitement and I grabbed Evelyn's head ... and the car ploughed straight into an oak tree.

1

Poor Evelyn choked to death ... and I'd just lost two of my best friends. I wouldn't want to be alive, knowing my sex life was ruined forever and with thoughts, only, of what might have been. Evelyn was pronounced dead at the scene and I was rushed here, where the surgeons tried all sorts of unpleasant things on my body ... all to no avail.

You might well wonder how I know what happened, but the thing is that I was watching and listening to the gossip ... each of the four times I died in this operating theatre. How they laughed about me and Evelyn afterwards, and I bet their friends and relatives will have fits when they hear the story. But I have news for them. As a ghost, I've returned as a whole person, with my tackle fully intact. Looking down at my pride and joy, I can't keep the grin off my face.

I don't know what happened to Evelyn after he choked to death. If he's a ghost somewhere, I might meet him, but if he's come back as anything else, it might as well be a Jaws look-alike after what he did to me.

Well, I'm standing here, gaping at my lifeless shape and wondering about what might have been. I won't miss work, although some of my former colleagues, certainly, gave me an uplift ... in more ways than one. Hmm ... I wonder if they'll miss me. I'll have to go up and see them sometime and, maybe, pay one or two a nocturnal visit, uninvited of course. I do like surprises; giving them and getting them.

I lift my hand up to adjust my glasses. Huh! They're not there, and, yet, I can see perfectly. It's just a natural reaction, I suppose. I'd been doing it most of my life and I wonder if I'll always keep doing it in death. I touch my eyes and, yes, I can feel them. Am I really dead? I lower my hand to my chin, and then my chest, and then my. ... Ah! ... Ah! It's there. I can feel it.

You might not understand this because some people say that seeing is believing, but believe me ... it's feeling what you can see that's important when you're a ghost. I place my hands over the whole of my body and everything's there, firm to the touch and not a bit lifeless. I look down at my naked body and its pink skin glows with excitement, and my thought-waves go into overdrive.

This could be better than I'd ever dreamt. I'd really thought that ghosts did not exist and that they were only a fanciful idea, but the reality of the situation is something quite different. My idea of a ghost was the same

2

as most people were led to believe – that a ghost is an apparition, and that ghosts float around and have no substance. At least, that's what I used to see in films and read about in books. Well, let me tell you … I can feel myself, and it's a really lovely feeling. And if I can, then so can other ghosts, wherever they may be … and I'm so excited.

It seems strange, really, talking about other ghosts. I'm here, inside a hospital, and you'd expect me to see some others around the place, especially in this room, but I don't. Look at it this way. Loads of people have died in hospitals over the years, including doctors, nurses and, of course, patients, so you'd think that there would be, at least, a few of their ghosts in here, but I can't see or sense any. I'll definitely have to do some poking around later on. I'm bound to find one somewhere.

Hang on! Something's happening.

It's me! They're moving my body. Two young nurses and a porter have just come in, and they're pushing me onto a trolley, and not very gently, either. What's the world coming to? They've got no respect for the dead these days. The sheet's fallen to the ground, and the porter is turning to one of the nurses – a small blonde one, and he's whispering something in her ear.

She's blushing, and gives him a dig in the ribs. *"Shut up, you little prick. From what I've heard … this guy's cock would be more use to you, than to me. And, apparently, it wasn't so small, either."* – I can't believe what she's just said … and out of the mouth of a nurse. And listening to her reminds me of Evelyn.

I watch while they re-cover my body with the sheet. They start pushing me away … that is, the trolley away, and I have to follow … don't I? This is, after all, a new experience for me, and I'm curious. I, sort of, slide along beside them as they make their way along the corridors. I know they can't see me or there would have been pandemonium, much earlier. The porter seems to be a sly little git … and I don't like him. He must have whispered something horrible about me or my body and I want to teach him a lesson, but what can I do?

Sliding up behind him, I push my hand forward, giving him a shove in the back. I don't, even, feel him, as my hand goes through his body, right up to my elbow. There's no reaction from him, at all. I don't understand this and wonder how I'm supposed to scare people if they don't know I'm here. I pull my arm back and as my hand comes into view, his body does a little shimmy. The two nurses turn and give him a funny look, little blondie saying,

"What's the matter, nerd? Got ants in your pants?" – Good for you, girl. She's got him taped.

"Shut up, you. I think I'm coming down with something," he replies.

"It serves you right; always talking behind people's backs." – I like her. At least she sticks up for herself.

I'm wondering about the effect I had on his body, but the strange thing is … I couldn't feel him or his clothes. I'd been thinking about getting something to wear, but now I know that I can't go covering myself with ordinary clothes. Having said that, it would look stupid, wouldn't it? Imagine me, walking around like the Invisible Man. It would scare people to death … or make them laugh. But surely ghosts don't go around without a stitch on, all the time for the whole ghostly world to see them? There has to be something, somewhere, or does there? I mean, I do like to go naked, sometimes, but not all the time, and, well, when you think about it, it's positively indecent. Besides, I don't want to be looking at lots of naked female ghosts, flaunting themselves in front of me. It'd put me off my breakfast.

The problem is that I'm new to this and although I'm excited, I'm also a wee bit apprehensive. I'm starting to have doubts about myself and my new found situation. I've got to ask myself some serious questions like – how long will I stay a ghost? Is it only until my body is buried, or cremated, and, then, that's it? I'm worrying myself to death now. Well, not quite to death – I've already done that.

You see, I don't want my dead self to be cremated, but I didn't specify it in my Will. I hope my sister has the good sense to bury me. After all, she'll inherit everything I've left, and quite a substantial lot it is. Oh god! I'd love to go back in time, if only for five minutes, and add a clause to my Will, stating my requirement for a nice cosy burial and for my body to be sprayed all over with Givenchy. My boyfriends always liked Givenchy. I'd like to think that if I'm buried, then my body will still be intact for some considerable time. Or else, I could insist that I was wrapped up like a Mummy, to make my body last even longer.

Isn't it strange, you know, what goes through your mind when you're dead … and a ghost, while looking at your former self being wheeled along on a trolley? I don't want a short life as a ghost. I've got so much

4

to do and see, and people to sleep with. I'd dreamt of this day many times – not the dying, but the coming back. Obviously, I didn't expect it to happen at all, but now that I'm here, I'd like to stay.

Eventually, we reach a dimly lit room underneath the main building. It doesn't have a sign outside saying it's the morgue, but as we go inside it is obvious. Along the walls are rows of slide-in boxes which hold the dead bodies until they are collected by the undertaker. I still can't see any other ghosts, and, of all places, I thought this would be the ideal room for a chance meeting. Perhaps there aren't many ghosts, or maybe everyone becomes one and they go somewhere else, quickly. You know, they don't hang around like stupid me. On the other hand, I might be the only ghost alive, and I don't like the idea of that.

I watch while my body is cleaned and then raised into one of the boxes. They push the box closed and then the two nurses and porter leave the room, shutting the door behind them. It seems such a final act for my poor dead body, and yet ... it isn't. There's still my funeral and I'm definitely going to it. I wouldn't miss it for the world. After all, I want to see who turns up and what they say about me; who really cared, and who will miss me. Of course, there'll always be those that turn up just for appearances sake. No, I'm not going to miss that part of my life and death and, right now, it seems the most important thing for me to think about. I've just watched my body get stuck in a box and I'm all alone in here.

Wait a minute! What about all the dead bodies in the other boxes? Surely, there can't be many here? And, what about Evelyn ... is he here as well? Perhaps he's gone straight to the mortuary. And where's his ghost, if he has one? It might still be down at the old oak tree, or it might have followed his body to ... wherever. I've no way of knowing. I'm going to look for the poor creature, anyway ... just in case.

Sliding over to the boxes on the wall, I push my head towards the first one. Huh! It won't go in. I try again, and again. I try a different box, then another and another, but still I can't get in. What's gone wrong? I know I put my arm into that stupid porter. I didn't imagine that. Let me think. Hmm ... . Perhaps I have to push my hand in first, so lifting up my arm, I try ... and I fail.

No! ... No! ... No! This can't be right. That's it then. I'm not going to hang around here, in this morbid place. I'm going to my sister's and I'll stay there until they bury me, and, maybe, a little while longer. I'm not, exactly, in any hurry to get anywhere, am I? At least, I'll feel a lot safer with Mary, and I'll be able to see and hear her. I know, deep down, that I can't go back to my house because I'd be as lonely there as I am here, and, after all, I need somewhere to relax and think. This isn't how ghosts are supposed to be ... surely?

I slide to the door and try pushing through, but I can't. I push against the wall, but there seems to be an invisible barrier that is stopping me penetrating anything solid. I look around the walls and then up at the ceiling. It's the only thing I haven't tried, so lifting my arms like Superman, I push myself off the floor. I start moving upwards and then stop. I'm about two feet off the floor, with my arms still raised, and I look down and around to see what's holding me. There's nothing there, so I push and stretch again, but it still doesn't work. Defeated, I sink to the ground.

Why can't I fly? All ghosts can fly – I've seen them. Oh, my god! Panicking, I slide to another wall, putting more effort into what I'm doing and when that fails, I try another and another, and all the time I'm becoming more frantic. What am I going to do? How did I let myself get trapped in here? I'm stupid. I should have followed that stupid porter. Everything is stupid.

Think, you stupid ghost, think, and as I listen to myself, I calm down a little. Okay, let's be rational about this. It's very late, now, so I'm pretty sure that the undertaker won't be coming here until the morning, and, unless another dead body turns up very shortly ... that's it. I'll be bloody stuck in this damn room for the night. At least it's only hours I'll be waiting and not days.

Jeez! What a way to start being a ghost? I'm beginning to think that my new career is not as easy as I'd dreamt. I can't even slide through walls. Some ghost!

CHAPTER TWO

Sitting down on my hunkers, I put my head in my hands. I feel really uncomfortable with myself for the first time in my new life. Talk about depressed, hunched down and completely naked ... I am so alone. I don't even know if I can talk. I have nobody to talk to anyway. Well, I suppose I've plenty of bodies in the boxes, but they're a dead loss. I shout out, "Is there anybody there?"

What do I hear?

Nothing. Nada. ... Yes, I do. I can hear myself, but I can't hear another damn thing, so I resign myself to waiting for the morning. Someone's bound to come in and when they open the door, I'll be out in a flash and they'll never trap me in a confined space like this again.

Something's wrong here. Why can't I walk like everybody else? I seem to slide everywhere, and I begin humming to myself and wondering about ghosts being here, there and everyw ... hats that?

Hwooooosh!

My god, there it is again. Quickly standing, I half-shout, nervously, "H..Hello! ... Hello!"

"You don't need to yell, you know," says an extremely soft voice, from above me.

I angle my head slowly upwards and see a young man, obviously another ghost, floating in mid air. I'm most definitely afraid, and, with this chap hovering over my head and the fact that he can get through walls, I'm a little curious. What's more, he has more clothes than I do – a lot more.

"H ... h.hello," I say again, almost in a whisper. "Who are you?"

The ghost lowers himself to my level and I'm afraid to move. He places his right hand on my shoulder and calmly turns me towards him. The warmest blue eyes that I've ever seen in my life seem to melt into mine, as he answers, "My name is Simon. I know you're scared but I'm not here to hurt you." His mouth opens into a lovely, yet cheeky smile, as he goes on, "I am here to give relief."

My eyes open in surprise and a naughty little grin spreads across my face, as I ask, "Relief?"

My god! He's gay. He's certainly pretty enough ... and so young, and still smiling at me. He has such wonderful teeth. And then, very sexily

7

and so softly, he moves forward a touch, whispering into my ear, "Yes, relief."

I'm on cloud nine. Can you believe that? Imagine being trapped somewhere dark and so alone, and then this Adonis appears and wants to give you the thrill of a lifetime.

Slowly, lifting his other hand, he reaches out towards my body, but doesn't quite touch me. He lowers his head, his eyes on my body, and I know what he's looking at. He holds his stare for what seems an eternity – watching me grow … and grow, and then, without lifting his head, he laughs and says, "I am your Reliever but, by the looks of it, I'm not the kind you need."

My smile slowly vanishes, as he continues, "I'm here to get you out of this place. I'll take you wherever you want to go and stay until your body has been buried. Then, I'll come back and collect you from the graveyard … after your funeral of course. Mind you, if you don't want to go to your funeral, I'll take you with me now." Gesturing, he swings his arm around the room. "You see, lots of new ghosts end up in morgues like this, and also in undertakers, tombs and other miserable buildings that they can't escape from. That's why ghosts like me are sent to assist, as and when we're needed. We are called Ghost Relievers."

I'd been fully erect a moment earlier, but now I can feel myself starting to droop. "Okay. I understand," I acknowledge. "So, how am I supposed to get out of here? I've tried and tried, but I just can't."

"You don't have to worry, that's up to me." He pulls his other hand from my shoulder and steps slightly away, letting me have a good look at him. He walked. … I saw him walk.

Simon has short, but well styled, blonde hair and his eyebrows are just a tiny shade darker. He's about five feet ten – the same as me, and he's so slim and lovely. I don't know, but perhaps it's my age that's put him off and more than likely he likes younger men. Simon can't be a day more than twenty and I begin to wonder how he'd died. He's such a young man. His clothes, an aqua-marine colour, are a perfect fit, but perhaps these are a standard ghost issue and every ghost gets the same. I do like his shoes though – so fashionable, and they look like real leather.

Simon's watching me studying him, and he still has that cheeky little smile on his face. Perhaps he does fancy me, just a tiny bit. Maybe he has another boyfriend somewhere else, or, more likely, a girl. And thinking of this is making me feel depressed. "I'm sorry, Simon. I seem so down at the moment. Look, is there any chance of getting me some clothes – some jeans and a jumper like yours, perhaps? I don't fancy hanging around my sister's place like this," I add, using my hands and eyes to point to my naked body.

"Of course I will, Mick. As soon as we leave here, I'll take you shopping."

I look at his face inquisitively. "Simon, tell me, how do you know my name?"

"In exactly the same way that we knew you were here ... and when you died, and, of course, how you died. Tsk, tsk. ... Nasty," he replies. "And, may I add, if you hadn't picked Evelyn up tonight ... you wouldn't be here. It was his time, not yours. We all have our time to die and Evelyn was supposed to choke on his food. But, there again, you wouldn't have known that he was dreaming of chewing on one of those great big German sausages when he was, ah, well, how shall I put it ... .?"

"The bastard! The dirty rotten little bastard! Where is he? I'll kill him!"

"Too late for that now, I'm afraid, but, to answer your question, at this precise moment, Evelyn is an egg in some farmyard in Norfolk."

"He's a what?"

"An egg! You know ... an egg. He'll probably be collected tomorrow and end up as someone's breakfast in the not too distant future."

"You mean to tell me that he dreamt of coming back as a chicken? I don't believe a word of it."

"No, he didn't. The thing is, as far as I'm aware, he didn't dream of coming back as anything, but we all have to come back as something, Mick, to keep the cycle going. Strange, isn't it?"

"Well! He deserved it." My eyes glance down between my legs. "A sausage, indeed? That'll teach him."

"Come on Mick, let's get out of here; it's too depressing. It's knockin' the stuffing out of my system."

"Alright, so how do we go about this?"

"All you have to do is hold my hand very gently, but don't let go ... . Okay?"

"Okay." So I take his hand and he eases his way upwards, with me in tow. When we reach the ceiling I shut my eyes, afraid of bumping into the plaster, tiles, or anything else that might be there. We float through the lot, and within seconds we're sky high and speeding towards Newmarket High Street – my eyes, once again, wide open. We come to an abrupt stop in mid air, but I don't feel any sort of jolt at all. Simon lowers us through a roof, an upstairs room, and on down until we settle on the shop floor. I immediately recognise the inside of Fergie's Fashion House.

"How did we do that?" I ask.

"Never mind for now, you'll learn that at Uni'."

"Uni'? … University?"

"Yes. All new ghosts have to go. How do you expect to fly on your own or pass through walls? That is what you want, isn't it?"

Keeping mum, I study Simon's face and am quite happy to let him guide me through the art of ghost shopping. I can't fathom out why the lights are on in the shop. It's the middle of the night and the shop is supposed to be closed. Although Fergie's is a real life clothes shop, which I used when I was alive, it also exists as a ghost shop, with the same clothes I would normally have worn, except that some of these are ghost clothes. There are so many of them hanging about the place that I'm spoilt for choice. There are even some old-fashioned clothes, going back at least fifty years. Fergie's definitely didn't have these on show when I last shopped there, and that was only a couple of weeks ago.

While I'm looking over these relics, I remember my dad and the time he came home from work with a Beatles haircut, and my mum went spare. He'd only gone and bought himself the suit that went with the haircut, and she was laying into him and telling him he should grow up. It was my dad who got me into all The Beatles' songs, back then – I must have been seven or eight, at the time – and I start singing their song … *Love Me Do*.

"Shush! Will you keep quiet? And hurry up with those clothes," Simon orders. So I stop singing, but carry on humming quietly as I check out the goods. After browsing for a while, I choose a pair of grey slacks, some socks, boxer shorts and a shirt.

"And don't forget your shoes."

When I hear his voice, I automatically look over and, at that very moment, he's pushing down his jeans. I'm gobsmacked. He has no underpants on, and … he's huge. And I can't take my eyes off him. All I

10

want, right this second, is to go over and touch him, but do I dare? I'm in love again. I'm in love with a ghost and I can feel the ache between my legs.

Simon looks at me, throws his head back and grins ... a massive come-and-get-me grin. He watches me staring and then laughs a really loud and dirty laugh. He picks up a new pair of jeans – this time dark blue, and pulls them up very slowly, teasing me and deliberately fondling himself, until he squeezes into them. Then, still laughing, he just turns away and shrugs his shoulders.

I can't concentrate on anything. I'm still in a wonderful state of shock and I can't do a thing about it. I stand there for a while, but eventually I snap out of my trance. I know I'd better get my clothes on. I pick a nice pair of brown leather boots and then choose a very warm looking jumper. Slipping into the clothes, I suddenly feel like a whole new person, and this wonderful sensation courses through my body. I slide over to a long dressing mirror, in one of the corners, and admire myself in my new found ghostliness.

I can't believe what I see. I've lost more than twenty years off my other life in my death. From being a middle aged man of forty-eight with receding and greying hair, I've turned into a reasonably handsome twenty-five year old ghost with dark brown spiky hair which needs the use of a comb. I don't understand why my hair is so messy – and where did the spikes come from? I check out my face, and all the wrinkles have disappeared, and my double chin has changed back to the single one I remember from my youth. Even the whites of my eyes sparkle clear and free of any bloodshot, and this in turn makes my deep brown eye colouring glisten. I turn around and check over the shelves, nearby. I can't see any combs, so I slide along the shop floor, trying, but failing, to open the drawers. Simon comes over, placing his hand on my arm, and asks, "What are you looking for?"

"A comb."

"Hang on. Let me do it."

He moves in front of me and lays his hands on the top of my head. He gently strokes my hair, first one way and then the other. It's such an odd feeling and my head seems to be getting heavier and then lighter, then heavier, then lighter. He searches my face and then winks at me. He leans so close that I want to grab him.

"Mick, please close your eyes and keep them closed until I say otherwise."

"Yes, Simon, I will." And I do, as I imagine him being with me for the rest of my life. Simon places his lips on mine and softly kisses me. He opens my mouth with his tongue and I feel the most delightful sensation as he moves it around inside. I nearly faint with the sheer ecstasy of his kiss, and I start kissing him back. He doesn't try to stop me, so I lift my hands to his face, wanting to kiss him even deeper, but he pulls away … so fast that I'm shaken. His hands fall from my head and, putting one of them in one of mine, he leads me along the floor, turns and positions me, and, giving my shoulder a friendly squeeze, he says, "Now, you can look."

My eyes open and the reflection from the mirror is unbelievable, so much so that I could fancy myself. My hair is slightly longer but it looks really cool and fashionable. I smile and let my tongue run over my teeth. Opening my mouth wide, I'm amazed to see how beautiful they are, and I push my lips up and back, on both sides, to inspect my teeth further. This can't be true – not one false tooth and not a filling to be seen. I've got a perfect set. Things are getting better by the minute and I love the feeling. I can honestly tell you, I'm a better looking ghost now, than I ever was a real man of twenty-five. I want to kiss Simon again.

"Come on, Mick," he encourages me. "Stop flirting with yourself and let's get going. There's a lot more work to do and I'm running out of time."

"Why? What do you mean by running out of time?"

"I have another relieving to do, in Norwich. As soon as I drop you at your sister's, you'll have to look after yourself, until Friday."

"Why Friday?"

"Your funeral, stupid! And don't forget that you can't get through walls yet, but those boots I just bought will help you to walk. So practise, okay?"

"Yes, dear."

"Now don't start getting fresh with me, Mick. I am not gay and it doesn't bode well for you to be saying, or doing, the wrong thing to the wrong ghost. You'll end up regretting it, so be warned. I'm here to help you and not every ghost will. They're not all as nice as me."

I'm dumbstruck and stand still, reflecting on what's just been said. I honestly thought that he was gay – the way he kissed me and the way he looked at me. He had a hard on, and I thought it was because he'd seen me naked. I had visions of him being my first ghost, but now ... I'm shattered. I don't feel I know him at all, but I think I still love him.

Simon stretches out his hand, once more taking mine. We leave the shop through the door and I don't say anything until we start flying. "Oh, Simon! My sister ... she lives in Ely. I'll show you when we get there."

"I know, Mick. I've been given all the instructions I need. Will you just stop worrying?"

"Okay, but wait a sec', there's something else bothering me."

I'm still clinging to his hand as he smiles at me, saying, "And what's that, Mick?"

"Simon, can you tell me why I'll regret it?"

"Regret what?"

"You said that I'd regret saying or doi ... ."

"Oh, that! The simple answer, I suppose, is for me to ask you a simple question."

"You want to ask me a question?" I ask, and he nods, a funny look on his face.

"Do you want to end up as an egg sandwich in somebody's lunchbox ... yes or no?"

I think for a few seconds before answering. "No ... er, no, I don't." I don't know, as yet, how this could possibly happen, but I'll make it my business to find out. I don't want it happening to me. Now, having a lot more to reflect on, my mind starts wandering back to the oak tree. The mere thought of Evelyn being served up with bacon and sausage doesn't amuse me in the slightest.

We fly on, and shortly after we start slowing down and dropping from the sky. Simon guides us to the island and goes directly to Mary's house. We hover outside for a minute, and then he pulls me through the wall and straight into the spare bedroom. How did he know which one was empty? It doesn't make sense.

"I like this room. It's so fresh and airy," observes Simon, "and it has some lovely colour tones."

"I agree. Mary's pretty handy at the old decorating lark."

Simon releases me and moves around the room, sometimes walking and sometimes floating. Stopping by the side of the bed, he turns about and sits down. Then, grinning, he pats the bed covers beside him, beckoning me over to try it out. Is this it then? Is this what he's been waiting for, all this time … to make love to me in my own sister's house? Yes. I know it is, and I'm happy once more.

I move towards the bed and, standing directly in front of him, reach out for his hands. Simon takes mine and then stands up, pulling my body gently towards his. He puts his beautiful lips on mine, this time giving them a little suck. He opens his mouth, still kissing, but sucking a little harder. I'm going crazy with happiness and getting harder by the second, and, just like that, he pulls away again. He is still holding my hands. And I'm so frustrated.

"Why?" I ask, a lump in my throat.

He smiles sweetly, saying, "That'll have to do for now, Mick. I have to go to work." He looks down and grips me firmly, adding, "One other thing. I must insist that you keep very quiet while you're here, and make sure you get a complete rest. You're going to need it." Simon lets go, walks to the window, and then waves as he eases through the glass. I mouth my goodbyes as I watch him float away, disappearing into the night.

I think about my lovely Simon and what he did for me and to me. I won't see him 'til Friday, at my funeral, and it isn't soon enough.

CHAPTER THREE

Lying here on the floor, picturing Simon in that shop and in this very room, I can't help it … I start touching myself. I gently rub my hands around my groin and then another memory flashes before my eyes – the terrible state my body was in. And all that blood.

Evelyn? Why couldn't he wait until we were back at my place? He was always so impatient. I can't say I wasn't enjoying it, but if only we'd known the consequences. This thought makes me pull my hands away from my naked body, and I try thinking of something else. I wonder about my new ghost clothes and whether they'd have creased. I'd taken them off because it was the natural thing for me to do, and does it really matter? Who's going to see me here, anyway, naked or not … and I smile? Perhaps I should go to Fergie's and get some more clothes. After all, I'll need something different for my funeral; maybe a new suit.

You might be wondering why I'm on the floor, but when I tried sleeping on the bed I sank through the sheets … and the mattress, and I only stopped when my body reached the wooden base. I was, and still am, confused. When Simon had sat there he didn't sink in, so why should I? And I don't have any covers on me. My hands had slipped through them when I tried to pick them up.

I have to ask myself some questions, such as – how come I can put my hands, and now my backside, through clothes, other materials, and through the porter, but not through solids? Can I even turn the door handle to get out of here? I don't want to be trapped, but I suppose that's hardly likely. Mary is bound to come in for something – maybe to use her computer, which is sitting on its desk, in the corner. Looking at the computer reminds me of Simon, and him saying that I'd learn all about this going-through-the-walls business at University, but what University, and where is it? Surely, it can't be a ghost Cambridge College like that ghost clothes shop? That's too stupid for any ghost to believe.

And why don't I feel hungry, or don't want to go to the loo? You know something … I don't even sweat. I wonder whether I can feel water, have a wash or, being a ghost, do I even need one? I sniff underneath my arms. Hmm, they seem okay to me but, there again, what's a ghost supposed to smell like? I didn't smell Simon, either, when he was so close to me, but, having said that, I wasn't thinking of smelling him; my mind was on something else at the time. The funny thing is, I don't even know if my nose actually smells – you know, does the job it's meant to. And another thing – my mouth is slightly moist all the time, in a nice tingly sort of way. It's been like that, ever since Simon first kissed me.

"Oh, my dear, dear Simon, I've got so many questions to ask you."

And Evelyn? Is he going to be fried, or boiled, or poached, or … .? Hang on a minute! If he's going to be taken from his hen tomorrow, then Evelyn will die again – that's obvious. Does he then come back as another egg or something completely different? Perhaps he won't come back at all. That's another answer needed from Simon on Friday. He's got to give me some info', surely? He can't leave everything for the Uni'.

"What the hell's that?" I can hear a tap, tap, tapping on the window. The noise is getting louder and more consistent.

"Hailstones!" I remember, now, checking the weather reports. I had to. It was part of my job. The experts said it would get very cold, with the possibility of snow. And thinking of snow, it makes me want to shiver, but I'm not cold and, come to that, I don't feel any warmth either. I have such an unfeeling feeling, and, yet, I know that my mind works just as it always had.

I wonder who's going to get my job. They'll probably give it to my assistant, Stan. He's on the ball, but, there again, they might bring someone in from outside. There's quite a lot of that going on these days. Anyway, why should I worry now? Give them a few weeks and they'll have forgotten all about me, especially with the amount of work they have to do.

I'd been working at Stansted – in the offices. I was a communications manager, liaising with other departments and airports about traffic flow; getting the planes in and out, supposedly on schedule; keeping up to date information regarding the weather, and any other problems that might interfere with the running of the place. I had a very responsible position and I enjoyed the variety it gave me. It also gave me the opportunity to mix with lots of different people, and many a time I met someone who took my fancy. It was quite rewarding … in more ways than one.

One thing's for sure, though … I've got to get some sleep. I can't spend the rest of my ghost life thinking about this and that – it'll drive me mad. I don't know if I can sleep, although Simon did tell me to rest up for a few days, but why was he so insistent?

I can't stay shut up in here for the next three days, just resting – it will do my head in. I, obviously, have a brain of some kind because I can see and hear things, use my imagination, and I can move around. I just can't go through walls and a few other little things. I mean, once I do learn how to fly and go through solids, I'll be laughing. I won't need the Uni' or Simon then, will I? I'll carry on doing the things I want to do; all those lovely things I dreamt about.

I must stop thinking, but I can't. The biggest problem I seem to have is that I'm lying here, on the floor but I don't feel the damn floor and I don't go through it. It doesn't make any sense. It's like being suspended in mid air, and yet I'm feeling comfortable. It's like lying on an air bed without the bed. And what happens when I do learn to go through solids? Will I fall through the floor and then keep going down and down and never stop? That can't be right, because Simon didn't. He was able to walk around the shop and he was standing on the ground in the morgue, and in this very room. Well, if he can then so can I, and the sooner the better. At least the thought of this has taken the weight off my mind. Turning to face the window, I try to relax. I close my eyes and make some effort to sleep.

What seems like five seconds later, I open them again and I can see light. You won't believe this but it's morning. I remember shutting my eyes and telling myself … sleep, sleep, for god's sake sleep, and then … nothing. I don't remember a thing after that. I'm awake and it's broad daylight outside. I've absolutely no idea of the time, but who cares. I don't have to go to work, do I? After all, I'm dead and I'm a ghost. I get up, stretch myself, and then pick up my clothes.

Before putting my socks on, I give them a big sniff. Aah! … Nothing! They're okay then – fresh as a daisy. I'd like to think so anyway, and it's certainly a lot different from the past. I wouldn't have dared to stick those socks anywhere near my face. My feet were terrible. I'd have to wash them and change the socks three times a day. I tried everything known to man, believe me. They used to stink something rotten when I was younger, and someone once told me that it must be my hormones and that I must have a high sex drive. Well, I'd like to think so, but they still smelled awful. Sometimes, I'd throw the socks away rather than stick them in with the rest of the washing. It might have seemed a waste, but it was probably worth it in the long run.

Finally, I slip the jumper over my head and slide to the window for a gander at the world from a ghost's angle. I've left my boots off for now. After all, I'm not going outside just yet, and it's just as well.

Would you look at that? ... White everywhere. A heavy frost has settled in, and I'm telling you that I won't be the only one sliding around today. I watch the people for a while, some going to work, others with their dogs, and I wonder if animals really can sense the presence of someone like me. I smile at the thought. If I could get outside, this very second, I'd prove it once and for all. I wonder if my sister will go out in this weather.

And what about Mary? Have they told her about me yet? I suppose it's hard to tell, but I doubt it. We'd had the crash late yesterday evening. It must have been ten o'clock, or thereabouts. I'm guessing that, by the time they'd pronounced me dead, it would have been too late to get in touch with her. You see, I'd never ever carried any of Mary's details with me. I had no reason to, so the police, or whoever else it is that deals with that sort of thing, would have had to go to my address. It would definitely take some time and, knowing the circumstances of my death, they'd probably wait until today to tell her. That's what I'd do and, no doubt, that's what they'll do.

Uh, huh! I can hear the telephone ring – once, twice, thrice, four, five, si ... .

"Hello," I hear Mary answer, quietly. Well, it seems quiet, with this door being closed.

"Yes, I heard last night," she says.

She goes on. *"No, I couldn't do anything when they told me. They said it was quick and that he didn't suffer."*

"Yes, I will. Hang on for just a minute. No, wait ... I'll ring you back."

"Yes, straight back. Look, let me go for a pee or I'll wet myself. Yes! I promise." How wrong can a ghost be? Didn't suffer! That's an understatement.

I can tell you ... it's not that easy trying to understand a one sided call, but that one I could. I can hear Mary dashing to the loo. Come on

Mary, hurry up. I'm keeping my fingers crossed that she just might open this door. I hear her flush the toilet and now the water is running. It's stopped. It's started again. My god … what's she doing in there? It stops again after another few minutes and she's walking, walking, and … damn it, she's going downstairs.

How am I supposed to hear anything, now? I slide to the seat by the computer and sit down. Oh, what the hell, I might as well check out the things on her desk while I'm here. I know I'm nosy, but how do you expect me to keep tabs on my funeral. I put my hand out to pick up a copy of an email, but stop. I realise that I can't feel it, so why bother. I read it anyway.

It's from Samantha, her daughter. She's a sweet girl, and clever too.

'Hi Mum,
Just a line to let you know we'll be arriving at Heathrow, Terminal
4, on Thursday. Plane's due in at 3.15pm. Hope it's on time and
we don't keep you waiting. We've had a grate holday and I'll tell
you all about it just as soon as we see you. I've got some brill'
news for you – it's a surprise.
Love, Sam and Jack xxxx.'

Great! I can't wait until Thursday. … Holday! I can excuse that one; it could easily be a typing error, but not the other. I really don't know what they teach them in school these days. School! … Sam's at Oxford now. I hope she's not going to teach English.

How's Mary going to tell her about me? One thing's for certain … I won't be going with her to collect them because I've decided to go to Newmarket for that suit. There are bound to be people calling here on Thursday, asking questions and consoling her, so Mary will have to open this door before then, and I'll be out of here as fast as my legs can slide me. I might even be walking by then. She'll probably have some other visitors, as well, so I'll be able to come and go as I please. Hmm, that's better. I'm thinking more sensibly now. It's marvellous what a night's sleep does for you – if it was sleep.

I hear footsteps on the stairs. Mary's on her way up and she's talking on her mobile. I can only hear her mumble the odd word, unfortunately. Come on Mary, come this way. Closer, closer, closer … and she's passed. Wait a sec' … she's coming back.

"Yes! Yes! Yes!" I shout.

She walks in, barefoot. Yuck! Mary is wearing a full length orange housecoat. What a horrible colour. Whoever she was talking to has gone, and her mobile is dangling from a strap around her fingers. She goes to a closet in the corner and, while she's busy doing that, I'm sliding over to the door. Keeping my eye on her, I see that she's picked out a dark blue suit. She turns, with the suit over her arm, and goes to the desk. She picks up the email I've just read and carries it and the suit towards the door.

Backing onto the landing, I wait at the top of the stairs. What's she going to do now? She's left the door to my room open – which is a blessing, and is going into her own bedroom. Mary throws the suit on the bed, lifts the email … and reads it.

"Oh, Mick, you bastard! Why did you have to go and die now;" she asks me, *"just when Sam's coming back from holiday? Didn't you know she was getting engaged?"* She shakes her head, drops the letter on top of the suit, and turns to me. She stands there for a minute, and I can see that it's crying time again as the tears run down her cheeks. A lump comes to my throat and I want to cry myself, but I can't. We were very close as children. I was only a year older than her.

Mary comes out of the room and walks straight towards me. I thought she was going to walk right through me, but she turns to the bathroom, goes in, and shuts the door slightly. She's a bit like me, I suppose. What's the point in closing doors when you're on your own? Brian, her ex, left her four years ago for another woman, eleven years younger. Mary went through a really bad time and it's only in the last year that she started going out on the odd date.

I think back to when we were teenagers. There was this place we used to go to. I'd go off with some mates playing football. We all used to pretend to be a top player and I used to be Peter Lorimer from Leeds United. When we'd finished playing, we'd go messing around with and teasing the girls. If the weather was fine, we'd find them sitting on some huge stones on a local hillside. Sometimes they'd be lying down and we'd sneak up on them.

One particular day – Mary would have been about sixteen or seventeen at the time – she and two of her friends, Liz and … and … drat, I've forgotten the other one; well anyway, they were lying down on their bellies, looking up the hill. We were slowly creeping up behind them and, as we got closer, we could see them peeping at someone or something, and we could hear them sniggering. So, being inquisitive, naturally, we crept back down, went to the other side of the hill and came across from there. We knew that the girls couldn't see us, but we could see them, and we could see what they were looking at and why they were getting so excited. We lay very quietly and watched both parties.

It was a man, in his thirties or forties, who was well known, in the area, for doing what he was doing at that particular moment. No wonder Mary and her friends were keeping the noise down. It was Dave the wanker, and he was looking at something and playing with himself, at the same time. He was given that name purely by reputation. Anyway, to cut a long story short, Dave was there with his hand going up and down, when two older and bigger lads came along the top of the hill and saw what was going on. They could also see us from their vantage point. We watched them both stoop down and pick something up.

That was it. ... They ran at Dave, throwing stones and shouting, "Dave, you dirty bastard. Fu ... "

"Hey, what's going on?" I ask myself, and try again. "Fu ... . Fu ... . I can't say fu ... ." I don't understand. Oh, never mind, I'll come back to this later.

On with the story. These lads were telling him, in an impolite way ... "go away you wanker." They chased Dave down the hill, past the girls and out of sight. I'd never seen anyone get up and run so fast, with one hand trying to stick his knob back in his trousers and his other held up, behind his head, trying to ward off the barrage of stones. We pissed ourselves laughing. We stood up and saw the girls, who were now turned the other way, sitting on the grass and watching the chase. We went over and joined them, all of us still roaring with laughter. I can tell you ... we cried ourselves laughing. I used to take the mickey out of Mary and her friends, for a long time afterwards. That is until the day she found out I was gay, and then the boot was on the other foot for a while.

I can hear the bath running, so I slide down the stairs for a nose around. No point in being up there while she's washing herself, I've seen it all before. Then, I have a brainwave, so sliding back upstairs, I go into the spare room, grab my boots and skedaddle back down again, placing them by the front door. Well, it's not as if they're going to trip anybody up, is it? It's just a precautionary move on my part. If Mary has to go out to the shops for something, I might as well tag along to get some walking practise.

Both the living room and kitchen doors are open, but which do I choose first? It has to be the kitchen; just a quick look and I'll be out again. I go in and see what kept Mary down here for so long. The nearly empty cup of coffee is still standing beside a plate, which has some half-eaten toast on it. Mary has always been a tidy person. The times she used to tell me off for not bothering to carry cups back to the kitchen … and for not washing them. There's no way she'd have left them there all night. I take a look around and notice a small CD player on the shelf. There's nothing else of interest, so I slide to the living room.

This room is well decorated. She has a light green coloured carpet with an even lighter, and nearly matching, wallpaper; no flowers on it at all. Instead, a couple of well placed oil paintings hang either side of the fireplace. She has a lovely looking old gas fire but it's just for show, as Mary now has full central-heating. There are a few photos over the fire and around the other walls. I inspect one after the other, trying to remember when, and where, they were taken. There are some of Samantha, taken at different stages of her life. One of them is a photograph of Sam, Mary, and yours truly, when we all went to Versailles. In the picture, we're standing in the flower beds with the Palace directly behind us. I remember Brian nearly falling in the pond when he took that one.

I smile. I'm sure Sam was only ten or eleven, at the time, and I remember us going to visit Disneyland, in Paris, on that particular holiday. Mary doesn't have any photos of Brian, anymore. I didn't like him anyway. We'd had this blazing row about sex and freedom of choice, and he'd gone on about morality. We never really talked after that, except to please Mary.

There's a half-sized wall mirror behind the sofa and I move closer to admire myself. Sure enough, I see my reflection and my hair is still in place, and I smile again, thinking of Simon. I am so taken up with my own image that I don't hear Mary come down. She's still in her dressing gown. I don't move, but watch, as she walks right up beside me, lifts a brush she's carrying, and starts tidying her hair. I don't know how she keeps it so brown, unless it's from a bottle. Mary still looks fairly attractive for her age; mind you, she'd always kept herself in pretty good shape.

She obviously can't see or hear me. If she had, she'd have jumped and yelled when we were upstairs … and so would I. I look at her in the mirror, then at myself, and then back again. Mary, very quickly, turns and walks straight through my body. As she passes out of me, she stops, shrugs her shoulders a little, shakes her head, and then carries on. I felt the briefest of sensations at the exact moment that Mary was in my body … or was I in hers?

Hmm … I wonder, as Mary sits down by the hi-fi. She hasn't bothered buying one of the latest music systems. She told me, once, that she didn't like them very much, and that hers fitted in nicely with the furniture. She picks up a bag, from beside the sofa, and pulls out a small black book. Addresses and phone numbers; I know – I've seen it before. She begins searching through the pages … stops, picks up the phone and starts dialling. Here we go – relaying the bad news.

"Hi, it's me."

"I'm fine. Well, to tell the truth, I'm not. The thing is, Mick died last night and … ."

"A car crash." Mary begins to shed a tear.

"I don't know. I have to go to the hospital in Newmarket today, to identify him, and I'm already upset. Will you come with … .?"

"Thanks, Ben … you're a love. And will you do the driving? I really don't feel up … ." Why doesn't he let her finish a sentence?

"Okay, I'll see you soon. Love you! … By-ee!"

"Who's Ben?" I ask, staring quizzically at Mary. He must be another new boyfriend. I don't know … she'll be catching up on me soon. I know one thing though – I'm not going back to that bloody morgue. She's on the phone again. I do wish she'd bought a speaker-phone.

"Hi, Alice. Are you okay?"

"Not really, there's a lot to think about. And thanks for coming 'round last night."

"Yes, I did. There's only a drop left."

"There is, actually, if you don't mind. Can you, possibly, pick up Sam and Jack on Thursday afternoon?"

"That's great. It'll give me time to sort things out here. Oh, and, by the way, Ben is on his way over."

"Yes. He's taking me to see Mick."

"Yes. To identify him – you know; next of kin and all that."

"Okay. I'll give you a ring when I get back."

"By-ee!"

Alice has been Mary's best friend since college. I like her myself, but she used to pull my leg every now and then, especially when we all went out for a drink. When she could manage it, she'd deliberately sit with her arms around me and crack jokes about 'us girls'. And, other times, she'd put her hand in my lap, squeeze my knob, and suggest that we go back to her place for a bit of nookie, or else she'd make some other sexy comment. All the time, her husband would be there, watching and laughing. I used to wait at the bar until she was seated and then I'd deliberately sit on the other side of the table, but it didn't always work. All of Mary's friends knew I was gay, and they knew I knew, and that's why we got on so well.

Mary reaches across and turns on the hi-fi. After choosing a tape, she puts it in and presses the play button. A few seconds later I can hear The Rolling Stones singing their song *I can't get no, satisfaction.*

I don't join in. The Rolling Stones weren't one of my favourite bands when they first started out, but I've learnt to appreciate them over the years. Mary turns the volume down low, gets up, and goes to the kitchen. I can hear her filling the kettle, the splash of water, and then the noise of dishes being washed. I told you she was tidy. Going to a corner of the living room, I sit down on the floor, wrap my hands around my knees, and then lean back against the wall. I start to hum along with the song, nodding my head to the beat, and the phone rings. I hear Mary's voice straight away. Huh! I didn't see a phone in the kitchen. Jumping up as fast as I can, I slide to the door so I can listen. I've missed a bit.

"No, I can't. I'm sorry."

"I'll be back about three or four o'clock."

"Yes, if you bring them here. I can go over to my brother's, this evening, and sort something out."

"Okay ... about four. Goodbye."

What's that all about, and who was she talking to? If she's going to my place, she's not going without me, and that's for sure. It's just as well I didn't go chasing dogs – I'd have missed that phone call. I'm about to go back to my corner when it rings again. This time, I'm on the ball and outside the kitchen door when she answers. I knew it would get busy.

"Hello."

"*Oh hi, Joyce.*" Joyce is another of her close friends. She's quite a few years younger than Mary and a little bit flighty. I've met her several times at the pub, with Mary and Alice.

"*No, Joyce, I'm not. To tell you the truth, I'm a bit miserable. You wouldn't expect anything like this to happen, would you?*"

"*I'll be alright, but I'm a bit worried about Sam.*"

"*No. It's just that, you know, she loved Mick – we all did, but I don't know how she's going to take the news. I can't even get in touch with her.*"

"*No. She didn't say which hotel in San Francisco.*"

"*Hawaii, but I don't know which island they went to.*"

"*I know. The thing is, I'm going to be out most of today and if anyone calls at the house, I won't know about it, and if Sam phones, then I won't know that either, will I?*"

"*I should have. I keep putting it off.*"

"*Will you?*"

"*It won't mess you up … no?*"

"*Thanks, Joyce. You're an angel. By-ee!*" – Why do they always say 'by-ee'?

Mary makes some coffee and then I slide, ahead of her, back to the front room. She sits down in the same seat and sips her drink. The expression on her face changes several times while she thinks. Sometimes it's a frown and at other times a tiny smile appears … and then she laughs. How can she be laughing at a time like this? She finishes her coffee, leaving the empty cup on the carpet. She's not like the Mary I know. She gets up, walks out, and then runs up the stairs. I decide not to follow and sit down in my chosen spot, in the corner.

About ten minutes later, Mary comes back down holding something in her hand. Now dressed in the suit and a pair of black shoes, she goes up to the mirror, leans close to, and applies a little lipstick. She's just about finished when I hear a car pull up outside. Getting up, I slide to the window, avoiding all contact with Mary.

I don't know the man, but it must be Ben. He's tall and dark but definitely not handsome; at least, I don't think so. He's pushing the gate open when Joyce runs up behind, smacking him on the bum. He turns and smiles and they exchange a few words. A couple of minutes later, they walk up the path.

'Ding-Dong'

Mary's already gone. She'd heard the car and the banter outside, and I'm right behind her to see what goes on. Ben gives Mary a big hug and a peck on the cheek. – It doesn't look that serious to me.

"I'm so sorry," he says. She lets him pass into the hallway, and then Joyce does exactly the same. None of them have noticed my boots, and Ben even stood on one as he came in.

"I'm sorry, too. He was much too young to die. Oh, poor Mary."

Joyce hugs Mary again. There are a couple of tears rolling down her cheeks, and I think Joyce means it.

As Ben comes into the living room, I slide away, backwards, to my corner. I notice Mary and Joyce whispering in the hall and not long after, they join us.

"Sit down … I'll get us a drink," Mary offers.

"No, I don't want one, thanks. Not now," says Ben *"and besides, I'm driving."* Joyce looks at him, kind of funny; you know … funny weird.

"Tea or coffee, then?"

"No. No thanks. Nothing," he replies.

"Joyce?" Mary asks, pointing to the brandy.

"I will, but only if you're having one."

"You bet I am. I need it. There's some left over from last night."

"Last night?" quizzes Ben.

Mary, already at the drinks cabinet, is pouring out two big slugs of Remy when she answers him. *"Yes, last night. When the police came, I phoned Alice. They said they had bad news and that I should have someone with me. You can't imagine it, Ben. All sorts of things were going through my head. Sam … the plane … I didn't know what to think. I was so worried."*

"Why didn't you call me?" he asks, nervously.

"Ben, sometimes a woman needs to have another woman to hold her. Alice has been my friend for so many years and she's the first person I thought of." She passes Joyce her drink, and turns back to Ben. *"Samantha's not here and … and anyway, Alice knew Mick. Ben, you didn't know him at all."* I don't understand and I'm not sure that I want to. Why is she defending herself like this? She shouldn't have to. You'd think that he'd think before he speaks. I've decided … I don't like Ben.

26

"I'm so sorry, Mary, I didn't realise. And, yes, you are right … I didn't know Mick."

Joyce is watching and sipping, and still eyeing Ben weirdly. I'm watching too, as Ben closes on Mary and gives her another hug. Mary's tears start again. She lifts her spare hand and wipes them away, and then eases slowly back from him, softly saying, *"We have to be going. The police are coming here with Mick's keys and things this afternoon, and I'll have to go over to his house this evening."*

"We'll make it," he says, his eyes in Mary's, *"and, I suppose Joyce is here to keep an eye on the place. That's the plan, I take it?"* He is now looking at Joyce.

"Yes," Joyce answers. *"Now, go on … the pair of you."*

They all make a move, Joyce leading the way to the front door. I stay put and listen to their goodbyes, and then hear the door closing. Joyce comes back, goes straight to the brandy bottle, and pours herself another shot. I don't blame her. I'd have done the same thing myself.

I've always liked Joyce, and I study her as she changes the tape. I don't know her real taste in music because she used to sing along to anything in the pub. She presses the play button and I relax, hoping it's something good. I'm very happy with Joyce as we start listening to Bob Dylan singing *Absolutely Sweet Marie*. At this second in time, I'm watching Joyce's face as she turns to the hi-fi, giving it a what-the-hell-is-that look.

"Don't touch it. It's brilliant – leave it alone," I shout at her. While the first verse continues, she seems even more shocked, staring hard, with her mouth wide open, and she moves her arm towards the player. "No-o! Put it back on," I plead. She's stopped the tape and is looking through others. I drop my head in disappointment. "How can you not like Bob Dylan?" I ask her.

What's the point? I know she can't hear me, and I still have my eyes lowered when I hear The Rolling Stones, once more, singing *I can't get no satisfaction*. It's no wonder they're mates – same taste in booze, same taste in music. I stare at her and wonder. What if … .?

I stand up and slide in front of her. She's still holding her brandy as I crouch down and lift my hands. Smiling wickedly, I push them slowly towards her blouse. I watch her face and then wrap my hands around her boobs … and squeeze. My hands disappear.

And would you credit it? At exactly the same time as Mick Jagger is repeating *I can't get no satisfaction* ... what do I get? – The same.

Damn it! She's now looking straight at me, eyeball to eyeball, and hers – well, actually, they're quite lovely ... for a girl. I lower my eyes and study the connection. Boobs for hands? Nah! I don't think so. I look up at her face and very, very slowly pull back. Her eyes open wide, her mouth opens slightly, and then lifting her free hand she rubs it across her breasts. I now know that whatever she's feeling, it's only a sensation, but I don't know whether it's a discomfort to her, or a pleasure. I must ask Simon.

I think about my experience with Mary, and how she reacted when she walked through my body and, of course, the odd feeling that I had. I stand up and move away from Joyce while I consider what to do. Should I? Will I? ... You know what I'm thinking, don't you?

No. I think I'll wait. After all, I don't know if it might do some permanent damage to her, and Joyce is okay. She stands up, goes back to the brandy and refills her glass. She carries it to the window and is taking another swallow when another little melody can be heard. It's her mobile. Joyce takes the few steps to her bag, pulls out the phone, and answers.

"Hello, Harry."

"Yes, I am mad at you."

"No, I'm not bloody pregnant." I look at her, in amazement.

"Well, it's no thanks to you. Is it?"

"No, but you shouldn't have been so rough. It wouldn't have bloody well burst, would it?"

"On the pill! Why should I? You men – you make me bloody sick."

"It was your fault. Anyway, why should we women have to do everything? You could always get yourself a vasectomy."

"Children? You want children? You're not bloody havin' them with me, that's for sure. I don't want any little brats yet – I'm too bloody young."

"Get yourself someone else then."

"Well, okay then, but don't you ever go mentionin' kids again."

"No, I can't on Friday. Got this funeral to go to."

"Mary's brother."

"Are you? So why don't you come?"

"Yeah! There'll be plenty of drink there ... and it should be a gas. He

was gay, you know."

"Joyce, you don't have to tell everyone." Does she?

"Yeah! We can have a laugh. You know, see how many of his boyfriends turn up." And I thought you were nice. I can't believe she'd want to make fun of me.

"No. Don't you be mean to him. It was a crash. Killed on the spot, apparently. Well, that's what Mary said and, anyway, I happened to like Mick. If he wasn't the other way, I could've fancied him." – Hmm, well, that's okay then.

"Yes, I could. He had a good body on him. Hey, Harry, guess what?"

"I've got this weird feeling he's around here somewhere." My god! She did feel me.

Joyce laughs.

"I'm not stupid. Oh, never mind. I'll give you a ring to let you know."

"Okay. See you now. Bye."

Can you believe that? Joyce thinks I'm here – in spirit anyway. She replaces her phone, lifts her drink and throws the brandy back her throat. Joyce moves to the hi-fi and changes the tape; and then turning about, she rushes upstairs – to the loo, I suppose. While I'm thinking this, the tape starts. Perhaps she's psychic, because I'm now listening to Bob Dylan singing *I Want You*. And I'm going to keep a very close eye on Joyce.

I sit in my corner and can hear the toilet flush. A few minutes later, Joyce is back and topping up her glass. She relaxes on the sofa – her shoes off, and taking the odd sip. I lie back, relaxing and enjoying the music … and I fall asleep.

CHAPTER FOUR

It's Thursday evening and I'm looking out the window, remembering the events of the past couple of days. You may well be wondering what happened since Tuesday, when I fell asleep with Joyce. In actual fact, it was Joyce who woke me up ... with a bang.

My eyes opened to the noise of breaking crockery and an almighty scream from the kitchen. I went to investigate, as one would, and there sat Joyce, in the middle of a broken plateful of cheese and tomato sandwiches and a smashed coffee cup. She was sobbing and holding her left arm which was getting redder by the second. Joyce was soaked ... in more ways than one. Her eyes looked bleary from the brandy, and her blouse and skirt were wet through. She picked herself up, turned to the sink, and ran some cold water over her arm for a few minutes.

Joyce eventually got around to clearing the place up and then went upstairs to the bathroom. I was tempted to follow, and I did. I watched her throw off her blouse, bra' and skirt, and she then proceeded to wash her face and upper body.

If you must know, Joyce has a very firm body. For a woman, she is quite attractive. She has a cute face, long dark wavy hair, and an ample, yet very firm, pair of boobs. If I wasn't the way I am I could fancy her. With a body like hers, it's no wonder she doesn't want any kids.

While I watched, I thought again about entering her, just to see what would happen, but once more I relented. Nevertheless, I couldn't resist moving towards her, reaching out and tweaking her nipples, the tips of my fingers disappearing and reappearing as I did so. I smiled as I watched them fill with blood and grow erect. Joyce's mouth opened in shock.

What I wasn't expecting was her response. *"Mick! Leave me bloody well alone. You don't want me to tell Mary that you're spookin' her house, do you?"* She was looking in the mirror – not at herself, but directly at me. I didn't have anything to say. It was me who was taken by surprise and I had some thinking to do. Is she a medium of some sort? Joyce ... of all people?

She finished in the bathroom, carried her clothes with her, and searched Mary's room for something to wear. She didn't bother with a bra'. Mary's wouldn't have fit her anyway, but she did choose a baggy wool top and a pair of black jeans. They were just long enough, but she had to find a belt to tighten them. After all, Mary is a few sizes bigger.

I led the way downstairs, just in time to see Mary opening the front door. Ben didn't bother to come in. Apparently, there were other things he had to do before driving Mary to my house that evening. I listened to Mary and Joyce, as they related their experiences of the day. How Mary had got upset at the hospital, and how Ben can be a pain in the neck now and then. Joyce told Mary about her accident and apologised for getting drunk. She didn't mention me, or her phone call from Harry.

Later on, Ben returned and took Mary over to my place. I tagged along, but it wasn't as exciting as I'd first thought it would be. Ben is such a slow driver, and it not only drove me mad, but also annoyed Mary. She seemed so anxious to get back home to make some phone calls.

I thought I'd get some time to roam around my house, but Mary was in such a hurry that she quickly found my address book, picked up a few letters from the hall floor, and took some of my paperwork. I went with her to choose my burial outfit, but she wasn't very selective. She grabbed an old, charcoal-grey suit from my wardrobe, a shirt, underwear, socks and shoes, and was heading out of the bedroom, when I chased after her, pleading, "What about my tie?"

It's not that my dead body would need it where it was going, but it's the thought that counts. I edged ahead of her and led the way back to Ben. He was standing in the hall, waiting, and after Mary had folded my clothes into a large Sainsbury's plastic bag, we made our way to the car. Mind you, I had to be pretty quick diving in and out of his car, because there wasn't much space to play with. On the way home, Mary insisted on Ben buying a Chinese takeaway for their and Joyce's dinner. He wasn't very happy.

After stuffing herself, Joyce left for home with her dirty clothes in tow, and Ben soon followed. Mary then made a few phone calls to some of our relatives. I rested in the living room overnight, rather than the spare room, just in case Mary shut me in. I settled down in my corner, but sleep, if that's what it is, was hard to come by. It had been a funny old day in some ways, but not as funny as Wednesday turned out to be.

I did conk out in the end, and it was Mary who woke me up the next morning with another re-run of Sergeant Bilko on the television. I enjoyed watching Phil Silvers trying another one of his get-rich-quick scams, but when it finished Mary turned the TV down and started on more phone calls. She phoned my workplace and gave them the news. This was followed by calls to some of the names that she knew from my address book. I was sure the word of my demise would get around very quickly.

Alice turned up mid-morning and helped Mary arrange the funeral details. Joyce joined them soon after and volunteered to house-sit again. Mary was only too happy with this arrangement, as she had to deliver my clothes to the undertakers and then collect the death certificate. They drank coffee and yakked about this, that and t'other, in between the phone calls.

Mary decided to do some shopping for food and drink first, in case some of the mourners came back to hers, and both she and Alice agreed that they'd need the drink for themselves, anyway. Alice said she'd go with her and this lifted my spirits, as it gave me the opportunity to go out for a bit of walking practise. I immediately fetched my boots and put them on.

When they were ready to leave, I was right behind them, and, after the usual cheerios to Joyce, we were out and about. I followed them for a while, struggling with my feet, but when we reached the shopping centre I decided to disappear. I needed to be on my own to try this walking business because, on a couple of occasions, I had tripped over and nearly fallen straight through Alice's backside.

I found a good stretch of road to start off. It was well tiled and pretty level, and, more importantly, not too many people were about. This was it … and I let myself go. I pushed out my right leg, in a long sliding motion, and then followed through with the other. It was like skating on an ice-rink. I shortened my stride and slowed down, yet I kept to the same rhythm. This became easier and I gained confidence with every stride. Very soon, I felt I was as good a walker as Simon, and the thought of him returning to me on Friday made my face crease with happiness. I couldn't wait for him to see me in action and I so wanted to talk to someone again. Except for Joyce, nobody knew I was here.

It must have been half an hour later when I stopped, took a seat on a bench, and rested. I realised that I wasn't even breathing hard. In fact, I didn't seem to be breathing at all. I didn't feel the cold, yet I knew that the passers-by did, all wrapped up in their heavy coats and scarves. I could see the air escaping from their mouths, but nothing came from mine. One thing's for sure, I won't have to think about going to warmer climes for the winter.

I hadn't been sitting for very long, when I noticed a man and his dog approaching. I couldn't believe my luck. The dog, a blonde coloured labrador, was pulling the arms off this guy and, every now and then, the man would pull the dogs head back, quite physically. I had sympathy for the dog, but I wasn't going to let it stop me experimenting.

When they closed to within spitting distance, I jumped up and straight at the animal. I pushed myself right up to its face, without touching, and the poor labrador went crazy. It swerved violently to one side and then to the other, barking its head off, and then it ran like the clappers down the street. The man had absolutely no chance. He tried so hard to keep a hold of his pet, but both the speed and the strength of the dog were too much. He fell face down on the paving, crying out for his dog and then for himself. He was up fairly quickly, still calling for his dog, but he didn't try to follow. He bent down and rubbed both his knees, one of which could be seen through the newly made tear in his trousers. He limped to the bench that I'd been using, turned his head, and searched with his eyes. I could see the labrador careering up and down, still howling and running at other people.

Well, I couldn't believe my eyes. The dog was running back towards us, when it crashed into another man who was carrying a shopping bag. The impact sent this chap ... and his bag, flying in different directions, and the bag was heading our way. All of its contents were falling out, and I couldn't help but laugh when I saw a box of eggs smash upon the pavement. You know who I was thinking about.

I watched from a distance, while everyone sorted themselves out, taking care not to upset the dog again. A few bad words were exchanged between the labrador's owner and a few of the shoppers, while others just pointed and laughed.

Shortly after, I made my way to Mary's, perfecting my walking style on the way, and I even tried to run. I found the running extremely difficult and it caused me to topple over several times. On the way back, however, I stopped at a bus stop. I'd noticed a young couple, in their early twenties, waiting and holding hands. I just had to have some more fun, and, besides, he was good looking. I approached them from behind and was so close to touching him when another, older man, walked up behind me. I moved slightly to one side, and still behind my target, as the second man closed in on both him and me. My man was chatting away to his girlfriend when I reached down between his trousers and pushed upwards, into his groin, and made a fist. I held this position for at least a minute before pulling my hand, quickly, both backwards and upwards, and out of his body. This guy ... well, he jumped, he yelled, and then turned around, releasing his girlfriend's hand, and then he took a swing at the fellow behind. The older man fell, clutching his jaw, as my man shouted, *"What the hell do you think you're doin' ... you dirty pervert?"*

The girl caught hold of her boyfriend's arm. *"What's up, Dan? What's he done?"*

"The dirty little bastard was feeling my nuts. I'm gonna kill 'im," he answered, as he raised his shoe towards the older man's head.

His girlfriend quickly pulled him away, just before contact was made, and said, *"No, Dan! Let's get the police."* She had her mobile handy and was already dialling.

At the same time, the man on the ground was backing away, scared to death, and denying everything. He then jumped up and legged it. I heard the girl ask her boyfriend if the other man had really grabbed him, and he told her, *"I felt something, like a pull and a burning feeling in my balls, and I know you didn't do it."*

I felt rather bad, at the time, about what I'd done. I didn't know, but I thought that it might have caused some permanent damage to him, for no other reason than my own personal pleasure. But, there again, isn't that why I wanted to be a ghost?

I walked slowly back to the house and had to jump over the wall. Fortunately, it is low. I studied the wooden gate as I waited outside for the door to open. It was about fifteen minutes later, when Mary and Alice came out, now on their way to the undertakers in Newmarket. I dived in as soon as I saw the gap, accidentally pushing through Mary in the process. I didn't see how she reacted, because my back was to her. I hurried to my place in the living room and relaxed, hoping Joyce would play some more music, and preferably something I liked.

Joyce did join me shortly afterwards, carrying a hot drink and some biscuits. I still hadn't felt hungry and I sat there and wondered. I stayed awake, watching her and listening to tapes of Billy Joel, Elton John and Madness, until Mary came home ... alone, and resumed the calls. Joyce stayed with her, talking and drinking for a few hours. They ate together, their trays on their laps, watching Bart and Lisa watch Itchy & Scratchy.

Joyce left soon after, and I could see that Mary was getting ready for an early night. She was just about to go upstairs when the door bell rang. ... It was Ben. I wasn't going to hang around, listening to him prattle on, so I went upstairs to Mary's room and lay down on the floor by the window. I never heard him go, nor did I hear Mary come to bed. The next thing I remember, it was daylight again, and a new day in a ghost's life was about to begin.

This morning, I was determined to go to Fergie's so I waited for the first opportunity to escape the house. It wasn't long in coming, either. Joyce arrived about nine-thirty to take up her duties, and, as soon as Mary opened the door, I slipped by her, but I couldn't help walking head on and through Joyce. I turned, and she'd stopped and was shaking all over. She half-turned and glanced at me, angrily saying, *"Right, you! That's the last bloody time."*

I looked on, as Mary, still holding the door, asked, *"Joyce, who are you talking to?"*

"Nobody, Mary. Most definitely, nobody at all. It's just this damn weather. It's so cold." – I thought she was going to drop me in it, but what could they do, and, anyway, who'd believe her? Mary gave her a funny look.

I stood in the pathway until they'd gone inside. I hopped over the wall and headed towards the town centre and the bus station. There were more people than I'd expected waiting for my bus and the hopes I'd had of getting a seat to myself were diminishing. When it did pull up to the stop, the bus was empty and I darted on first. I walked the length of the bus to the back seat. I'd thought hard about this in advance, as the long back seat gave me the opportunity to move quickly to another if I saw someone approaching. I observed the other passengers climbing aboard, and, fortunately, most of them stayed either near the front or close to the middle set of doors. It was an uneventful journey and I arrived in Newmarket without encountering any mishaps.

I made my way along the main road and waited outside Fergie's until someone else was going in, and when a fellow shopper came along, I followed close behind. I went straight to one of the shop's corners and looked at the range of ghost suits available. There were different styles, from many eras, but when I tried to pick one up, I couldn't. I tried again with another suit, but this effort was also in vain. I went over to the jumper section and saw the same type I'd previously chosen. I couldn't pick it up. I didn't understand what was going on, but then I thought I knew the answer. It had to be that ghosts can only shop at night. Then I remembered Simon and what he'd said. He'd mentioned that he'd bought the clothes. But how can that be? He didn't have any real money or ghost money, and nor was there a ghost attendant or a ghost cashier in the shop. And, anyway, ghosts can't buy things. I had no choice, other than go back to Ely.

I left the shop, and while I was returning to the bus stop, it started snowing. Having just missed one, I had to wait, so I passed some of the time by trying to catch the snowflakes but they fell through my hands. The snow was getting heavier and the scenery was changing all around me by the minute. Eventually, the bus showed up and, again, I was the first to get on. I'm sure you can imagine how easy it was for me to jump the queue. This time, though, I was joined on the back seat by two young children, about eleven years of age. Two boys, and they were making a right nuisance of themselves; flicking bits of paper at other passengers; arguing with each other very noisily; and jumping around, annoying me. I didn't do anything, but I noticed that as the bus stopped at its stops it picked up more people than it let off. This caused me some concern because the new passengers were now filtering towards the back of the bus. It was only a matter of time before someone would need my seat.

It had to happen. These boys seemed to be going the distance and were becoming even more rowdy. A lady had taken the middle seat on the back row with us. She was getting frustrated with the boys and, rather than tell them off or tell the driver, she moved away from them, as far as she could. The problem was that she was closing in on me and I tried to move, but she was in my way.

"No-oo!" I shouted, as she squeezed herself right into me. I do mean squeezed, as this lady was big. She had to be in excess of twenty stone, and so wide that one seat hardly seemed to do. I was trying to move out of her when another two people took up the spare seats alongside us. I had to stay inside her and watch what she watched, as the bus rode along. Fortunately, she tended to keep her eyes on the countryside and the ever changing scenery. It was now becoming so like a Christmas card. All we needed was the reindeer and a Santa look-alike. During the course of the journey, I felt the motions through her hands when she took out an inhaler, and I watched through her eyes as she pulled it to her mouth. Then both her lips and mine gripped the implement. I heard her take a very long and very hard suck. Asthma, I presumed. Soon after, though, my body started getting tired and my head became a little woozy, but I put this down to the strain of carrying this woman. The reality was that she was carrying me, although, at the time, my mind could not accept this.

It wasn't long before both she, and I, noticed the two boys stand up and move to the middle door, pressing the bell on the way. It was also the time when my body was released from its captivity. The fat lady rose, very gingerly, and as she moved away from me, she shook like a jelly and screamed. The boys turned to the noise, saw the wobbling woman, and roared with laughter, pointing at her and making disgusting jokes. I felt so sorry for the lady, but what could I do?

I still don't understand the different sensations that people are getting from me. Some seem to get a mild one, while others get sensations that are more prolonged, causing more movement. I have to find out why.

Anyway, not long after, we entered Ely and I soon disembarked from the bus. I didn't have any problem with the snow but as I walked along I saw that others were slipping and sliding. Despite my tiredness, I too started sliding along, this time deliberately. I became quite proficient at it in a very short time, and I was happy. You see, when I was alive, no matter how many times I tried ice skating, I always fell either flat on my face or doing the splits and sliding along on my bum.

My arrival at Mary's coincided with the return of Joyce, who had obviously been out shopping somewhere. She was laden with three heavy bags of groceries, and I'd have helped her if I could. I was lucky, I suppose, in not having to wait around to get in. I sidled up beside her and as Joyce walked through the gate I sneaked in, keeping as close as I could to her body without entering her. I followed the same routine when Mary opened the front door.

Home again, I thought ... safe and sound. I now regard Mary's as my home, even if it is only temporary. Once inside, the two women talked their way to the kitchen, while I went to lie down in the living room. The television was switched on, but I didn't bother with it. My mind was elsewhere, thinking about being squashed to death, and how easy it is for me to penetrate other people's bodies. I also recalled my failure to acquire new clothes, yet Simon had so easily changed his jeans. I thought about Sam and Jack, and their imminent return from holiday, and this gave me a brainwave. I could travel the world by plane, ship, train or coach and nobody would ever know. I'd probably be restricted in the desert though – the camels would get the ... you know. The more I wondered about these possibilities, the happier I became. Soon after, my head had cleared and I felt alive again.

Joyce came in, sipping a glass of white wine, and sat on a soft chair close by me. Mary soon followed, carrying a mug and a plate of buttered scones. She sat down by the hi-fi and placed the scones between the two of them. I used to love scones with tea, and I looked on enviously, even though I can't eat. They discussed my death again and Mary picked up my address book. She found a pen nearby and started ticking off the people she'd called, telling Joyce who they were, what they did and whether they were my boyfriends or not. I listened to them laugh and joke at my expense, as they tried to imagine what I would get up to sexually. This banter was nothing new to me, as they both knew me so well, but when Joyce lifted her middle finger and moved it back and forward in her open mouth, she wasn't aware of the relevance of her action to my death. They both creased up laughing. I had to smile myself, at the time, and I'm smiling even now at the thought of it.

Both of them finished their food and then Mary called some more of my acquaintances. When I heard their names, I wished she hadn't bothered. She then turned up the volume on the television. I joined them in watching Countdown, and I couldn't get over the similarity in appearance between Joyce and Carol Vorderman. If only Joyce had Carol's brains ... then they could be sisters. I was only thinking this, when Mary pointed out, to Joyce, exactly the same thing. They laughed, and I laughed.

After the programme, she lowered the volume and they both went upstairs. I went as far as the hallway and could hear them moving the bed around in Sam's room. Preparing for tonight, I thought, so I left them to it. I went back in the room and looked out the window at the falling snow.

CHAPTER FIVE

It's getting dark in here, and I wish I could put some music on if only to liven up the place. It's not that it's like the morgue, but Sam and Jack should have been home by now. Where the hell are they? And why's it taking Joyce and Mary so long to make a stupid bed? You'd think that they'd have left the lights on down here.

Moving behind the settee, I turn to face the mirror and my reflection hardly shows itself in the gloom. Lifting my eyes to the ceiling, I shout, "Come on, you two. Hurry up!"

I can't believe it. As if by magic, the sound of flip-flops … flop, flop, flopping on the stairs, makes me turn as Joyce walks in, flicking on the light, and she nearly passes through me as she heads to the window. She's no sooner there, than she turns around and rushes back to the hall, shouting, *"Mary! Mary!"* And I follow and watch her fling the door open. Joyce is out of the gate in a shot, and … .

"My god, it's Sam," I shout. Sam drops the case she's lifting and wraps her arms around Joyce as Joyce gives her a welcoming hug. Joyce takes Sam's arm and escorts her inside, leaving Alice and Jack to cope with the luggage. I back away and let them follow me. Mary hears all the commotion and flies down the stairs. She pulls her daughter to her, squeezing and kissing her – tears of happiness in Mary's eyes.

"Oh, Sam! Sam!" she cries. At the same time, Joyce is greeting Jack, while Alice just stands there, smiling at everyone.

"Mum!" Mary's hanging on for dear life, not wanting to let Samantha go.

Then she does, and turns to Jack, grabs his waist with both hands, and gives him a kiss on the cheek. *"Hello Jack,"* she says softly. *"I'm so glad you're all back safely."*

"No thanks to this snow," chips in Alice. *"I'll tell you about it later – after we've had a drink. It's bloody freezing out there."*

"Come on you lot, get inside and I'll put the kettle on," urges Joyce, *"and there's a bottle of Remy to get stuck into while you're waiting."*

Alice joins Joyce in the kitchen, chatting to each other, while Mary, Sam and Jack do as they were told. I take my place in the corner and study Jack more closely, as he makes drinks for everyone. Now that he's going to be my niece's husband … if they do eventually marry, I want to know more about him. I can see that he's handsome in a rugged sort of way, and I know that he's twenty-nine, the same as Joyce. I wouldn't mind betting that Joyce has taken a fancy to him. If you'd seen the look in her eyes when she gave him that peck on the cheek, you'd know what I mean. Jack's quite tall, just over six feet, and has the build of a rugby player. He looks as though he plays the game, or does some other physically demanding sport, and I know that Sam gets involved in various games. Maybe they are well suited.

The three of them are sitting down, drinking and making small talk, when Alice and Joyce come in with the cups of hot coffee. After passing them round, Alice sits on the only other chair in the room, while Joyce perches herself on its arm. I look on, from my usual vantage point, and I'm wondering when the news of my death is going to come out.

Alice is the first to open the real conversation.

"It was terrible on those roads today. We almost came a cropper. Didn't we Sam?"

"Oh, God! Yes. And what about that bus?"

"Yeah! Skidded right into a ditch and toppled over. Lucky no-one was killed," chips in Jack.

"Where did this happen?" asks Mary.

"Just this side of Little Thetford," answers Alice. *"They were so lucky. There were two ambulances, as well as loads of police."*

"I can imagine there'll be lots of car accidents in this weather," predicts Jack. – "Don't remind me," I say quite loudly. Pity they can't hear. Of all topics, why pick this one? But, I suppose, it's a way to let the bad news out.

"Oh, poor dears," offers Mary, shaking her head. She starts crying softly. And then the tears really start to flow.

"What's wrong, Mum?" asks Sam, now holding Mary's hand.

"It's ... . It's ... . Oh, Sam! My little Sam. It's so terrible. Mick! It's Mick. He's de ... ." And she sobs her heart out.

Sam's eyes and mouth open wide, and her tears start falling. *"Uncle Mick?"* She shakes her head. *"No!"*

Alice, seeing the state Mary is in, has come over and is comforting her, and she quietly says, *"Sam, Mick's had an accident. I'm so, so sorry. He's passed on to a better place."* – So that's what she thinks. If she only knew the truth, and, yet, perhaps she's right. I don't really know enough about this ghost business to pass judgement on whether it's better or not. Joyce, by now, is behind Sam and is gently holding her shoulders, and Jack also looks stunned. He had already put down his drink, and is now holding Sam's hand.

There's nothing I can do, and I feel sorry for them feeling sorry for me. I watch their faces and listen as they explain my death. After a few minutes, Jack gets up and tops up their glasses, while Joyce stands with hers raised, and proposes,

"Let's drink to Mick. He'd want us to. And .... And he'd want us to think that he'll always be with us ... er, you know, to keep us safe. God bless him."

I couldn't have put it better myself. And it works. Everyone stands up, Mary and Sam still teary eyed but now quiet, and they all join Joyce.

"To Mick, God bless him."

They down their drinks and hug each other, then all, except Joyce, sit down again. She brings the bottles over and refills the glasses.

I like Joyce more, each time I see her. Seeing that everyone's quiet, Joyce goes to the hi-fi and selects a tape, and then she holds it up, adding, *"I think Mick likes this kind of music. Let's play it for him."* The others nod. So she puts it on and soon we can hear Bob Dylan singing his song *I Want You.*

"Joyce. Oh Joyce. You're not joking, are you?" I'm looking at her, as she looks at me in the corner ... and she winks. I don't know what to think, except ... I love her. Not for the sex, you understand, but for the ... oh, I don't know, the ... the ... being a medium kind of thing. The way she said *'likes'*, as if I'm not dead.

The music isn't loud, and I'm quite content as I close my eyes and listen to the tape, while the others talk over the music. I don't mind, and sometimes I hear the odd bits of conversation. When the news of the engagement is announced, I look over and see that they're all so happy. At least the bad news is forgotten about for the time being, and Mary comes to life. I knew that she'd heard, in advance, about the so-called surprise, but she pretended that she hadn't. Shortly after, the door bell chimes. Alice is the first from her seat and answers it. I recognise the voice of Ben, saying his hellos, and then they come in. Jack gets up, followed by Sam, and Ben shakes their hands.

"How are you? Did you have a good holiday?" he asks.

"We did. We had a great time. Beautiful weather," says Jack. Sam nods with a little smile. I wonder if she likes him.

Joyce cuts in, on her way to the cabinet, *"Ben, would you like a drink?"*

"Er, no. I better hadn't. Driving you see." Does this fella' ever have any fun? I don't think he's going to last too long.

"Go on. Have one … just a small one." Joyce is giving Ben a you-better-bloody-well-have-one-under-the-circumstances stare as she says this. I know he will, or she'll kill him.

"Okay, then … a very small one." He forces a smile. Joyce fills a glass to the top with whisky but doesn't bother adding any mixer, and then she hands it to him.

I laugh as I watch the pair of them, and say to her, "Joyce, you're brilliant. Now make him drink it."

She is so quick witted, it's unbelievable. In a flash, she fills the rest of them up again and proposes another toast. *"Now that Ben's here, let's have another one for Mick, and let's drink to Sam and Jack on their safe return … and their engagement. Come on, now – down in one."* She raises her glass and the others stand, raising theirs … Ben tentatively.

"To Mick," they all join in. *"To Sam and Jack."* They all swallow their drinks … in one.

Not long after, I can see that Mary and Sam are getting quite drunk, and that Jack isn't far behind them, and then he asks Sam, *"Any chance of a sandwich?"*

"You make it. You've got legs. I'm shattered," she replies.

Alice jumps in. *"Don't worry about it kids. Anybody else for food?"*

All, bar Ben, are hungry, and after Joyce makes another drink for herself, she follows Alice to the kitchen. They aren't there for very long before returning with some plates full of beef and salad rolls, chicken drumsticks, and a bowl of egg and mayonnaise dip with Melba toast on the side. It looks fantastic … and I wish I was hungry. Ben and I watch the others stuff themselves, and Mary takes his hand, encouraging him, *"Ben, please eat something. Just a little, but you must eat."*

"I don't know," he replies.

"Now look, Ben, don't go making me upset again. I'm concerned about you … . Please?"

"Very well. I'll have some of that egg and toast. That'll be enough."
– And I laugh as Mary hands him the bowl and the toast, and when he

puts the egg mixture in his mouth, I wonder if it's Evelyn's egg. When they finish, Joyce takes the dishes away. Alice chats to Mary and Ben, while Sam and Jack cuddle up together.

I get up and go after Joyce. I'm standing in the kitchen doorway, and she's singing to herself while washing up. She makes some more coffee and two mugs of tea, placing them on a tray with sugar and spoons. Then lifting the tray, she turns to me, so I edge back into the hall, letting her pass. She doesn't do or say anything as she goes by me. I don't follow, and, instead, sit down on the stairs, my head in my hands. I'm not here long when a mobile starts ringing. It's Joyce's, and she carries it to the kitchen before answering. I move closer to listen.

"Hi, Harry. What you up to?"

"No. I'm still at Mary's. Got to go soon, though."

"Yeah! Course it's still on. They're not likely to cancel a funeral."

"About eleven, they said."

"I don't know. Depends if I'm getting a lift or not."

"Would you?"

"You mean, you really want to go?"

"Okay, then. Pick me up at my place."

"About ten."

"See you then. Bye."

Joyce gets herself a drink of water before going back in the room. I step inside the door and notice that Ben is standing and saying his goodbyes to Sam, Alice and Jack. He walks ahead of Mary and I let them pass by, untouched. Mary sees him out, with a hug and a kiss, and I think. … Yuck! She tells him to drive carefully, waves, and then shuts the door. I turn around and hear Alice saying,

"See you in the morning, bright and early." She's coming towards me, but is looking at the others and waving gently. I back up the stairs a few steps, while Alice grabs her coat.

Mary is watching her, and saying, *"Alice, thanks for today; you're a godsend. Look, before you go, I've something to tell you."* Mary beckons her to the door, but keeps it shut.

Alice smiles, knowing it's got to be something interesting, and whispers, *"What is it?"*

"I made a phone call today."

"Yes. And?" Alice asks, egging Mary on.

43

"It was to you know who."

"No!"

"Yes, and I told him about Mick."

"You didn't?"

"I did. I had to."

"Why, for heaven's sake?"

"Samantha, of course."

"But he didn't like Mick, so why bother?" I've been trying to guess who she's talking about. Now I know.

"We never discussed Mick in front of Sam, and I don't think she knows how much her dad disliked him. Besides, Sam would expect him to be there."

"Oh, I suppose you're right, but I hope he doesn't show up." So do I. I don't want him at my funeral.

"So do I, really. What, with Ben and that."

"He won't care about Ben. Not now. Anyway, he's got a partner."

"That's just it. Someone told me that she threw him out." My eyes light up at this latest revelation. It's music to my ears ... and it serves him bloody well right.

"She never?"

"She did! And I think it bugs him that he still has to pay some of the mortgage on this place, while he's reduced to a bedsit."

"Does he still see Sam?"

"Now and then. She tells me when he does."

"Never mind, Mary. It'll be alright ... you'll see."

"You're a rock." Mary gives Alice a big hug and opens the door for her.

"Get a good night's sleep. I'll be here at nine. Is that okay?"

"Yes, of course," and as Alice treads down the path, Mary follows adding, *"and you take care. We don't want any more accidents."* Mary waves goodbye to Alice, comes inside, and re-enters the front room. I join them, this time leaning on the wall by the door.

They're watching News At Ten, and the footage of the traffic hold-ups, due to the snow. The picture changes to one of Luton airport, where an aeroplane has skidded off the runway, and it shows the efforts being made to help. I look on with interest. Then Mary suggests a cup of tea, and both Joyce and Sam insist on making it. Mary lets them, while she stretches out, yawning. Jack asks some more questions about me and the funeral arrangements. He, actually, does it in a calming way that doesn't upset Mary anymore, and she seems quite cheerful and safe with him. Jack seems like an okay guy. Shortly, the girls are back with the drinks. Sam turns down the tele', and they join in the conversation, changing the subject several times.

Joyce empties her cup, and asks, *"Anyone else finished? I'll wash up and then I'll have to shoot off."*

"No! Leave them Joyce. I'll do them in the morning." – See, I told you Mary's not herself.

Joyce doesn't agree. *"No, no, Mary. You've enough on your plate, and it'll only take me five minutes."*

"Don't be daft," says Sam. *"I'll do them."*

But Joyce shakes her head. *"No you won't, you're tired."* Sam is already up and collecting the glasses, so Joyce offers, *"Okay then, I'll wash and you dry."* Sam nods agreement and they go off to the kitchen. Jack excuses himself and goes up to the loo, while I stay behind with Mary, and she is soon nodding off.

A few minutes later, Joyce is back and tries coaxing Mary to go to her bed. Mary agrees, and slowly rises from her seat, saying, *"You're a great girl. I hope I haven't messed you up, with all this."* They make their way into the hallway.

"Of course not. You'd do the same for me, or for Alice come to that. Now go on, up those stairs and I'll see you in the morning."

"Thanks. By the way, if you like you can come with us tomorrow."

"No, but thanks anyway. I've got a lift. Harry's picking me up."

"Oh, I meant to ask you – you know, about the other?" Mary's eyes are inquisitive, and she's smiling.

Joyce pats her tummy, and laughs. *"Yeah, three months gone and still growing."*

"What?" Mary's face changes to one of shock.

"No, only teasing. Go on you, don't be daft. Go and get some sleep. I'll be off home myself, in a minute or two."

Mary blows her a kiss. *"Goodnight then,"* she says, and turns to see Sam coming from the kitchen. *"I'm off to bed, love."* She hugs her daughter and turns towards the stairs. Jack's on his way down, and they exchange their goodnights. Then she leaves us.

As they enter the room, Jack asks, *"Do either of you want a nightcap?"* – I relax in my corner.

"Just a quick one," answers Joyce, pointing to the brandy.

"Not for me, Jack. I'm knackered. That jet lag has really set in." And Sam does look worn out. Jack looks okay. I suppose he must have slept through the flight.

Sam and Jack sit down together on the sofa, while Joyce takes the seat by me. We're so close that if she reaches out her right hand, she'll be able to slice it through my head. They talk, for a few minutes, about their lives in general, and then, out of the blue and to my utter amazement, Joyce asks, *"Do you believe in ghosts?"*

Jack laughs out loud, shaking his head. Yet Sam gives Joyce a very strange look before answering. *"Yes! I do, as a matter of fact. But, Joyce, what made you bring it up?"* – I know, but I can't tell them, and Jack's now looking at Sam in disbelief. He obviously doesn't know everything about her.

Joyce tells Sam, *"Oh, I don't know. I just get these feelings sometimes, that there's someone present."*

"There is," I say, reaching up and placing my hand in hers.

Sam turns from one to the other as she explains. *"If you must know, I made a study of supposed ghostly appearances and hauntings in my first year at University. I did it out of interest, to take my mind off the serious stuff. I found it quite fascinating."* – The three of us stare at her, as she continues, *"It started as a bit of fun, after watching films. Some of us started talking about them, just as we're doing now. So we did some checking up on a number of these haunted buildings, but answers couldn't be found for some of the goings on. My friends gave up after a while, but I carried on and, yes, I do believe there's something there."*

"So, do you think that ghosts only come back and haunt people because they've been murdered, or something like that?" asks Jack.

Joyce adds, *"Yeah! Or is it the soul of the person who's died that's in turmoil? Maybe it can't go to heaven, or hell for that matter, until it's been released in some way?"*

"God! ... You two. I'm not an expert you know. I only did it out of interest. It's hard studying to be an English teacher. We do have to read a lot anyway, and it took my mind off the course." Hmm. English teacher is she?

"So, you haven't really learnt much about ghosts," implies Jack.

"No, I suppose not, but I will tell you something odd. No, I'd better not."

"Go on," says Joyce, *"don't stop now. If you start something, then finish it. We're not going to say anything to anybody. Are we, Jack?"*

"It's okay, you don't have to Sam." Jack accepts the point that she's had enough. I don't. I want her to carry on, as long as possible. I mean, I'm a ghost and even I don't understand why I can't do everything I'd thought I'd be doing.

Sam looks at Jack's face and holds her stare for a good while, and then turning to Joyce she stares at her. Joyce looks back, urging Sam on, saying, *"I need another drink. How about you two?"*

She stands up and, as she does so, her right hand starts to shake.

Both Sam and Jack are watching, and Jack says, *"No, I've had enough drink for one day, but, Joyce, what's up with your hand?"*

Sam is still looking at Joyce's hand when the shaking stops and she says to Jack, *"Leave Joyce alone. We don't ask you men personal questions about your health."*

Joyce doesn't answer, goes to the bottle and takes another drink. *"It's okay,"* she answers. *"I've got this small problem at the moment. I'll sort it out. Now, are you going to tell us what's odd, or not? Come on, Sam, be a sport."* Joyce resumes her seat.

Sam looks at them both again. *"Well, the thing is, I keep having this dream. I know we don't usually remember dreams, but this one recurs quite often, and it's fairly vivid."*

Joyce is nearly off her seat, mouth wide open in anticipation of the next words from Sam. I'm damn sure I know what she's going to say, and Sam goes on, *"In the dream, I'm a ghost. I'm a happy ghost because I'm doing the things I want to. I look after children – keeping them safe. Of course, sometimes I – that is, me the ghost – can't be everywhere at once, and I can't save a child or something like that. I get so sad when this happens. What I like best is doing something to these nasty people who hurt kids, and I always get to a point in the dream where I'm in a difficult situation and can't get out of it. Then the dream stops."*

I knew it. I knew it. As soon as she mentioned having a dream, and we're all talking about the likes of me, it had to be similar to my dreams. Not the same, of course, because we all think differently and we want different things.

Jack hadn't finished. *"Is that it? You do know that it's only because you've read about them quite seriously, and it's always in the back of your mind. We never really forget much, Sam. These memories are always there when we need them; in the subconscious. You know this. And we all dream of different things, and you've probably dreamt of falling down a never ending pit or something like that, but it's still only a dream."* I must admit, Jack's reasoning is very plausible, but I know the truth.

Joyce adds, *"Yes, Sam, Jack's right. He makes a lot of sense. Even I've dreamed of being a ghost and coming back to haunt somebody. It doesn't make it real – it's a dream, and that's all it is, as Jack says."* – I can't believe my own ears. You could have knocked me down with a feather.

"You're both right, and I have been down that pit as well. But it's still odd." Good on you girl. You'll find out eventually, but not too soon I hope … and so will Joyce. No wonder I like her … and Sam, of course. Joyce finishes her drink and tells them she's going home. I follow her while she collects her coat and bag, and hear them saying goodbye. Then, just as she's going out the door, Sam adds, *"Take care, Joyce, and pleasant dreams."*

Jack closes the door and turns out the lights in the living room and kitchen. They both go upstairs. I have to go after them. I'm tempted to see what Jack has going for him when he goes for a shower, but I don't. Following Sam to her bedroom, I watch her undress. She's very fair like Brian, but she's taken her Mum's brains – of that I'm sure. When she gets down to her underwear, I turn away. After all, she is my niece. When Jack comes in, Sam, now wearing a long white nightie – and nothing else by the look of it, takes her turn in the bathroom. I watch Jack, as he gets down to the raw.

Hmm … I've seen bigger. It seems so out of proportion to his tall strong body. Still, Sam seems happy. She comes back soon after and joins Jack, who's already under the cover. They haven't bothered to turn the lights off, as yet, and Jack is wrapping his arms around Sam. He starts kissing her, and, as I watch the cover sliding off them, his right hand is fondling her left breast. He moves his hand lower and she slaps him away. *"No. I told you … I'm wearing red tonight."*

That'll teach him. Anyway, being next to Mary's room, they shouldn't be making a racket. He's still kissing her on the mouth, then the face, and is starting on her neck when she whispers, *"Oh, Jack, I can't, honestly, but if you're very quiet, I'll give you a five knuckle shuffle."*

"What the hell is a five knuckle shuffle?" I ask her, but it doesn't take long to find out. Jack's agreed, and Sam is pushing her hand way down his naked body, the duvet moving with it. – I know now. Well, I should have guessed, and I start counting mine. "Why five?" I ask myself. When I see her grab hold of him, and then her face joins her hand, I look away. I can't watch anymore, so I head for the door.

"Oh, no!" It's shut! I'm locked in again. That's three times in four days, and now I have to listen to this carry-on. It wouldn't bother me, ordinarily, but she is family ... and she is going to be a ghost. I still don't understand this idea of dreaming, and Simon could be having me on, but I'll find out for certain. I have to.

I sit by the wall – my eyes closed, wondering about my predicament, and I can't help but hear the panting and moaning. I push my hands over my ears, but that doesn't work. I try concentrating on Dylan, on Joyce, and even on the Rolling Stones, and it does help a little. However, in what seems a very short time – two to three minutes at most, I hear his stifled yell. Shortly after, Jack rolls over, crawls out of bed, and I see that his erection's a thing of the past. He ties Sam's dressing gown around his waist and heads for the bathroom.

No sooner is the bedroom door open than I'm off and down the stairs to safety. I'm lying here, now, with my eyes closed, thinking about everything that's gone on today, about my funeral tomorrow, and then ... .

CHAPTER SIX

I don't know what made me get up so early today. There weren't any noises or anything like that, but when I opened my eyes I knew, immediately, it was one of the most important days of my death. I had to look forward to finally putting away my body. I went to the kitchen to see what the time was. You see, Mary has this thing about clocks – she hasn't got any. Well, not a proper one, so I had to check the time from the clock on the micro-wave oven; one of those combination types.

It was seven-thirty, and outside the snow was even thicker on the ground, and it was still falling. They'll all be wearing white today, I thought at the time – snow white. As for me, I have this thing about funerals. I think that all this dressing in black makes them seem such miserable occasions. Anyway, I sat down at the kitchen table and waited for Mary to make an entrance. I knew she wouldn't be long. After all, Alice was coming at nine and the hearse would be here about ten.

I'd heard Mary giving out the details and am quite happy that there isn't going to be a big church service. She's arranged to use the small chapel at the cemetery. I've been to a burial at one of these before and they're very quick and easy; no messing about at all – in, out, down, and goodbye. As I've said before, not being a religious person, I couldn't really care where they bury my body, so long as it lasts, but as they're seeing me off, so to speak, in my charcoal-grey finery, I'd like to see myself go down well.

I thought about that stupid Brian coming and hoped he might get stuck in a snowdrift somewhere, or maybe his bedsit is in a basement and he can't get out. I could tell him something about that ... couldn't I? I wondered about my own travel arrangements; about whether I'd be able to squeeze into one of the cars or perhaps enter one of their bodies, but then the answer struck me and it seemed so obvious.

About twenty minutes later, Mary came down and put the kettle on. I didn't move from my chair while she made herself some toast and threw a tea-bag in a mug. She was pouring in the water when we both heard Sam coming downstairs, coughing. Mary greeted her, then opened the fridge and took out some bacon, liver-sausage and a tub of low-fat spread. They talked about their immediate plans while Mary buttered her toast and prepared a breakfast for the other two. When Jack joined us he seemed in a very happy mood. After his and Sam's exploits last night, it's no wonder.

The door bell rang and I looked at the micro-wave. If I hadn't checked the time, I could have guessed it. I'd always known Alice to be a punctual person.

Sam answered the door and brought Alice back in with her. She was dressed entirely in black. I stood up and, sneaking by them, went to the doorway. When the breakfast was cooked, they all sat down to eat. Mary added a couple of slices of the bacon to her toast, but only after some stern advice from Alice with regard to eating before drinking alcohol. Afterwards, Sam and Mary went to change while Alice talked to Jack about his holiday in Hawaii. I left them to it and went to the front room.

Not long after, Mary's neighbours turned up and were shown into the lounge. I knew two of them fairly well, Nigel and Doreen Temple from next door, and they brought with them a large spray. The other man, Ron, lived across the road, but I'd only met him once before, at the pub. Mary and Sam reappeared, both wearing black coats, hanging open, with matching hats. At least their dresses weren't all black. Mary's had a purple flowered pattern on it, while Sam's was coloured a deep red with thin black horizontal lines. She looked a picture.

Jack came in, apologising for not having anything dark to wear. He had dressed in brown shoes, medium green slacks, and a sports jacket over a cream shirt. Mary took one look at his brightly striped tie, dashed upstairs, and returned with a black one, saying, *"Brian's,"* as she gave it to him. I sneaked around them all and went to the window.

I was looking out when the funeral cars drew up, and inside the hearse I could see flowers on top of my body's coffin. Ben showed up just after, and was no sooner in the door than he was out again. Mary led the way outside, holding his arm as they went through the gate. The others followed ... and so did I. I listened while they discussed who was travelling in each car, and then Mary and Sam climbed into the first one. Doreen gave the spray to the driver of the hearse, and as he opened the back, I took the chance that I'd been waiting for. I ran, and, while he was placing the spray on the coffin, I jumped in beside it. When he closed the door, I looked out of the back window and saw Ben offering Ron a lift. Jack, Alice and the Temples took their places in the second car. We were about to pull away when another car stopped alongside Mary's.

Inside were Pat and Patricia McHugh, the landlords of the local pub, and Mary talked to them for a minute. They then reversed and waited for us to move off.

The hearse pulled away and I found that there wasn't much room to move around, but, eventually, I managed to lie by the side of my own coffin. It was the very last time I could be with myself and I wished my body a long and happy burial. I was pretty confident that I would remain a ghost for some considerable time, as I could see that the coffin looked very solid, with nice looking clasps at the top, sides and bottom. I had no idea of the cost of my funeral but felt that Mary had done me proud.

We were moving ever so slowly, and every now and then I popped my head up to look out. People were stopping and staring at me. Some would cross themselves, bow their heads, and then glance at me again, as we passed by. I was taking another peek outside, at the very moment we turned into Beech Lane, and I knew we were close to the cemetery. I got myself into a good position, and when the car stopped, and the door was opened, I hopped out. I walked to the chapel entrance and waited for the others.

And I'm still here now – there's been a delay. I search the faces of the people as they approach and hear Mary say to both Sam and Ben, *"Fifteen minutes. There's another getting done in front of us. They're running a little late."*

Some gather outside the entrance, talking about me, while others stand alone, smoking that last ciggie before going inside. It's like that everywhere now. They'll be banning smoking in your own house soon, and thinking about this reminds me of the time I was nearly killed, and all because of a cigarette.

I'd been doing an extra night shift, as a favour for one of my colleagues, when the police turned up at work; about two in the morning. They asked me to confirm my name and address, and then brought me home. They told me there'd been a fire at my house. At that time, I was living in Edmonton. I used to have a first-floor flat in a two-storey building, and the fire had started in the bedroom above mine.

The guy who lived in this room had returned home – drunk apparently, and had gone to bed, and to sleep, with a lighted cigarette in his gob.

He'd also placed his electric fire close to his bed and switched it on. He was a very lucky man – the cigarette burnt down, burnt his lips, and then he'd panicked. The bedspread had fallen on the fire and the place went up in flames. The man had managed to get out of his room and into the bathroom before he collapsed.

Don't worry – he didn't die; just some minor burning to his lips from his fag. The thing was, the fire became so fierce that it not only destroyed his room, but also burnt through the floor boards, into my bedroom and onto my bed. Apparently the smoke and heat were so bad that I wouldn't have had a chance. That's according to the firemen. So, I survived – by accident I suppose. Until now, that is.

From my position I have a good view of the mourners as they approach. I can recognise most of the faces in front of me. Four people, friends of mine, are standing together exchanging small talk. I know them well from my local in Newmarket – Alan and Irene French, and Megan and Carl Thomas. Mary approaches them, shakes their hands, saying, *"In a few minutes."*

Behind these are two of my mates, Andy and Brian from Jack Straws in Hampstead. Pity it's closed down now. I'd have liked to visit there, spiritually of course. I could tell you a few stories about that place, and what went on behind it.

I'm still grinning, when three relatives walk towards me, and my Uncle Oliver asks, *"Young man, can you tell me which hymns will be sung during the funeral?"* I'm dumbfounded. I'm not visible, surely?

I'm about to answer when a voice behind me says, *"Yes, of course. We have some pamphlets with the order of the service."* I turn to see a really attractive man looking through my face at my uncle and my Aunties, Dot and Maisie. I get out of their way, step into the snow, and go to join some of the others. As I'm walking through the snow, I look down and see it's so deep that I can't even see my feet. They've disappeared. I lift my right foot up and check it out. It feels fine, neither cold nor hot, so I put it down again and carry on. The first group I meet is comprised of my own next door neighbours from Newmarket, Colin and Sylvia Phelps, Paul Scott and his girlfriend Marie. Joyce and Harry are standing nearby and she's telling them about the drinking plans for later.

Paul says, *"The doors are opening."*

And they all make a move forward.

What is now a quite sizeable crowd makes its way inside the chapel. I stand to one side, studying them as they pass me by. I knew that someone from work would come. Actually, there are three of them and except for Susan Bates, my secretary, the others are only here as a gesture of courtesy. They are Freddy Beasant, my overall boss, and the office creep, Luke Jeeps. I can't stand him, and neither can anyone else. He's always into everybody else's business and hanging around Fred, trying to make himself feel important. I used to wonder about those two. There had been rumours, but they'd proved unfounded.

Mary and Sam had already gone in, but then Ben came walking along, talking to two men who I didn't want to see at my funeral. These were former partners of mine – that's boyfriends, not business – Brendan O'Neill and Maurice 'spit' Hall. I won't tell you why he's called spit, but I'm sure you can guess.

I'd had a thing going with Brendan about nine years ago. I always liked his rich Irish brogue, and he had the most wonderful huge hands and he certainly knew how to use them. He probably still does. At the moment, they are in his trousers pockets – keeping them warm, perhaps. He used to play the field and this annoyed me. I used to get so jealous.

One day at my place, after some drinks and a curry, we went to bed. We were really getting into it and I was so turned on when his mobile rang. His hands stopped doing what they'd been doing, and I was in agony – begging him to ignore the call, but he didn't. He lifted his naked body out of bed and I remember watching him cross the room, pick up his phone and start talking. When he put the phone down and started dressing, I ran to him, pulling at his trousers, but he just pushed me away. He swore at me, saying we were finished and that I shouldn't pester him anymore. I was gutted and didn't know why.

I bumped into him a couple of times after that, by accident. We frequented the same clubs and bars, on occasion, and it was in one of these, a few months later, that I saw him with Maurice. I wish I'd never introduced them. I'd known Maurice before Brendan and although we'd had a fling, it wasn't serious. When I started going out with Brendan I thought it was going to be forever and that we might have a gay marriage. It was that lousy Maurice who told me later, it was him on the phone on that particular night. I could have killed him. I hope they both come back as slugs, each and every time, and that people keep pouring salt on them. It would be so nice to see them squirm after what they did to me.

I watch Ron crushing out his fag-end and walk towards the entrance. I can't see anyone else, so I rush ahead of him and get inside before they close the door. Ron walks down the aisle and joins the Temples, while I sit in the rear. I can observe everyone from here and I'm so happy that Brian hasn't shown up … and I smile.

The service is just getting under way when I hear the door open again. I look across and start to frown. He's here, and he's got a big cheesy grin on his face. He's wearing a big pair of wellington boots and is shaking off the snow as he makes his way into my aisle. Having no desire to be anywhere near him, I move to a seat further back and on the other side. From here, I can see the two Pats sitting behind Sam and Jack, and then I notice Joyce looking up at a huge engraving of an angel.

Seeing what Joyce is engrossed in, it makes me think about Simon. I'm wondering whether he'll turn up for me now, or wait until my body's in the ground. I'd really like to go to Pat's pub and finish my do off properly but, knowing Simon, I don't think I'll get the chance.

I can't help but listen as they say a little prayer for me – the Twenty-Third Psalm. Most of them join in … *"The Lord is my shepherd"* … and I switch off. I don't pay much attention to the other prayers and hymns, but when I hear music coming from some speakers, I perk up.

"Good for you Mary," I say, as we listen to *My Sweet Lord*. She knows how much I like the Beatles so, I suppose, hearing the voice of George Harrison is as close as I'm going to get to them, and his song does seem fitting.

The service soon finishes, so we all stand while the pall-bearers, led by the vicar, carry my coffin outside. We follow, this time me first so I can watch as the rest come out. They have to pass a collection box, right by the door, and I'm surprised by how many donate some cash, but, needless to say, Brian's hands don't leave his pockets, and he's still grinning.

Alice compliments Mary on her choice of song, and Mary replies, *"I wanted them to play John Lennon's Imagine, but the vicar thought it inappropriate. At least we got one of the Beatles for Mick."*

Slowly, we make our way to a corner plot and I take a position away from the crowd, but close enough to inspect my body's new hole in the ground before they place me in it. It's so cold looking, completely covered in snow, both inside the hole and all around it. I step closer to Mary and Sam, taking care not to enter anybody. Mary is explaining to Sam about the type of burial this is.

"No. There won't be a headstone." I look at her, surprised. Doesn't she want to remember me? Is she ashamed of me, after all this time?

"Why not, Mum?"

"It's a new type of burial … a green one. It's what they call a woodland burial."

"I've never heard of it," Sam replies.

"When they release Mick's body into the ground, it will decompose far quicker. Then, after the earth has settled we can plant a tree where his head is." I'm afraid, I don't understand this and don't like it one little bit. I want my body to last. What *does* she think she's doing?

"Honest?" asks Sam.

"Yes. And the coffin will decompose very quickly too, so it won't be long before we can do it. Well, when it's planting time, they'll tell us." I'm getting worried. Even I don't know what's going to happen to me as a ghost, and maybe I should have asked Simon how long I'm likely to last, but I'm sure that coffin is strong. I aught to know … I rode with it. I'll last a hell of a time before the bugs get me.

"Mum, that coffin will protect Uncle Mick for a long time." You see, Sam knows.

Mary shakes her head. *"You'll see. Mick would prefer to be back to nature sooner. You know what he was like. He was always in a hurry."* – In real life, Mary … in real life; certainly not now.

"Oh, Mum! Are you sure?"

"Of course, my love. If he could hear me, he'd thank me for it." I think you're wrong about that, Mary, and you don't know what you're talking about.

Other people are mumbling around us. Ben is complaining about the cold, and Alice tells him not to be such a wuss. At least she's got him sussed. The vicar starts talking again and the others close in. He prays silently, occasionally shaking his hands at the coffin, which is sitting, over the hole, on a couple of wooden planks and specially designed ropes. I watch but don't really listen as the vicar says a final prayer and then crosses himself with his, *"Amen."*

They all say, *"Amen."* Two of his helpers come forward and are about to pull the planks away, while others hold the ropes, and the vicar is still praying to himself when a couple more start messing with the coffin's clasps. I can't believe what I'm seeing. These last two pull the coffin away, to reveal another coffin.

"My god! ... It's made of cardboard," I shout.

My body, in its cardboard sleeve, is lying on the ropes, practically defenceless. The others pull the planks away, while me ... well, you can imagine, I'm in a desperate state. I don't know if I can watch.

"Mum! What's that?" asks Sam, pointing at the cardboard coffin as it gradually goes down. Everybody edges forward, looking and listening.

"It's bio-degradable."

"I can see that, Mary," I say, sarcastically. "You don't give me a ghost's chance, never mind a cat-in-hell's chance, do you?"

"Bio-degradable?" asks Ben, now alongside Mary.

"Yes, Ben. It's new, and I'm going to get it for myself – when it's my time, of course. Everyone should. It's good for the environment and, let's be honest, a tree is much nicer to visit than a headstone. Think about it – Mick will be here, so close to the Nature Trail. He'd have loved it if he'd known."

Mary picks up some soil, from a tiny pile close by, and throws it gently on top of my bio-degradable encased body, and then she steps back. Others copy her.

I move away, disappointed and worried. I don't even look where I'm going and end up by Brendan and Maurice. I look around and watch them all – some mulling over what they'd just seen and others chuckling, including the two I'm now listening to. Brendan, in his not too quiet voice, is speaking. *"Yes, Evelyn! He bit it right off and choked to death."*

He can't know. It's impossible. "It's bloody private, for god's sake," I shout, noticing some of them, Brian included, cocking their ears to listen. He'll be happy to hear this, the prat.

"You're winding me up," says Maurice.

"God's truth, Mo! My cousin is a porter in the hospital. He was there on the night and he helped to wash Mick's body, and, I'm telling you now ... not all of his body is being buried here today."

"Unless they've let him keep a hold of it, and if they've done that," Maurice sniggers, *"he can play with himself whenever he likes, can't he?"* They both laugh ... and Brian laughs, and I cry inside. By this

time, Andy and Brian from Hampstead, having overheard, have come closer, smiling.

"Not you as well! You were my mates."

"No, he can't," goes on Brendan, *"It's been thrown away in the incinerator, I think. Anyway, that's not all the news about this Evelyn. He had a bit of a reputation, you know; especially with his mouth."* – At least he didn't do a Joyce demonstration.

"Let's hear it then," Maurice urges.

"He should have died the week before. To tell the truth, I don't know how he escaped."

"Go on." By this time, most of the mourners have gathered around.

"He was nearly drowned."

"Drowned? What's that got to do wi ... ?"

Brendan cut in. *"He was underwater, in a swimming pool, giving this bloke a blow job."*

"No?"

"Yeah! And when this guy started to – well, you know, he grabbed Evelyn's head and held him there, underneath the water." I'm having visions of Evelyn's head and my hands.

"Oh, my God!" exclaims Maurice.

"It was touch and go for a while, but they blew air into him and he came round. I wouldn't have given him the mouth to mouth, though. Not after what he'd been up to." They roar with laughter again. And so do Andy, Brian, and Mary's Brian. The others look on with disgust. Mary, who's now crying, has a quick word with Ben. He comes over to her Brian and quietly tells him to shut up, or else. He mentions Sam, and how ashamed she'll be of him. It works. Brian clams up and my mates follow suit.

Susan, my secretary, is shocked at what she's just heard. She couldn't help but hear the story being repeated by a few of the others. She'd only been with me for a year, and those who knew had kept my sexual preferences under their hats. She was always giving me the eye and knew I was single. This news has shattered her and she's crying out loud. She turns to my boss and then my ex-colleagues approach Mary. I follow them.

"We're so sorry about Michael," says Freddy. *"We've had a collection at work and hope you'll accept it from us."*

58

"*Of course I will. It's such a nice gesture,*" she says, still sobbing quietly. "*I do hope you'll come back with us to our local. We're having a drink for Mick – you know, to send him off the way he'd like.*" Mary's putting on a brave face in front of the others and, by this time, Susan has only a few tears in her eyes.

"*We should really go home. Susan doesn't feel too well.*"

"*Don't be silly. You'll do nothing of the sort,*" chips in Ben. "*A good stiff whisky will see her alright.*"

"*I ... I'll be okay,*" says Susan.

"*If you insist then,*" adds Freddy. "*We'll follow you.*" In the meantime, Sam has gone to her dad and is talking to him. And she doesn't look at all pleased.

"*We're leaving in a few minutes,*" says Mary. "*I just want a little time alone with Mick. If you'd like to wait by the cars, I'll be along shortly.*" She gives Ben a knowing look and whispers to him. Ben takes the hint and goes around telling everyone of Mary's wishes.

They all move off, leaving Sam, Alice and Joyce to comfort Mary. The girls talk among themselves, and then Mary and Sam walk back to the graveside. I see them mouth a few words to each other and then to my body. Mary crosses herself and then takes Sam's hand before rejoining the other two women. The four of them talk for another few minutes, and Joyce points at my two ex-partners. She's grinning while the others softly smile, and then they walk, heads held high, towards the cars.

As I tag along behind the girls, I'm not sure what to do. Simon should be here by now, but there's no sign of him, and I'm wondering whether to go to the pub or wait by my grave. Everything's been running late because of the delay to the service, so there's no reason I can think of for Simon not to have shown up. Mary and Sam have caught up with Ben and Jack, while Alice and Joyce are making their way to Harry's car. There is a gathering by the cars, and I hear people arranging lifts to the pub, but Joyce pulls both Harry and Pat McHugh to one side and whispers something to them.

Whatever she's said, has led to the three of them crossing the car park towards Brendan and Maurice. I'm not too far away and can just make out what's going on. Pat, who's not very big, closes in on Brendan, saying, "*You two ... go home. You're not welcome at my pub. And, after upsetting Mick's sister with your foul mouths, I suggest you get out of Ely .... Now!*"

"Hey, pal. There's no need to get shirty. If you don't want us at your place ... fine. But you can't stop us having a drink somewhere else in the town," answers Brendan. By this time, a few more have gathered round, and both Joyce and Harry have moved directly in front of Maurice.

"I can and I will," says Pat. "You don't know the grapevine we have in this city. So go, before it's too late."

"Too late for what?" asks Maurice. Joyce turns away, bends down, and picks up a handful of snow.

She turns again, moving up close to him, saying, "This, you foul-mouthed little creep."

She quickly pulls out the front of his trousers with her free hand, and then stuffs the snow-filled one down, inside, and around his precious triangle.

"Aargh! You bitch," he shouts, reaching down to scoop the snow out. Brendan makes a forward move but Pat manages to hold him back, despite the difference in their size.

"Now do as Pat says ... and piss off. The pair of you," Joyce advises, pointing her finger straight in Maurice's face. While this is taking place, Ron has moved, unseen by the two of them, to the back of their car and is filling the exhaust pipe with snow and ice.

'A nice bit of team work,' I think.

"Come on, Mo," orders Brendan, turning to open his car. "I know when we're not wanted."

"Yeah, right," Maurice replies, and when he turns away from Joyce, he makes a fist, threatening her, "We'll be back, you'll see."

"Just try it," says Joyce, now gathering more snow. Harry grabs her and tells her to simmer down. The rest of the onlookers start clapping and then go back to their own cars.

Mary and Sam are saying cheerio to our uncle and aunts, who've obviously decided to go straight home, and I'm still on the lookout for Simon. I'll have to make a decision soon. Do I stay here and wait, or find a space in one of the cars? Some of them are moving off, so I make my choice.

I run for Freddy Beasant's car because I know that they're definitely going to the pub. When he opens the rear door for Susan, I dive in quickly, flinging myself across the back seat before she can get in my way. Now, feeling safe in their company, I look towards my burial site and search the nearby area for any last possible sighting of my favourite ghost. The only person I see is a young lady in a red coat, looking down at another grave. "Well, Simon, I'll be in the boozer when you want me. I hope you can find it," I say to him, wherever he is.

Freddy and Luke are still standing outside their open doors, looking and laughing at something behind me, so I turn around to see what's amusing them. Brendan and Maurice are knee deep in snow, poking a stick up their exhaust pipe. Brendan turns to his pal, giving him what for. We watch for another couple of minutes, and then Freddy decides he's seen enough, climbs into his car, and Luke follows. We pull away and turn out of the gate.

"It's a pity Stan couldn't come," says Susan.

"He's covering for Mick. Someone has to," replies Luke.

"I suppose you're right. Mind you, if you were clever enough, you could have done it."

"What do you mean, clever enough?"

"Well, you're not, are you? You just hang arou ... ."

"Stop it! The pair of you! If you carry on like this, I'll swing the car around and head back home," interrupts Freddy.

"You'd better not," I tell him. That's the last thing I need. Imagine ending up at Stansted while Simon is searching for me in The Three Oysters. What would he do? ... What would I do? Fortunately, Susan and Luke stay quiet for the rest of the journey to the pub.

CHAPTER SEVEN

As soon as Susan opens the door, I'm up and nearly inside her as I follow her out of the car. I walk beside them and then go inside, where we are greeted with a drink by Patricia, who then directs us to a buffet. It seems so sad and lifeless in here, despite the amount of people. And I can't believe that there isn't any music playing … and this is a pub.

Mary is talking to Colin and Sylvia, and I join them until I get the drift of the conversation. I've had enough of coffins for one day, especially the bio-degradable kind, and Mary can't stop going on. She must have shares in the company. I notice Joyce having a drink with Harry and Marie, so I head in their direction. I want to thank Joyce, personally, for what she did at the cemetery, but I don't know how. Not unless I. … No, I'd better not.

Marie offers them cigarettes, but Harry declines. I know that Joyce usually smokes when she's drinking, and the two women light up. I don't know, as yet, how ciggie smoke will affect me, so I lean in and take a whiff. I neither taste nor smell anything, which is a big difference from the past. I couldn't stand to be around smokers, although I had to now and then, and the only reason Joyce hadn't indulged at Mary's is because it's a no-smoking house. Paul comes over with a tray full of shorts and lagers and lays it on the table. Marie gives him a questioning look.

He smirks, saying, *"Saves time, doesn't it?"*

"I suppose so, but remember … we have the car," answers Marie.

"Don't you worry, about a thing. You can always stay at my place," suggests Joyce.

"No, we're alright. As long as we eat enough and watch ourselves, we'll be okay. Anyway, I've just decided that, for a change, I'll do the drinking and Paul can do the driving." Paul looks at her, nearly dropping his pint. I've known them for some while now, and Marie has always been the sober one of the two.

"What's got into you?" Paul asks, while the others take their glasses.

"I'm celebrating," she replies. *"The thing is … . Mmm, now, how can I say this? Well, you know that belief about when someone dies and then another takes their place."* Marie smiles, and then pats her tummy.

Paul's jaw drops open. *"Marie! … You mean it?"*

"Of course, I mean it." She then turns to Joyce, saying, *"We've been*

trying for ages and I only found out late on Monday night ... about the same time Mick died."

"*Congratulations!*" exclaim the other two, as Paul throws a large short down his throat. He puts his glass down and gives Marie a kiss. When the two of them move apart, others gather around, including Colin and Sylvia, Alan and Irene, and my old two muckers, Andy and Brian. News spreads so fast and now everyone is congratulating the couple. I step back, so as not to get caught up in anybody accidentally. It's not that I'd mind, but there seems to be plenty of excitement at the moment. The drinks start flowing even more and there's no way those two will be sober when they leave.

A short while later, things start to quieten down, and people are beginning to move away, but party-girl Joyce gets them going again.

"*Hey, everyone! I've got another celebration.*" The crowd regroup, waiting. And then Joyce makes a big show of patting her stomach, all the time watching as they open their mouths in amazement. "*Guess what?*" she says. "*I'm not pregnant, although Harry gave it his best shot.*" She bursts out laughing and everyone joins in. Harry doesn't look too pleased, but then starts chuckling himself. He kisses her cheek, smacks her bum, and then heads off to get a refill.

I follow him to the bar and Mary's Brian is already there. He's got the most miserable look on his face, and, occasionally, he glances over at Ben. I can feel something brewing and I do wish he'd go. I'm surprised Mary let him come here in the first place, but when I consider Sam and her feelings, I can understand it a little. Speaking of Sam, both she and Jack are now approaching her dad, so I hang around to listen.

The first thing I hear is music, and observe the two Pats selecting discs with help from Andy and Harry. At least we'll get plenty of variety and my party won't be ending too early. Sam quietly tells Brian to behave himself and not to drink too much, but he seems reluctant to obey. Then she drops the bombshell. "*Dad, I know we've talked about Jack, but now I'd like you to meet him.*" They say hello to each other, shaking hands, and she adds, "*And I have something else to tell you. Me and Jack are engaged – well, sort of. We haven't got the ring yet, and I'd have told you before, but we wanted to make sure of our relationship.*"

"*Sam! Jack! This is good news. Congratulations!*" I thought he'd go into one. Brian kisses Sam and then shakes Jack's hand again, not wanting to let go. *"Sam says that you're an estate agent?"*

"Yes," replies Jack. *"I'm doing quite well, at the moment."* I wonder what's going on in Brian's tiny mind. He must be after something; maybe a way out of his bedsit.

"Well, good for you. We'll have to get together sometime. Let me buy you a drink." I knew it. He's always up to something. I listen to their small talk for a few minutes and then explore some more.

More people are coming in – some I've seen before with Mary and Alice, while others are new to me. Patricia has left the bar and is engrossed in a conversation with Alice, Susan and the Temples, so I step closer and take an interest. I study Patricia while she rambles on about rambling. She's giving them information regarding nature trails and pub strolls. I haven't got the foggiest idea what she's going on about, except that it's a keep fit, have a pint, and enjoy the countryside kind of exercise. I quite like the have a pint part … if only I could. I realise now, just what I'll be missing, but I'm determined to make up for it somehow. My life as a ghost has only just begun and it can only get better. Patricia looks pretty fit, herself. She's only thirty, and even though she's already had three kids, her body says otherwise. Joyce should take her as an example if she ever does fall foul of another faulty condom.

I notice some of the people making their exit, among them my Newmarket drinking buddies, Alan and Irene. Colin and Sylvia are also disappearing. I don't suppose I'll see them again.

Moving on to another table, I find Megan and Carl chatting and singing with Ben and Mary. Every so often Carl vanishes for five minutes, so on one occasion I follow him. He makes his way towards the toilet but then turns towards the rear door. Once outside, I watch while he rolls a joint, lights up, and then takes a few hefty puffs. When he turns around, he has the grin of a Cheshire cat. He's about to come back in when Megan rushes right through me, charges out of the door, and suddenly she starts to shake. Carl grabs a hold of her, whispers something in her ear, and then offers her a drag. She takes his spliff and sticks it in her mouth. Carl takes the last pull before coming back in, and she's saying,

"I don't know, Carl, I've never felt so weird. I hope it's not this wacky-baccy."

"Course, it's not. I'm okay. Maybe you've drunk too much."

"No. It wasn't like that. I think I was spooked." Now, that's interesting.

I wonder if she's like Joyce. The thought of someone being spooked reminds me of Simon, so I go back to the bar and check the time.

It's four-thirty and there's still no sign of him. "What's gone wrong?" I ask myself. There aren't many people left and those who are are nibbling away at sandwiches, crisps and cocktail sausages, or else they're drinking themselves into oblivion. My mates, Brian and Andy, are legless. They have a row of glasses, full of spirits, and they're having a competition to see which one of them is the first to die of alcoholic poisoning. Andy gets up and lifts a glass, swallows its contents, and slurs, *"Shee yun min't,"* and he slopes off to the toilet. I can't help but follow, can I?

He staggers from side to side, now and then, reaching out for a wall to support him. He, eventually, makes it to the loo and I go in with him, and in the process enter his body. It's purely by accident, as he stops to hold himself up in the doorway. I decide to stay inside him for a while, just for the experience. It could be my last chance for some time. After all, I don't know what Simon has in store for me when he does turn up. A minute later, I doubt whether Andy is the right choice, as he leans over the urinals and spews up … and spews up … and I'm not feeling too good. I'm watching as his eyes inspect the bits of sausage, tomato, coleslaw, and the browny-yellow liquid that's pouring from his mouth. I want to throw up myself … and I'm getting dizzy.

Andy carries me back to the bar, sits down opposite Brian, and asks, *"Whooj nex?"*

"You," Brian replies, seeming the better for wear of the two of them. Andy doesn't argue, and my head is going to pieces while I watch him lift the next glass towards both his and my mouth. I don't feel the drink touch my mouth, nor feel it go down, but my eyes are closing and I'm getting weaker by the second.

"I've got to get out," I shout, but no-one hears me. I try moving, but I'm so tired. I push myself again and shout into Andy's brain, "Let me out."

I manage to release the right side of my body and Andy falls away from me, onto the floor, and I fall the other way, collapsing in a heap. My body is in agony and I'm so sick, and yet I know I'm free. I open my eyes a little and try to get up … but I can't. I'm helpless, and just then two female stockinged-feet plant themselves in my chest and stay there. I hear voices all around me but I can't make out what they're saying. The feet don't move, and soon they're joined by a pair of Wellingtons which make my neck and face their stamping ground. I feel worse than ever and close my eyes again. My head is aching even more and I feel myself passin ... .

'Don't ever stop,' I think, as the lips that are kissing me keep caressing mine, and are blowing, what seem like little bubbles, into my mouth. I haven't got the strength to open my eyes, but I know it's Simon and he's here to save me. My mind is getting more alert, but still I can't move. My head still aches but, right now, I don't care. The lips just keep on kissing and they are so soft. I can feel hands wrapping themselves around me. My mind is telling him, 'Simon, dear Simon, I knew you'd come,' but I'm sure he can't read minds.

I feel his body so close to me now, and it feels so soft, gentle, and so warm, whereas, before, I couldn't feel any heat or cold. He kisses me tenderly and I can feel myself start to move, but my eyelids are still so heavy that I can't raise them. He can have his way with me and I'll love him even more for it. Will my new life always be so wonderful, like this, I wonder, as he lifts me up, his lips still pressed on mine, and carries me off somewhere. I don't care where he takes me, so long as we're always together.

I lift my arms, achingly slowly, and manage to put one behind his back and the other on his arm. He lays me down and lies on top of me, all the time kissing and blowing into my mouth, and he's sending me wild. And ... I start getting excited. My body is waking up and I'm getting hard. I must be getting better. My aches and pains are going and still he kisses me, and I reach out, wrapping my arms about him, pulling him even tighter into me.

'He's got boobs!'

Simon's got small pointy breasts and they're sticking in my chest. I don't know if it's shock, or what, but I open my eyes ... wide, and see a pair of beautiful hazel eyes smiling at me.

They are not Simon's ... and neither are the pointy bits that are still rubbing up against me. Nor are the lips that are still glued to mine and won't let go. I haven't got the strength to push her away, but I know that this is not a man, and I'm wondering if it's Megan. I know she has hazel eyes, but I also know she can't see me ... so it can't be her.

'Who are you?' I ask, mentally. If she lets me speak, I'll ask her properly. I can't even move my head; she has such firm a hold on me. 'Where am I?' I think. I know we haven't moved far. Raising my eyes to the ceiling and beyond, I see the same light blue paint and the dark blue velvet curtains of the pub.

Suddenly, I'm free of her lips. She moves her face away, but only inches, yet still she holds me close, and says, "Mick, whatever you do, don't move. That's an order."

"Who are you?"

"I'll tell you shortly. Meanwhile, do as I say. That is, everything I tell you, even if it sounds stupid."

"Why?"

"If you don't, you'll never get enough of your strength back to recover properly. Is that understood?"

"We're still in the pub. I'm not imagining all this, am I?"

"No, you're not imagining anything and if you want to get better, faster, then try to forget about having a nice warm body next to you ... and get that stiffy down. It's sticking in my ... er, well, where it's not supposed to be, and, while it might be making me feel a little hot and horny, we haven't got time for sex right now. ... Perhaps later."

I can't believe what I'm hearing and she's still lying on me ... and my stiffy, as she calls it, is still stiff ... and it won't go down.

"Mick, I'm going to kiss you for some considerable time, but when I stop, I want you to enter your friend, Ben, completely, and don't argue. I'll be close by so we'll be able to talk."

"Ben? Why Ben, of all people?"

"Don't argue. Just do as you're told."

"I don't like it. Not Ben, and, anyway, why should I enter anybody; what's the point?"

"His body will give you that strength I was talking about."

"Well, Andy's didn't do me any good."

"I've told you, now, Ben, and only Ben. That's if you want to live."

"Okay," I answer, feeling down.

"Oh! And don't get upset about it. It will only make you miserable and I can't perform miracles. Think of something that will make you happy."

"I'll try. By the way, what's your name?"

67

"Jana."

"Yana?"

"Yes, Jana … with a Jay, and not a Wi as everyone seems to think."

"Jay, ay, en, ay … Jana! That's different. Where does that come from?"

"Where I'm taking you to. Now shush, shut your eyes, and think of somewhere exotic, but not people. You're still hard, and I want you to relax, so don't go thinking of me and sex. Think of fish swimming freely, or a south sea island, or somewhere else you might like to visit."

"I'll try."

I close my eyes and do try to take my mind off her, especially when she starts kissing me again, but my thoughts go to Simon and Fergie's Fashion House. Then doing as suggested, visions of a long forgotten holiday come to mind. I start remembering one of the last times that I ever had sex with a girl – in a field in France. Okay, I wasn't always gay. Actually, I didn't know what I was at the time. I remember Cathie's face and those bloody cows, and I can't help it and start laughing through Jana's kiss, and she stops. I open my eyes.

"Mick! Whatever's on your mind … forget it. Think of something else." So, I close them again and try thinking of fish, but it's not easy. I remember my holiday in Sitges, and fishing from the rocks for hours – spinning with a silver lure and catching them one after the other. I was throwing them back but some of the local kids were going mad, so I started giving the fish to them. I was only wearing a pair of skimpy shorts and that's when my holiday was ruined. I nearly died from sunburn. I wasn't happy then, I can tell you.

I think of great whites and Jaws springs to mind … and so does Evelyn, so I stop thinking of fish. Maybe I should go to Hong Kong and join in with all the hustle and bustle of the place, or visit Australia. I think of the sand, the sun, and the laid back way of life, and all the time Jana is kissing and blowing into me.

Eventually, she takes her lips from mine, rolls off me and sits down. Jana looks into my eyes again. "You know what to do. I'll be along in a minute. Now, go!"

I don't want to go inside Ben – he's such a dullard, but Jana must have her reasons. There aren't many of the mourners left, and these are now gathered together around two of the tables. Fortunately, Ben is on one of the outer chairs, so it won't be difficult to gain access to him. Shrugging my shoulders, I get up and cross the room. The aches and pains seem to have gone, but my legs feel like lumps of lead and a slight dizziness still remains. I take another peep at Jana and she just waves me on.

Ben is just getting up when I reach him, and he's fishing in his pocket for something. He turns towards the bar and this gives me the opportunity to make my move. I step inside him while he's walking and he doesn't feel a thing. He buys a few shorts and a mineral water, and as soon as Patricia places them on the bar he lifts the water to our lips. Now I'm beginning to understand why Jana chose him and nobody else. I'd watched most of the people get reasonably drunk, and others paralytic, but I hadn't been watching Ben. We carry the drinks to the tables and dish them out before resuming his seat.

"How is he?" asks the voice behind me. I can't turn around, because I'm facing where Ben's looking – at Joyce, but I know full well that it's Jana's voice and that she's very near.

"He's as sober as a judge," I reply.

"Don't kid yourself. He's had a couple, but that was early on. He'll have to do for the next hour or so."

"Why so long?"

"We need you at maximum strength, and I have to look for someone to enter, also."

"Why you?"

"Do you think it's easy giving you all my energy?"

"What are you talking about?"

"You don't, honestly, think I was kissing you because I love you?"

"Huh! Then … Simon? He was kissing me. You're wrong, Jana. I didn't need any of his energy when he kissed me in the shop, or at my sister's house."

She laughs at me. "Was he sucking or blowing?"

"I don't remember."

"He was sucking you, wasn't he? Tell me, Mick. Don't be shy."

"Perhaps, he was. Anyway, where will you find someone around here? They're all a bit tipsy."

"There are three children upstairs. I'll use one of them – probably the oldest, unless he's ill."

"The children! You can't use children. They're too small, and, anyway, that's an awful thing to do."

"You've a lot to learn, Mick. Now stay inside Ben, unless he decides to go home. If he does, then hop out and wait for me here ... . Okay?"

"Okay." I don't see Jana leave, because Ben and I are still ogling Joyce. Our eyes focus on her thighs as she crosses and uncrosses her legs. I know she knows he's watching her. Joyce is deliberately tempting him, and he only lifts our eyes up when she speaks.

"Ben, do you believe in ghosts?" I hear gasps of surprise to our left from Jack and Sam. They're obviously wondering why Joyce has brought up the ghost topic again.

"No, of course not. That's for children and fairy stories." We look into Joyce's face, and then at Mary and Alice.

"I don't either," says Mary.

"Well, if you must know, I think you're a ghost."

Joyce is leaning forward and looking straight into Ben's eyes as she intimates this, and then winks at us. She knows I'm here, inside Ben, and her wink is for me.

Before Ben can respond, I ask her, "If you're this receptive to me when you're half-cut, then what are you like when you're sober?"

Ben asks, *"Me? A ghost? Joyce, go home. You're drunk."* She opens her eyes wide, glaring at us, and then bursts out laughing.

"Don't worry about her, Ben. She was on about stupid ghosts last night," adds Jack.

"Leave Joyce alone! At least she's more entertaining than most other people. Besides, it's an interesting subject," says Sam.

"Let's drop it or we'll only end up arguing, and that's not right. Not today of all days," demands Alice. I can see Mary nodding her head, and Ben keeps our eyes off Joyce for a while. I listen while they carry on talking about trivial things, and I'm getting bored. Soon after, Harry asks Joyce if she wants a lift home and she accepts the offer. She gets up rather awkwardly and falls forward, landing on top of me and Ben.

I'm looking straight into her eyes when she lifts her head, saying, *"Well, now that you have me, you might as well give me a goodnight kiss."*

"Go on," urges Mary, laughing, and Ben has me looking down at Joyce's puckered lips. We give them a little peck and she grabs us, planting a great big sloppy one on ours.

She pulls away, asking, *"Did you like that, ghostie?"*

Ben just glowers at her, while I answer, "From you, Joyce, yes. You're magic … and I wish you could hear me." When Harry and Joyce head for the door, some of the others follow. The only ones remaining are Mary, Sam, Ben, Alice and Jack.

"Well Alice, it looks like we've got all that booze at my place to ourselves," says Mary.

"I'll have no problem helping you get rid of it, believe me," she answers.

"And don't forget us," says Sam. *"We might as well finish our holiday in style. It's back to work next week."* They drink and talk a while longer before deciding to go, and when Ben stands up, I make my escape. He shivers and shakes, and I smile. Walking over to Sam, I give her a big kiss on the lips. Mine sink slightly into hers, and when I pull away she licks hers, saying,

"Mmm, that's nice."

"What's nice?" asks Mary.

"I don't know. My mouth feels so lovely – all tingly and fresh."

"I could do with some of that, especially after all the drink," suggests Mary. So I oblige, and she, too, is soon licking her lips. Ben helps Mary with her coat and then gives her a hug. Jack and Sam are not only ready to go, but are holding Alice up as they leave the pub. The two Pats come to see them off, and they both wish Mary well. I wave my family goodbye … and I want to cry.

CHAPTER EIGHT

When the pub door closes behind Mary, I turn away, dejected, and take an empty seat in the corner to wait for Jana. A few minutes pass by and then I notice her casually approaching Patricia, who is busy serving a young couple. Jana stops and stares at her, and it looks as though she's waiting to do something. And then I watch her lips move as she starts talking to Patricia. She gets no response, but I can't believe my eyes as she moves forward, putting her head completely inside Patricia's, and within seconds it's out again.

"Pat, will you finish this round for me?" asks Patricia. *"I'm going upstairs for a while. I've got this blazing headache and, anyway, I want to check on the kids."*

Jana comes over and, without even mentioning what she's just done, says, "Look Mick, it's getting late and I'm still feeling shattered. We'll travel in the morning, after a good nights rest, and a rest wouldn't do you any harm, either."

"We are supposed to be ghosts you know. Ghosts do come out at night – at least I thought they did."

"That might be so sometimes but we do have a long way to fly, and by daylight you'll be able to see some of the beautiful scenery from all the countries as we cross them. We might even stop somewhere, on the way home, and drop in on some of my friends."

"And where's home?"

"My home … Slovakia! Actually, we ghosts don't have one country, as such. We can journey anywhere we want to, or where we're needed, and, if we ever get lucky enough, we can travel back in time. Well, some ghosts can … in a fashion."

"That's ridiculous."

"It's true. I wouldn't lie to you, Mick, not after the way you felt for me earlier." She thinks I had the hots for her. She obviously doesn't know very much about me.

"So, how can ghosts be so lucky to do time travel? Do we have to win the ghost lottery, or the phantom jackpot at Cheltenham? I don't think so somehow. You're just winding me up. And do you really expect me to believe that we can go back in time like Dickens' ghost of Christmas past?"

"Never mind then … . Unbeliever! Not that you need to know, but I haven't got that kind of ghostly power. There aren't many ghosts lucky enough to achieve that distinction, and when they do … it's by accident and not by design. And, as regards Charles Dickens' characters like Bob Marley and his spirit, they were only in fiction, whereas we are real life ghosts. And going back in time is not the same as you might imagine it to be. We don't have a time machine."

"I still don't believe you but you certainly have my interest. Oh, and by the way, that Dickens' character was Jacob Marley. Bob was a singer."

"Okay! Okay! So many names. How am I supposed to remember them all? Anyway, Mick, forget that for now. They should be closing the pub soon and we can get our heads down. We can lie down together, if that's alright with you. What do you think?" I don't reply.

"Well?"

"Yeah, I suppose so." I had to think about that one. If I'm not friendly towards her, then I'm not going to get the answers to my questions, and Simon isn't here to help. I just hope she doesn't want sex. My god! It could set me back years, and I don't know if I could do it now with a woman; pretty as she is.

"You don't sound too enthusiastic. What's bothering you?"

"It doesn't matter. Just so long as we're resting, then it's fine, and you're probably right. I do need to relax for a while."

"Come on," she says, "let's move over there." Jana is pointing to a long sofa type seat at the back of the lounge. I get up first and, of course, being the gentleman I am, take her hand and help her up. It's not that she needs any but I'm only trying to appear keen to please. She flicks her ash-blonde hair off her face and gives me a lovely warm smile. We cross the floor and she sits down at one end of the sofa while I deliberately sit at the other. It is quite firm and I only sink in an inch, if that, and she laughs. Jana slides her bum along the sofa and cups one of my hands in hers. She searches my eyes, saying, "Hi, Mick, I think it's time we got to know each other. You must have loads of questions to ask, and I'll answer those I can, but I won't be able to explain everything. I hope you understand this." I nod my head. "So, what do you want to know?"

"We should start at the very beginning, but I've got so many questions that we could be here all night."

"I'll do my best, but we do need some shut-eye. I know. Start from this evening while it's fresh in your mind and any others we'll sort out tomorrow. How's that?"

"Okay. So, what happened to Patricia?"

"Patricia?"

"Yes ... the lady behind the bar."

Jana smiles at me. "So that's her name! What about her?"

"You know what I'm talking about. You stuck your head inside hers and gave her a lousy headache. I heard what she said to her husband, and I'm not stupid. What did you do to her?"

"Oh that! The thing is, her youngest girl isn't too well and she was crying for her mummy. I had to tell her. You must understand. It wouldn't be right ... not to help."

"How can you talk to her? She's human. I mean ... she's alive."

"You'll develop these abilities in time, if you listen and learn. Actually, you've already used them, even though you weren't very quiet about it."

"What are you talking about?"

"Your friend, the drunk."

"Andy?"

"If that's his name, yes. You shouted 'let me out' while you were inside his body."

"He could hear me?"

"Of course he could. You were inside his head at the time, and you must have really got to his brainwaves. Mick! You could have died in there. Andy let you go ... . Don't you get it?"

"No, I don't. What do you mean by – he let me go? I got out by myself."

"No, you didn't. You were too weak to move. You were dying and I was about to push my arms in and pull you out when he set you free."

"Huh! I didn't see you here today."

"You saw me twice, as a matter of fact, but you weren't looking for me. Think about it – we might be ghosts, but we do look like the living. If you didn't know I was a ghost, this very second, and I was up the other end of the bar ... would you think I was one?"

"To tell you the truth ... no, I wouldn't. So you've been here, all the time, mingling with the customers?"

"Yes, I have ... and at the graveyard. You were in the back seat of a car, looking at me. I was pretending to take an interest in another grave, but my eyes were on you."

"Bloody hell! You're the girl in the red coat."

"That's right. My coat's over there." Jana points to a seat near the entrance. I hadn't twigged it, at all. I'd been on the lookout for Simon.

"Why didn't you pick me up at the graveyard?"

"Well, I think it's only right that a ghost should enjoy its body's last day, if it so chooses. You wanted to give yourself and your family a last goodbye ... unlike me and my body."

"Why ever not? I mean, if you wanted to be a ghost, why wouldn't you want to see yourself off?"

"I was too young. I was only just fifteen when I was mur ... er, when I died, and the circumstances were horrible." Jana is looking downcast.

"Oh, Jana, I'm so sorry. Fifteen! You never really had a life at all, and I'll understand if you don't want to tell me what happened."

"I can't tell you. No, that's not exactly true. I can but I won't."

A couple of tears, or what look like tears, come into her eyes, as I go on, "It doesn't matter, Jana. I think I understand, and it couldn't have been that long ago; a few years at the most. What are you now ... .twenty-two?"

"Mick, please leave it alone. You're going to find out anyway, so I may as well tell you now. Ghosts don't age. You come back as you appeared in your dream. If you've had more than one dream of being a ghost and your appearances have been different in each or some of them, then it's pot luck as to which appearance your ghost will take."

"That's amazing. So, when you had your dream, you dreamt of you as you are now."

"Yes." Her funny looking little tears show again as she continues, "I dreamt of being married, and of being a ghost, and I dreamt about other horrible things ... and my dream was all mixed up. Now please stop talking about it. You're upsetting me."

"I'm sorry. I didn't mean to. Do you mind if I ask you something different?"

"Of course not, as long as it's nothing too personal."

"No, it's not, but I'm confused. You see, you say we're going to your place, but Simon said I'd be going to Uni' and, well ... which is it?"

"What are you talking about? What's this Uni'?"

"University! Simon said I'd learn everything there; everything about being a ghost."

"We don't have Universities. He's teasing you. He teases every ghost he can. That's Simon all over. I don't know him intimately, but he has a reputation."

"So, he lied to me?"

"I think he only exaggerated the truth, so's to make himself feel important."

"Exaggerated the truth? So how am I supposed to learn to be a ghost?"

"Mick, you are a ghost. You're not a baby crocodile or a penguin."

"I can't fly. I can't go through walls. I can't lie on a bed without sinking in. There are so many things I can't do. Why?"

"You're learning Mick. You really are. I've been keeping an eye on you since Monday night when Simon left."

"That's impossible. I'd have seen you. Please ... don't tell me you're lying as well?"

"I'm not lying. I'm a Ghost Monitor. I have certain abilities that can make me invisible to other ghosts. That's to say, not really invisible but, less conspicuous. You would have noticed me at your sister's had you explored a little more, or been a bit more observant. Fortunately for me, you tended to stick to the front room, and, I might add, I'm a much faster and far more experienced ghost than you."

"Don't be crazy. You don't think, for one minute, that I believe you. You're as bad as Simon."

"No, I'm not, and don't you ever call me crazy. It's not very nice. I don't go around insulting other ghosts, or people for that matter. What I do have to say though, is very important – well, it is to me."

"What's that?"

She takes her hands away, points her index finger at me and, surprisingly quietly, says, "Mick, don't you, ever again, scare another animal the way you scared that labrador. You could have killed that poor dog. And, another thing – although I know it wasn't your fault, but – the next time you see anyone approaching who might cause you to enter them by accident ... get out of the way. That lady on the bus was ill and on medication. She might have had a heart attack the way she was shaking."

"I couldn't help it. How was I supposed to know? That's what I mean by me needing to learn to be a ghost. I'm sorry, Jana. I'm really sorry ... Okay?"

"Okay." – I feel miserable now and, turning away from her, I stand up. I want to go out and walk around for a while. I'm still confused and I'm thinking of the other things she's seen me do. Jana can sense this, saying, very softly, "Come here, Mick. We can rest soon, and tomorrow we can make a fresh start … together."

The way she said 'together' makes me turn to her, and I don't know whether to laugh or do as she asks. I'm still not smiling when I sit down again, my hands on my knees and my face pointing towards the bar. She doesn't reach for me but I can sense her looking. We remain quiet for a while longer but the silence is broken when she asks, "May I tell you something?"

"If you like."

"I like you, Micky. You don't mind me calling you Micky … do you?"

I turn to her. "I don't mind. Lots of people used to." My mother often called me Micky.

"You're so different from the other ghosts I've met," she adds, placing her hand on my arm.

"How so?"

"Many are stubborn, stupid, vindictive, or too intellectual for their own good. Some are dreamers, some are poets, while others seem happy all the time. You'll like the last ones when you meet them, but you, Micky, have a good all round character about you."

"Do you think so?" She's definitely getting to me and I can't help but let a tiny smile escape my lips.

"Yes, I do. From what I've seen and heard, and who you admire, and even your choice in music, you are most definitely different from the norm'. And you have a lovely family and some funny friends – especially Joyce. She made me laugh."

"So, you like Joyce? Do you know if she's a medium?"

"You know about mediums then?"

"Of course, I do. There are lots of supposed clairvoyants and psychics around – most of them wanting money; and then there are the séance meetings, and, of course, the mention of them in films. Why wouldn't I know about mediums?"

"It appears as though she is one, and so is Megan."

"So, I was right. But how do you know Megan's name?"

"I told you I was close by. Megan and Carl introduced themselves to

Mary at the graveyard. And then they were singing in here. Why wouldn't I take notice, especially when you followed them? Do you think I'd want to miss out on whatever you're up to?"

"You saw them with the spliff, then?"

"Spliff? What's a spliff?"

"Never mind. I'll explain later." She's never heard of a spliff. That doesn't make any sense. I'll make her wait for the answer and remind her when I need to know something interesting.

"No. Tell me now." She's interested alright.

"It's not important, Jana, and look," I say, pointing to an empty bar. Pat has closed the pub and is making his way upstairs.

"Thank goodness for that. Now let's get some rest." I don't move. "Come on, Micky, lie back."

"I'm fine. I'll lie on the floor. I'll be more comfortable there because I won't sink in."

"Don't be daft. You don't have to sink in."

"What are you talking about? I always sink in, unlike you or Simon."

"You have to think for yourself. Tell your body to lie on top of the sofa. Implant the idea in your brain, just like you did to Andy. You don't have to shout, or talk, for that matter."

We stand up and, looking at her, I ask, "Now?"

"Yes. Do it now." I close my eyes and concentrate. "You don't need to shut your eyes, Micky. Just think about what you're doing."

"If you say so." I start again and order my body to lie on top of the sofa. 'Lie on top ... on top ... on top' I keep stressing as I move forward and place my hands on the seat. They stop just above the cloth and, still concentrating, I turn, sit down and stretch out. It's amazing. It feels just the same as lying on the floor – like a cushion.

Jana comes closer. "Are you comfortable?"

"Yes. It doesn't feel any different from before, but now I don't feel so stupid. I was afraid of drowning in that bed at Mary's. I didn't know what to do."

"I know. I was watching you from the door and I nearly burst out laughing. It's just as well I didn't – you'd have been scared to death." Both of us start laughing at this, but I stop when she says, still chuckling, "You have a lovely body, Micky. Believe me, I was tempted to come out of hiding and screw you silly when I saw you playing with yourself."

Now I remember, and I'm hoping my embarrassment isn't too obvious. I realise that she must have seen lots of naked ghosts before, and I've done far worse than strip off in front of a woman, but to be spied upon by Jana, in a very private moment, has taken me aback and I know I have to pretend that it hasn't.

She pushes me further in and lies alongside, facing me. She places her right arm around my waist and her left hand is curled beneath her head. Her body presses into mine, so I turn onto my side, giving her more room. "I can go and lie somewhere else, Jana, and then we'll both get a good night's sleep." I can't get the idea of her wanting my body out of my head … and I'm scared.

"Micky, right now, I need you close by. I need to feel safe."

"I can't sleep like this," I plead.

"You will. Now shush, and please hold me."

So, reluctantly, I do, and she makes herself more comfortable, snuggling even closer, her eyes smiling into mine. I really don't know what to do. Despite what she said, I feel quite comfortable with her, and, yet, if she were to, somehow, turn into Simon this very minute, I'd be so happy. I'm still a little worried about this situation. Wouldn't you be, if you were me? A couple of seconds later, I'm even more worried when Jana whispers, "Micky, aren't you going to give me a goodnight kiss?"

To keep her quiet, I move my lips to hers and give her a little peck. She gives me an is-that-the-best-you-can-do look and then kisses me properly. She moves her right leg over mine, still kissing, and then she starts sucking, just as Simon had. I try closing my mind to what she's doing but my body starts to respond. I can feel myself starting to twitch and then grow. Seconds later, I'm fully erect and pushing against my trousers, but no matter what I try to think of, I can't stop reacting to her advances. We both seem to be getting extremely warm and then she stops sucking, kisses me softly, and then our lips part. With her lips moving so close to my ear and sort of tickling me, she whispers, "That was lovely, Micky. You're so sweet to me."

"What have I done?"

"Ssh! Lets try and get some rest." Jana closes her eyes but I can't sleep. I stare at the ceiling wondering where all this is taking me. What's going to happen next? Several things run through my mind. At least Jana did show me how to lie down, but why, for heaven's sake, didn't

Simon explain things to me? I still have so many questions for her but, with her looking so peaceful and pleased with herself, they'll have to wait. I watch over her for, what seems, an eternity until I close my eyes, dreaming and ... .

CHAPTER NINE

"Jana! Where the hell are we going?"

"I've told you already – Slovakia."

"What's so special about Slovakia? Surely there's somewhere in England I can learn?"

"We're going to a very small and specially rebuilt village that shows how life was many years ago. We'll be staying there – you in the big house and me in one of the small worker's houses. There's even an old school room. I know you'll like it, Micky, so stop going on."

"But why Slovakia?"

"There aren't any Ghost Tutors in England. You seem to think that ghosts are created every minute but that's just not so, and it was quite amazing, actually, that two of you came into being in the same night, and only a few miles apart. Sometimes we wait months before a New Ghost turns up."

"You mean to tell me that there's only one ghost school, or whatever it is?"

"No. There are others, of course, but they're too far away, and, anyway, I want the best for you. Besides, the ghost you're going to meet is, without doubt, the most accomplished instructor in the art of ghosting. That's what I believe and that's what matters."

We're talking while flying, hand in hand, across the English countryside, following the M11, towards London. There's snow as far as the eye can see and the cars beneath us are crawling along, obviously due to the hazardous conditions. We seem to be making good time – that is, if a ghost can make good time. I don't have the slightest idea how fast we ghosts can move but Jana seems to be putting her foot down. She's flying a lot faster than Simon did on Monday night.

"So, you want the best for me. I take it then, that my final destination is your individual choice and not a predetermined arrangement by some superior ghost?"

"Not really, Mick. I'm your Ghost Monitor and I do have the right to decide which Tutor is likely to benefit you the most. And, besides, I don't fancy taking you to another one outside Europe. If you'd been a bit of a dullard then I might have taken you to a more reserved instructor. A lot depends on your personality and where you live."

"That's logical, I suppose, but what about this other ghost? Will he be there?"

"In the first place, the ghost might be a female, and, secondly, where he or she goes is up to its own Ghost Monitor."

"So, how long's it gonna' take us?"

"A couple of days. Maybe three … it depends."

"On what?"

"We might make that stopover I mentioned, and there's also the weather to contend with."

"We're ghosts, so why should the weather bother us?"

"You do ask so many questions. Look over there. Those clouds are moving towards us very quickly and I don't like flying in the wind. I've had some bad experiences." I look and see what she's talking about. I want to ask her about last night but decide to keep quiet for a while. I can't understand why we didn't fly from Stansted, by plane. It would've been so much easier. We could have cadged a lift in somebody's car, or taken the bus or a train, but Jana insisted on flying to London.

"We'll have to go down soon. I don't want to take any chances." Turning to Jana, I notice the worried expression on her face, but don't understand what the fuss is about, and I'm still looking when we're thrown sideways by a fierce blast of wind. It's so strong that Jana loses her grip on my hand. I try clinging on by my fingertips but both our bodies are being thrown over and over until we eventually separate. Pushing my arms and legs out like a free faller, I'm afraid to close my eyes as I start gliding through the air. I'm beginning to enjoy this feeling of flying on my own, but when I look down I can see that I'm ever so slowly dropping from the sky. There's no sign of Jana anywhere, and I don't know if she can see me. The last time I'd noticed her, she was face upwards and kicking out, and looking panicked.

Seconds later I, too, panic as the snowy ground below seemingly rises up to meet me … and I do close my eyes. I'm scared shitless and try convincing myself … "I can't die. I'm a ghost. I can't d … " but, just as suddenly, I feel an almighty tug from behind and open my eyes again. My body twists and turns while I'm being pulled along by my leg. It's extremely uncomfortable in this position as I watch the snow white fields pass away behind me, no more than ten feet from my face. It has to be Jana who's saved me, and as we slow down the picture I have of snow white fields is gradually replaced by one of a pair of railway lines. I can feel Jana working her hands, one by one, along my body until she grabs my arm. She gently guides me to a small railway station and, quite honestly, I don't know where to put my face. Jana is naked except for the smallest pair of bikini briefs I've ever seen on a woman.

"Don't be embarrassed," she says, as we land on the station platform. How does she know? I didn't think it would show on a ghost's face, unless it's my look of surprise that tells its own story. The thing is that I'm feeling embarrassed for her – not me, but she doesn't seem the least bit concerned. I study her slim body and the small pointy breasts which were sticking in me the previous evening.

"I'm not. I'm … I'm only thinking about you; that you might be embarrassed."

"Of course I'm not. I've done this many times. I'm so much faster flying naked and I had to catch you."

"What'll you do for clothes? Are you going back for them?"

"You must be joking. I'll get some in London."

"How? I tried the other day but I couldn't pick any up. My fingers went right through them."

"I know. I watched you. I could have bought some for you, but then you'd have known I was there. Let's go inside the waiting room for a while, or, at least, until the wind dies down. I haven't made up my mind as to whether we'll fly the rest of the way or get the train. Which do you prefer?" Taking my hand, she guides me into the empty waiting room and we sit on one of the three small benches.

"It's up to you really, although I do think that, with you being naked, going by train would be the sensible option. I would if I were you."

"And why's that, Micky?" Jana eyes me inquisitively.

"I'd go inside somebody. I wouldn't feel so out in front, as it were." Jana is watching me looking at her erect nipples as I speak.

"Ooh! Kinky! I see your point though." Jana gives me a naughty look and then laughs. It's the first time that she's laughed today and it relaxes her. "By the way, where are we?"

"Harlow Mill. This line will take us straight to Liverpool Street Station," I inform her.

"No. I've decided that we're going to fly, but we'll have to wait until the wind has dropped. I hope that's okay with you and that you don't mind flying with a couple of naked boobs dangling down from the sky, not that I've got much to show."

"I don't mind if you don't, but you shouldn't criticise yourself. There's many a female who'd die for a body like yours. While we're waiting, can you tell me how you can buy clothes? You see, Simon said he bought these for me and you said that you'd have bought some, and I'm somewhat confused."

"Once you learn the basic rules for ghosts and your Tutor is satisfied that you'll adhere to them, you'll be credited with the ability to buy various things a few times per year. If you need more credits then you'll have to earn them. We don't have ghost money, but these credits are associated to a ghost's abilities and are automatically earned by ghosts each time something good is achieved. Does this make any sense to you?"

"I'm not sure. Give me an example."

"I might have just saved your life. If you had fallen into water and didn't get out within a minute or two, then you – Mick the ghost – would have died; just as you would have if you'd stayed inside Andy. The point I'm making is that I might have earned some extra abilities for saving your life. I don't know if I have as yet, but no doubt I'll find out sometime or other."

"On that basis then you *must* have earned some credits."

"It all depends on the type of ghost you turn out to be. If I've saved a prat then I might get nothing but grief for a while. On the other hand, if you turn out to be some super-hero of a ghost then I could go places."

"You're confusing me again."

"That's why I'm taking you to the best Tutor in the business. She wasn't always a Tutor and, at this moment in time, I'm not going to elaborate. You'll find out about her soon enough."

Jana's smile has been replaced with a frown again, and I'm determined to find out about her. "You sound a bit apprehensive. Is it something personal, or to do with this teacher? You seem to praise this ghost highly and yet seem afraid of her."

"I'm not afraid. She's only a ghost and I know her very well, but I don't want to talk about this anymore, so let's change the subject." I don't know. She seems irritated – the way she snapped at me. I wonder what went on between those two. Whoever this woman is, she must have upset Jana at some time; probably when she was being taught the rules. Jana doesn't look as though she could hurt a fly, nor that she'd have been disobedient, but something must have happened between them. Whatever it was is beginning to intrigue me.

"Jana, I have a problem understanding this dying in water business, and I also want to know whether I'd have died if I'd crashed to the ground."

"I don't know why ghosts can drown. Other ghosts have, so we take it for granted that it's the same for all ghosts if they put themselves in that type of danger. As regards your dropping from a great height ... no, you wouldn't have died. It would have been like landing on a cushion, but I was concerned that there might have been a pool, iced over and covered by the snow. After all, ice is only frozen water and you could have gone through. That's why I hurried to save you. ... Okay?"

"Yes." At least that's answered some of my questions, but ... . "Jana, don't you think Simon should have told me some of these things?"

"Now, look, Simon has his own job to do. He's a Ghost Reliever, and I've told you already that he's a teaser, especially with New Ghosts. Besides, he probably had other jobs to do, and it's the work of other ghosts, like me, to put you right in the ways of ghosting. I wish you'd stop worrying."

I'm about to ask her another question when the door opens and five young Arsenal supporters, in their full regalia, push their way inside. A couple of them approach our seat while the others make their way towards the empty benches. Jana pushes me away while she dives in the opposite direction. Two of the men open their rucksacks and pull out some cans of beer, while another offers his ciggies around.

They start talking, but before I can take an interest, Jana says, "I'm going out. I'll be back in a jiff', so stay here and keep out of their way." I don't even get the chance to answer, as she's through the wall in a flash.

"What do you reckon, Ken ... five-nil?" asks one of the men.

"Against Chelsea! ... No way. Three will do, and then Arsene can make his substitutions. So long as we win, I don't really care, providing we don't get any injuries."

I wish Jana hadn't left me with these lads. It's not that I don't like football – I do, but I've got other things on my mind. I like watching football, especially the players. Some of them are really pretty boys and they're so athletic – lovely legs and bums. This makes me smile because I realise that I can go to as many matches as I want to now, without a season ticket, and then I'll be able to watch the players in the showers afterwards. And I'd join them except that I'd be worried about the water; especially after what Jana's just said. But that doesn't make sense. I've just been flying through falling snow, and I walked through snow the other day and it didn't have any affect on me, so why should water?

"Come on, Micky. The train's coming." Jana is back and holding out her hand, and, as soon as I take it, she pulls me across the room and out through the door.

"I thought we were going to fly."

"The weather's too bad. The wind's too strong and I want to be on my way."

"I don't want to be stuck in the same carriage as those Arsenal fans. I'd probably end up in another nice mess if any of them sat on me, especially with them drinking lager."

"One of my friends says that, Micky. Quite often, as it happens."

"Says what?"

"Another nice mess."

"What's so special about that? Lots of people say it."

"That may be so, but this ghost is funny, and when he speaks, everyone usually laughs."

"Who's this ghost then?"

"Everyone calls him Ollie."

"Ollie?"

"Yes! His name is Oliver, but he likes to be called Ollie."

"Do you fancy him?"

"Why, Micky, I do believe you're jealous. But, no, I don't fancy him. He's a bit too podgy and not my type, although he and his friend do make every ghost feel happy when they visit."

"Who's this friend of his?"

"He's called Stan."

"Don't be stupid, Jana. The next thing you'll have me believing is that Laurel and Hardy are ghosts."

"They are, Micky. Stan Laurel and Oliver Hardy are ghosts, and, what's more, you'll probably meet one or maybe both of them while you're in Slovakia. They often make visits to speak to the new arrivals. What do you think of that? Did you like their films? Wait a minute … here's the train. Let's jump in the guard's car. It will be quieter in there."

The train stops and we make our way to the back car and hop on. Quite a few of the compartments are empty but Jana insists that we sit with the guard. We wait for the train to move off, and when the guard appears, we follow him into his compartment. We sit closer to the window, while he sits by the door. We watch while he picks up his Daily Mirror and a pen, and he then starts doing the crossword.

"Mick, did you ever think you could influence the outcome of something or other?"

"No, not really. I always wanted to win the football pools or the lottery but, as far as I'm concerned, winning is all down to luck."

"Things can be manipulated, you know. Think about what happened to the poor labrador and how Patricia reacted to my thoughts." And as I reflect, now smiling, Jana once more interrupts my thoughts. "Anyway, forget that for now because you haven't answered my questions about Stan and Ollie."

"Of course, I liked them. Laurel and Hardy films were absolutely fabulous, just as Charlie Chaplin's were. I suppose you'll now tell me that he's a ghost as well. And I just can't believe that both Laurel and Hardy dreamt of being ghosts. It's highly unlikely."

"Maybe Charlie is – I don't know, but if so then I'm sure someone would've mentioned it by now. Nobody knows all the ghosts' names – that's an impossibility, but we generally hear about any famous ghosts. As to how Stan and Ollie both dreamed of being ghosts, that's another story and not for me to tell."

"So, how did you get to meet them?"

"Like I said, they visit the village now and then. I lived near there when I was alive, and it's where I monitor ghosts like you. You know, showing them the ropes and the local places of interest; that type of thing. When a ghost becomes proficient and can do their own tasks, then I go on to the next new arrival or some other job."

"Why bother with another job if you're a Ghost Monitor?"

"New Ghosts don't arrive every minute, or every day, and sometimes we don't get any for weeks, so we have to help out with other things. You'll learn this as time goes by. Now listen, I'm going to nod off for a while so please give my ears a rest. In a way, I'm glad I didn't fly, or I'd have been totally shattered. I suppose it must have been the stress of saving you. I hope you don't mind."

"Not at all, and thanks for looking after me."

"Give me a shove when we're near London ... and don't go wandering around." Looking out the window at the falling snow, I wonder about all the things I have to ask. I wish I could pick up the guards pen and newspaper to make a few notes. I'm starting to forget some of the things I wanted to ask both Jana and Simon, and I don't even know when I'll see him again. The train starts slowing down and very soon pulls into Cheshunt. More Arsenal supporters are among the people joining the train and when it starts moving again the guard returns. Instead of sitting down though, he picks up his ticket machine and leaves to check on the passengers.

Not long after, we arrive at Tottenham Hale so I nudge Jana, waking her up, and she decides to leave the train straight away. She takes my hand, leads me through the doors and away from Tottenham in a westerly direction. Jana certainly seems to know her way around London, so I just let her fly me wherever she wants to go. The wind has dropped and very soon we, too, are dropping, down and into Brent Cross shopping centre.

The amazing thing is that Jana has managed to guide us directly into the middle of Dorothy Perkins, and turning to me, she points to an empty corner, saying, "Wait there ... and don't go sneaking into the changing rooms." She throws her head back, laughing, and I do as instructed. She, though, has no need of the changing room and I watch while she tries on several outfits. Eventually, she makes her way back to me, dressed in a black roll-neck top with matching trousers. "What do you think, Micky – do they suit me?"

"You look terrific, but what about your feet?" Her feet are still bare.

"They don't have what I'm looking for. Let's try somewhere else."

"It's up to you. There are plenty of shoe shops in this place."

"I know. ... I know."

The way Jana drags out the words 'I know' reminds me of Sybil Fawlty, so I ask, "Have you been watching Fawlty Towers?"

"I have, as a matter of fact. It's brilliant. I only saw it for the first time a few years ago and I think it's so funny." Jana takes my hand and flies us in and out of several other shops until she finds a selection of boots she likes. Soon after, we're on our way out and flying into central London.

"Where are we off to now?"

"I don't fancy flying across the Channel, so I think we'll take a trip on Eurostar, to Brussels."

"Is it the weather that's bothering you?"

"Yes, it is, and crossing the Channel. The water is wide, and while I might chance it in fine weather, I won't while it's windy."

On our arrival at Waterloo we join the train and make ourselves comfortable in a nearly deserted first class carriage. I must admit that Jana certainly knows the quickest way to travel to the continent from London but I have to ask, "Do you ever fly by aeroplane?"

"Of course I do, silly. Most ghosts do. Flying by plane is the most economical way to travel. We also go by boat, but it depends where we are and how rough the water is."

"If I'd had the choice I'd have flown from Stansted, but you were determined to go this way, weren't you? And, also, why do you say flying is economical? We don't pay."

"You're quite right, Micky. We could have gone from Stansted. But aren't you forgetting the weather and what happened at Luton Airport the other day. There will be delays everywhere and I didn't fancy hanging around for hours, or mess about changing flights. And, besides, they'll mostly be full. As far as economy is concerned, I wasn't talking about money or credits. I'm referring to the matter of conserving our energy ... our life. Don't you realise that every bit of work you and I do – whether it's running, flying, pushing through walls, and everything else as it happens – saps our life, and if we don't rest when we can or get our strength from somewhere else ... we'll die."

"Thanks, Jana. At least I'm beginning to understand some of the things you said earlier. It's suddenly sunk in."

"And about time too!"

"You could teach me all I need to know." Before she can reply, the train starts moving.

"I can teach you some things, but you'd have to acquire the basic abilities first. The only reason you can go through walls, or fly with me, is because I hold your hand and pass some of my ability through to you, but each time I do it saps my strength. I wouldn't be able to carry you around for the rest of my life. It would be impossible with the job I have to do. So go and earn your abilities and credits with Madam Majerniková from Myjava."

"Who's she?"

"Isn't it obvious?"

"I suppose it is. She has such an unusual name, though."

"Names don't matter, Micky. You'll get along fine with her, I hope."

"You have doubts?"

"Not really, but you have to behave, and I think you're sensible enough to do that."

"Does she speak any English? And how come you speak it so well?"

"Of course she does. There'd be no point in bringing you to Slovakia if she didn't. As far as I'm concerned, I learnt my English by listening to people and reading lots of books. I think you'll develop these abilities very quickly. You seem fairly intelligent, and you certainly ask enough questions. That'll go down well with whoever is teaching you."

"Thanks for the compliment. By the way, why don't I get thirsty?"

"That's another silly question. I think you know the answer to that one already ... don't you?"

"Yes, I suppose so. We're ghosts, and ghosts don't eat, drink, nor sweat, and we don't feel the cold and we don't get hot. On second thoughts though, we do get warm as you well know. We both got warm last night. I meant to ask you about that."

"What? When you wanted my body? Tell me the truth, Micky. I know you did ... and stop blushing."

"I didn't, honestly, and I'm not blushing."

"Yes, you did. You had a little stiffy all for me, and you were getting me worked up as you well know. Why do you think I stopped kissing you?"

"I thought you were coming on to me, and I'm flattered, but I'm ... it doesn't matter. You wouldn't understand. It still doesn't answer the question about us getting warm or going red in the face."

"Yes it does. When two ghosts become sexually active they exude a feeling of warmth and the skin starts to show this, even though we don't have any blood. The fact that this thought embarrasses you a little has caused you to do exactly the same now, and I can see that you're blushing. It makes sense, Micky. We are still people, albeit in a ghostly way, so why shouldn't we have and show feelings for one and other?"

"Okay. You're right. I was turned on but I wasn't thinking of …. Can we forget it?"

"It's Simon, isn't it?"

"If you must know, yes. I'm gay and I was thinking of him. Now do you understand?"

"I do, although you seem to have some sexual attraction for the female form. Have you ever had a girl?"

"Why do you want to know? I've told you I'm gay."

"I know lots of bisexual ghosts who thought they were one thing or the other when they were alive, but most of them were sexually active with both sexes when they were young. The thing is, unfortunately for you, they're all female. Were you, Micky, going with both girls and boys? I'll know if you try to lie to me, and you know I'll know, so tell me the truth. Your future could depend upon it."

What's she on about? Why should my future depend on what I say? She's put me on the spot and I don't answer immediately. Jana is watching and waiting very patiently. I have to tell someone, and if what she says about Simon is the truth – him being a teaser and all that – then I'll have to trust her. I have to trust someone.

"Micky, I know you're gay," she continues. "I was in your sister's house. I was at your funeral. I heard what that disgusting man had to say about Evelyn, so I know how and why you died … and do stop blushing. It is history. It is not now. We are here … now, and at this present time it is we ghosts that are important. If I can help you remember at least one little tit-bit from your past associations with women then it might help you to get along with other ghosts besides me. I'll tell you what. Just tell me about the girl with the cows and I'll leave you alone."

"What? How do you know?"

"When I was first kissing you in the pub, I couldn't read much of your mind because I was concentrating on saving your life, but I did manage to read a little bit when you tried to laugh. You were thinking about some girl called Katka, I think … and some cows. Tell me, Micky. Please tell me. I'm dying to know."

"Promise me you won't tell anyone else."

"I promise."

"It seems like such a long time ago … when I was eighteen. I'd …. Oh, blast it, Jana, I can't tell you. I will, but it's just that I'm embarrassed and you've caught me off guard."

"That's not fair, Micky. I've told you what you wanted to know."

"You've told me more than I wanted. You've been watching me without me knowing. You've heard about me from my relatives and friends, and my ex-friends, and you even know what I was doing when I died. Isn't that enough? And you don't tell me anything about yourself. When I ask about you and this Tutor, you become subdued, and then I feel sorry for you, so I shut up. You say that I'll find out later, but everything in my ghost life seems to be … wait 'til later."

"Alright, Micky, I understand. I can't tell you much about my life, but I'll tell you where I came from and some of my early life. Will that do for now?"

"Yes, so long as you tell me the truth?"

"Of course, I will. One thing you must realise is that ghosts can't lie. We can pretend to be other than we are and we can pretend to do things. We can tease as Simon does, and we can interpret words and meanings differently to save embarrassment for other ghosts, but not for ourselves. We can't deliberately and maliciously lie to one and other."

"So, when Simon said he wasn't gay … he was telling the truth, and his erection was a figment of my imagination. And his kissing me the way he did was likewise. Is that correct?"

"Simon was kissing you to draw out some of your life to build up his own. I've explained this. When I was kissing you initially, I was giving you some of my life. His erection problem is well known and that's why he teases New Ghosts. Once they find out that he has a permanent stiffy, he loses interest in them and the teasing stops. He does it to both male and female ghosts."

"What's up with him then? I'd die for a problem like that."

"I don't mean to be rude, Micky, but you did die … while you were sexually active, and so, too, did Simon. He used to experiment with Viagra and the end result was as you've seen. He was an eighty-three year old man having sex with his extremely young wife when he had a heart attack and died … on the job, as you might say. He was the first and, as far as I know, the only ghost, as yet, to start his new life as stiff as he left the last one. Some ghosts reckon that the drug will wear off eventually, but he's been here five years and there's no sign of it going down."

"It's still a nice problem."

"Do you really think so? Don't you like the joy of touching yourself when you're soft and feeling it grow in your hand? ... I know you do. And think of the pleasure and the lovely sensation it gives you and whoever you're with when it starts to stiffen while kissing and cuddling each other."

"You're right you know. I hadn't thought of it that way, and sometimes I don't have to be touching anyone to get excited. Last week I saw this young man on a train and I wanted him there and then. He was so dreamy looking, but there was nothing I could do because I was on the other platform watching him through the train window. If only I'd found out where he lived, but it's too late now."

"Oh, poor Micky. You're a lost cause. The boy might have been straight and then you'd have been wasting your time, and, even if you had been able to speak to him, he might have knocked your block off. Okay, just answer a question before I tell you something about myself. How old were you when you died?"

"You'll think I'm a dirty old man, although I am surprised that Simon was eighty-three when he died."

"I won't think anything of the kind. All of us have died at varying ages and I've already told you how our ghostly appearance happens, so nothing surprises me nowadays. I've been here too long and seen so much."

"I was forty-eight, and, knowing you were only fifteen, it makes me feel like a sugar-daddy when I think about you and me, even though there's nothing going on between us."

"Micky, you'll have to stop thinking of what age you were and think only of how you look now. Then we'll respect each other a lot more. You'll have to treat all ghosts in this way because you might recognise some of them. I can only tell you some of my story if you will accept this."

"I will, Jana. I promise. And I do respect you, and in some way I feel sorry for Simon and his affliction."

"I don't think it's giving him too much distress; he seems to be enjoying his life. We're so used to it. We can tease him now and again, and he doesn't seem to mind."

"So then, tell me about yourself?"

"What I'm going to tell you is for your ears only. Some of the other ghosts know but they're ones of my choosing. You'll find that this is one of the rules we ghosts have. That is, we don't relate other ghosts' life stories. That's for the individual ghost concerned to do, if he or she so wishes." Jana takes my hand in both of hers as she starts to speak in a soft, yet serious sounding voice. "When I was alive my country was part of the old Hungarian Empire." I can't believe my ears. That would mean she's been dead for centuries and yet she still looks so young, and I'm contemplating my decomposing body while she continues. "I came from a little village in the north of Slovakia and my family was very poor. People didn't have the education then, as they do nowadays, unless they were from rich families. We lived off the land as best we could. Micky, I was born in the year 1594 and I died in 1609, and my mama and papa didn't know that I was dead for another two years. As people were so poor, young girls like me had to go into service for wealthy landowners, to work as housemaids or do other menial jobs. The person I worked for was not of good character, and that's putting it nicely, and the last thing I'll tell you, for now, is that I didn't die of natural causes. The rest you'll find out when you get to the village. I don't want to say any more until you're told the history by your Tutor. I'm sure she'll tell you because she always likes the truth to be known about her life and death. Both our deaths are related so, I'm sorry but, you'll have to wait for the rest."

The fact, that Jana didn't die naturally and that there's more to this story, has me intrigued. My god! Jana has lived as a ghost for nearly four hundred years … and I suddenly realise that being buried in my bio-degradable coffin won't make the slightest difference to my own ghost life. I should have realised this earlier, when she spoke of Simon's death and her talk of other, more experienced, ghosts. It didn't dawn on me until now. I feel so content, and the smile that forms on my face reflects this, and Jana says, "Why are you looking so happy? I shouldn't think what I've just said could please anyone."

"It's not that. I really feel for you. I do … honestly. I can't possibly imagine what happened to you, and I understand, in a way, why you get so upset, but what you've said has made me realise that I can be a ghost forever, no matter what."

"You won't be if you don't do as you're told. You have to obey the rules and be careful about who you decide to enter. And, also, you have to look out for unscrupulous ghosts. We're not all saints you know."

"Simon said something about bad ghosts. Is it them you're talking about?"

"Yes, it is. You'll find out about them soon enough."

"Go on. Tell me."

"No, I won't. I don't like to be reminded of them. All I can say is that it's not only nice people who dream of being ghosts, so you can work it out for yourself, and if I tell you everything, there won't be much left for you to learn. Now shush and let's rest a while." Jana snuggles up close and shortly afterwards shuts her eyes. Meanwhile, mine are taking in the last few minutes of English countryside before we reach the Channel Tunnel. I start wondering when I'll be back on English soil, and as we enter the tunnel my eyes, like hers, start closing.

"Wake up, Micky! Wake up!"

"W … What's going on?" My arm feels as if it's coming out of its socket as I do indeed wake up. Her look of anger has me worried, so I ask her what the problem is.

"We're here … in Belgium! Now come on, we've another train to catch."

"What time is it?"

"What does it matter? Trying to wake you is like trying to wake the dead, and I want to get to Munich before nightfall."

"Okay! Okay!" I answer. "Why go to Munich? Surely, we can travel right through, or else we can fly?"

"If you want to fly, then go ahead, and don't forget to flap your wings, but I'm going by train and there's one due to leave in ten minutes." Is she trying to be facetious or something, although, from her expression, I don't think so? I take her hand as we jump off the train, and then Jana leads me to another platform. She certainly knows her way around the place, but, when I think about it, she's had plenty of time to learn.

"This is the one," she says, as we approach a train that's loaded with cars on the rear trailers. "We'll be able to relax in a Bentley or a Jaguar if we're lucky, and then we won't be disturbed. The problem with these inter-city trains is that they're so full and I don't fancy sitting inside someone I don't know."

"That's a good idea," I agree. We walk down the platform until Jana decides on our resting place for the next part of my journey into the unknown. Still holding my hand, she gently pulls me as she floats up and into a deep blue Astra. Not quite a Bentley, I think, but it'll do. Jana jumps in behind the wheel, while I climb in the back. I ask her to join me.

"You know what, Micky," she replies, "this is the only chance I get to pretend I'm driving a car. You've been driving for years, but there was no such thing as a car when I was a child."

"That's fair enough. So, why do you want to stop in Munich?"

"I was thinking of going to a pub tonight, if you're up to it, and some of my friends hang out there. They're usually around the Schwabing area … that's the Latin Quarter, and it's a great place to visit. There are always plenty of guys around, and women too if they take your fancy." And she laughs.

While we are chatting away, the train starts pulling out of the station, and I can't help but notice a young railway worker walking along the platform. He looks so attractive in his uniform, and I want to climb out and join him. My eyes follow him, and I'm so taken with his features that I don't hear Jana.

He's gone, or I should say the train has taken me away from him, so I turn back to see Jana's face right in front of mine and she is giving me one hell of a disgusted look. "If you want to get involved with someone you don't know, then by all means do, but remember that you do so at your own risk, and you'll have to hope that some other ghost will come to save you if you get into trouble. Is that clear?"

"Yes, Jana." She doesn't realise how disappointed I am. "That's perfectly clear, but you don't need to go into one. I was only thinking."

"And wishing!"

"Was it that obvious? I only saw him for a few seconds."

"I was trying to tell you that you might meet someone you fancy in Munich, but if you want to switch yourself off, even when our conversation is getting interesting, then let's keep quiet and I'll take you straight to Slovakia. What do you think of that?"

"I'm sorry. Can we start again?"

"No! Not now. You've put me in a bad mood so let's just give it a rest."

"Okay." I shut up, and Jana obviously means what she said because I don't hear a murmur from her, and I watch as she grabs the wheel, pretending to drive us along. I lie down on the backseat, close my eyes and relax. I keep thinking about her; her anger at me; the knowledge she must have acquired over the years; but, more than that, I wonder whether she was jealous of the lad. I think about this place she wants to visit in Munich, or whether she really means it about going straight through. Maybe she's right, and that I have to stop thinking about myself all the time.

Time passes and neither of us speaks. I know that I'm not going to be the one to open any conversation. Jana has stopped her driving practise and is now lying down across the front seats. She starts humming and, having no option, I listen, but I've no intention of joining in until she speaks to me. I can't help enjoying her version of Offenbach's *Barcarole*, and mentally I think along with her, imagining Elvis singing *Can't you see that tonight is so right for love*. She carries on humming or whistling various other tunes, some of which I don't know, but when she starts singing *Imagine* incorrectly, I can't help but sing along, putting her right. She doesn't seem to mind and, although we aren't really speaking, this musical interlude helps to ease the tension.

We arrive in Munich in the late afternoon and I decide to break the ice. "You have a very nice voice, Jana. I wish I could sing as well as you."

"I used to sing when I was at home with my mama and sisters. We all used to sing when we did the housework, or to pass the time away before snuggling down to sleep. If we weren't singing we were listening to stories – what you'd call fairytales these days, except there was always some concept of truth in them. Oh, and by the way, I apologise for what I said earlier. If you must know, I'm a little jealous of you being gay. I find you attractive and funny, and I think it's such a waste of a good looking ghost. There aren't that many sexy ghosts you know, and some of those that are sexy looking still have their minds in the dark ages and they don't want to change."

"I'm sorry too. I like you a lot, and if I felt differently then you'd be my first and probably only choice. You seem very intelligent and I'm a wee bit envious."

"You shouldn't be, Micky. You'll learn so fast that I should be the one to envy your capabilities. Anyway, enough of the niceties, we have to get off soon. I know a good Irish pub with music. You don't mind, do you … being English and that?"

"Not at all. I like a bit of the craic, now and then."

"Okay, let's go." She lifts herself up and as I move my body forwards she grabs my hand. As soon as the train stops, we're floating out of the car and down onto the platform. Jana checks her bearings and then hoists me up and over the city. Soon after, we're descending and as our feet near the roof of a building, I close my eyes again. I don't know why I'm afraid to look, yet, in only a few seconds we stop moving, and I open them to find us hovering above a huge red-bearded man drinking a pint of Guinness.

"They're not here."

"Who's not here?"

"My friends, but, there again, we are a little early. Will we watch them drink while we're waiting?"

"We might as well, but I'd rather join them."

"So would I. What does that black stuff taste like?" she asks as we float towards a couple of empty chairs. There aren't many people in the pub and finding seats in an out-of-the-way corner isn't difficult.

"Guinness" I tell her, "is like liquid silk trickling back your throat. It has such a fulfilling feeling and when you've had a few, you know you're full and totally satisfied. Mind you, I know some men who drink one pint after the other, not stopping until the pub closes. I don't know how they do it, and some of them don't get a beer belly. It's amazing."

"It sounds heavenly. I tried a glass of champagne once, unsuccessfully."

"How?"

"I can move things; only small objects like glasses, pens, books and that sort of thing. You'll be able to do the same. Anyway, I managed to tilt a full glass into my mouth, but, just like rain, it went straight through me. I couldn't taste anything."

"That's a pity. You might have enjoyed it."

"I don't know. I never tasted alcohol when I was young. People used to brew stuff from fruits, or rye and wheat but it was usually the men who drank it."

Jana and I talk for a while and listen to music. She tells me more about the village we're going to, and its name, Pribylina. How it reflects a time, long after she had died, more akin to the nineteenth and early twentieth centuries but also with some earlier effects. She's making it sound interesting and I'm quite keen to get there.

More people drift in, and one of them – a small black haired man with a violin case, joins red-beard. Jana tells me that they do a little turn, and shortly after the big man goes behind the bar and returns with a guitar and a mouth organ. They set up their equipment and then treat us to a session of Irish tunes. They stop every now and then for a refill, and time passes while we listen to them playing their versions of *The Fields of Athenry, Loves Old Sweet Song*, and a few other old tunes.

"They're not coming," says Jana, pointing to a clock. "I bet they've gone home."

"Don't they stay here in Munich?"

"Sometimes, but Luisella told me that if she and Petra weren't here tonight then they'd be at home."

"So, what will we do?"

"We'll go to a big plush hotel and get ourselves the best room available. How does that sound?"

"I'm going up in the world," I answer, smiling from ear to ear. We leave the music and Guinness behind and make our way over the rooftops to a hotel. Jana tries a few places, via the roofs and ceilings, until we find an empty penthouse suite.

We eventually settle into a huge double bed, Jana insisting we take our clothes off. I refuse at first, but after a few threats and the likelihood of another, maybe longer, silent stint between us, I reluctantly give in. She pulls me to her, wraps her arms around my neck and throws a leg over mine. I'm scared stiff as she pushes her breasts into me, lifts her head and plants a kiss on my lips. I move my head slightly back, looking at her with fright – and if someone hadn't left the bathroom light on then Jana wouldn't have noticed the fear on my face.

"Don't worry ... I'm not going to bite," she whispers. "I do want you though."

"Please stop. This isn't fair and you know it."

"Ghosts aren't gay, Micky. Most are straight and others are bisexual but I've never met a completely gay ghost in all my time here. Besides, you admitted yourself that you've had women."

"That was a long time ago as you well know, and I don't want to try again."

Jana is not deterred as she puts her hand down between my legs and takes a very gentle hold of me. I try easing away, but she is strong. She crooks her other arm firmly around my head as her right hand continues trying to arouse me. I close my eyes and think of the past ... and of Gwen. I keep the memory of Gwen's face in my mind and about ten minutes later Jana gives up, defeated. She pulls away from me, lies on her back, and then I open my eyes.

She's staring at the ceiling as she says, "You're going to be one hell of a lonely ghost if you don't make an effort. How can you just switch yourself off like that? How do you expect to get your sexual thrills? ... By looking? By moving and shaking yourself about inside a live person's body? ... How?" I keep staring at her as she rants on. "If you think that you'll meet, by some magic formula, a gay ghost to suit your needs, then your badly mistaken. I've been here too long and I don't know of any gays. Who knows? You might get lucky if you ever bump into one in Africa, Australia, or Never-Never Land ... and pigs might fly."

Jana stops her blast at me and I think hard about what she's been saying. I'd never considered that things could be as difficult as she's suggesting. There again, although I'd dreamt of being a ghost, I'd never really believed it was going to happen, so why would I consider the implications? It was only a dream – a repetitive dream. If what she says is true then I'm knackered ... amn't I?

"Micky?" she says softly.

"Yes."

"How come you fell on the other side of the fence?"

"What?"

"Being gay and all that? Why didn't you choose girls instead of boys? Was it something to do with the girl Katka or whatever her name is?"

"No. It wasn't Cathie. Why'd you think it'd be a girl's fault?"

"I'm not stupid, Micky. I can read you like a book. There's no way you wouldn't have got a hard on if you hadn't been thinking of something, or more likely someone, and that someone had to be a girl or what she did to you. I wish I'd been kissing you while you were thinking – I'd have found out. Wouldn't I?"

"Why should I tell you?"

"You do want my help. You do want to get out of here. You don't want to be left stranded, high and dry so some other ghosts can take advantage of you ... or worse. Do you? And you have to confide in someone, and you know I can be trusted. I wouldn't be your Ghost Monitor otherwise."

"A moustache."

"A moustache! What do you mean, a moustache?"

"She ... that is, Gwen, was the last girl I ever went out with. I was twenty-three, and I didn't know which way I was going to fall. I'd always enjoyed sex with girls as well as men, and it was natural for a man to have a moustache, but I couldn't stand it when I was kissing Gwen. She turned me off women for good. I assumed she'd been shaving and, even worse than that, she had bristles – coarse, hard, stick-in-your-skin bristles. Kissing her was the biggest turn-off I've ever had in my life. I made some excuse and left, and until you kissed me I'd never kissed another female ... properly that is."

"That was it! You gave up on girls because of one bad kissing session. You made your life choice because of a kiss. You're crazy! You're really crazy! The only mistake she made was to shave ... that's obvious. She probably had thick hair and tried to do something about it, but the poor girl did the wrong thing. Poor Micky, you don't know what you've been missing. You could have married and had a family, and you probably wouldn't be here now. You mightn't have dreamt of ghosts ... but there again you might. But what's the point of being a gay ghost if you're the only one in this hemisphere? I pity you. I really do."

"After that I imagined all women shaving on the quiet – you know, as they got older, and the thought of them doing that put me off. When I made the decision to stick with men I felt it was right, and, anyway, I was having a ball ... until Evelyn that is."

"Do I have a moustache?"

"Not that I know of but I can't see in this light."

"You know I don't ... you'd have felt it."

"Okay, you don't."

"Am I a good kisser?"

"For a girl, yes."

"Make love to me."

"No."

"Aw, come on. Give me a kiss."

"No."

"You'll have to sooner or later. If it's not me it'll be some other girl."

"Not if I can help it."

"I give up. Let's get some rest." She turns, puts her arm over me and snuggles up. I don't stop her even though her boobs are pressing into my side. "Mm-mm," she sighs.

"Nighty-night."

"Nighty-night."

I lie quietly, thinking about our day and things I haven't yet understood. Remembering Gwen again, I know I made the right choice. Why would I want a marriage and family anyway? Look at Mary. She couldn't make hers work and now she has Ben. At least she has Samantha. I shut my eyes.

CHAPTER TEN

When my senses are awoken the next morning I'm afraid to open my eyes in case what's happening isn't really happening, and I don't want to stop the sensational feeling running through my body.

It's not unusual to wake up as stiff as a poker, but this time it's not for the want of a pee, nor the result of an erotic dream. Jana's head and body are lower down the bed, lying across me, and she's ever so gently playing with me. The fingers of both her hands are like feathers as one of them lightly caresses me one second while the other delicately squeezes my balls the next, and what she's doing with her teeth is reminding me of Evelyn ... and I'm worried.

The trouble is that even with my thoughts of a second dismemberment, I'm in a state of utmost pleasure and I don't seem able to stop her ... and I don't want to. My arms are lying, weak, by my sides, but as my body tenses up with the near explosion I'm taken by surprise. Jana, still holding me with one hand, lifts herself up and over my body with such speed that I don't get a chance to react. She pushes herself down, guiding me inside her, yelling with delight as she forces me deeper and deeper. She moves up and down, faster and faster, gripping me tight, and I look at her. My hands go to her hips as my body starts moving in time with hers.

It's not long before an extraordinary heat builds up in my loins. Jana's nipples seem to have trebled in size on her small firm breasts. She pushes herself forward across my body, biting into my shoulder when she orgasms. Immediately, I feel a fantastic sensation of release and I wrap my arms around her body, holding on to her for dear life. I kiss her hair and then her face as she clings to me. We remain in this position for a long, long time, until she finally moves backwards, freeing me from my delightful prison.

Jana climbs up my body again, pulls me on my side, and starts kissing me over and over again. It's only when we pull our lips from each other that she says, "You were beautiful, Micky. Did you feel the heat?"

"Oh, god! Yes! I've never felt anything like it. I thought I was going to burn up. And then that lovely warm feeling."

"It's the same for me. Shall we do it again?"

"What ... now?"

"Yes, of course. And why not?"

"I can't. I need time to recover."

"Of course you can. We're ghosts."

"But I'll need time to build it up again."

"Build what up … the sperm?"

"Yes."

"You don't have any, just as I don't have any love juice. What we have is a ghostly feeling of moistness, created by our minds from our movement and sexual sensations. And the beautiful heat we feel is the start of our climax. We can achieve this anytime we want until we burn out."

"What do you mean … burn out? And, anyway, I did feel myself come."

"Well, using too much energy depletes our life, but we can always go for a top up inside somebody, or else we can rest in a state of pure bliss for quite a while. And, no, you didn't come and neither did I. It's just a wonderful imaginative wet feeling we ghosts are capable of." I wonder about this, and wish my imagination had reached these heights when I was with my boyfriends, and thinking about them turns me on.

"I know that look, you bad boy." She turns her head, sees that I'm excited. "Hmm. I'll have to make you comfortable." Jana looks back at my face, smiles, moves her mouth to my chest and kisses me gently as she slides back down my body. Within seconds, she's throwing herself about again and making whooping noises, while we screw the life out of each other. I'm totally knackered when we finish, and we lay in each others arms, first kissing and then sleeping.

It's dark again when my eyes open. Jana is at the window, fully dressed, and when she hears me moving about she turns. "How's my little toy boy this evening? For someone who's supposed to be gay you didn't do a bad job, did you?"

"What do you expect? You practically raped me. And what's with the toy boy business?"

"I'm only joking, Micky, but I am a little older than you – about four hundred years, give or take a year."

I get up and start pulling on my clothes. She comes over, plants a big smacker on my lips, and whispers, "Thank you, Micky. You're the best ghost I've had and I've only ever had ghosts."

Eyeing her quizzically I want to ask her how many, but don't. If she wants to tell me, that's up to her, but I imagine it's an awful lot given the amount of years she's been around. "What's next?" I ask instead.

"To start with, I'll have to sort out your hair. Sex always makes a mess of it."

"You're joking!" I must have a look. I cross to the mirror and am amazed at my reflection. My hair's all over the place. The rest of my body seems okay; the clothes are fine and my skin still looks perfect. Jana approaches, and pushes her hands through my hair until she's satisfied that it's back to its former glory.

"I don't know why. Orgasms always do that to men, so you'd better remember that. We'll know when you've been playing with yourself or screwing around. Anyway, there's a train to Vienna shortly, so move it." I pull my boots on, tell her I'm ready, and, hands held tightly, we're off again.

Not long after, we're on board and chatting away inside an empty compartment. Jana explains more about her village and the nearby places of interest. She goes on and on, promising to take me here and there. By the time the train crosses the border and stops in Salzburg, Jana has conked out, her head resting on my shoulder. I make her more comfortable, lifting my arm and wrapping it around her, and I close my eyes, smiling.

When I finally wake up, Jana is still in exactly the same position. I gently pull my arm away, get up, stretch, and then move to the window. Morning has broken on the snow-filled fields as we head towards Vienna. It seems like I've been travelling forever since I left Ely. Looking at the occasional houses and the snow-topped trees, I think of Christmas cards and brandy trifle, and how Christmases will never be the same. I think of some of my past boyfriends and the presents; the parties; my Mum and Dad. I wonder if they are ghosts, and if so, then why didn't they come to meet me. I wonder if Jana knows.

"Morning, Micky, are we there yet?" Jana's voice makes me jump.

"No, but we're approaching some town or other. The houses are coming up thick and fast."

"Let's have a look." She joins me at the window and says, "We're here. I know this place like the back of my hand."

"For a Slovak, you know an awful lot of our expressions."

105

"I've been there … done that. I've told you I'm well read and I'm a good listener. One thing about being a ghost is that we don't forget very much, unless we forget to top up our nectar."

"What has nectar got to do with us? We don't eat, do we?"

"Of course we don't. We take it orally and store it in our system. It gives us life and strength for long periods. You've a lot to learn about ghost life, so don't be in too much of a hurry. Now, where's my morning kiss?"

"Don't be daft. It's a wonder you don't want sex again, after yesterday. You took advantage of me … twice, and I know how horny you feel when you're being kissed."

"I'm only trying to be nice, and, besides, I did you a favour. If you must know, a kiss at the start of a day sets it off perfectly. It makes a ghost feel alive."

"What would you do if I wasn't here?"

"Sulk! Sometimes it's miserable doing the same thing every day, especially when there aren't any New Ghosts to look after, and some of the old-timers are a waste of space. To be honest, I wouldn't bother my arse with them. Micky, you're different. You're gay and yet you're not gay, and I feel sorry for you because you don't know what you want to be. You only think you do. Okay, so I took advantage of the situation, but you don't know how long it's been since I had sex. I'll tell you … two years, and that's a long time by some ghosts' standards. And, regarding sex … you'd better watch out."

"Why? You said there weren't any gays."

"I'm not talking about gays. It's those other ghosts – the bad ones. They want sex all the time and they don't care whether you're gay, straight, male or female. To put it crudely, they'll fu' … er, screw you to death. And I mean … death. I know what some of them look like and I wouldn't be seen dead in their company. I'd probably end up dead if I didn't have the protection of my abilities."

I'm surprised by her language and still don't understand why we can't say fu … . I'd have got her to teach me and then I could tell Jana about my sister and her friends. I can't believe that any female could kill me, just from having sex. Okay, it's tiring, and I did feel weak yesterday, but that was a pleasurable weakness.

"So, where's my kiss?" I move forward and press my lips on hers.

She gives me a little suck and afterwards, smilingly says, "Thanks, you know it makes sense."

"You've been watching Delboy too often."

"Not often enough, you mean. Anyway, are you ready?"

The train slows down, but Jana doesn't wait for it to stop, grabbing my hand and pulling me outside. We fly away and I don't know which direction we're headed. She tells me to hold tight and I watch as she seems to close her eyes. Within seconds we're flying so fast that I'm frightened. We soar on and on, over frozen streams and small rivers, and then we follow what can only be the Danube as our journey to her home country continues. I don't have the foggiest idea of how long it takes us – my sense of timing has gone to pieces with our unbelievable speed – but Jana gradually takes her foot off the gas and starts dropping towards some old grey stone walls on the top of a hill.

As we land in their midst, she says, "Welcome to Slovakia, Micky. This is the castle I told you about – Čachtice hrad. This is where my life ended before I had the chance to marry, have a family, or feel what real sex was like. I missed all that because I came to work and die in this god-forsaken place." Jana has such a serious and angry face, and I wish she'd tell me the story. I keep hold of her hand, giving it a squeeze of comfort and support. She turns to me, smiles, then laughs, and waving her free hand around, starts trying to imitate Julie Andrews, as she sings, "The hills are alive, with the sound of music … " and then she stops for a second before saying, "but not these bloody hills." Her eyes look angry and she seems agitated. Just as quickly, she faces me again, with an appearance of calm and a casual smile, as she asks, "So what do you think?" I'm not sure how to reply after what she's told me and her reactions, yet I can't believe my eyes as I look out over the great expanse of snow white fields that surround Čachtice hrad. If ever it needed defending in the Middle Ages, then its archers certainly had a terrific advantage. "It was built in the thirteenth century you know," she goes on.

"Was it?" I didn't know, but I wanted her to carry on, hoping she'll say more about her time here.

"Yes. I've studied the history of the place since I died. In the year 1392, it changed hands and was extended. I remember going up to a tower in the shape of a horseshoe. The castle seemed more like a palace with a tower, but it was later destroyed by a huge fire."

"A fire?"

"Yes, and it wasn't me who started it, although I had every reason to." She walks me across to a rear corner of the plot and stops. "I was born here ... well, not born as such, but I started my ghost life exactly where we're standing. You'll do the same. That is, you'll remember exactly where, when, and why you came into being." And I think of the hospital; of that evening with Evelyn; and, as I look down at my trousers ... at my stupidity.

"I don't know what to say," I say.

"I'm expecting company, and I don't think we'll have long to wait."

"Who's coming?"

"Those friends we were supposed to meet yesterday. If they aren't in Slovakia yet, then some others will come to take us the rest of the way."

"But you know where we're going."

"It's not safe. While we're within a few kilometres of a changeover place then we're safe, but trying to get you to the village, on my own, is far too dangerous. It's those other damn ghosts, you see. They hunt in twos or threes, and while I might be able to fend off one or two, it's impossible when there are three or more. They are too strong. If we tried flying on our own, they'd find a way to part us, keep me busy, and, as you can't fly, the other one would get you."

"So, how do they know we're coming? How do your friends know we're here, now ... this very minute?"

"All ghosts earn the ability to sense others within two hours flying time, and I've been afraid of an attack since we passed close to Trenčín. They'll know that my friends will be coming to meet us, so I doubt that they'll bother us now, but we can't take any chances."

"Is this changeover place a collection point of some kind?"

Jana laughs. "No, silly. It's where my body changed into me. Wherever a ghost is born is a changeover place. I know lots of them. Like Simon, I used to be a Reliever, so I know some funny changeover places; little nooks and crannies; and being a Monitor helps even more. The point is that knowing an exact changeover spot is safer. There's another one around here, and that belongs to your Tutor."

"My god! They could have attacked us earlier, then, while we were in England or Munich, or on the train."

"Don't you listen? They have to be within two flying hours to sense us, and as far as travelling is concerned, they wouldn't know which route I'd be likely to take. What's the point of them wasting their energy, flying over Europe or Asia, looking for fresh blood, when they can wait around the ghost villages?"

"Villages? You said villages ... plural."

"There are lots of ghost villages, all over the World. There's probably some other ghost class going on elsewhere, at this very moment. Some ghosts take forever to learn while others, like you if you pay attention, will take no time at all. Oh, and by the way, don't keep saying my GOD. While I don't mind, others do, because it sounds as though you have your own personal GOD, and that, perhaps, you're in league with him or her."

"What are you on about? I don't believe in God. Not since some old choir singer tried to grab me in the stalls while the service was going on. He was a pervert. And I was only eight at the time. Obviously, I didn't know anything about sex at the time, but if I hadn't been such a fast mover he'd have grabbed my little willy." Jana gives me a funny look, mouthing the word 'willy'. "Well, that's what I used to call it when I was an innocent little boy, and God didn't protect me then. And the clergy believed this guy when my parents put in a complaint. He was a respected member of the community, they said, and they insisted that I was making it up, and that I should be disciplined by the church ... and by my parents. I didn't go back to church after that, although my mum and dad used to send me. When they found out I wasn't going, that's when they punished me. Where was God then, and how come you're talking as if God exists now?"

"Micky, I don't believe in the god you're on about, but I know we have GOD here because I've met quite a lot of them."

"You're not making any sense. You make it sound as if there is more than one, and, anyway, how can ghosts have gods?"

"If you're ever lucky enough, you might become one. They're not the same as you think. Our GOD is just a short way to say Ghost or Ghosts Of Dreams, and we have many such ghosts. I'm a Ghost Monitor; Simon's a Ghost Reliever; and so on. These are our titles."

"I can understand your job, but what do these Ghosts Of Dreams do?"

"They read dreams. They've been doing it since they earned the ability to do so. I don't know how a ghost reaches that status – no ghost does except, possibly, the ones directly involved in helping a ghost get these increased abilities. When this happens, the helpers gain extra abilities too, as part of the natural process. These Dreamers, our Ghosts Of Dreams, can read dreams as they are being dreamt by people like us when we were dreaming of being a ghost. Does that make any sense to you?"

"No, but, there again, maybe it does. I'm here and I did dream of being a ghost. I just thought it happened, but if these ghosts are listening … how did they get here in the first place?"

"You're right. It does just happen, except they aren't just listening, they're also reading your mind. When a person dreams of being a ghost then he or she becomes one. The Dreamers, as we sometimes call them, know where a ghost is likely to be born – such as you in the hospital. They know who has dreamt as we did and, I don't know how but, they also know the moment we died. It's as if they are tuned into the person that had the dream, so they'd have been psyched into your brain in some way, at the time you died … and mine of course. On the other hand it might be the Mindbenders that tuned into us on instruction from a Dreamer. It's hard to tell unless you're one of them."

"Stop it! Stop it! This is too much to take in. Can we go over it again … slowly?"

"Not now, and, anyway, you'll learn all about it in the next few weeks. The girls will be here in a few minutes – I can sense them."

"I wish I could."

"You will, Micky. And sooner than you think."

Jana takes me by the hand and leads me through the snow to an opening in, what once was, the front of the castle. She points to the sky and a few seconds later I notice two shapes moving towards us. Moments later, these show themselves to be the girls. They slow down and ease themselves to the ground in front of us.

"Ako si sa mala celý ten čas?" – They're all speaking at once, hugging, laughing and kissing each other.

"Čo si zo sebou robila?"

"Kde si sa flákala?" – Jeez! I thought they'd speak English, and it's so fast.

"Stale to isté bez zmeny."

"Mala som zopár somárov." – What's a somrov? Well, at least I'll remember one word for Jana to translate.

Then taking one of the girls hands, she points to me, saying, "Lucia toto je Micky. Come here, Micky. Say hello to Lucia, or give her a kiss." So I shake her hand, nodding hello with a smile. No point in being rude even if I don't know what they're on about.

"Luisella toto je Micky," says Jana, now introducing the second girl.

"Hi, Luisella," I say, and she takes my hand, comes closer and kisses me on both cheeks.

"Luisella is Italian, Micky. Do you like Italians?"

"Yes. Of course I do," I reply, keeping an eye on Luisella.

"Ale dobre vyzerá čo?" Lucia says slowly to the others, flashing me a look.

"Áno. Ľubi sa mi ale je trochu prihriaty." They laugh out loud as Jana has obviously cracked a joke. I hope it's not about me.

Lucia, still laughing, turns to Luisella. "Mali by ste vidiet akého má."

Then Jana quickly speaks to them again. "Dala by som si povedat "

"I'm sorry about that, Micky, but you know how it is." While talking to me, the other two sidle up alongside, one taking one hand and the other the other.

"You're cute. I like you, Micky," says Lucia. She's about five-six in height, has blonde hair, light brown eyes, and an I-want-to-have-you-now look in her face. I don't know what Jana said, but it must have been good.

"You speak English?" I ask, amazed.

"Yes, we do. Luisella is fluent in seven languages but Jana's the best of the Monitors," answers Lucia.

"That's brilliant. How long did they take to learn?" I ask, my eyes now on Luisella.

"Five years, but the Spanish was easy … it's similar to my own. And the French wasn't too bad, either." Luisella is slightly taller than Lucia, with dark hair, brown eyes and a very shapely figure. They're both dressed in denim jeans and jackets, and while Luisella is wearing a pair of black shoes, Lucia's wearing trainers.

"I think you'll enjoy having Micky in the village," suggests Jana.

"Most definitely," says an excited Lucia.

111

"Me too, and I saw him first," replies Luisella, quickly glancing at Lucia and then back at me, and I begin to wonder whether they're all man mad. Then she adds, "Jana, another lad arrived a few days ago, about seventeen or so, and Moira's keeping him safe from the vamps." I assume these vamps are the sex maniacs.

"Shit! That's all we need. So how many New Ghosts are there?"

"Micky makes four – two of each, and Petra is guarding the women," Lucia informs her.

"We've got our work cut out. We'd better get going," Jana says, now frowning. The two young ladies lift me off my feet, fly straight upwards and then come to a stop in mid-air. Jana soon joins us and they talk a little more in Slovenský before we move on at a somewhat casual pace. Every so often they slow to a crawl, search the sky in all directions, and then carry on. It seems as if we'll take a lifetime to get there, and I still can't believe we're in so much danger.

Lucia turns to me. "They'll be after your body, Micky … and the other guy's, and if they haven't got him yet, they might have started on the women."

Luisella stares at Lucia, telling her, "Don't make him nervous. He'll never get a night's peace if you carry on like that." I'm beginning to wonder whether I'll get any peace at all. With Jana, these two, and the supposed bad ghosts … all after my body, I think I'd be safer in that hospital morgue.

Not long after, we pick up speed, flying hard for about fifteen minutes, and then Jana goes ahead to scout the area. She's back in a flash, telling us that the coast is clear and then down we go, landing in the middle of a seated area. In front of us is a large central wooden building that seems as if it was the focal point for the villagers in olden times, and the girls surround me while we walk inside.

"It looks as if they've gone; I don't feel their presence," says Luisella, closing the door behind us.

"More than likely" agrees Jana, "but we'd better be on our guard. Where's this new kid?"

"In one of the small houses by the school," Luisella answers. "Moira said that Anna might be coming today and, if so, the vamps will keep their distance."

"Let's hope so, but they are cunning bitches. Just watch your backs

"… Okay?"

"Okay," they reply.

"Right, Micky, you come with me. The girls will keep watch around the village. I'm going to take you to the manor house where you'll be sleeping. You should be safe there, and, as long as Anna's close by, you won't be bothered by those nymphos."

"Who's Anna?"

"Your Tutor, dummy, Anna Majerniková. She has the respect of most ghosts because of her knowledge and her personality. She has no more power than other ghosts, but she creates fear in the likes of any bad-minded ones. Don't ask me why, I don't know, but it's probably to do with the abilities she's earned. She might tell you if you ask her nicely … or if you're her type."

"What do you mean, her type?" We cross the snow, passing a few houses, and then turn right where a much larger house comes into view.

"Nothing, really. I mean, once she finds out that you're gay, she'll probably leave you alone. But there again, she might not. Anyway, she happens to like inexperienced ghosts." Jana chuckles to herself as we climb some steps and pass through a closed door into, what looks like, a reception area.

"Are you telling me that my … "

"Keep quiet," she whispers. "She might be inside the building."

My eyes take in the display of holiday literature – maps, postcards, brochures and historical books. There are displays of pottery, ornaments and other memorabilia for visitors to buy and take home with them.

"Does this place get busy?"

"Only in the summer months. This time of year, it's closed to the public – there aren't enough tourists. People tend to come to Slovakia for skiing in the winter because it's so much cheaper than Austria and Switzerland. You'd be surprised how many do come here. They usually go to Poprad for the slalom racing, or stay in one of the hotels near here, at Štrbské pleso, if they want the ski jump. You know, Micky, they had the Winter Olympics here one year and the place was packed. All the chalets and hotels were full and some people stayed with the locals. Most of the ghosts went to watch, and quite a few of us enjoyed jumping in and out of the spectators … and, of course, the competitors."

"You didn't?"

"You'd better believe it. There'll be jumpers up there now, and guess what?"

"What?"

"Women aren't supposed to go on the ski jump, well, not the high one. The powers that be reckon it's too dangerous for us."

"Us?"

"Not us ghosts. I mean women, as in live females. Have you ever been ski-jumping before?"

"No. I've never even tried skiing."

"I'll have to take you. Would you like that – it's fun?"

"When I learn to fly, and, anyway, where do we get the skis or are they like our ghost shoes?"

"Don't be daft. We don't bother with all that; we just hop into one of the jumpers and come down with him. Some of these men are so fit that I get hot all over. Actually, they're all fit, but some look sexier than others … you know what I mean?" Jana winks cheekily at me.

"Sounds good to me. So, when will we go?"

"Sometime soon, I hope. Look, when you've learned all you need to know here, I'll take you on a few trips. But when we do go we'll have to look out for you know who."

"I'll do my best."

"I know you will, Micky. I know you will." I like the way she has so much faith in me and I take her hand. Jana leads me up a wide stairway, along a corridor, and into a very large bedroom. There's a huge bear-skin rug lying beside an enormous double bed. Some very old paintings adorn the walls and the furniture appears to suit the period of the building.

"Go on, try the bed for size," suggests Jana, pushing me gently forwards. I climb on, thinking all the time about not sinking in, and lie on my back. I still can't get used to this idea of stressing what I have to do but it's bound to come naturally, eventually. I put my hands behind my head, close my eyes and relax. I reopen them when Jana joins me, lying on her side, facing me. "While you're here," she whispers, "don't make too much noise. We don't want to attract any unwanted attention." I nod my head and she smiles. "I have to go now. I must find Anna to sort out this safety issue."

"But don't these nymphomaniacs do this every time? You should have a permanent guard."

"There aren't enough of us, and if we did catch them, what are we supposed to do? We can't kill them or lock them up, can we?"

"I don't know. So, what do you want me to do?"

"Stay right here and try getting some rest, or read about our history." Jana points to a book that's sitting on an old dressing table.

"How am I supposed to open a book or turn its pages?" Jana looks at me as if I'm stupid. Jumping off the bed, she goes to the book, opens it, and starts flicking from one page to the next.

"Now, you have a go." And I try, and find that I can move the book about and lift it. I throw it gently and, in the process, nearly drop it. Jana scowls and, raising her voice, has a dig at me. "Micky, be careful with that. Treat our bedroom book with some respect."

"Huh! Ja ... "

And before I can say anymore, she bursts in again, "I'm sorry. I'm so sorry. I get so frustrated and forget how it was for me in the beginning. I really can't remember all the things I wasn't supposed to touch or do, and nowadays I tend to take things for granted. I think I'm becoming more critical with each New Ghost I get."

Jana stares at me, hands held out, and I feel for her. "It's okay, Jana. I am a bit of a dipstick, sometimes, and don't always think first."

"The bedroom book is just that – like your clothes, and we have to take care of it. It takes a lot of time to keep it updated, so we don't want any pages spoiled. Just wait until you have to move things that aren't made from ghostly materials. But don't worry, Micky. While you're here, you'll learn how to move objects from one place to another, just like in those ghost films where cups go flying through the air – that type of thing; much the same way that I tilted the champagne glass I told you about."

I'm amazed by this, and ask whether I'll be able to move parts of living people's bodies, and she answers, "Of course you will, but only when you're inside them. You'll be able to move their eyes, to make them look at something you're interested in, but it won't work every time. Some people are very strong willed and yours might not be as strong as theirs. That said, you won't know until you try. In the meantime, concentrate on your reading." I nod my head.

I start looking through the book, and when Jana sees me looking baffled she takes it, finds what she wants, and then replaces it on the table. "The English section," she points out. "I'm off now, but if you have any female problems … shout."

"I most certainly will." I bid her goodbye and then sit down by the dressing table. The book has some fascinating information and I can't take me eyes off it. I read for a long time, chapter after chapter, until my eyes get sore. So I stand up, stretch, and have a good look around the room. A book shelf stands in one of the corners and I cross over for a closer look. On inspection, I realise that most of the books are similar to the one I've been reading, except that each one has a different translation on its binding. Returning to the one on the table, I flick the pages back, to the very beginning, and notice that it is written in Slovak with translations in Latin, Greek, German and English.

From the little I've read, I can tell you that it's a book about ghosts, but it's not a book of fiction, and the interesting thing is the title … GOD. Turning over the next couple of pages, I see the title written again, but this time in full and in all five languages, and the English translation says Ghosts Of Dreams. This book, I imagine, is to a ghost what a bible is to a living person, and I think it's going to take me an age to get through it. I flick the pages forward and back to where I left off. I start reading once more but, after some time, I give it a rest and lie down. I close my eyes, wondering about my day, and the book.

CHAPTER ELEVEN

Waking up at seven o'clock to the chimes from an old antique clock instead of the electric alarm that I'd been used to, I glance around the room once more, checking out the rest of its old furniture, this time in more detail, but I can't resist going back to the book. It has me hooked. I used to love reading when I was alive, so I'm sure you can understand that old habits die hard.

I become so engrossed in the stories, that I don't notice the time flying by until I get up to stretch my legs. The clock says nine-thirty, and I haven't heard from Jana, or any of the others for that matter. Should I go down? Is it safe? I do wish to see what's going on, so I cross the room and putting my hand around the doorknob I try willing it to turn and the door to open, but this doesn't work. I move to the window, look out on the picturesque snow-topped old houses and reflect on what's gone on in my new life, and I also wonder about how the hell I'm going to get out of this room. What if I'm attacked? If I shout, will Jana save me in time? Why can't I do some things and not others? I can't wait to get started with this Majerniková woman. At least I'll find out how to do some of the simple things in life.

"Ahoj! ... Er, hello!" says a female voice, interrupting my thoughts.

"Hello! Come in." I turn around and start towards the door, and at exactly the same time part of the door seems to disappear. A body, in the shape of a lady in her mid-thirties, dressed in long and seemingly ancient clothes, passes through it.

She stops and offers me her hand. "Ako sa máte? Ooh, I'm sorry about that. How do you do?" she asks. "I take it that you are English speaking?"

"I'm fine, and, yes, I am English. My name's Mick. What's yours?"

"My name is Magdalena, but you may call me Maggie. Everyone else does."

"It's good to meet you, Maggie." She bows her head, giving me a pleasant smile. "Where's Jana? Is she up yet?"

"Oh, yes, some time ago, and she's waiting for you in the kitchen. Jana's such a lovely girl and we're all so proud of her. If you'd care to follow me, I'll take you to her." Maggie turns to the door, takes my hand and pulls me through. She leads the way downstairs, holding up her long billowy dress. She has such an old style pair of shoes that I can't fathom out what era they might have come from. From her dress sense she obviously prefers living in the past, whenever hers was, whereas Jana and the other girls appear to move with the times. I begin to lag behind as my eyes fall on some of the paintings, but Maggie soon realises and waits. When I'm alongside, she once more bows and smiles before we carry on. How quaint, I think. Once downstairs, we pass along a few more corridors until, eventually, arriving at the kitchen.

The kitchen has a very olde-worlde feel about it, with huge pots and pans hanging from its wooden beams, and yet it's spotless. It's plain to see, though, that Jana isn't here. I ask Maggie where she is. "Probably outside," she answers, pointing to a small external door at the back of the room. Holding my hand, she leads the way out to where we see Jana standing by a barn and talking to an older woman. "There she is," points Maggie. Jana sees me and waves, but carries on talking to this very well dressed lady. Maggie taps my elbow, saying, "We'd better wait here. The lady is your Tutor, Madam Majerniková, and we all treat her with great respect. And she is worthy of it, because over the years she's earned more abilities than most other ghosts."

"I'm slightly nervous, I'm afraid," I mutter through my teeth.

"Don't be silly. You've no need to be frightened, Mick. She's not an ogre. When you hear about her past, and read about some of the later years in the bedroom book, then you'll understand."

"Have you read the book?"

"Indeed I have. It's the most interesting book I've ever read. I never had the opportunity when I was alive. I couldn't read or write back then. Only boys from rich families were educated in those days. We villagers had to work the land or go into service for one of the land-owners. We didn't know any other way of life."

"Jana told me much the same, but she died so long ago."

Just then, both Jana and Anna Majerniková start towards us. Maggie says, "I have other things to do, Mick, so I'll see you later."

"Okay, Maggie, and thanks." As they near me I get butterflies in my belly, but it's too late to do anything about it – not that I could anyway. "Hello," I say, offering my hand.

She shakes it gently, eyeing me up and down. "Ako sa máš, Mick?"

"Er, I'm sorry, but I don't understand."

"Of course you do, Micky." Turning to my Tutor, Jana says, "See, I told you he's a bag of nerves."

"Calm down, Mick. We're all ghosts together, and perhaps one day you'll spend some time teaching other ghosts what, and what not, to do. I'm sure you'd like that. By the way, call me Anna." She seems pleasant enough, and I can see that both of the women get along quite well. In fact, they seem to enjoy each other's company. And then I think about Jana and how upset she was. If it isn't the teacher then who can it be?

Anna then suggests a walk around the grounds, and Jana hooks her arm into one of mine. Anna takes the other, and they let me escort them in a way I haven't seen for many a year. They seem very relaxed and appear to treat me as something of a novelty.

"When I was alive, everyone knew me as the healer Majerníková from Myjava, until it suited some of them to call me the wicked witch. I might as well tell you the whole story, Mick, because sooner or later someone else will. Looking at Jana, she asks, "Have you told him anything yet?"

"I've only mentioned the year I died and how old I was at the time. You know I don't like talking about my past."

"I can understand your anger – I'm the same myself, but you should have the courage, by now, to vent your feelings. And think of all the other terrible things that have happened over the centuries in our former world, and they're still going on. All the killing, and it's still all for money, power, or the silly beliefs that people have. It's one thing to have faith in something, but to kill for it, well, that's wrong. And if our Dreamers and Mindbenders don't manage to do something soon, then we won't have an earth to be ghosts in at all. Anyway, are you going to stay while I tell Mick, or not?"

Jana nods her head. "I'll stay."

"Very well, then. I won't beat about the bush, Mick. Jana and I met really horrible deaths nearly four hundred years ago." I can feel Jana's hand as she grips my arm tighter. I can't believe I'm going to hear this. It's not something I'd want anyone to know about me. We stop by a stone wall with a light covering of snow on top, and we make it our seat, the pair of them still either side of me.

"My life, Mick, was a fairly long one for the period we lived in. Everyone from miles around would come to me with their ailments and

I would treat them with herbs and poultices. We didn't have medicines then as they do now. I don't know if you are familiar with medieval history but people like me were eventually called witches when other people needed somebody to blame for one thing or the other. All the good things I, and people like me, had done were forgotten. We were easy targets. Anyway, let me take you back in time to a castle and some of its history. What I'm about to tell you is completely true and is a case of the rich getting away with murder on a grand scale. People like Crippen and that Ted Bundy, to name but two, would have nothing on the bitch that killed us, and that's a fact."

I look at her with complete surprise, and then glance at Jana, whose head is down, looking forlorn. I turn back to Anna's voice. "This castle, Čachtice hrad, was in the hands of the Batoriová family during the sixteenth and seventeenth centuries. Alžbeta Batoriová, who was the owner at the time of my death, was also known as Čachtiska Pani – the woman of the castle. This evil cow and her family had great wealth, and she would travel around several countries employing servants to do her bidding. That was the way of life, as I've said, but she wanted to appear young to her friends. I don't know where she got the idea, but this disgusting person came to believe that if she bathed in the blood of young virgin girls then she would stay forever young and good looking."

"During her travels," Anna goes on, "she'd find some of these young girls and employ them as maids. She'd take them from their families, sometimes for a few lousy coins, on the promise of feeding them and teaching them the ways of the world. You must realise that poor families couldn't afford to keep all their children. Girls married very young and became the responsibility of their husbands. People had large families at that time. Don't forget that there was no such thing as what you call a johnny or the pill, and can you imagine a man, in those days, believing in the withdrawal method. They'd never heard of it then, and they don't bloody believe in doing it now. You see, Mick, in life, nothing changes. Anyway, this woman used to bring these girls home, from her very frequent journeys, to do the cleaning, cooking and general work about the castle. The girls' families would probably only expect to hear from them if they ever got married, came into some money, or ran away from their new owner and returned home. Otherwise, they weren't missed.

"When she wasn't travelling she'd give live-in work to young girls from remote villages. The thing is, Mick, she wanted the girls for their blood. With the help of some of her loyal workers she'd cut a girl either over, or in, a bath of water and watch as the blood ran out of the poor girl's body. This bitch had no shame or mercy and was also clever enough to dispose of the bodies. She and her cohorts would take the dead girl and cut her up. She ordered that the body be cooked, then she, or, more than likely, some of the others, used to eat the heart, liver, kidneys and other parts of the dead girl. The rest they'd burn, bury, or give to the dogs."

I can't watch anymore as she angrily relates the story, and I'm too upset to look at Jana. I now know what happened to her and can only imagine her sorry eyes while she listens to this sad end to her very short life. I can't understand how Jana can even live in Slovakia, or go anywhere near those castle ruins, and why has Anna Majerniková stayed? If it was me, I'd be a million miles away.

Anna continues, "The crimes of Čachtiska Pani were found out in the year 1610. This woman, Alžbeta Batoriová, was brought to court early the following year, but they couldn't get a conviction against her, even though there were two hundred and twenty four witnesses to her wickedness. Her friends wanted a scapegoat, as you might say, and they let it be known that a witch was responsible for distorting her mind in some way ... and that so called witch, they claimed, was me, a healer. The powers that be went along with this and the bastards burned me at the stake only fourteen days after she'd been to court. The ones who helped her were beheaded on the orders of the King in the November of 1611, while she was kept a prisoner in her own castle pending more investigations. As she and her family were so wealthy and part of the in-crowd, Čachtiska Pani got away with it in a fashion. She was locked up in the small dungeon beneath her castle until eventually dying on August 21st 1614. I remember the date well. She was survived by her daughter.

"Can you believe that over nine years this miserable serial killer – if that's what you'd call her – killed over six hundred young girls and got away with it? What I'm saying is that locking her up was too good for her. It makes my heart bleed to think of it. And it's because of her that I'm a ghost. While I was being burned alive I vowed that I'd come back and haunt her, her family, and her so-called friends. I remember, to this day, starting to pass out and going into a dreamlike state, and still thinking of haunting them. I'm sorry sometimes that I did, because I'll always remember my past, and yet I'm happy being a ghost. Poor Jana was one of her victims. Her family was devastated. I'd already returned to visit the castle and the nearby village, as a ghost, when people turned up from other towns and villages inquiring about their daughters' whereabouts. I'd listen to the excuses and the details as the truth was made known. Some of Alžbeta's helpers tried to trade off information for amnesty, but they still lost their heads. Well, Mick, that's all there is to tell you, and I hope that being here and knowing the truth about us doesn't affect you too much. Jana and I have learnt to live with it, and it has made us stronger and more determined to do our best for everyone that comes our way."

"Thanks for telling me, but it's not something I'd like to have known, ordinarily. No doubt someone would have said something, but it's better from your own lips. And if I'd been you, then I, too, would have wanted my revenge." Turning to Jana, I take her hand. "Jana, I'm so sorry. Now, I realise why you wouldn't talk about yourself, but I can't help wondering what keeps you going or why you keep coming back here. You're such a brave person. I really don't know what else to say. I'm flabbergasted and, to be honest, I feel drained. God knows how you two must feel." Pulling Jana closer, I kiss her forehead. She turns, giving me a warm knowing smile, and I can't help thinking of how brave she is. If I'd been her, I'd have let my ghost-self die and taken the chance that I might return as something nice – a butterfly or a bird perhaps. But we dream what we dream, I suppose.

Anna stands up. "I'm going for a rest. You two can do what you like for today, but tomorrow we have to get started. And, unusually, three other ghosts have arrived in the past week, so we have our work cut out. Take care … the pair of you, and don't do anything I wouldn't do. There again, perhaps you should. It's just as well we ghosts can't get pregnant. … Ciao!" Anna winks at us before walking away.

"Ciao, Anna," says Jana, softly.

Jana stands up, pulling me with her, and we head off through the snow. She tells me that Anna has spoken to the nymphos and warned them to keep their distance, but Jana doubts that they will. She reckons that as Anna isn't here all the time, they might take a chance. It doesn't make any sense. Okay, it's not my style, but I'd bump them off. I have to ask, don't I? And so I do. "If they go around killing other ghosts, why then can't we kill them?"

"Try it and see. As far as we know, ghosts can't kill. These nymphos don't intentionally mean to cause death. They do it by accident really. One might jump on you, while the others hold you down, and she'll screw you and screw you until she's satisfied, and then they'll swap over. Remember how we were so shattered after our little bout of sex, and then imagine three of them having you time and time again. They're just after sex and they'll take what they can get. Sometimes they give ghosts a chance to recover, and then they'll start all over again. And they will kiss and suck some life from you so they can keep on screwing. Eventually, you'll be so weak that you won't have the strength to recover. Then they'll leave you to die. The thing is that if they were to attack, they'd take you to some isolated place to do their business. Who knows? You might get lucky and a passing ghost might see you, but the chances of that happening, or some living person lying down in your body at that precise moment, are in the millions. You'll die, Micky ... on the job."

"So, they're not deliberately trying to kill other ghosts?"

"No! And the reason they pick on ghosts like you is because you can't fly and haven't built up the strength to fight them off. Don't worry. We'll get you juiced up and then they might keep their distance. It's such a pity we don't have fuchsia growing here. The best place is in the west of Ireland."

"Don't be silly. Fuchsia grows all over the place. But why fuchsia?"

"It doesn't have to be fuchsia. It can be any bell flower, but fuchsia has the best type of nectar for us. Anyway, going to Ireland has other benefits."

"Such as?"

"Shamrock and clover. We know shamrock doesn't grow wild anywhere else, and it has a slight edge over clover, so, by going to Ireland, we can kill two birds with one stone."

All the time we're talking, Jana is showing me inside some of the smaller buildings. Some, like the carpenter's, are so tiny that it seems impossible to have raised families inside. They would have been so cramped. Others, though, such as the farmhouse, with its barns and sheds, would have housed quite a few people. We go into, what once was, an old school, with its small chairs and a blackboard on its easel, and I realise that the village shows the history over several periods. This is confirmed when, around another corner, we come across a building housing a fire cart, all ready to roll, with a horse stabled close by. Some houses have small barns on their plots, and I can hear the sounds of chickens, ducks and goats. Someone must look after these, even in the winter, so I ask Jana about them.

"Yes, of course they do," she replies. "Local people help out with the feeding and the cleaning of the village. They come here for a few hours and then check on similar villages in the area. Our country has a great history, Micky, and we need the tourists to come here, so the government department responsible employs site managers. And look around you. Forget the snow and, instead, imagine the spring and summer, the smell of the pine trees, the streams, the mountain flowers, and the panoramic view from wherever you are in Tatry."

"Tatry?"

"Yes. This is part of High Tatry. It's so beautiful. Why do you think I stay here, Micky? It's peaceful, and the people are friendly, and, besides that, it's my home."

"I must admit, you've got a point. I'd like to watch the snows melt and spend time painting waterfalls, but I won't be able to now."

"There's nothing stopping you watching the ever changing seasons, but painting might be a problem."

"Being a ghost, I'd say it's impossible," I respond.

"Nothing's impossible. Well, yes, I suppose lots of things are, but painting isn't. It takes a long time to learn, but, like me, you're probably a crap painter."

"I'm not. I used to enjoy painting – mostly still life. No, that's not right. It wasn't really still life. It was more like nude painting."

"Micky! … You painted nudes?"

"I tried to, but sometimes he moved. He couldn't keep it up, even though I was naked as well."

Jana bursts out laughing. "I'm trying to imagine it. Come on, let's find the others." As we walk off, she adds, "Wait 'til I tell the girls."

"You wouldn't?"

"I might, if you don't do as you're told."

"Please, Jana? Don't stress me out. I've enough on my plate with these nymphos of yours, and I don't need everyone knowing everything about me."

"Okay, but I'm telling you now that my friends have an inkling about you."

"How?"

"News like that travels fast, especially where Simon is involved. I'm not saying he's directly responsible, mind you, but it might keep the other girls away. And if those nymphos get it into their heads that you're gay then they'll probably leave you alone. They won't want to waste their time and energy trying to get your little cocky hard when there are easier fish to fry." I stop still, weighing up what she's just said, and it makes sense. I think she could be right about Simon. And then I think about the way Luisella and Lucia were arguing over me. Add to that the threat of being screwed to death. They are all situations which have been playing on my mind. "Anyway, Micky, perhaps it's for the best. Your safety is of paramount concern to me, so don't go getting mad at anyone."

"I'm not mad. Not now, and I'm glad you told me. And, Jana, at the moment, you're the only friend I have. Okay, so the others are friends, but I don't know them properly or what they might be saying about me."

We carry on walking, and minutes later Jana grabs me again and takes deliberate steps towards a tiny house. Once at the door, she pulls me inside. Lucia is on the floor in the far corner, which isn't very far when I consider the size of the room. Luisella sits close by, back against the wall and her hands cupped around her knees, while another lady is seated opposite. A young lad is perched between them and he seems very nervous.

"Hi, Micky," says Lucia, a huge grin on her face. She points to the third female, saying, "This is Moira" and then nodding towards the boy, "and this is Tommy."

"Hello, Moira, Tommy, nice to meet you." I shake their hands. "I believe you're new as well," I say to him.

"Y ... yes," he replies, and I don't know why but he appears to be scared. Then it dawns on me. They've told him I'm gay. The poor lad – if he is a lad – is frightened to death. He must think that either the nymphos will get him, or if they don't then I will. What can I say, except that he looks too young and he's not my type?

I decide to crack the ice. "When did you die?" All the girls stare at me, Jana included, with astonished expressions on their faces.

But they say nothing, and seem more surprised when Tommy replies,

125

"Last Monday night, in Norwich."

"You were trapped somewhere, weren't you?"

Luisella interrupts, looking at me angrily. "Leave him alone, Micky. We don't ask such direct questions to frightened ghosts, especially when they're new."

Surprisingly, Tommy lightens up, saying, "I was trapped, but how did you know?" And they all stare at him and then back at me.

"Because of Simon. I died in the hospital, in Newmarket, and he got me out. I was trapped in the morgue. When he dropped me at my sister's, he said he had another job in Norwich. So, it had to be you."

"It was Simon. Me and my friend, Jim, had been working late, fixing up a youth club for ourselves and our mates. The lights went out unexpectedly. We went to the basement to change the fuse and it was all this old wiring. Neither of us knew much about electrics, and we were fiddling around with the old fuses, but we must have touched the wrong thing 'cos the next thing I know ... I'm a ghost and I'm, like, standing over my own body and Jim's was a few feet away. I tried going back in, hoping I'd come back to life, but it didn't work. I didn't know what to do. I tried leaving the place, to raise the alarm, but I couldn't get out of the building. The next thing I see is this other ghost, Simon, and he took me home. I asked him why Jim wasn't a ghost as well as me, but he just said something stupid about squirrels."

"You say you were doing up a youth club. You must have been young."

"What are you on about? I'm only eighteen. I'd have been nineteen next month. Jim was only sixteen." I decide not to press him on the matter.

"So, who brought you here?"

"That's the joke ... some ghost who calls herself Anne Boleyn. She says she's a Ghost Monitor, or something like that, but it couldn't be her – she lost her head. And, anyway, she'd be nearly five hundred years old by now." I think someone needs to speak to our country's former Queen and that someone should be Jana.

"Didn't she say anything to you – you know, about ghosts and their lives?"

"No. She hardly spoke at all. Something else has happened, though, and it's crazy."

Jana butts in. "And what's that, Tommy?"

"It's embarrassing really. You see, this Anne Boleyn ... well, she saw me naked, so I don't suppose me telling you lot will make any difference. The thing is, I used to be circumcised but I'm not anymore, and I don't know why." – I do, and I'm not about to tell him what I lost or how I got it back. Then Tommy, looking at me, asks, "And what about you? How did you die?"

"A car crash." And that's all I'm prepared to say. "I know quite a few people in Norwich. What's your surname? I might know your dad."

"Smith, and there are loads of them in Norwich."

"Tommy Smith! Well, it's nice to meet you, Tommy."

The girls talk among themselves for a few minutes, and then Luisella comments again on how we English are so up front with our questions and answers.

Moira comes to our defence. "We're just the same in Ireland. We're certainly not backwards in coming forwards, and that's the truth."

"You're Irish?" I ask. Mind you, I should have guessed from her accent.

"I am, indeed," she says. "I died in the potato famine."

Tommy's eyes light up and his mouth falls open. "I studied that in History. Jesus! That was yonks ago ... eighteen hundred and something. It's impossible!" Moira looks no more than thirty, give or take a few pounds. I always find it hard to guess women's ages when they're slightly overweight, but she looks well on it.

"Don't tease him, Moira," says Jana. "What needs to be said is better said by Anna or Anne." Tommy stares from one to the other, not knowing what, or who, to believe. I still can't understand why our good Queen Anne didn't give him the low-down on being a ghost. Even I'm not fully aware of all the information, but at least Jana has explained most things when I've asked.

"When did you get here, Tommy?" I ask, trying to change the topic.

"Friday evening, by aeroplane and train, and then we flew from the station. How come she can fly and I can't? She held my hand ... even going through walls. It doesn't make sense."

"It will, Tommy. It will," Jana informs him. Then she turns to me. "Let's go and find Anne. I've got some questions to ask her. Anyone know where she is?"

"Up in the big house, I think," replies Lucia.

I look at Tommy, wait until he's watching, then deliberately make a show of grabbing Jana's hand before taking our leave through the closed door. You should have seen the look on his face. Once outside we make tracks through the snow towards my lodgings. Well, I'll be honest. We don't actually make any real tracks because we can't, but you get my drift, I hope.

We're about half-way there when we sight Anne, flying in our direction. She lands in front of us, smiles a radiant smile, and says, "Hello Jana, and what have you been up to? And this must be Mick. I've heard a lot about you." – I bet she has.

We say our hellos, and then Jana speaks. "Anne, why didn't you help that poor lad? You've told him nothing. He thinks you're a bit screwy in the head, bad tempered and unfriendly, and it's all because you didn't tell him about how we look as ghosts. He doesn't believe who you are. Well, he might now, especially after Moira telling him when she died, but you said nothing to him about the magical reappearance of skin on his penis."

"What are you on about? What skin?" Anne looks at her, quizzically.

"He used to be circumcised."

"How was I supposed to know? I don't go around asking New Ghosts. … 'Have you ever been circumcised my dear?' … when they look normal to me. And you wouldn't have mentioned it, either, unless he said something. He told me he was eighteen when he died and he still looks eighteen now, so his dream of being a ghost must have been very recent."

"Okay, I accept that, but why didn't you help him?" Jana keeps at her while I stand, hands in pockets, eager to hear Anne's explanation.

"Fine! I'll tell you. I'm fed up to the back teeth with men. If you must know, picking up Tommy brought back bad memories. I was nearby when Simon brought him to his house, so I took charge of the situation. Simon decided to fly along with us for a while, and we were having a laugh. Tommy was quiet, naturally. Anyway, we had to get him some new clothes, because his smelled of death, so we went into the city centre. As we approached the shops, Simon stopped, called me back, and said … 'Look at that'. I did, and then lost my temper, kicked him in the balls, and told him to piss off."

Jana eggs her on. "So, what got you so mad?"

"It was a block of flats – its name … 'Tudor' bloody 'Mansions'."

Jana starts laughing.

"It's not funny."

Jana's laughter has her doubled over and she can't stop. "Anne. Oh, Anne. You've got to get it out of your head." And she laughs even louder. I can't hold mine back any longer. We're having fits as Anne moves the few feet between them and starts hitting Jana on her chest and shoulders. Jana falls to the ground, still laughing and holding her stomach. Anne follows her down, still hitting, but not as hard, and then she starts laughing too.

"What's going on?"

"What are they doing?"

"Mama Mia!"

"Huh!"

I turn on hearing the voices, to see the girls and Tommy running toward us. And they aren't the only ones. Others have heard the excitement and are following close behind. Word gets round and pretty soon about twenty ghosts have either joined in the fun or are watching on in stunned silence.

Tommy asks, "What's so funny?"

"I can't tell you," I reply, now trying to control myself. With all these new faces, my attention is drawn to them. "Where have they all come from?"

"They live here most of the time."

"How do you know? You've only been here a couple of days."

"It's a small village, Mick. There are lots of foreigners here."

"We're the foreigners, Tommy. We're not in England now."

"I suppose we are. Anyway, what are they doing down there?" He points to the two women, saying, "I didn't think she could laugh, the miserable cow."

"You mean, Anne?" I ask, while Lucia and a huge male ghost try lifting the girls to their feet.

"Yes."

"She's not miserable, but however badly she may have acted with you, it wasn't your fault. We all get upset sometimes, don't we?"

"I suppose. She really is Anne Boleyn, then?"

"So it seems. When did you figure it out?"

"The other women. After you left, Moira told me more about her own life and death. I still didn't believe it, but then Lucia was beginning to tell me her own story when we heard the commotion. She stopped talking and we all ran out to have a look."

"One day, Tommy, Anne might tell you what was said here, but that's her decision."

I walk him over to one of the houses, lean on the wall, and tell him some of the basics. I'm not in the least surprised that Tommy is bewildered. He tells me about his family and funeral, and although I mention mine, I don't go into detail. Occasionally, I glance over at Jana and Anne who are chatting away with some of their friends, while others walk on by.

The rest of the day is spent being introduced to one ghost after the other, including the two new females, Nancy and Freda. Plans are made for a few trips once our learning curve is over, and I'm looking forward to them.

Later in the evening, Jana tells me to get some rest; that I'll have a few long days ahead and I'll need my sleep. She escorts me to my room, where we sit a while, discussing the contents of the books. This in itself raises a question in my mind – it's been bugging me since I first saw the books. But when I ask how ghosts can acquire them, and who brought them and the implements to write with, all she says is … "Ask Anna."

I can't accept this, but she insists that it's Anna's job to explain the more intricate work of the different types of ghosts. I'm still not satisfied, but eventually I lie down with Jana alongside … at her insistence and the promise of no hanky panky. I stay awake until she drops off, and then, feeling safe from one of her attacks, I close my eyes.

CHAPTER TWELVE

Jana is still sleeping when I ever so quietly climb off the bed. The first glimmer of daylight shows itself through the window, so I cross the room to peek outside. Everywhere looks so quiet and picturesque. There's not even a crow from the cockerels and I take a look at the time. Six-fifteen, and all's well. No sign of danger from any of the nympho ghosts, so it appears that the influence Anna has over them is working.

Going to the bedroom book, as Maggie calls it, I start reading again, this time inspecting the paper and ink. The pages are faintly lined, and the ever so neat writing seems to be in the same hand throughout. Going back in the book, to the Greek translation, I check the handwriting and compare it to that in the English section. Whichever ghost had written in Greek, had not written in English. So I study the German writing and find the same thing, except that in the latter chapters, a greater similarity does arise.

This is crazy. The more I see, the more I'm baffled. How, I ask myself, can any ghosts have written this and the other books, assuming they all have the same stories? The books seem modern … well, no more than fifty years old, but most of the stories are archaic, and it's only in the later chapters that they tell of ghost life from present times. It's as if the books are updated regularly, but if that's the case, who by? Even the ink is strange, and, sometimes, it too changes slightly, yet still maintains a reddish-purple colour as the book progresses. And what did they use to write with? There aren't any pens around, unless they're in a drawer. One thing's for sure. Whichever ghosts did the writing, they are exceptionally good at calligraphy. This, in itself, raises another interesting question. That is … how did they write? I mean, how did they hold their pens, quills or whatever? Now, do you understand why I'm confused? And the more I think about it, the more confused I am.

The only thing, I can think of, that must relate to this in some way, is something I remember Jana saying when I told her of wanting to paint. She said I could learn, but if I can't hold anything and we don't actually touch things, then how can a ghost grip something such as a pen, or a paintbrush, to do the job? It seems impossible, but she said it isn't. My thoughts are interrupted by her voice. "Morning, Micky. And what are you up to?"

"Just browsing through the book again. If I ask, will you tell me the answer?"

"It depends what it is."

"It's about the books – all of them, and the stories, and how and when they were written?"

"The Ghost Scribes write them. They write nearly all the dreams and stories down, and anything else we might need. You'll be seeing Anna soon, so don't be impatient. You've only got another. ... Blast! Is that the time?"

I glance at the clock which now shows eight-ten. Jana jumps off the bed, tells me to get my skates on, and starts rushing for the door. I'm right behind her grabbing for her hand. "What's the problem?"

"You should have been downstairs forty minutes ago. She'll go mad."

"Why? What's she going to do to me – smack my backside or something?"

"It's not you I'm worrying about. It's me. She'll have me monitoring the United States or some other far off place, and you know how I hate crossing water."

We're half-way down the stairs and she's panicking. "How can she do that? She's not your boss. I thought we ghosts are supposed to be the same, other than having different abilities."

"Never mind about that ... we're here."

She guides me through a door leading into a large sitting room, and seated around an extremely long table are four ghosts – a smiling Anna, a straight-faced Nancy and a weary looking Freda. But when I look at Tommy I burst out laughing. Jana tries not to laugh but she can't help herself, and then Anna joins in. Tommy's red hair is sticking up. It's a complete mess, and I wonder if he'd ever been laid before he died. I'm also wondering who was the lucky, or, perhaps, the not so lucky ghost. Anna, still laughing, casts her eyes at Jana, waves her away, and Jana's off like a shot.

"Sit down, Mick," Anna manages to say, pointing to a seat, in front of which are several pieces of paper. I take my place, still chuckling, but avoiding eye contact with Tommy. I know if I look, it will start me off again, so Anna has all my smiling attention.

"You're a bit late, Mick. I trust Jana didn't keep you up all night?" And she laughs at her own intimation.

I laugh with her. "No! No, she didn't."

"It doesn't matter. I've enjoyed the wait. In fact, I haven't had such a funny start to a day for a very long time." Still laughing, she says, "I can't even say why I've got the giggles."

The other three stare, but don't say a word. A minute or two later, both Anna and I control ourselves, and then turning to me, she says, "Mick, will you please take Tommy outside for a while? I want to talk to Freda and Nancy, privately."

"I would if I could, but I can't because the door's closed."

"Oh, yes. I forgot about that. Right, you take Tommy's hand while I hold yours, and I'll pass you through. When you're done, and have said what I think you ought to, give me a shout."

Anna, Tommy and I stand up, walk to the door, and, laughing again, she says, "Five minutes ... okay?" Then she pushes us ahead, Tommy first, and as we pass through the door Anna's hand frees itself from mine. Looking down, I see that the only part of her that's visible is her arm, from the elbow down. I wonder how her ability is so strong that it can pass from her to me and then on to Tommy.

Once in the hallway, I can't help but smile. "Who were you sleeping with last night?"

"W ... What do you m ... mean?" he stammers.

"Okay then, I'll rephrase the question. Which little ghostie screwed you last night?"

"What! How do you know?"

"Your hair! It's a mess. Where are all those red curls?"

"My hair is always a mess." He lifts his hands and feels the spiky points of his hair. "What's happened?"

"Would you like me to fix it?"

"No. I'll do it when I find a mirror." He tries patting his hair down but it's still all over the place.

"The mirror's in the lounge, but the women are there."

"Okay! Okay! You do it, but what's the big deal?"

"I know you've had sex with someone because this is what happens to male ghosts when they get their leg over. You see, Tommy, Jana told me, and if you don't say who your lady friend is then I'll leave it as it is."

"Don't," he pleads, but I shake my head. "It was Lucia," he admits. "She was guarding me last night because of some ghosts they all keep talking about."

"Were you willing?"

"She kept kissing me and wouldn't stop. I got all worked up."

"So, she took your virginity," I state.

"How'd you know I was a virgin?"

"I didn't, but I do now."

"You tricked me. You bastard!"

"Not really, but better Lucia than one of the nymphos. They'd have raped you and left you for dead. So, remember that." I tidy his hair as best I can, before raising my voice. "Anna! ... We're ready."

"I don't want to go in so soon. It's embarrassing."

"Don't worry. Anna's not likely to tell the other two. Is she? She knew I knew, that much was obvious, and she only wanted me to sort you out."

A sigh of relief comes from Tommy. "Thanks Mick, but you won't tell anyone else, will you?"

"I won't, and I don't think Anna will, but I don't know about the other two."

"The other two? But they don't know."

"Lucia and Jana!"

"Jana! Oh, no! She saw me."

I'm about to answer when Anna walks through the door, saying, "Time's up boys ... let's get to work." She winks at Tommy then takes his hand. "I hope you've explained what you could, Mick."

"As much as I know, and that's not a lot." She gives me a sly grin and closes her eyes slightly. And that one look tells me that Anna is a very perceptive lady. Once back in our seats, she re-introduces us to each other, as a matter of courtesy, and then says we should read the documents on the table.

There are five papers in total and, working from left to right, they list the types of ghosts on the first, and details of the known abilities of each on the other sheets. They are all written in the same colour ink, deep purple, as the most recent entries in the bedroom book. The word 'known' is underlined, and I wonder why.

I read the list again:

NEW GHOST
GHOST VILLAGER
HAUNTER
GHOST RELIEVER
GHOST MONITOR
GHOST GATHERER
GHOST SCRIBE – local
GHOST TUTOR
GHOST SCRIBE – dreams
MINDBENDER GHOST
GHOST OF DREAMS

Then I glance through the other papers which give the description of each. Well, I know I'm a New Ghost, so what's the point in telling me? I read a little about the life of a Ghost Villager and it doesn't inspire me. They must be thick. Imagine wanting to stay in a village all your life. Now here's something that might be interesting … the Haunter.

HAUNTER – A Haunter is a ghost that learns the skills needed to haunt buildings, places or people. Certain abilities must be acquired in order to move objects. A Haunter has to be able to carry and push an object with a degree of speed. These are basic abilities and are easily learnt by obeying instructions.

The purpose of a Haunter is to frighten a person, or people, but the Haunter must cease the haunting when it verges on real fear. Haunters must not scare anyone to death or near death. It is designed as an entertainment not a threat.

Objectives – To be able to throw a cup a distance of 20 metres.

To be able to … .

It's not worth reading as far as I'm concerned. The list is miles long with distances for this and that. I'd be here all day trying to learn them, and what's the point if you can't scare anyone properly?

I don't bother looking at the details of the Reliever and Monitor. I know what Simon and Jana do for a living. And I can imagine a Scribe. It's obviously a ghost writer, but what I don't get is the difference between the local and the dream Scribe. By the looks of it, they both seem to do the same job. I suppose it's down to where you want to work. Who wants to write for a living anyway? I realise someone had to write these papers but it's so much like being a clerk.

The Gatherer obviously gathers things and takes them wherever. Once again, there's a list of things to carry and the distances required, but this time in the thousands of kilometres. Fat chance of me doing that, I can tell you. I don't read it all, and why should I? The Ghost Tutor speaks for itself. After all, that's what Anna is and I never fancied myself as a teacher.

Now these look interesting, I think, as I browse over the Mindbender and the Ghost Of Dreams.

MINDBENDER - A Mindbender has the ability to read people's minds and, if required, to attempt to change a person's mind.

A Mindbender will have the ability of speed of thought - a requirement needed to make split second decisions and act in the same time.

A Mindbender can cause a person to do an action without that person knowing he or she is doing it. - See notes below.

A Mindbender can achieve all of its abilities by, some way, helping another ghost become a Ghost Of Dreams. Please note that this is an accidental occurrence.

A Mindbender has the ability of being multi-lingual in at least 6 languages after only a short time.

A Mindbender ... .

I'm interrupted by Anna, who says, "As you can see, there is quite a lot of information, but I don't expect you to remember everything. I'll be going over all this, so don't worry too much. Now then, before we start ... any questions?"

"I have several, but don't know where to begin," I say. I look across at Nancy and Freda, who have started a quiet discussion between themselves. Tommy sits, arms folded, waiting for my first question.

"Quiet ladies. Let Mick speak."

Anna then points at me, so I ask, "How long will it take to be able to pick things up? What I'm really saying is, do I have to become a Scribe or a Gatherer to do this?"

"How long is up to you. It depends on how quick you learn. Once you've finished here, you'll be shown how to collect juices with your mouth, and then you'll be taken away to acquire more strength so giving you the ability to fly, go through walls, doors and other man-made structures. But, Mick, you are getting ahead of yourself. I'd have thought you'd have asked about the Villager or Reliever first. After all, you are a New Ghost and its title speaks for itself."

"I have a fair idea what most of them do, but I hadn't heard of the Gatherer. I heard about the Ghost Scribes this morning and what they do seems obvious. After all, someone had to write the books upstairs and these papers, but I'm not sure what the difference is between the Scribe that's marked local and the other marked dreams."

"Jana has mentioned something – that's perfectly obvious, but I'm surprised you think you know it all."

"I don't ... honest! Yes, Jana explained quite a lot, but there are things I'm confused about, like – how the lights come on in shops at night when we're the only ones in them."

"They don't come on at night. Whichever shop you went into must have had them on for security reasons. You should know by now that many shops do this; especially, nowadays, with all the criminals about." I must admit, I hadn't thought of that, so I nod my head, acknowledging her answer. "Now, please Mick, don't get ahead of yourself. I appreciate that you might know some of the answers, but your friends here might not, so let's hear what they have to say."

Freda utters her first words since I've been in the room. "I have been meeting with Scribe Ghost before today. She nice and how say ... perty." I must tell you that Freda is from Finland and, although her spoken English isn't up to scratch, I did see her chatting with several ghosts while we were walking around yesterday.

Anna smiles at her. "Pretty, Freda. Pretty! You must have bumped into our special visitor. She'll be spending some time with us this afternoon and I'm sure you'll all enjoy her company."

"How do I become a Ghost Haunter?" asks Tommy. I grin, thinking how typical of a kid.

"Now wait a minute, all of you. You want to fly before you can float and that's not reasonable. But, regarding Tommy's question, I must point out that his phrase, Ghost Haunter, is incorrect. Haunters don't go around haunting other ghosts. They haunt buildings, places, or the living, so the title is just as it says on the paper – Haunter. Does that make sense?" She casts her eyes over us and we all nod. "Very well, then. I'll do the talking and you may interrupt if you're unsure of anything. Are you agreed?"

We nod again, answering, "Yes."

"We ghosts are the result of dreams that we had when we were alive. At some stage of our lives we dreamt of being a ghost. Most of the ghosts that I've met don't remember having the necessary dream, and why should they? Most people dream while they are sleeping, and sometimes it's a dream that causes them to awaken, but it's not always a dream of being a ghost. They might be running away from something frightening, or drowning. I know, because I used to dream regularly. I think that, perhaps, one or two of you may have done the same. The point I'm trying to make is that the wanting to be a ghost, or imagining oneself as a ghost while going about a person's everyday life, is not the same as having a dream of being a ghost. The wish; the desire – they don't matter. It's the real dream that counts. Do you understand?"

Once again we nod, but having read some of the book, I raise my arm slightly and ask, "Anna, do you know who the first ghosts were?"

"I don't, Mick. You see, the earliest ghosts we know of go back over two thousand years. We assume there were others before that but they must have died. When the first one originated it was probably on its own and, not knowing what to do or how to survive, it eventually died. Then others must have come along and then these died, and so on, until a time came when one, then two, and then more, must have met somehow, and learned and developed a system of survival. So, I'm sorry Mick, I can't really help you. Now, let's get back to the matter in hand. New Ghosts are expected to develop abilities that will give them extra life without resorting to re-charge every so often."

"What do you mean by re-charge?" asks Nancy, in an American accent. I'm wondering what the hell an American is doing on this side of the Atlantic. Nancy is small, about fifty, with light-brown hair.

"I'm coming to that. You four are weak in that you haven't got the strength to fend for yourselves as yet. You can, if you choose, remain as you are, but then you're easy prey for any unscrupulous ghosts." Nancy turns to Freda, lifting her eyebrows, while Anna carries on. "I want you to understand that not all ghosts have the same mental capacity. Some are so stupid that I still find it hard to believe that they ever dreamt of being ghosts in the first place. However, most of these work as Villagers – that's helping ghosts like me prepare things for ghosts like you, or they help the Gatherers or other ghosts that may need assistance. That's, of course, if they can or if they want to. If a ghost doesn't like another, for instance, then he or she might not help. There are other ghosts – no doubt you've heard of some of them, who prefer to play around, taking what they can get for their own enjoyment. There's nothing we can do about them except hope that one day they might change their ways. Occasionally, I try persuading them to do something constructive with their ghost lives and sometimes I succeed, but not always. It's possible that one or two of you will go the same way, but I hope you're intelligent enough not to. But, be warned, these bad ghosts can, and do, deceive others and lead them astray. And they can cause you to die, albeit accidentally, but they don't care. So be on your guard; develop some abilities and strengths; and then you'll be reasonably safe from them.

"One of the greatest abilities is speed in everything you do. That includes speed of thought, as well as physical attributes such as flight, writing, gathering things, and so on. As New Ghosts you are vulnerable; you can get trapped easily, and you are a burden on every ghost around you. We don't want to see you dead, so do something about it. Make a choice about which type of ghost you want to be and have a go. There are some ghostly positions you might never achieve because they happen by accident, but other abilities are earned automatically by doing something worthwhile, such as saving the life of another ghost, or helping a living person in some way prevent a disaster.

"We can teach you to hold and carry things, locate other ghosts, take residence in live people as hosts ... " – And I start chuckling.

"What's so funny, Micky?" asks Tommy.

Anna glares at me. "I'd like to know, as well. You've been inside somebody, haven't you?"

"Yes" I answer, counting my conquests on my fingers, " ... a few times."

"That's impossible!" Tommy exclaims. "What did you do?"

"I don't want to say, but I can tell you ... it was very interesting."

Anna, now with her hands face down on the table and lifting herself from the seat, says, "I bet it was, and I'd like you to shed some light on who you entered and why, and what happened when you went into these people. It might make my explanation to the others a lot easier. Do you understand?"

"I see your point, but some of the circumstances are embarrassing."

"Forget the embarrassing bits. I want to know the type of people you went into. Were they sick, drunk, pregnant, or in good health? Were your movements deliberate or accidental – that type of thing, and what were the people's reactions when you left their bodies?"

"All right! I'll tell you." And I do, starting with the hospital porter.

Both Nancy's and Tommy's faces react to my varying experiences. Sometimes they laugh, while other times they look at each other, mouths open. Freda stays quiet throughout, and gives me the impression she's been inside someone herself. Anna, on the other hand, walks up and down the room, hanging on to my every word, occasionally looking at me kind of funny-weird, and other times laughing with her head in the air. And when I finish the account of my time inside Andy and what Jana did to save me – including my entering Ben, Anna turns and walks back to the head of the table.

"Is that it?" she asks, staring me in the face.

"I'm afraid so, but you must realise that I didn't know of the possible consequences, beforehand. It was only later that Jana explained the danger I was in."

Anna, now stern-faced, says, "Well, ladies and Tommy, have you learnt anything from Mick's mistakes? And, while we're on the subject, has anyone else been inside a body? We might as well know now."

Freda raises her hand, and answers sheepishly, "I did Ma'am, but only for Ivan tell me to."

Anna is quick to speak. "Ivan … your Ghost Monitor? Were you tired, Freda?"

"Yes, Ma'am. Ivan kiss me and make me tired. He lick my teeth and suck mouth."

Tommy, with a wry expression, repeats, "He licked and sucked you – Ivan, that big gangly fella?"

"Tommy, surely Anne must have licked your mouth, or, if not her then, Simon?" asks Anna.

"No way! She tried to, and so did that Simon ghost, but I pushed them away. What do you think I am?"

"Very well, Tommy. What does your mouth taste like right this minute?" I'm enjoying the banter between them, but I don't know why she's asking this question.

"I don't know what you mean," he says.

"Does it feel or taste musty ... like death?"

"It did feel a little funny, I suppose, but it's okay now." I didn't think we could taste anything but, having said that, I can't remember what mine tasted like when I was in the hospital. I had other things on my mind.

Anna winks at me. "I suppose it is, Tommy, especially after last night. Never mind, I'll come back to it later." And with her face, once again, on Freda, she asks, "Did Ivan tell you he was tired, or give a reason for what he did and what he told you to do?"

"Yes, Ma'am. He say he tired and he have to kiss me as welcome. He say I must go to woman's body for strength. He show me how."

"How did you feel when you left this lady's body?"

"I feel good. I laugh with Ivan and give him more kiss."

"That's good. Now let me explain. When New Ghosts are born, for want of a better term, they bring with them the staleness of death. Ghost Relievers and Monitors, who are responsible for collecting them, should always take away this staleness. They do this by kissing the mouth and licking the teeth, the gums and the tongue. They will then suck the mouth, drawing out the staleness from inside. The Reliever's and Monitor's bodies can absorb this mustiness and cast it out as if by magic, but it isn't magic. I'll explain about nectar and its uses later, but it is the nectar we take inside us that dispels the bad tastes and feelings we might encounter."

We look at each other and then back to Anna, who seems to be enjoying herself, as she goes on, "Furthermore, the kiss that Ivan gave as a welcome was his way of doing what he had to do, trying not to embarrass Freda. Ivan had told her he was tired and that's why he sucked for, probably, a longer time than necessary, but if his strength was down then it makes sense. By sucking life from Freda he gained in his own, enabling him to do his job. Believe me, that's what these nymphomaniacs will do if they catch you. They're too lazy to gain life properly. And one of them used to be a Mindbender."

On hearing this, we all start muttering, asking each other how that could have happened. Anna lets us chatter for a couple of minutes before asking for silence. She rests her eyes on mine. "Come here Mick. You seem to be more familiar in the ways of ghosts."

I get up and stand close to her. She lifts her hands, gently pulls my head towards hers, and puts her lips on mine … sucking. Minutes later, she lets me go, waving me back to my seat.

"That, ladies and gentlemen, is how to suck life from another ghost, and sometimes it may be necessary to do so. On the other hand, if you know that a ghost is weak and needs life, then you do the opposite. Instead of sucking you blow, for however long it takes."

She calls Freda to her side, and, although hesitant, Freda obliges. This time, Anna demonstrates her blowing technique and for quite a long time. We watch and wait … and wait … and wait, until, eventually Anna releases her. Tommy shakes his head in amazement, while Nancy looks as if she wants a go, but, having been there and done that, I'm not fazed at all. Freda, on the other hand, is delighted, a smile beaming across her face. She sighs a contented sigh, and I wonder if she's a lesbian. As Freda walks back to her seat, Anna says to her, "I'll go over this with you afterwards, in Finnish. I know your English isn't perfect as yet, but you'll learn quickly enough. Oh, and Freda, please call me Anna; you keep forgetting."

"Thank you, Ma'am … I mean, Anna," and if we could see her blush, she'd be as red as an English letter box. She has to be gay. I can't be the only one. She seems so happy to be seeing Anna later.

Anna picks up her papers. "Now, back to the list. I want to finish with most of these today, so let's continue. A Ghost Reliever is one that comes to the aid of a trapped ghost. The trapped ghost doesn't have to be a New Ghost. It could be any ghost in a place where it can't escape from. The trapped ghost might be one that's lost its strength, due to an attack by you know who, or else it might feel sorry for itself and deliberately try to die by hiding and thinking mournful thoughts. You see, ghosts can die by being unhappy – it saps their strength. And, although it takes a long time to die this way, a ghost *will* die unless something is done to prevent it. We don't like to see an unhappy ghost, but now and then something happens in life that might make one depressed. If you ever feel this way, then please let one of us know. We can help … honestly. There's a famous example of a ghost trying to commit suicide because his best friend – when he was alive – was dying. This ghost didn't want to live without his friend, but I don't want to elaborate, because he might want to tell you himself. These things are personal.

"Anyway, Relievers have the ability to locate trapped ghosts and save them. They have an extra sense. They also have more life in them, in case they have to top up the trapped ghost. You might think that all he or she has to do is pull the ghost free and put it in some living person, but that's not strictly true. If the trapped ghost is too weak, it won't be able to pass through walls, doors or windows – even with assistance, so it has to be given mouth to mouth resuscitation. Also, if you were the Reliever and you did manage to pull a very weak ghost free without blowing into him or her, would you then try and use a living person that you know nothing about? If you did, then you'd be wrong. You might be responsible for putting the ghost into a drug addict, an alcoholic, or worse, and the ghost you've just saved would die very quickly, perhaps in seconds. Could you live with that? What if you were the trapped ghost? If a Reliever does cause a death in this way, then its abilities are lost … immediately. The same applies to any other ghost that does something drastically wrong. Just as an ability can be gained by accident, it can be lost through ignorance or stupidity. It just happens. Now, do you understand what a Ghost Reliever is?"

"Yes," we reply, and it gives me food for thought.

"Let me add," she says, "that not all New Ghosts are found by Relievers. Mick, Tommy … I know you were both trapped, but you two ladies weren't. You were easily found in accessible places. Nancy, you were found near your body at the foot of the Eiffel Tower, and you, Freda, were in your own home with plenty of your family around you. So in your cases, Ghost Monitors picked you up. They do the same type of job as Relievers. In fact some of them were once Relievers – Jana for instance – but they have the responsibility of bringing ghosts here or to other villages. Monitors look after you from the moment they meet you. It's up to them to keep you safe from other ghosts, or from yourself."

Anna turns, opening her hand towards me. "Take Mick, for example. When Jana saw him in danger of dying, after entering his friend, she gave him some of her own life. Perhaps she should have brought him straight here when she first met him, but we leave those decisions to the

Ghost Monitor. She waited with and got to know him and what he wanted. We're not your bosses; we can't and don't dictate to you; you've got a ghost life of your own; and any choices you make or desires you might have … we try to oblige. And I'd like you to treat other ghosts in exactly the same way. Jana realised, after staying with Mick, that he wanted to go to his own funeral and so she let him, observing him all the time." As she mentions this, I remember Jana telling me about that first night in the bedroom, and me on the floor thinking of Simon.

Tommy gives me a nudge, smiles, and I'm wondering whether he's heard anything about it, but, on hearing her voice, we both look back at Anna. "Monitors acquire great speed, excellent sight, and a wonderful knowledge of geography. They are also multi-lingual, and quite a few can suit their voices to the local dialects from many countries. For example, I can speak in many of the Uralic languages and their dialects, but as Freda is the only one here that would recognise one of her country's variations, it's pointless me showing you. This is one of the abilities that Monitors possess. They can learn several languages and dialects fairly quickly – four to five years at the most. Monitors can also sense danger from great distances and can find changeover points at the drop of a hat. These are safe places. I won't dwell on them now – we have too much to cover – but ask one the Monitors and he or she will elaborate. I used to be one myself, after doing some haunting. I started out as a Haunter, and, as I've already explained how I came to be here, that's hardly surprising."

"How long were you a Haunter?" asks an excited Tommy.

"Just over a hundred years. I lost interest after the castle burned down. All the people responsible were dead and their children too. So, also, were the King and his cronies. I stayed in the local village for a while, and then came here. I'd developed a few other abilities in my haunting years, and these helped me to become a local Scribe and, later, a Monitor. Becoming a Monitor can either be earned by performing good deeds, like saving lives, or it can be the result of how well you've trained. In other words it happens accidentally. Think about this. Just as we *happened* to become ghosts as the result of a dream, so too can being a different type of ghost just *happen*. Who knows, Tommy, next month you might *happen* to be a Mindbender, and with it comes all the knowledge. You don't have to learn how – you'll know immediately – although it might take a while for your mind to adjust. I must point out, though, that becoming a Ghost Of Dreams is not gained as a means of promotion in any way. This too just happens, but you must have done something quite extraordinary to achieve this ability."

"That's incredible!" Tommy's face lights up. A minute ago he was excited at the thought of doing some haunting. Now he'll want to change the world.

"Being a Haunter is a lot of fun. It's like playing a game all the time. Sometimes Haunters work together, and when they're not haunting they enjoy themselves in other ways. Quite honestly, if I had started out treating haunting as a game instead of a vendetta, I might never have become a Ghost Tutor. I never scared anyone to death, but I did come close on occasion, and this surprised some of the other ghosts. I didn't lose my ability, and I'm happy about that, but I could have. Later, I went out on some trips with other Haunters, and it was on one of these that I found myself in a position to help another ghost. In doing so I gained extra abilities and I've never felt better. Life's worth dying for sometimes. Once you've been trained you'll be able to throw things, turn paintings back to front, and move curtains, but you'll have to practise. Check out the description of a Haunter and see what you have to do. Haunting is a good way to learn. It also teaches you about people. The funniest times are when the so-called ghost experts or exorcists believe they can get rid of you. Some use machines in trying to prove our existence. They're so stupid."

Tommy asks, "Did you lose your ability to haunt when you became a Tutor?"

"Not at all. Once you have the ability to do something, you keep it. In actual fact, if you progress in some way to be a Mindbender, as others have, then you'll also be a better and faster Haunter. You'll also have the ability to teach, to scribe, and do other ghostly things. You won't be able to read dreams though. Only a Ghost Of Dreams can do that, as yet."

"Have you ever come across any mediums?" I ask.

"My, you have been busy. Yes I have, on many occasions. Tell me, Mick, have you?" Anna leans forward on the desk.

"I don't know, but I think so. Jana says I've met two of them."

"Now listen, all of you. A medium is someone who can sense ghosts, and some of them can see us. I'm not sure how they come about but there has been talk of mediums being the result of ancestry, but not ancestry in its proper form. How can I explain this? All the gossip, and it is only gossip, says that if – let's say you, Mick, were having sex while you were dreaming of being a ghost … and your partner gets pregnant from the sperm of that particular sexual encounter, then it's possible that the child will be a medium. But this isn't guaranteed. This medium might be able to see us. If this child later has offspring, then they in turn might become mediums but their ability to notice us is weaker. Eventually, with each new generation, the medium strength fades and eventually disappears. I must stress, though, that we can't be sure about this. Some of the Ghosts Of Dreams seem to know, but they can't tell us."

"Why not?" I ask. "Surely, knowing how is beneficial to all ghosts? We could learn so much more." I'm desperate to find out so I can visit Joyce and watch, knowing what I now know about her.

"There is a problem, Mick. I can see you're anxious, and you must know this medium very well, but the Ghosts Of Dreams can't tell us. It's not because they don't want to – it's because they're not able. They have tried telling their Scribes and Mindbenders; they've tried writing it down; but for some reason or other they find it impossible to tell their story. It doesn't make sense, and it's an extremely interesting subject. We should talk about this again. You can tell me who these mediums of yours are and how you came to suspect their ability."

"I'd very much like to." One thing's for certain though: none of my partners are, or ever have been, pregnant … and they're not likely to be.

"Have you any more questions … ladies … gentlemen?" Not getting any response, she continues, "We seem to have jumped ahead of ourselves because I haven't explained what the Gatherers do. We value the Gatherers very highly, because without them we'd have a very hard time. This paper in front of us, and the ink and pens used to do the writing, would not be readily available without the Gatherers. The bedroom books, our clothes – with all the latest fashions, and our footwear, would take forever to make because we'd have to find the materials ourselves. And we can't forget the flowers for our nectar. We have to keep a small supply for emergencies, and in order to get enough supplies for the Villagers to work with, the Gatherers have to travel long distances at great risk to themselves. They are very fast and very strong ghosts; fast enough to make their journeys by night, and strong enough to carry heavy loads.

They also have perfect vision – having said that, I suppose we all have – but they can see in the dark as well as they do in daylight. They also help the Villagers with the workload. One thing I can say is that the vast majority of Gatherers enjoy what they do because it takes them all over the world. It's easy to become a Gatherer – just by learning the skills, and there are plenty of them here to help you. I'm telling you now that when I was new we had a bad time of it. We had Gatherers, Villagers, and other ghosts, but only a fraction compared to nowadays."

"Why's that?" interrupts Tommy. I wish he'd shut up. I don't dislike him, but I prefer the women because they don't get involved. I know I do, but I don't ask stupid questions – at least I don't think so.

"There have always been wars throughout the ages, Tommy, and also plagues like the Black Death. And, of course, the diseases you take for granted like tuberculosis, typhoid and smallpox, to name but three, used to wipe out populations. These diseases have been virtually eradicated in the past fifty years. That's modern medicine for you. I didn't have the luxury of penicillin, for example, in my time as a healer. Another reason for the shortage of ghosts is that while we might have told ghost stories, not many people dreamt of being one. Nowadays, there are millions of books and films about ghosts. And with the rapid increase in the world's population, and people living nearly twice as long as we did, there are bound to be more ghosts. There are more people to dream of being one of us. And if you need proof of what I'm saying, then look at your own circumstances. You and Mick died on the same night, not far from each other, and you're both here. Does that answer your question?" Tommy nods.

"Anyway, I'd like you to spend some time studying the Ghost Gatherer's information. I bet you thought homework was a thing of the past. Now, remember, the quicker you learn ... the quicker you get your nectar." Tommy is about to open his mouth again so I dig him in the ribs, telling him, quietly, to shut up. He takes notice.

"Goodness me! Look at the time." Anna's eyes are glancing behind me. Turning around, I notice a small wall clock showing eleven-thirty. "That's all for now, and I'll see you at two o'clock. Oh, stupid me. I nearly forgot again." She goes to the window and makes a loud hooting sound. Within seconds, Jana and Moira float through the door, take our hands, then lead us outside.

147

CHAPTER THIRTEEN

Once out in the open, we are joined by Lucia, Luisella and a few other ghosts. Lucia approaches Tommy and his face takes on an appearance of embarrassment.

"What's up, Tommy?" she asks. He whispers in her ear, and when she glances at his hair I can tell what's on his mind, and so, it seems, can the other sniggering ghosts. Lucia takes his hand, whispers a reply, and he, too, starts smiling. I know who's sleeping in whose bed tonight.

Discussions go on about the morning's topics, with the odd questions thrown up and answers given. It all seems pretty basic and I don't sense any difficulty in being a ghost so long as I keep to the rules. Obviously, I need to know more, and am about to speak when Tommy asks, generally, "When will we get this nectar we've been told about? Why do we have to wait?" I must admit that I've had similar thoughts. If there is a supply, as Anna has indicated, then why not give it to us?

"For Pete's sake, use your common sense," Moira retorts. "If you're allowed a small amount now, it won't be long before the effects wear off … perhaps a month or two, and that's if you're lucky. You should know that this is a bad time of year for flowers and our winter supplies are running low. As long as we're around to protect you then the later you get your fix, the better. And there's another reason. In the past, ghosts were given their share of nectar on arrival, and then, rather than stay and learn what they needed to know, some took it upon themselves to leave the village and explore.

"Quite a lot went missing and, more than likely, died. We can't be certain, but nobody has seen hide nor hair of them since. So, to deter this we've made rules regarding the distribution of supplies and we all agree that these rules are fair. At the end of the day, we're looking out for your well-being and you should be grateful." I'd never heard Moira make such a long statement and her strong Irish brogue made us all sit up and take note.

As time goes by, various other questions are asked by Nancy and Freda, some pertaining to the nymphos and some about work around the village. While sitting here, I notice several ghosts walking to and fro, chatting and watching us. Some join in and everyone seems so relaxed and interested in our new faces. Meanwhile, Jana and Lucia have stood up and taken a place on the edge of the small crowd. My eyes linger on Jana and, noticing me, she beckons me over with her index finger.

I approach her, and she says, "Micky, Lucia wants to know if you'd like a new hairstyle."

Turning to Lucia, I ask, "What are you offering ... the same one you gave Tommy?" Those close by laugh, and it's just as well he's not listening.

"Come on you lot. You've got work to do," says Jana.

Back inside, Jana and Lucia keep us amused, while we wait for Anna. Presently, she appears in the company of an extremely young dark-haired girl, probably no more than sixteen years of age. Anna shoos our minders away before starting her introduction.

"Ladies and gentlemen, I'd like you to meet a personality of sorts." I'm studying the young girl's freshly toned skin, which appears to come from an outdoor lifestyle. Her long glossy hair falls all the way down her back, emphasising the strength of her features. Her clothes are conservative, in a fashion. She is wearing a long-sleeved white blouse with the top button undone, and a dark blue pleated skirt. Over her left shoulder swings a matching jacket, while on her feet she wears a smart pair of blue suede shoes.

Anna points to us individually, saying, "Freda, Nancy, Tommy, Mick ... I'd like you to say hello to one of our favourite Ghost Scribes. This young lady is Matoaka, but you might know her better as Pocahontas."

She looks at us, mouthing her hello, and we all answer in unison, "Hello." The shock on both Nancy's and Tommy's faces is there for all to see, and I am equally amazed. Freda, having already met her, just sits back smiling.

"Matoaka is going to tell you about herself and her work as a Scribe. She'll give you an insight into some of the most important aspects of our life as ghosts." Anna takes a seat beside me, while Matoaka sits at the head of the table.

"Thank you Anna, and good afternoon to you all," she smilingly says. "To be honest, I'm not really a celebrity, except, I suppose, in folk-lore. If you wish, you may call me Pocahontas, but please don't call me by my later name, Rebecca. It's not that I don't like it, but when I dreamed of being a ghost I had not taken that name." There is a look of confusion around the room as this little Red Indian girl explains about her early life in the Algonquian tribe.

"How did you get the name Pocahontas?" asks Nancy, excitedly. She seems in awe of her.

"It was a pet name given to me by my parents. I was always playful and sometimes a bit of a tomboy, jumping around and doing wheelies before I knew they were called wheelies. I was always asking questions and getting involved in everything. I'm from the Powhatan Indian family of Tidewater, Virginia, and, at the time, my family was quite large. When I was at home, I lived as an ordinary Red Indian, living in a tepee, and we'd sing our songs, dance our dances, and work around the village. Life wasn't always pleasant because we'd have to move our homes according to the season and the hunting. My father had several women as his partners. We Indians didn't marry as people do nowadays, although we did have ceremonies to celebrate partnerships. In the end, though, I did marry a Christian – a very religious man by the name of John Rolfe. He was a tobacco planter. That's when I was baptised with the name Rebecca. John brought me to England where I met King James and the rest of London society and that's why my name is so well known. We had a son, Thomas, but I died so young that I didn't get the chance to enjoy his life."

"That is sad. How old you be?" asks Freda, a little down-hearted.

"I was twenty-two, Freda. I had a terrible sickness that they couldn't cure, and when I died, in 1617, they buried me in Gravesend. I'd always been healthy before coming to England. It's only now that we can find out why diseases spread so rapidly. Before the foreigners came to our country, there wasn't much in the way of sickness, but the white man and later the black man brought all sorts of illnesses that our people weren't immune to. Since becoming a ghost, I've watched lots of Indians die and many wrongs being done to our people over the years. Even present day, some of the Indians are still suffering as second class citizens. That's another reason I prefer my Indian name. I don't dislike the white man. Heaven knows, I saved some of their lives when our people took them prisoner."

"I don't blame you for keeping your name," says Anna, who I didn't expect to say anything.

"I wish I could write this down," says Nancy. "It's so interesting, being from West Virginia, myself."

"You don't have to," replies Matoaka. "You'll find that as long as you keep taking the nectar, your memory will improve and you'll start remembering everything we tell you and everything you read. As a Ghost Scribe, I work with the Ghosts Of Dreams and that's one of the reasons I am here giving this talk. We have Dream Factories where these ghosts sit and relax and listen to some of the dreams that people have. I won't go into detail just yet, because you will soon be going to visit one of these places."

"Dream Factories?"

"Yes, Tommy, but they're not what you might think. In fact, it will probably surprise you, but don't be alarmed if you meet one or two Red Indian ghosts. We don't want you to be afraid." Not only is my interest taken with this, but so is that of the other three. She continues, "You probably won't know any of them, with the exception of Tutanka Iyotake, who was better known as Chief Sitting Bull. You might even bump into Hiawatha and his holy-man Deganawida, but they aren't Dreamers, as we sometimes call them. Hiawatha is a Scribe and his friend is a Mindbender.

"Let me explain why so many Red Indians are ghosts. Try and imagine the films you've seen, and then visualise the Indian dances, our chants, and our centrepiece, the totem pole. Our beliefs were such that if we sang and danced for our dead spirits – that is our ancestors, then they'd help us find food and take care of our well-being. Whereas you might have prayed to your God or to Jesus, we didn't because, to us, they didn't exist. Our prayers, if that's what you want to call them, were sung to the spirits of our dead families. Our Medicine Man would go into a trance and he could hear these spirits, or so we were led to believe. Indians like Hiawatha and Sitting Bull, in their tribes, would be able to understand the messages as told to them by the Medicine Man, and then they'd translate these for their people. These Indians would relate the stories about our ancestors believing them to still be alive, although we knew they were dead. The spirits they talked about were what people would now regard as ghosts. Of course, at that time, we didn't know the word *ghost*, but it was the same thing. Indians, like me, would sleep and dream, and, to us, it was the natural thing to do because we lived by that creed.

"We didn't have television in those days," and all, bar Anna, chuckle on hearing this. "What I'm saying might confuse you. I don't want you to think that all Indians have returned as ghosts … they haven't, but some, like me, have because in my dream I dreamt of being a spirit and living with my ancestors. We don't have more ghosts than other peoples, but if you consider the percentage of us in relation to our living population as it was back then, then we are many, especially when you realise that the Red Indian tribes were nearly wiped out. So please, don't be afraid of us; we're not going to scalp you." Matoaka starts laughing.

"How come you're only a Ghost Scribe?"

"Nancy, being a Scribe is an important position to have. We can't choose the type of ghost we want to be. We have to earn the ability and that can be done through learning or by accident. If, as I did, a ghost helps another ghost achieve a higher ability, then the assisting ghost automatically gains new abilities. I was a Monitor and was responsible for the care of a New Ghost and taught her as much as I could. I saved her life on one occasion and somehow, some time later, she became a Mindbender. I found that I'd earned my scribing ability as a circumstance of her achievement. It could happen to you.

"My work takes me all over the world, taking notes of everything a Dreamer reads. They can read dreams at a phenomenal speed and, as they do so, they relate these dreams at the same time and at the same speed. My ability allows me to write as fast as they speak. There's no difficulty with this. Mind you, I don't do it full time, because there are many more Scribes than Ghosts Of Dreams. I can take a break whenever I fancy, and sometimes I go haunting for a change. It's all very interesting."

"Who are these other Ghost Scribes … the local ones?" asks Tommy.

"They are as the title says. They write all the necessary information that we need to know on a local basis. They write the bedroom books in different languages and all the paper work we use, such as the leaflets in front of you. They don't have my super-fast speed, but that's not necessary for a local Scribe. They can take all the time they want, and some do. However, when they want to write at speed they can. And when they're not writing, they help the Gatherers, do some Monitoring if they can, or assist the Villagers, depending on their abilities. You can always train to be a Scribe, unless, of course, you acquire the ability by some other means. One of the advantages in developing your abilities is that you can become multi-lingual. It takes time, naturally."

"Where are the Dream Factories?" I ask.

"They can be anywhere a group of Dreamers want them to be."

"That doesn't make sense."

"No, I suppose it doesn't, Mick. Okay, let me put it this way. At the moment we are using this village, Pribylina, as a ghost village. There's another one further along this mountain range, and many more throughout Europe and the rest of the world. We take advantage of situations and places where very few people live or work. The Ghosts Of Dreams do exactly the same. They've been known to take residence in parts of castles in Scotland, England, Germany and elsewhere, which aren't open to the public or when the owners aren't at home. These buildings have marvellous bedrooms and sitting rooms in which the ghosts can relax. Sometimes, they use holiday complexes or bungalows which are closed for the season, or they take rooms in quiet hotels. Wherever a Dreamer is, a Scribe is close by in case someone's ghost dream comes into the mind. It's quite common for Dreamers to read dreams while travelling, and so, of course, we travel with them. The Dreamers do try switching off but it's not that easy. And Dreamers are no different from the rest of us – they too like to be alone at times, but sometimes their ability to ignore dreams fails them, and if it's not written down then a dream can be forgotten. They don't read all dreams; sometimes only parts of dreams; because if there's no reference to a ghost in the dream then there's no point in recording it. There are other circumstances where they'll read the dreams that powerful people may be having, such as leading politicians, presidents, dictators and their adversaries. You'd be amazed at some of these dreams and the corruption that's going on in their minds, but there's nothing we can do. We don't have the power to manipulate as yet, but, one day, perhaps we will."

"Hmm!" nods Nancy. – I wonder what she's thinking about.

"Now, then, are there any other questions?" asks Matoaka.

"What does a Mindbender do?" asks Tommy. I knew he was going to ask that, especially the way his eyes lit up when Anna mentioned the possibility of him becoming one.

"In fact, Tommy, most of what you need to know is in the description on the paper. You can't just work your way to being one. It happens by accident. They work very closely with the Dreamers and Scribes, but they also work alone. Mindbenders might go on assignments to try and make some things possible, but they're not always successful. The title should give you a clue as to what they try to do, however, where they have most success is in the gift of healing. They speak to the brain of a living person, and if a person responds to a Mindbender's words then we deem that to be a good result. You don't need to be a Mindbender to tell someone something, but their superior ability – to force thoughts on both the living and other ghosts – is more likely to achieve the desired reaction." I think about Jana and what she did to Patricia. "Now, is there anything else you'd like to know?" she asks, searching our faces.

We ask her more about her life and she happily obliges us. Our discussion soon ends with her thanking us for listening. Joining her at the head of the table, Anna turns to us, saying, "Tomorrow, ladies and gentlemen, you may spend the day relaxing, but don't forget to spend some of that time reading these leaflets. And when we do resume, I'll explain how we ghosts can use the living to our benefit."

With the help of both Anna and Matoaka we pass through the window where we meet Ivan and Jana. Not long after, Matoaka says her goodbyes and walks off with our Tutor, leaving us gabbling on about her life. Freda seems happy with herself, while Nancy keeps going on about Matoaka and Virginia, as if she and our new Red Indian friend were next door neighbours.

CHAPTER FOURTEEN

Jana brought me back to life, this morning, by viciously pinching the little bit of fat that's left on my stomach, and then chastising me for sleeping in. I don't know what the hurry was because no-one else has turned up. Perhaps they don't want to go ski-jumping.

I slide my leg over one of the benches, asking, "So, who's going besides us?"

"Moira's bringing Tommy, and Luisella is coming along to keep watch," she answers. "They'll be here, soon. Moira's gone to change her clothes."

Minutes later, Tommy and Moira join us, her wearing a skin-tight outfit and a woolly hat. We talk over the plans for avoiding trouble, and Jana explains how we should manoeuvre our bodies into those of the skiers. Tommy, not experienced in entering a human – I mean, a live person, is somewhat wary, so when Luisella shows up a decision is made to indoctrinate him in the ways of using hosts.

The girls take our hands and we fly off and up the mountain to Štrbské pleso. On our arrival we land on the edge of a small crowd of spectators. Their attention is taken up with the flight of a ski jumper as he soars through the air. I'm quite keen to get started, but I also want to watch Tommy at his first attempt to enter somebody. Fortunately, plenty of people are readily available, some drinking coffee and others sipping from hip-flasks. Jana tells him not to use anyone drinking from hip-flasks, because the contents are more than likely to be vodka or brandy. Having listened to her, Tommy is now aware of the potential outcome regarding alcohol, but he's also worried in case someone maybe taking drugs.

"Don't bother your head about that," Moira tells him. "When you go in the body, make sure you speak to us. If you start feeling a bit queer, then come out immediately. And if your head feels woozy straight away … shout out, and we'll pull you out. The chances of that, up here, are unlikely. Most of these people tend to be the sporty type, and we usually use older, more sensible looking people as our hosts. And as for the ski jumpers, they wouldn't dare use drugs or drink alcohol, so we'll be safe inside them."

"Okay then, pick someone for me," says Tommy, excitedly rubbing his hands.

"Try her," suggests Luisella, pointing to a young lady wearing spectacles whose hands are holding those of two young children.

"Why a woman?" he asks.

"It doesn't really matter, but a young mother is as safe as you're likely to get," replies Jana, "and all you have to do is move forward and push your whole body through her back. Once inside, tell us how you feel. She won't know you're talking but we'll be able to hear you."

Tommy edges forward, and, with a gentle push from Moira, he slips into the young mother. A minute goes by before he asks, "Can you hear me? Hey, you out there … can you hear me?"

"Of course we can," says Moira. "What's she like?"

"I feel kind of weird, but she's okay. It feels kind of strange because everywhere her eyes go, mine follow. It's as if I'm alive again. I feel as though I'm responsible for her movements."

"You're not, Tommy," says Moira. "Now, be careful when you leave her body. Back away very slowly and steadily."

Following Moira's advice he does as he's told, and I study the lady's body when Tommy steps free. She shakes, but hardly that you'd notice. And it seems as if she hasn't noticed anything unusual either. Hmm, I'll have to remember to be gentle; at least with the people I like. Then I tell him, "Now, Tommy, you've got to do it all over again."

"What?" He sees me pointing at the ski jump, and confidently replies, "Oh, that's no problem. I could get used to this woman entering business." Tommy turns his head, winking at me, and whispering, "Don't tell the others, but the lady turned me on."

"You're joking?"

Before he can answer, Jana enquires, "What are you two up to?"

"Nothing, honest," says Tommy.

"Well, whatever it is, it better hadn't involve me. Alright, let's go."

Jana takes my hand, Moira … Tommy's, and Luisella flies alongside, her eyes everywhere. In a few seconds, we're at the top of the highest jump and standing in front of some seated skiers who are awaiting their turn. Luisella hovers around outside, watching which partners we select. Jana pushes me towards someone in an all red outfit, while Tommy slides into one dressed in yellow and blue. Making myself comfortable inside, I don't notice which partners the girls choose. My host slides his backside along the seat, and, as he looks about, I see that we're the next to jump.

"Jana! Where are you?"

"Right beside you, you idiot. And stop worrying. I'll meet you at the bottom."

"Okay." My host moves us along the seat again and I'm getting butterflies in my stomach. It'll be the first time in my life that I'm going to fly without Jana or an aeroplane, and my first time on skis.

Seconds later, me and my partner look down, check his boots and skis, and edge to the top of the slide. We bend our knees up and down, and then I feel the effect of him swallowing great gulps of air as his chest inflates and deflates. We start sliding, ever so slightly, forward and back, and then push hard with our legs.

Down, down, down we go; gathering speed every split second, and the ground beneath my feet disappears as we soar out ... out, and still further out, and then down, all the time with our bodies stretched forward and our arms held back along our sides. It seems as if I'm doing this all by myself, but I know I'm not. My feet, in his, are bent forwards, as the boots hold the skis, keeping them perfectly still and slightly splayed beneath us.

We keep dropping and my arms seem to be glued to my body as the slippery ice approaches. At the very moment we hit the ice, our arms move out for balance and we slide forward, coasting and turning towards the onlookers. Everyone's clapping like crazy. I don't know if my ears are deceiving me, but the shouts of joy are everywhere to be heard as the adulation goes on. The next thing I feel are vibrations on my back and shoulders as people are hitting my host, congratulating him.

"Micky! Micky! You've broken the record." Luisella appears in front of our eyes. "Come on, get out of him, but do it slowly," she orders. I do so, at the same time asking what all the commotion is about.

"You! That is, your host here, with a little help from you, has broken the local ski jump record. Everyone's going mad because he's improved about four metres on his previous best."

"That's crazy. Do you think I'm responsible?"

"It's more than likely," she replies.

"Well, I'll be blowed." Luisella takes me in her arms, kisses me, and, when we turn around, another skier is completing his jump. Just as he hits the ground, he slips and slides into the curved barrier. He tries picking himself up, but can't. Others, first aiders included, rush to help.

"Poor sod," I say. "He might have broken his leg."

"Yes, and it's just as well you weren't inside him because you'd have to stay there until the man's heart rate comes down and the pain eases off."

"What for?"

"In case you cause him more distress by trying to get out. Ghosts have to be very careful inside people, especially these sporty types."

"Jana never mentioned that."

"I don't suppose she thought of it. Why would she consider the possibility of one of us taking part in a ski jumping contest? Besides, she doesn't think this is dangerous. And speaking of Jana, where is she?"

"Oh, no! He's her host!" I exclaim, pointing to the stricken jumper. "She was the next one down."

"I'll go and check," says Luisella, turning and walking away. While my concentration is taken with the immediate events, I ignore everything else around me. In the back of my mind, I hear the faint sound of someone calling my name, but I assume it to be a very worried Jana as Luisella closes in on her and her host.

Luisella bends down and I watch her mouthing something to Jana, and, suddenly, I feel an almighty push in my back. I begin to fall over, but before my body hits the ground, two pairs of hands grab my arms. The next thing I know, I'm being forcefully lifted up … and up … and into the sky, and when I turn to my right, one of the ghastliest sights I've ever seen is smiling back at me.

She is totally naked, and her huge dangling breasts are swaying from side to side as she manoeuvres me alongside. Looking down at the folds of fat on her short stumpy body, I want to be sick. Turning the other way, I see that the other pair of hands belong to an attractive, yet equally naked, black girl. She too is smiling, and then she calls out, "Helga! Are they following us?"

And with that, a third naked female swoops down in front of us, saying, "No, Affiong. We took them by surprise." This ghost is flying backwards, facing me, and says, "I do believe you're Mick and that you're gay."

I can't bear to answer as my eyes take in the enormity of this strongly built abductor. I can't think of the best words to describe her, except to say – well, if you can imagine an extremely tall, harsh looking testosterone-induced-shot-putter, with a moustache, then you'll know what the hell it is that's scaring me to death. How can this be happening to me?

Coming to my senses, I try pulling away but they are far too strong and are squeezing my arms like crazy. Beyond the shot-putter's body, I can see that we're flying further up and across the mountains and away from the village. I wonder about my capture and how they made it possible. They must have been waiting for the perfect moment, and the whole rotten incident with Jana's skier gave it to them. Luisella and I were so engrossed with the fall, while the other two – Moira and Tommy, were still inside their hosts at the top of the slope. If Tommy had come down next, it could have been him, but until the injured person was taken away, both he and Moira had to stay up top.

"Where are you taking me?"

"Some place they'll never find you," answers fatty, to my right. "I've never had a gay boy before. Lesbians, yes, but not a male gay ghost. I think you're the first of your kind, Mick."

"Shut up, you fat bitch."

"Hark at him. I'll make you suffer for that, you dirty little poofter. That's what they call your kind in England, isn't it … always mincing about like a fairy?"

"Shut up!"

"Hmm … he's got a temper to go with his nice physique," says the black girl.

"You're right, Affiong. I like it when they act tough. I like the struggle," replies the shot-putter, before turning about and flying on ahead. We appear to be flying the mountains lengthwise, instead of over them, and, looking down, I notice the outline of a river in the very high valley with, what look like, huge snow-covered rafts tied up at various points on its banks. We follow the river as it trickles between the ice flows, and I don't know whether we're still in Slovakia or have crossed into Poland. But, with all the snow and ice stretching out beneath us, I've no way of guessing. And, to tell the truth, when I look from one ghost to the other, I'm more worried about my immediate future.

Not long after, they pull me downwards and the outline of a small wooden chalet comes into view. It's within the trees and close to, what looks like, a very narrow road. It's hard to make out with the blanket of snow everywhere, but what is very noticeable is an absence of car tracks leading to this chalet.

Down and down we go until we reach the ground, and, on landing, I try taking advantage of the situation. Kicking out at the fat ghost, I catch her above the knee and she squeals like a pig, releasing her grip and holding the injured leg. I try as hard as possible to pull away from the black girl, and swinging my fist, it crashes into her shoulder. She yelps, but still manages to keep hold of me, giving the third member of their party time to close in. Miss shot-putter races over and behind me, grabbing me by the waist and trapping my free hand to my body. She has the grip of a bear, and, with her strength and Affiong's assistance, they manhandle me into the air once more. I've no chance of escape, and they know it, as they fly me through the chalet wall and into a fair sized bedroom.

"Throw him on the bed, Helga, and stay on top of him," orders Affiong. Turning to her other mate, I hear her say, "Dorothy, you get his legs and pull his boots off. I don't want any bruises."

"Too right I will," replies fatty in the faintest of Scottish accents. "Nobody kicks me and gets away with it."

I try stopping them, but my actions are limited. Once on the bed, the black girl starts pulling at my trousers while Dorothy fiddles with the boots. Meanwhile, testosterone Helga's body has me firmly held underneath her manly chest. Her hands are huge and her arms are extremely well muscled, giving me no chance of moving my upper body. I feel one foot after the other being set free from my boots and socks, and then feel my trousers being coaxed down my legs.

"Oh, my god! No! Stop!" I shout, and then continuously yell, "No! No! No! No!" My shouts of anguish only stop when Dorothy slaps me across my mouth. I attempt to bite her, but she pulls my jaw upwards, not giving me the chance.

"Now we've got you, we're going to play with your little Moby until it drops off."

While Dorothy is threatening me, Affiong is pulling at my boxers and I lift my knees to stop her. I swing my legs about, making things as difficult as possible, but she slaps me hard across my thighs, saying to her fat friend, "I told you to hold his bloody legs. How do you expect me to get to work?"

"Okay! Okay!" she replies.

I watch Dorothy's folds of skin move away and back down the bed, and I'm about to shout again when Helga's hand takes Dorothy's place across my mouth. And then I feel my feet being pulled and held apart. More panic sets in when Affiong's fingers take hold of my penis.

"Come to Affi. Come to Affi. Come on," she says, while tickling and playing with me. I can't stop myself growing as both her hands bring me to life. "At last, he's up, and it's my turn first this time, girls."

They laugh and encourage her, while Affiong moves her body across mine, and when her thighs are either side of my hips and she's about to force herself down on me, I raise my head slightly. One sight of Helga's face and moustache makes me close my eyes and concentrate on the memory of so long ago, and I compare it to the manly appearance of this shot-putter look-a-like. I can feel Affiong lower herself gently and her hand still guiding me in, when I start to soften.

"What the hell's going on?" she asks herself. I can feel her trying frantically to get me hard again, pulling and pushing with her fingers, but I know I have her beaten. She lifts her body away from mine and tries every way possible to coax some new life into me. I concentrate, ever harder, on Helga's moustache until, eventually, Affiong gives up and pulls away. "It's true! He's a bloody gay," she states.

"No, he's not. I saw him. He was as stiff as a poker," says Dorothy. "Here, let me have a go. You grab his legs." They swap places, but the longer that Dorothy tries, the more frustrated she gets. "What the hell will we do with him? If he can't fuck us, then he's no bloody use. The little shit."

"You're not trying hard enough," says Helga. "It's my turn. You two hold him and he can shout 'til his lungs burst, but, one things for sure, I'm going to raise his little fairy pecker if it's the last thing I ever do."

When she takes the weight from my chest and her hand from my mouth, I yell for help. Affiong and Dorothy each take a leg, pinning me down, while I watch the monstrous shape of Helga moving towards my midriff. She grabs me by the balls with one hand and squeezes, and then, lifting my head, I watch her face go down on me. And I'm so afraid that she'll do an Evelyn, just for spite.

Closing my eyes again, I start thinking about Jana and then shout her name. "Jana! … Jana! … Jana!" And this time, they let me shout. I can't move from under Helga's heavy body while she tries one thing after another. Surprisingly, the other two release me, leaving Helga on her own. I'm too scared to move, though, and keep shouting Jana's name at the top of my voice, until an almighty slap across my face causes me to stop and open my eyes. The look of hate on Helga's face is petrifying. She balls her fist and is about to strike me again when Affiong grabs her wrist. Helga gives the black girl a filthy look, but, now, with her body straddling my body and her sex over mine, she squeezes her legs and thighs into my hips. Pulling her arm away from Affiong, she grabs me by the shoulders and twists me around so that I'm now on top of her. Wrapping her legs around me, and still squeezing, she takes a firm grip of my wrists and pulls me into her.

"If he won't get hard any other way, let's try something he might enjoy," she suggests.

"What's that?" asks Dorothy, excitement in her voice.

"Play with his bloody arse, you idiot. You know, tickle it. Use your fingers. Do anything you want."

"Good idea," Dorothy says, and then I feel a couple of soft podgy fingers touching my bum.

"Help! Help! Help!"

"Oh, shut up, you wimp," orders Helga, "or I'll shut your mouth with mine. I'm telling you now that if you don't come over and let us have what we want, then I'll suck the life out of you."

"You can't do that, Helga," says Affiong.

"Who says I can't?"

"I do. Ghosts can't kill and you know that," the black girl answers.

"I'll do as I damn well please, Miss Goody-two-shoes."

"No you won't, Helga. Even the thought of killing could cost you dear, and maybe us as well. Isn't that right, Dorothy?" I can hear Affiong, but she has slipped from my sight.

"I couldn't care less about him," answers Dorothy, as she continues trying to excite me. "Is he ever going to get it up?" she asks. "Because if he doesn't, then Helga's got a point. After all, what kind of life is he going to have; a useless fairy all on his own, with no-one else like him around? They're no good to us ghosts, are they?"

"You're wrong, both of you, and I'm not going to stay here and be responsible for his death."

"Help me then," I plead. "Affiong! Help me! Don't leave me at their mercy. Please!" Between concentrating on staying soft and listening to them argue over my life or death, I don't notice the black girl disappear.

"She's gone, you stupid tosser, but she'll be back," says Dorothy. "Now, let's see what magic my fingers can do."

"No! No! Help me, Affiong! Help!"

I've no sooner finished shouting when Affiong returns, panicking. "They're here! They've found us. Leave him you two, and let's go. Quick!"

Dorothy is the first to move, taking her hands away and diving for the far wall, followed closely by Affiong. Helga's muscled body relaxes, releasing me slightly, but I try holding her down, pressing for all I'm worth into her body, groin to groin, nipple to nipple. She's far too strong and gradually pushes me off, but I still manage to grab her legs from behind as she tries moving away. Falling over, like a rugby player, she lands with her head disappearing through a cupboard, while the rest of her body lies flat, belly down.

Pulling herself backwards and onto her knees, she yells, "You dirty shit. I've told you before, I'm going to kill you." She throws her fist back, cracking it into the side of my head, making me let go. I feel faint, but can't mistake the sight of a massive naked foot swinging towards my face. I pull back, but far too late, and stars flash before my eyes before they shut, involuntarily. Her body pushes down on mine, covering my mouth with her lips as she sucks the life from me, and, being so weak and concussed, I have no defence to her attack. As the sucking goes on, I seem to go into a dreamlike state, and glimpses of Jana, Mary, Joyce and Evelyn come into my head, over and over again, until even these begin to dim.

Suddenly, I feel as though I'm floating, and all the weight has left my body. I must be dead again, but I can't be, because I'm still thinking and having strange fantasy feelings. Then the weight returns once more and my head begins to clear and, yet, I feel her lips still locked on mine. My head clears slightly, and I realise that the lips and attached mouth are not sucking any more. Helga has changed her mind and is now blowing. It must be a trick, so using my new found strength, I try pushing her away, opening my eyes at the same time.

"Lucia! It's you! Thank god, it's you. I thought I was dying."

"Shush, Micky. Let me sort you out and then I'll take you home." She pushes me back on the bed, where I now find myself. Lucia kisses me again, gently and with affection. I realise, now, that the floating feeling was me being lifted from the floor and carried, and I wonder what became of Helga. Did she get away, or what? Shortly after, Lucia pulls her lips away and lies beside me.

"Where is that cow?"

"Helga? … She's on her way to Pribylina in the firm hands of Ivan and Lun. We'll have to do something about those three nymphomaniacs, but what? Even Anna has problems with them. We can't punish them – we don't know how, Micky, and they always fly off when they get their energy back. It's not fair on the rest of us. We shouldn't have to worry about those lazy bitches making life difficult. And if they were the only ones, it wouldn't be so bad, but there are others."

"Did you catch the other two?"

"Yes. We saw Affiong from a distance. She seemed to be flying about in circles, and when she flew back to the chalet, we followed. You're very lucky, you know. If we hadn't spotted her, we might have been too late. Affiong gave the game away and I don't know why, but her movements seemed calculated."

"She didn't want me killed. She argued with the others, saying that she wouldn't get involved in a deliberate attempt to kill anyone."

"But ghosts can't kill, anyway," Lucia says, in a puzzled voice.

"I know we're not supposed to be able to kill, but Helga was determined to either rape me or do me in, and the fat one was happy to help her."

"It's just as well we came when we did then, isn't it? She had you by the short-and-curlies, didn't she?" Lucia chuckles, lifts her head and stares at my body. "Hmm, not bad for a little roll in the hay. So, tell me, Micky, which one screwed you first?"

"None of them."

"Pull the other one. With the start they had, you could have been dead already. Those three are fast little fuckers, and strong with it."

"I'm getting dressed." Jumping off the bed, I pick up my boxers and slip them on.

"Don't you want me, Micky? After all, I've just saved your life."

"Give me a break, Lucia. I'm pretty sure you know about me and, besides, I'm still shattered."

"I suppose you're right," she sighs.

In no time at all, we're ready to roll and Lucia holds my hand tightly for our flight home. On our return to the village, we are greeted by Anna who ushers us into the manor house.

"Mick," she says, "Jana and Luisella have explained what happened and I'm really sorry, but we did warn you about these stupid ghosts. They're such a pain in the backside. Excuse the pun, but you know what I mean. Anyway, how are you? They didn't hurt you too much, I hope?"

"No, they didn't really hurt me, but Helga nearly killed me. It was a close call. And thanks to Lucia I'm alive and well, but I need some rest and time to think."

Anna gives me a very strange look. "Think about what?"

"What we can do to stop them doing this again."

"Oh, that. It's difficult, Mick ... very difficult. We can't lock them up because they can simply fly through the walls. We don't have any way to secure them, we can't kill them and neither do we want to. Even thinking of killing can affect us."

"How?" I ask. "That shot-putter not only threatened to kill me but damn well nearly succeeded, so what's likely to happen to her? Does she lose any of her abilities?"

"That's the problem, but, before I go on, what do you mean by shot-putter?"

"Helga! She looks like one, doesn't she?"

"Hmm ... . I hadn't thought of her like that. You know, Mick, once upon a time, Helga used to be a Haunter and ... ."

I quickly interrupt. "With looks like hers, she'd scare the pants off anyone."

"There's no need to be like that. It's not her fault that she dreamt the way she did. Apparently, she was never the best looking of girls, but she had talent. Helga only died recently – in the nineteen-eighties, if I remember correctly. When she was younger she was an athlete of some sort, and was forced to take steroids and all that kind of junk. It's such a pity she didn't dream of being a ghost when she was a young girl. She might have turned out okay. Now, what was I saying?"

"You said she was a Haunter."

"Oh, yes. Anyway, she got into trouble and did something bad. It caused her to lose her haunting ability and she became angry with all of us. Helga has this idea that we are to blame, but the poor girl doesn't

165

understand. She's lost a lot of her speed and her sense of humour, and she thinks that revenge is the only answer. As a ghost, she knows how to maintain her life and keep her strength topped up, whether it's by sucking the life from other ghosts or entering a host. And then there are the bell flowers which can be found everywhere at the right time of year. Most aren't as good as fuchsia, but they serve their purpose, and so long as she keeps sucking nectar then our Helga won't have any problems in keeping herself going. Dorothy, on the other hand, is more of a problem because she influences the others so much. She's been around for quite a while longer – longer than me in fact, and not only does she have more experience than the other two but she's always been sex mad. She used to be a Villager and at first we all thought that she was only playing with the New Ghosts, but then she started getting rougher and her attacks became more frequent. In the end we had to warn her off. Dorothy has also lost her speed, but that's all. The other girl, Affiong, is a bit of a mystery. She hasn't been around this area very long – four or five years, at the most – but she never tells anyone about herself. And please remember, Mick, that these ghosts always have their brains ticking over, and they know that New Ghosts are easy targets, so we have to be careful."

"Why don't you put them in an open prison?"

"We don't have prisons, Mick. And, as I've said, there's no point because they'd just walk out."

"I don't mean a prison, as such. Put them somewhere they can't fly away from. Jana told me that she's afraid of crossing water. She said that ghosts can drown. Is that true?"

"Yes it is, but why do you ask?" asks Anna, while Lucia looks on, curiously.

"If we, well … I don't mean me because I don't have the ability, but what if these ghosts were placed, forcefully, on an island somewhere, far from any mainland and with most of their life sucked from them, then, maybe, they wouldn't have the strength to escape."

"We can't leave them without a means of life, such as nectar bearing plants or flowers, and once their strength is restored, they'd take the chance and fly away. They'd probably wait for a passing ship, and once on board they'd have the choice of several people to use as hosts."

"I understand that but you're assuming that they can fly. I'm aware that ghosts are in need of clover or shamrock to give us our flying ability, so why can't we take them to an island, depleting their flying ability on the way. Surely, the only reason that Gatherers and Mindbenders can fly as far and as fast as they do is because they've achieved that special ability to do so? I don't know if Ivan can fly indefinitely without recharging his body with shamrock, or whether he has earned the ability to store surplus flying ability in his system, but if Helga and her mates have only a limited flying time, can't this be drained from them as well as their strength. The way I see it, they'll have to be flown an extreme distance by several ghosts – perhaps a relay of ghosts – until they haven't any flying time left. Then place them somewhere they can gather nectar, but not clover or shamrock. They'd have to be kept on separate islands, though, and preferably in different parts of the world."

"Now let me think about this. We'll have to see how weak they are. I know they've been in this area through the winter, and we've had snow on the ground for months. They haven't had access to clover for quite some time, and shamrock doesn't grow here, so what you've suggested has its merits. Thanks, Mick. I'll talk to some of the Gatherers and see what they have to say."

"Where are Helga and her mates?"

"We're keeping them under guard – separately, of course. None of them knows in which buildings the others are kept. Why do you ask?"

"Affiong tried to save my life. She didn't want to kill me and argued with the others. I'm not sure, Anna, but I don't think she should share the same fate as Helga and Dorothy."

"If we decide to do as you suggest, then I'll bear in mind what you've said about her, but I can't promise anything. Now, Mick, go and get some sleep. Lucia will take you up and see you're well rested. And, Lucia, don't go taking advantage of his tiredness."

"Who, me?" asks a wickedly smiling Lucia.

"Yes, you! Now, be a good girl and look after him." Taking my hand, Lucia leads me away and up the stairs. Once inside my bedroom, I'm so shattered that I head straight for the bed and lie down. Lucia hops up with me, resting her head on the pillow, facing me and smiling.

"Don't get any ideas," I tell her. "I know about you and Tommy."

"I'll think about it," she laughs.

We talk and talk until, eventually, my eyes start closing.

CHAPTER FIFTEEN

"Good morning. I hope you're all well rested after yesterday's exploits," says Anna, her eyes settling on me more so than the others. We respond in the affirmative, and then she says, "Today, we're going to talk about the use of live people as hosts," Tommy glances in my direction with a silly grin on his face, obviously thinking of his first effort inside the young bespectacled mother, and his sexual turn on, "but before I do, I want to discuss the outcome of yesterday's events.

"At Mick's suggestion, we've decided to place two of the attackers on a couple of tiny islands from where they'll have the dickens of a time trying to escape. I must admit that this is the first time anyone has thought of such an ingenious plan – to isolate these girls, giving them the chance to think about their lives and whether they want to rejoin our community as productive and friendly ghosts. They might escape, of course, if luck and a small boat come their way, and that's a chance we'll have to take, but the islands we've chosen are remote and virtually inaccessible."

"Why can't they fly away?" asks Nancy.

"Most of their life has been sucked from them so reducing their strength, and they won't have the means to top up their flying powers because both shamrock and clover are unavailable. They might find a different kind of grass that gives this ability, but, as far as we know, no such vegetation exists. There are bound to be flowers available and whatever nectar they take from these will keep them alive and healthy. We wouldn't dream of putting them somewhere without nectar. That would be murder. We'll monitor them, to see that they're okay. After all, we have to give them the opportunity to mend their ways."

"But how will you know they won't have sufficient power to fly off somewhere else?"

"That's a good question, Nancy. To tell you the truth, we won't, but seeing as Helga and Dorothy have spent all winter here, where the fields have been covered in snow, they haven't had access to clover for a long time, and as they spend most of the time flying around looking for easy targets, then their own resources must be nearly depleted. I doubt that they've enough flying time left to reach the islands, but some of our Gatherers are escorting them, so they'll make it. You see, the Gatherers can always top themselves up, en route, while others restrain the girls,

168

preventing them from doing likewise."

"It sounds rather cruel to me."

"You have to realise, Nancy, that it could have been you that these three ghosts attacked, and if it was then you might be a rattlesnake this very moment."

"Huh!" exclaim both Nancy and Tommy, while I burst out laughing.

"There's nothing to laugh about, Mick ... nothing at all." All eyes are now on me, as Anna says, "You have no idea about reincarnation, no idea whatsoe ... ."

"I do," I interrupt, still chuckling. "A friend of mine came back as an egg. Simon told me."

"And do you believe him?"

"I do now. For a while, I thought Simon might have been teasing me, especially after what Jana said about him, but you've just confirmed it."

"An egg?" asks Anna. "It's possible, I suppose. He must have been very fond of his food." I was just going to add something, but decide that it's better left unsaid. Anna puts her hands up, palms forward, saying, "Anyway, let's change the subject for now. I will come back to it, but we must get on with the important business. Regarding Helga and Dorothy, I hope they have the sense to stay where they are and not try flying across a great expanse of water. If they do have any flying time left, it will be insufficient, and they won't make it. They'll, more than likely, drown. They know that – we've drilled it into them. On the other hand, they might feel sorry for themselves and then their energy levels will drop. This, too, can cause them to die. The more miserable a ghost feels, the more life is lost. So, you lot better remember this. It's no good going around feeling sorry for yourself, but if you do, make sure you top up with nectar. Don't do as those girls did by trying to steal life from others.

"This brings me back to today's topic about hosts and a ghost's life in general. I have some information here," says Anna, picking up some leaflets and passing them around, "and I want you to read these notes carefully and remember what I tell you. You'll be able to keep these papers for reference, but, in time, this information will become second nature to you. Take a few minutes to browse through them before we start."

Quickly scanning my eyes over the papers, I notice that they tell us who, and who not, to enter, reasons for bodily entry, and the possible repercussions for both the ghost and the host when the wrong host is chosen. Already knowing some of the details, I'm not surprised by their content but, while reading, my ears can't escape the mutterings and gasps from Nancy, Freda and Tommy. What's new to me is a paper titled Long Term Host which outlines the preference for New Ghosts to use people as hosts for years at a time. Another paper details the best types of bell flowers, and their order of strength, from which ghosts can obtain nectar.

"Have you had enough time to digest anything interesting?" Anna asks us, glancing at me, and probably recalling our previous conversation on the topic.

"How's a ghost supposed to enter a child? That's impossible."

"Answering your own question, eh, Tommy? And you're wrong."

"But we not fit," says Freda.

Anna lifts her finger to her mouth, shushing Freda. "Let's start at the beginning, shall we? Nancy, have you experienced an entry into a body since you became a ghost?"

"No, Anna, I haven't."

"Very well, then. I'll speak to your Monitor and later today you'll be given the opportunity."

"I'm not sure I want to."

"Nancy, I think you'll find it's beneficial to know how, whether you want to or not. You must enter a living person at least once, even if it's the only time you do. There's always the possibility, as Mick experienced, that you enter a person by accident, so you have to be prepared."

"Yes, Anna."

"And what about you, Tommy?"

"Yes, I have. I went in twice, yesterday."

"Of course you did. You went on the ski-jumping trip. Right then, we'll get started. On page one is a list of the types of people in which it is advantageous to enter and the reasons why. Let's go over these." – I look, once again, at the first page.

GOOD HOSTS

FEMALES – Teenage to Mid-Life – Better hormones
MALES – 25-35 years – Hormones/Sensible men only
CHILDREN – 8 years and upwards – Reliable, but only
in emergency

MALES – 36-45 years – Must be fit/Sensible
OLDER MALES & FEMALES – Fit and happy
MALES – 18-24 – Hormones/Must be selective

Anna continues, "As you can see, females should be a ghost's first choice when selecting a host. The reasons are obvious, because their hormone levels are higher and longer lasting than men. The higher the hormone level, the quicker our recovery when we need to top up our life and also our strength. Please be aware that we should only take hosts in an emergency. People are not playthings, except when we do a little haunting, and then allowances are made.

"Our second choice of host is the young male, from twenty-five to thirty-five, again for the hormones, but these must be sensible people."

"That doesn't make sense," says Tommy. "The hormone levels in lads of my age are higher than the twenty-five year olds. So, why isn't the eighteen year group the second choice?"

"Tommy! Don't be so impatient. While you're quite right about the hormone levels, our choices are made from experience. If you needed to enter someone in an emergency, would you really choose a very young man without knowing where he's been, what he's been doing, or where he's going? I wouldn't, because he's likely to be getting on with life as a young lad does: going to the pub, maybe dancing, clubbing, and possibly on drugs. None of this is good for you, Tommy. Okay, the dancing doesn't sound too bad, but will he drink while he's there, or take something he shouldn't? It's not worth the risk, and nor is it worth taking the risk with girls of that age, but at least girls have the better hormone values, and, as long as ghosts are selective, girls and young women far outweigh the boys. If, on the other hand, you were in a position to know that a young man is fit, healthy, a non-drinker and not abusing drugs, then, by all means, use him. The same applies to the twenty-five and upwards men. You must be selective. By this age, most have settled into proper jobs and have some ideas of responsibility, and their heavy drinking days are over. But you still have to be careful because not all men become responsible human beings. Some still go on drinking binges, take drugs, or get into trouble, while others still act like ten year olds.

"Okay," agrees Tommy, nodding his head.

"Now we come to a touchy subject, and this is the use of young children, from the age of eight, as hosts. I know they're smaller than us, but when ghosts enter hosts their bodies adjust to the size of the chosen hosts. To prove this, I'd like Mick to answer a question." Looking at me, she asks, "When you were inside the lady on the bus, did you feel that your hands and arms, your legs and feet, and your head were not where they should be? Could you see through her eyes properly or were hers too wide apart for you to see?"

I hadn't thought about this before, but the reality has caused me to have other concerns. "To be honest, I felt uncomfortable with the thought of being trapped inside her, but I didn't feel any smaller than her."

"You told us the other day about your full body experiences inside your sister, this lady, and your friends – Andy and Ben. Weren't they all different shapes and sizes?"

"Yes, that's correct, but this, in itself, poses another question." Anna tilts her head and lifts her hands, urging me on. "When I went inside them, did I take their shapes, completely? I mean, with me being male and, you know ... er, my sister being female?"

"No, Mick, you didn't take their actual shape. However, your body size did alter to suit each of your hosts." The noises from the four of us and our looks of bewilderment don't deter Anna from adding, "The same applies to our use of children, and, if I had it my way, I'd have children as my first choice."

"Why?" asks Freda.

Anna places her hands on the table, before answering. "Because, Freda, they are young, vibrant, full of excitement, and they eat heartily. They might not have the hormones that older people do, but the entertainment they bring me, when I do use them, makes me so happy. And happiness is nearly as good as any amount of hormones to the life of a depleted ghost. Jana thinks like me and prefers using children. Children sleep better than adults, unless they're sick, but we should never use hosts that are ill or on medication. I'm jumping the gun here, but you can read about this. In fact, the only time you should use children is when you are in desperate need of a host and there's no other satisfactory choice available. Yes, I know I prefer them, but I never use children unless I have to.

"Our fourth choice of host is the male between thirty-six and forty-five because, as long as he's sensible and reasonably fit, he can't do you any harm. His hormones will have taken a dive, but at this age he probably eats well, has a set routine and is very responsible. Again though, I'd be selective, because quite a lot from this group suffer from stress, are easily upset, and are, perhaps, going through a mid-life crisis. If they're miserable, then they're a waste of time. Watch what, and how much, they drink or smoke before selecting them. You must get to know your future host before taking the plunge.

"Next, we have the older adults, both male and female, and great care must be taken before entering any of them. Check them out, properly. If Mick had known, beforehand, that the fat lady's medication could do him harm, he'd have jumped out of the way. Wouldn't you, Mick?"

"Getting out of the way was harder than you think. I didn't like the idea of being squashed." And this response brings a round of chuckling from all quarters.

Anna carries on, "As long as the older adults are fit, energetic, and are happy individuals, then use them to rest in when they're going to bed. It shouldn't be often that you'll need to use this age group – there are so many others to choose from, but be careful when you do. Men get moody, and women go through the menopause. Heart problems, diabetes, and other nasty ailments sneak up on them, and some don't know about it. So watch out. You're not going to catch any of these ailments, but you might have an adverse effect on your host, and we don't want this to happen. It's our job to look after our hosts when we're inside them.

"Finally, but not as you see our last choice, we come to our eighteen to twenty-four group of males. I've already discussed this with you, so, remember, be very selective and, if your choice is a wise one, then you'll reap the reward of a quick replenishment of life."

"Why don't we just suck nectar? It would save all that messing about," suggests Tommy.

"Tommy, think of your own situation. You died late at night in the middle of winter and, fortunately, you didn't need a top up. Furthermore, you didn't exert yourself before your funeral, unlike Mick." All eyes turn to me, as she continues. "However, had you been in need of some life, there weren't any fresh flowers to get the nectar from. Were there? Simon was tired and couldn't have given you any of his life, and, besides, you wouldn't let him or Anne near your mouth. In emergencies, we ghosts need hosts. Now, do you understand?"

Tommy nods his head, but still not done with, he asks, "You know when you said we can reduce in size when we enter children … well, I had a problem trying to get out of that club. I thought ghosts could go through keyholes and tiny spaces, but I couldn't. I'd like to know why." All our eyes and ears are on Anna. I'm especially keen to learn why I couldn't escape from the hospital.

"Tommy! You've been reading too many comics or watching films, because you're acting like an eight-year-old." Anna seems mad as hell and I'm so glad that it's Tommy who's put his foot in it and not me. He folds his arms, bites his lip, his eyes afraid to move from Anna's face, as she goes on, "We might be able to take residence in smaller people's bodies, but we can't change our human form and become some phantom-like shape as you seem to think. Go through keyholes, indeed? Listen, all of you, I want to finish as much as I can, today. We missed yesterday because of a meeting, so it would be nice if we could crack on without interruptions or silly questions. However, If you have anything sensible to ask, then, by all means, do so. " Tommy doesn't flinch or open his mouth, while the rest of us just nod.

"Right, let's get on. On page two are a list of bad hosts and these have nothing to do with age. They are people with bad or excessive habits, some with illnesses and others on medication. I must specify that the terminology – bad host, doesn't mean that the person is bad. It means that it would be bad for us to use some people as hosts for one reason or another. Look at the list and tell me what you think." – My eyes scan the paper in front of me.

BAD HOSTS

DRUG ABUSERS - People taking drugs of any description. Effect on ghost - possible death in a short space of time. See list below.

ALCOHOL IMBIBERS - Alcohol in a host's body has a weakening effect on the ghost. Alcoholic drinks of all types are damaging. Ghosts have a toleration point and this varies with each ghost. Possibility of death.

UNDERWATER WORKERS - Possibility of drowning.

SMOKERS - Slight weakness to ghost.

PEOPLE TAKING MEDICATION - Some medicines are damaging to ghosts while others have little or no effect - such as Aspirin taken in moderation, most cold remedies and mild tranquilisers.

PEOPLE WITH SERIOUS DISEASES - Their weakened bodies cannot aid a ghost and may cause a ghost's life to reduce. Avoid using as the host may also suffer from a ghost's carelessness.

OLDER PEOPLE - Avoid for their sake. No advantage to a ghost.

CHILDREN - From birth to 7 years. Possibility of damage to the child.

DRUGS TO AVOID -

Marijuana - slight weakness to ghost.

Ecstasy - causes dizziness in ghosts and weakens steadily.

Amphetamines - weaken ghosts rapidly.

Cocaine - causes an immediate loss of consciousness and then rapid loss of life.

Crack Cocaine - as cocaine.

Heroin - causes instant death to ghosts.

Many other drugs cause varying degrees of weakness and eventual loss of life, including LSD, Opiates (opium related - such as Laudanum), morphine.

Note: A mixture of alcohol with any drugs can cause rapid loss of life.

"How are we supposed to know what a host is taking?" asks Nancy. Anna replies, "There's no point in going into someone unless you're reasonably sure that you'll be safe. Check the person out; follow him or her; go into his or her home and search for evidence of sickness, drugs, or anything else. If you are thinking of entering a person in a club, a pub, or anywhere else for that matter, watch, listen and study your target and any of their friends or family. There are clues everywhere if you look, but always be careful."

"You no have prosutes on list," states Freda. Anna looks confused.

"I think she means prostitutes," I intervene.

"Oh, prostitutes! Actually, Freda, unless they were to catch something deadly, like AIDS, or are on medication for something or other, then they're as fit as the next person. The only drawback is in how much energy they lose during the course of their working day. Personally, I wouldn't enter one because she might be too tired to do me justice. Also, I wouldn't enter what you call gays" – she turns to me and cocks her eyebrows – "or swingers, because of all this talk about sexually transmitted diseases. Of course, that's my own preference, but you have to use your own judgement. Are there any other questions on this subject?" Anna watches us shake our heads, and then says, "We have to stop for a break, and, Mick, I want you to come with me to speak to Affiong. It seems as though she's taken a shine to you since saving her from the same fate as the other two. Right then, I'll see the rest of you in a couple of hours."

With that, we all rise, join hands and Anna leads us outside. Shortly, after a shrill noise from Anna, Moira and Luisella show up to keep the others occupied while I toddle off with our Tutor.

We enter the old school room and find Affiong, now in a tee-shirt and jeans, sitting in the company of Lun, a Chinese ghost in his early twenties, and Maggie, dressed once again in her old-fashioned clothes. After a few words from Anna, they leave us, and we sit down on the extremely small children's seats in front of the African ghost. Anna leads the way with question after question, but Affiong doesn't respond. I don't know what to ask and can't understand why we're bothering.

And then Anna loses her temper. "Let me tell you, Affiong, that if you're not prepared to say why you became a sex-mad nymphomaniac, then you might as well become an outcast on some far-flung island like your friends. Is that what you want?"

"No! Don't send me away. Please!"

"Are you going to tell us?"

"I … I'll speak to Mick. I know something about him and I've heard how he died. I won't be embarrassed with him and he might understand.

Please, Anna ... please," she begs. How the hell did she find out about my death? It must have been Simon doing all the talking, and if so, then I'll give him another affliction to think about.

Anna warns her, "If you attack him, then you're out of here and off to the South Seas."

"I won't. I promise," she says, her eyes showing signs of tears.

"I'll be right outside, and I want you to know that Mick will tell me everything, anyway." Affiong nods her head, and, seeing this, Anna passes through the door, leaving me with a task I have no idea how to handle.

A sobbing Affiong asks, "Mick, can I trust you not to tell anybody else about me? I've kept this bottled up inside for years and I'm ashamed of what I've become."

Feeling uncomfortable on the tiny seat and with the situation, I stand up, walk around scratching my head, and then squat down in front of her, saying, "I don't know you, Affiong. I didn't like what you tried to do to me, and, initially, I thought you were the leader of your little gang, but if you want to confide in me, then I promise that only Anna will hear what you have to say. The question should be, though, can you trust Anna?"

"Yes, Mick. Anna's not allowed to relate anything told in confidence or she could lose her abilities."

"Why not tell *her* then? That way, even I won't know."

"I can't. She has this aura about her that scares the living daylights out of me. I'd never be able to explain things properly," she answers, her eyes pleading and searching mine for help.

"Okay, but I'm not happy with this. You used to be a Mindbender, so you must have been a good ghost at some time in your life."

"I was never a good ghost. There again, perhaps I was, but I've always had this problem."

"Problem?"

"Yes, Mick. It all started when I was alive. The thing is ... I hate men."

"I'd better leave then. How will I know if what you say isn't made up?"

I start to rise, but she reaches out, holding my arms gently. "Please listen, Mick. Ghosts can't lie, and I've no-one else to talk to. And I need a friend." More moisture creeps into her eyes.

Resting on my haunches once again, I take her hands, softly saying, "Okay, Affiong. You can call me Micky. I prefer, Micky. Now, start at the beginning."

"I don't know if you'll understand, but where I was born, in Nigeria, the people – especially the men, have this belief that everyone should be circumcised, girls as well as boys. Micky, it's still going on nowadays, and it's so cruel. I can understand boys being circumcised for health reasons – well, that's what they say – but I don't really believe them. As for girls, their reasons for cutting off the clitoris are sexist. The men insist on it because they think girls will be promiscuous if it's not done. Micky, when I was a baby they circumcised me and, although I later found out that this was wrong, I grew up not realising what I was missing, in more ways than one."

"I don't understand. You must have found out about circumcision when you became a teenager, from talk amongst your friends and family, but what do you mean by saying … in more ways than one? You're not making any sense."

"It will, Micky. Just let me tell you." I nod my head, looking at her inquisitively. "In all my married life I never had an orgasm. No matter how many times that my husband and I had sex, I never felt comfortable and never achieved any sense of fulfilment. He always managed to come, and he had this idea that I'd enjoyed his lovemaking and that he was the perfect stud, and that I wouldn't trade him for anyone. I assumed, at the time, that this was normal. There were occasions, though, when other women would brag about having orgasms and they'd try to explain the thrill it gave them, but I never had one, no matter what I tried to do."

"Yeah, but what's that got to do with you being a nymphomaniac? If you didn't like men back then … why go sex mad now?"

"Listen, will you? My husband used to tell his friends how good he was in bed and how I enjoyed him so much that I couldn't get enough of his body. You don't know how much I hated having to do my wifely duties, but as the years went on and I still hadn't borne him any children, his friends started to disbelieve him about his sexual prowess. Eventually, he tired of this and threw me out of his home. I went to live with my mother – my father had already died – and other men shied away from me. You see, my husband divorced me and then took another wife who gave him three sons in consecutive years. Some people said a witch had

178

put juju on me and that I'd never be able to have kids. Men, and even a lot of my former friends, spurned me after that. Soon after, my mother died, so I left the town and went to Lagos. I didn't have any brothers or sisters so I grew into a very sad and lonely old woman."

"I'm sorry, Affiong. You seem to have had a rotten life."

"It wasn't always bad. When I was small, I had a happy time playing around with other children. My mum and dad used to take some of us for walks and tell stories about animals, witchcraft, ghosts, and all that. Sometimes, we'd go down by the river and watch the boats and the fishermen. I used to dream about going on trips and about the stories they told me, and even after I married I used to dream nice dreams. I loved my early life as a child and a young woman. I never knew why I didn't enjoy sex until I died and came back as a ghost. Just like you, Micky, I came back fully intact. I'd never known what it was like to have a clitoris, or the thrill it could have given me if they hadn't chopped it off. I don't know if I can tell you the rest, but I suppose I'd better or Anna might not understand. The thing is that my clit is sensitive, and when I wear underwear I'm easily aroused. If I'd had a clitoris when I was married I could have made sure of my husband's happiness, kids or no kids. I'd like to think so, anyway. One thing's for certain ... I wouldn't have been so lonely."

"But why did you become a nymphomaniac?"

"I'm not a nymphomaniac, Micky. Others only think I am because of who I mixed with and what happened to me. It didn't take me long to attract other ghosts, both male and female. We enjoyed sex together and, to tell the truth, I couldn't get enough at first. This seemed to please the ones I dated, so there wasn't a problem. Eventually, I acquired the abilities of a Mindbender and I took a fancy to one of the GODs, but I couldn't leave him alone. He enjoyed my body as well, but on one occasion I was so sexed up that I couldn't stop myself screwing him, time after time, and even when he begged me to stop, I didn't. When we'd finished he couldn't move and was so drained of life that he needed help, but I didn't give him any. I was on such a high, and totally consumed with my own satisfaction, that I ignored him ... not intentionally, though.

"I was in seventh heaven and, although quite tired, I flew off, leaving him lying by the side of a lake. I wasn't away very long, but on my return I saw three other ghosts pulling my boyfriend from the water. I

179

don't know how he fell in, unless he, somehow, turned over and dropped in by accident. I didn't mean to burn him out. I loved him, and I still do, but that didn't make any difference. I still lost the ability to read minds. It vanished from my system."

"You say that you still love him, but if he's been dead so long, can't you find a way to forgive yourself and find somebody knew?"

"He didn't die, Micky. He's still a Ghost Of Dreams. I have seen him on a few occasions, but he won't have anything to do with me. He blames me for his near death situation, and I don't blame him."

"If he didn't die, then why did you lose your ability?"

"I shouldn't have left him alone. I'd left him in a defenceless state and if the other ghosts hadn't come along when they did he might have died."

"Now I understand, but why did you go off with Helga and Dorothy, doing what you've been doing?"

"When the rest of the ghosts found out what happened, they thought I'd left him deliberately. It wasn't enough that I'd lost my mindbending powers; they treated me like a leper, and this reminded me of my former life with my husband and how the people treated me for not having children. I was lonely once again and I felt so much anger towards men, and how their sex has been responsible for everything that's happened to me."

"I'm a man, so why are you telling me all this?"

"You're gay, Micky. I'd never met a gay lad in my life until I became a ghost, and the living ones with whom I have come into contact aren't as gay as you."

"How do you work that out?"

"After what we did to you in trying to get you stiff ... and your not so little pecker wouldn't stay erect, what do you think? If you're not gay then you must have been a very lonely person when you were alive. Not even a devout virgin can resist our sexual advances, but after some initial expectations you didn't even twitch." And I'm not about to tell her why. "Micky, I feel safe with you and I don't want to be lonely anymore. Please help me."

"I'll see what I can do, but I'm only new here. Perhaps, though, you should try helping other lonely ghosts."

"I don't understand you."

"There are bound to be other ghosts like me, such as Tommy, Nancy and Freda, who feel lonely now and then, and we're going to need help, more new friends, and questions answered that a former Mindbender, like you, might know the answers to. Join us, Affiong. Start again and see what happens, and when the other ghosts notice how you're trying to belong, they'll accept you. Find a partner and, as long as you control your mind and don't fly off thinking about your own satisfaction, then you'll start enjoying sex as a lover and not a rapist."

"You make me sound cruel, putting it like that, but you're right. I wish you weren't gay, Micky. You're so easy to talk to." Affiong smiles ever so innocently, and I can't help thinking how much she looks like Halle Berry. She, certainly, has everything going for her in the looks department.

"Is there anything else I should know?" I ask, gently squeezing her hands.

"No," she replies, shaking her head, her smile now withdrawn.

Releasing her, I stand and she does likewise. "I'll tell Anna what you've said – privately of course, and I'll keep my promise not to tell anyone else. I *do* hope the ghosts accept you, Affiong. Perhaps you'll tell some of them your story when you're ready. It doesn't hurt to explain things. While everything is bottled up inside, then you're going to find life difficult, but I know that if you tell them the truth then Jana and the others will treat you well." Leaning forward, I peck her on the cheek. "Thanks for not wanting to kill me yesterday, and for trusting in me today."

"Thanks Micky." A few more tears, of either worry or joy, enter Affiong's eyes when I back away, calling out for Anna.

Anna walks in, quizzically raising her eyebrows, and when I nod my head, she asks Affiong, "Have you told Mick everything you need to?"

"Yes, Anna," she replies, still looking forlorn.

"What do you think, Mick? Are you satisfied with her reasons for being the way she is, and, more importantly, is she likely to change her way of life?"

I think for a second or two, before replying. "Yes, Anna. I'm convinced she's telling the truth and that she can change, but everybody in the village has to help and accept her. I know this might be difficult at first, but I'm sure that, after listening to her reasons for being the way she is and her responses to my questions, Affiong will be an excellent addition to the local community."

"I'm not so sure," replies Anna, "but if you think so, then I'll talk to our committee and see what they have to say." Affiong seems apprehensive and looks to me for support.

"Anna! What Affiong has told me is extremely personal and, I believe, deeply hurtful to her, and it explains an awful lot about the way she has acted. I'm sure that, when I tell you, you will not only be surprised but also accept it to be the truth. I have first hand knowledge of particular circumstances in her life, when alive and on her return as a ghost, and if you can understand what these are, then you'll appreciate how difficult life has been for the girl."

Affiong looks at me with the tiniest of smiles, as Anna responds, "I'll tell you what. If, as you say, she has a valid excuse for acting and living the way she has, then I'll accept your word and relate to the committee that an advantageous outcome has been reached." Looking at Affiong, she continues, "I don't want to hear your reasons, Affiong, but I want you to try and become part of our life without resorting to antics that demean the personalities of ghosts. If Mick wants to tell me about your life, that's up to him. On the other hand, you might want to tell me about yourself, and I'd much prefer that. I don't like what you and your so-called friends have been doing and if it was left to me, I'd send you packing with your mates, but I respect what Mick has said. He can't lie and seems intelligent, so maybe one day you'll tell me what is, or was, ailing you."

"Yes, Anna. I've told Micky everything and he's given me some sound advice. I wish I'd met him before I met Dorothy. I wouldn't be in this mess." She glances at me, now slightly more confident and, seemingly, with relief that what she's told me is going no further.

"Very well, Affiong. Stay here for the time being, or at least until the others are made aware of the situation. I don't want you roaming around scaring the pants off them." Affiong agrees and sighs with relief, as Anna takes my hand and leads me from the school room. On the way out, she says, "Go and join the others, and tell them that Affiong is staying in the village, but don't say anything you shouldn't."

"Certainly, Anna." I feel proud of myself having accomplished something positive for the first time as a ghost.

182

"And, by the way, Mick, you can tell them to take the afternoon off. I'm going to call this committee meeting now, to let them know of my decision. I'm sure they'll accept it. There's many a ghost that's been given a second chance, myself included, so I don't envisage any problems. I can only hope that the girl doesn't let us down." Anna shrugs her shoulders and walks off. I make my way to the seating area where Jana has joined Luisella, Freda and Nancy.

Their faces light up, expecting a detailed report, but I only mention that Affiong is being allowed to restart her ghost life in the village. Nancy and Freda seem disappointed that the whole story can't be told. Luisella, however, explains to them the rule of privacy and what can happen to a ghost if he, or she, spreads the personal details of another. I give them the happy news of a free afternoon and this puts the smile back on their faces.

"Tommy'll need to know," I say. "Where is he?"

"He went off with Moira, ages ago," answers Nancy.

"He's not with Moira now. I was only just talking to her," says Jana. "Micky, you stay with Freda and Nancy. You'll be reasonably safe now that Helga and her mates have been sorted. Come on Luisella. Let's go and find him."

Jana and Luisella waltz off, leaving me with the two women. After a while, there's still no sign of them coming back and Nancy's conversation with Freda has changed from one of an interest in ghosts into that of a typical woman's. I'm bored to tears listening to their worries about how they look without lipstick and mascara, and the type of clothes they should wear. They become so involved, discussing their shoes and hair-dos, that they don't notice me sloping off.

Once round the corner and out of sight, I relax, walking along and whistling softly with my hands in my pockets. Thoughts of Jana and her search for Tommy come to mind, so, for something to do, I decide to seek him out. Peering through the windows of each house I pass reveals nothing and nobody. My curiosity takes me to the edge of the village and, not having found him, I sit down on an old log. I'm not here long when a funny whooping noise disturbs my peace. Do I investigate this disturbance, or not? I know the nymphos are no longer a threat, but the possibility of there being more of their ilk is putting doubts in my mind.

Oh, what the hell. As long as I shout, someone's bound to hear me, so

I creep forward and crouch down behind a clump of trees and bushes. Still the noises persist and, on lifting my head, I'm gobsmacked. I'm not afraid of moving forward but I don't know that I want to. The sight of Tommy playing with himself has me transfixed and I'm getting as excited as he is. I'm so tempted to join him and replace his hands with mine. I'd never thought of Tommy as a partner – he didn't seem my type – but seeing him here, within spitting distance, I must admit he's turning me on. While his hands make love to himself, mine move to my trousers. Just as I'm fumbling my fly open, Tommy yelps so loud that it causes me to jump. He turns and, on seeing my face, scrambles away behind another tree.

Re-doing my fly, I follow him. "Tommy! Tommy! Talk to me, will you?"

"Go away."

"Tommy! Speak to me. I'm not going to tell."

"Just go away and leave me alone," he sulks.

I'm about to do as he wants when another voice surprises us. "You wouldn't want me to tell everybody, would you?"

I look up and see Jana hovering above us. Tommy, in shock and now fully covered, emerges from behind his tree, as I reply, "Don't tell on him, Jana. That's not right. How would you like it if everyone knew about your intimate moments?"

"Please don't," begs Tommy, as Jana floats to the ground.

"Tell on Tommy? Yes, I would, and on you too, Micky. You're no innocent in this. Are you?"

Tommy turns to me. "W … What've you done? How long have you been standing there?"

Jana winks at me, saying, "He's not been here long, Tommy. At least, not long enough to get himself too excited. I'll tell you what; let's do a deal … the three of us."

"What do you mean?" I ask.

"I'll say nothing if the two of you answer some questions."

"I don't understand," says Tommy.

"First of all, Tommy, you can tell us why you prefer the company of your own right hand instead of having sex with one of us females."

Tommy looks aghast. "B … But I do like s … sex with g … girls."

"We all know about you and Lucia, Tommy, and she'd have been more than happy to satisfy you, so why the need to play with yourself? And tell me, when did you start wanking in the first place – you know, how old were you?"

"Jana, don't you think that's a bit personal?" I ask. "Besides, I bet you play with yourself … it's only natural; and we shouldn't go around asking questions like that."

"I do, Micky. It's part of the enjoyment of being a ghost. I like watching people have sex, either by themselves or with others, and don't tell me that you don't," she says, looking at me, accusingly. "Now, Tommy, are you going to tell us, or do I open my mouth?"

Tommy sits down, leans back against the tree and folds his arms. Looking up at Jana, he says, "Go on then … tell everybody. I don't care."

"Very well, then." She glances at me and then makes to fly off. Tommy shouts, "Wait! I'll tell you, but promise that you won't tell anyone else."

"Why the sudden change of heart?" she asks.

"It might not matter to you, but I don't want all the others looking at me and pointing their fingers every time I walk by. As long as you both promise to keep quiet, then I'll tell you." We both agree to keep his secret. "I can't stop playing with myself. I've always enjoyed the feeling it gives me. I'm not sure how old I was when it started; maybe eight or … ."

"Eight?" I interrupt, surprised, and Jana's mouth is open, mouthing the same number.

"Yeah! I used to get into trouble because my little brother, who shared my bed, always used to go to the top of the stairs and shout down, '*Mum, Tommy's fidgeting again*'".

"Fidgeting?" asks a chuckling Jana.

"Don't laugh. It's not funny. I didn't even realise that what I was doing was supposedly wrong. I had this habit of rubbing my, you know," Tommy points to his crotch, "against the top of my leg, because it always made me go to sleep. It was like my mum, when she was rolling soft pastry into sausage shapes, and she'd keep on rolling it until it was perfect. I used to keep rolling my whatsit along the top of my left leg. It never got hard, but at some stage it would give me a lovely fulfilling sensation, like an electric shock, and then I'd be able to sleep. Sometimes, though, my brother used to give me a thump so I'd hit him back, and this always led to our mum coming upstairs and slapping me. It was worse if my dad was home because he'd belt the two of us just for being awake. I don't know why I started to fidget. It was like a comfort thing." Tommy shrugs his shoulders and I think he's finished, but then he starts again. "It wasn't until I was thirteen or fourteen, and still fidgeting, that it started getting hard, and this electric shock feeling changed to a wet one instead. I didn't know why, but it was no less a thrill, so I got into the habit of doing it as often as I could. My awakening to sex was just beginning and I didn't need any girlie pictures to set me off. I could just think about the thrill it gave me and I'd start."

"Oh, Tommy, you amaze me. I've never thought of rolling a man. Have you, Micky?"

Giving her an annoying look, I answer, "No, I haven't, and nor will I." But the thought of trying doesn't escape me. I can't believe her. That's twice in a matter of minutes that she's alluded to my sexual preference.

Jana, with her eyes still on me, asks, "So, Tommy, when did you find out the proper way to toss yourself off?"

"You don't expect me to say any more?"

"Of course! You weren't, exactly, rolling pastry into sausage shapes just a minute ago."

"How long have *you* been here?"

"Long enough. Now, carry on. You said you'd tell us everything, so let's hear it."

"That's not fair."

"Aw, come on Tommy. You've told us this much, so you might as well tell us the rest. If you weren't so interesting, we wouldn't bother, would we, Micky?"

I wish she'd leave him alone but, not wanting to get on her bad side, I agree with her, saying, "No, we wouldn't."

Tommy glowers at me. "It was at my mate's house when I was fourteen. There were three of us, and we were having a race to see who'd be the first one to come." Jana looks away, her hand to her mouth, trying not to laugh. Tommy goes on, "It was the only time in my life that I ever saw other boys playing with themselves and I couldn't understand why they weren't rubbing themselves against their legs. They were pulling and pushing and I was wondering what the hell they were doing. We never finished because we heard his mum coming up the stairs. I was so embarrassed when she walked in the room ... and so were the others. We never raced again, but after that I stopped rubbing myself and copied them instead. Now! Are you satisfied?" Tommy glares at both of us and then looks away, and Jana can't hold back her laughter any longer. I don't laugh at all, and feel sorry for him in a way. It's not that his sexual awareness was any different from that of other boys, me included, but having to tell about it is something else.

"Let's go back," I suggest.

"Not so fast, Micky. Tommy's told us his story, so how about yours?"

"What are you talking about?" I ask.

"I want to know about your girlfriend ... and the cows."

Having listened to Tommy and having been through the mill in the last few days, telling about Cathie isn't such a big deal. "Okay, but remember you two ... don't tell anybody else." They both agree to keep silent.

"It was a long time ago. I'd been going out with Cathie, an attractive long-haired brunette, for about three months – clubbing, drinking in pubs, going to the pictures and that – and we were getting along fine. She wouldn't let me make love to her, though, and I was getting more and more frustrated." I don't want to mention my relationships with other lads at that time in my life, because Tommy doesn't know and I don't want him to. If he's not aware of me being gay, then I'd rather it stay that way. "I knew Cathie wasn't a virgin, but that didn't matter. I liked her a lot. We enjoyed each other's company, and, for a change, I decided to take her into the countryside. I called at her place and when I saw her, my heart skipped a beat. She looked very chic, dressed in a red top and a tight-at-the-bum figure-hugging skirt. We carried a small picnic, some wine, a transistor radio and Cathie's new camera, and took a couple of buses to Weeting Castle and Grime's Graves. Afterwards, we walked around more of the Breckland area, eventually stopping near Thetford Warren."

"I've been there," states Tommy, excitedly. "Did you go to the Priory?"

"Jeez, Tommy! No! I had other things on my mind."

"Oh," he says. Jana grins, lifting her eyebrows, letting me know how naïve she thinks he is.

"Anyway, the weather was beautiful, and to get some privacy we climbed a gate and sat down in an out of the way corner of a field. We ate, we talked, and we drank the wine, and then we lay down together, talking some more and listening to my transistor. We started messing about, kissing and cuddling, and gradually getting ourselves worked up. Cathie then said she had something to show me. She picked up her bag and pulled out a packet of three. You can imagine the look in my eyes, and I took hold of her, easing off her clothes. She helped me off with mine and, after a little foreplay, she coaxed a condom onto my stiffy, as you call it," I say, looking directly at Jana.

"Stiffy?"

"Shut up, Tommy. Let him finish," snaps Jana.

"The thing is … while we were making love, Cathie decided that she wanted to be on top, so she squeezed her legs around me and we turned over, knocking the radio to one side. We heard the volume change from quiet to very loud, but, honestly, at that particular moment, we didn't bloody care. We were in heaven – Cathie with her eyes closed; the radio blaring; and us … we were so busy banging away that we couldn't hear the other noise approaching. Very soon, though, I felt the ground vibrating through my back. I couldn't see a thing because Cathie had me pinned down in the long grass, and she seemed to be in the throes of orgasm until I squeezed her arms. She opened her eyes and, still bouncing, looked at me before looking up. *'Shit'*, she cried as she jumped from my body and pulled me to my feet. As I rose, I could see what she'd seen and I shouted *'Shit'*.

"A herd of cows was bearing down on us at a ridiculously fast speed and there was no bloody sign of it stopping. We grabbed what we could of our clothes and legged it through a nearby hedge. Even then we weren't sure if we were safe, and kept on running, leaving the radio, the camera, the hamper, and some of our clothes to their fate. Fortunately, we had enough clothes to cover us, and we had our shoes, but the cuts and bruises we'd incurred, by throwing ourselves through that hedge, put a dampener on our sexual activity. Initially, we laughed about it and sat in the next field until the cows went away, but the blasted animals stayed in that corner for ages and were making a hell of a noise, mooing and stomping on the ground. I'd always thought cows were placid creatures that would shy away from people, but these cows were a breed apart.

"When the cows eventually moved on, everything went deathly quiet. We couldn't even hear my radio. So I made Cathie wait while I went back for the rest of our gear. I threw what wouldn't break over the hedge to Cathie, and then, carrying the rest, I returned to her and we inspected the damage. The hamper was crushed; the clothes we'd left were filthy; my transistor was smashed to pieces, and so was Cathie's camera. When she saw the camera, she went into one, hitting me, yelling and telling me it was a present from her grandfather who'd just died. She was not a happy bunny, to say the least, and when we got home, her mood hadn't altered. She wouldn't go out with me after that, despite my apologies and endless phone calls. She wouldn't accept the fact that it wasn't my fault; that the cows had spoilt our day and broken her camera. Not long after, I heard she was dating some fella' from Bury St Edmunds, so I gave up on her." Looking questioningly at both Jana and Tommy, I ask, "Well, what's a man supposed to do?"

"Nothing, Micky … nothing. It wasn't your fault and you shouldn't have let her blame you. If she was so obsessed with the camera, her grandfather's present or not, and not concerned about you, then that was her mistake and she wasn't worth the trouble."

"I agree," says Tommy. He then asks, "Was she your first … er, girl?" Tommy clenches the fist of one hand, moving it back and forward, and I want to thump him.

"Don't be so bloody nosy."

"Go on. You can tell us," urges Jana.

"No, I won't. Don't you think you've heard enough for one day?"

"No, Micky. I love hearing stories, sexual or otherwise. You should know that by now."

"I do, Jana. I do, but I've told you all I'm going to about my sexual life."

"We'll see," she says. "Come on guys, let's get back. We don't want them sending out a hunting party." With that, we leave our space between the trees and make our way back to our usual meeting place. "By the way, Micky … it was the music."

"What are you on about?"

"The cows! They didn't like your taste in music."

CHAPTER SIXTEEN

"Hello, you lot. Where have you been?" asks Moira, who is standing between Anna and, to my surprise, Affiong. "And, look at the state of Tommy's hair. Whatever have you been up to?" Moira and the others start laughing, and I can't suppress my smile.

"Shit!" explodes Tommy. "Why didn't you tell me?" he asks, turning angrily to me.

"Sorry, Tom. I forgot," I reply, but then Tommy pushes past me, running off in a huff.

"We're waiting," says Anna. "You wouldn't want to keep a nice bit of juicy gossip from me, surely?"

Jana casts me a glance before answering, "We found him behind a tree. Nobody knew where he was, so we went looking for him. He's probably been playing with himself, but what's the harm? We all do it, don't we?" Clever answer, I think, and it will put the others on the back foot.

"I think you know more than you're telling, but we'll let it pass," replies Anna.

"Where are Freda and Nancy?" I ask.

"They've gone to a restaurant with Lucia, Anne, and a few of the others. Nancy has to learn how to enter people and Freda wanted another go. She's only done it the once," replies Moira.

"Fair enough." Then, turning to Anna, I say, "I've been going through some of the leaflets you gave us, and on the subject of entering people it says that we shouldn't use underwater workers as hosts. I can understand the drowning aspect, but are there any exceptions?"

"Hmm. You know, Mick, I'm going over these topics in the morning, but, I suppose, giving you a few titbits might keep your mind occupied, rather than gathering new hairstyles every five minutes." We start laughing again, while she continues, "Water can be dangerous to ghosts. Rain water is okay when it's falling down, and so is paddling in the sea and going in a shower, but complete submersion is life threatening. If a ghost becomes fully submerged, then he, or she, should try and get out within two to three minutes, or death is the outcome. It's happened on many occasions. For goodness sake, Mick, isn't that the reason we've sent Helga and Dorothy to live on a couple of isolated islands ... and at your suggestion?"

"Yes, I know that, but I was relating my question to people who work underwater, such as divers."

"Why on earth would you want to choose a diver, of all people? And, anyway, divers aren't the only worry. Sailors, deep sea oil-rig workers, or any other people working on, in, or near, the water are potentially bad hosts. There's a classic example of a ghost drowning when one of our Dreamers went down with the Titanic."

"The Titanic?"

"Yes, Mick. You must have heard of Plato, the Greek philosopher?" My eyes and mouth open wide, in shock. "We don't know whether he went down with the ship, or drowned in the water with his host. All we know is that Plato was determined to travel on the ship's maiden voyage, and, with it being supposedly unsinkable, he felt safe. Unfortunately, the ship didn't know it was unsinkable and our good friend Plato is no longer with us. We also lost his Scribe at the same time, so we suffered a double loss. You must realise that famous as Plato was, to us he was just a normal everyday ghost – the same as you or me. Being a Ghost Of Dreams was only an ability he acquired by accident, as they all do, but I've already explained this to you."

Affiong starts sobbing at the mention of drowning and moves away to hide her face. I know what's on her mind, but the others don't. Moira quietly remarks, "Why's she so upset about Plato? It was a long time ago." The others shrug their shoulders.

"Please leave her alone. She's got somebody else on her mind," I reply. Thinking of Affiong and her new clothes, I look at the others and, while discreetly pointing to Affiong and keeping my voice down, I ask, "Did they deliberately fly around naked … to scare us?"

"Of course not," answers Moira. "Once your clothes deteriorate, they start falling off. You have to check them every so often, but so long as you've been working to help other ghosts or the living, then you automatically earn the ability to pick up new ones, wherever you are in the world. You might be working as a Villager, a Gatherer, or any other ghost, but you must do your fair share. Other ghosts don't decide whether you've earned enough credit; it's one of these things that happen. Affiong and her friends didn't do any work. They only caused problems, as you found out. Some time or other, their clothes turned to rags and fell off, but by that time they'd lost the ability to pick up new ones."

"Couldn't they just steal them from one of their conquests, or from the drawers in the rooms?"

"No, Micky," Moira goes on, "they couldn't. Just as ghosts can't deliberately kill, neither can they steal or lie. They might have tried, but if they did, they failed."

"How come Affiong has new clothes?"

Jana looks at me as if I'm stupid, before replying, "We gave her some, and the other two. How do you think you got yours? We don't want ghosts flying around naked ... or do we?" She smiles, lowering her eyes to my nether regions.

"No, I suppose not."

"I'm going for a lie down. Who'd like to keep me company?" asks Anna, winking at me, but I'm surprised when Moira accepts her invitation. My eyes follow as they walk off hand in hand.

"Let's go and find Tommy," says Jana.

"Not again."

"Come on, Micky. As long as I know he's safe, I'll be happy. Not knowing bothers me."

"Can I join you," asks Affiong, sheepishly.

"Of course you can," replies Jana, and we move off towards Tommy's sleeping quarters. "Tell me, Affiong, how come you're so far from Africa? I'd have thought you'd be ghosting in the southern hemisphere."

"It's a long story," she answers.

"For goodness sake, Affiong, I don't want a long story. I've had enough of those for one day. Just give me the abbreviated version."

As we tread through the snow, she gives Jana a brief account of what she told me; of how her Dreamer nearly died and how she was shunned. She tells us of her travels to America, and then Europe, to escape the gossip, and how, after bumping into Dorothy, her life went all down hill. Jana doesn't push her for any more details, and soon after we meet Tommy, who's made himself at home with some of the Villagers.

Tommy's hair is back to normal and he seems to be in his element, talking about films. He stops, turns to me, and I'm expecting him to go into one about his hair, but he doesn't. "Hey, Micky, what's the name of the actor in that ghost film, It's A Wonderful Life?"

"James Stewart, I think, but it wasn't a ghost. It was an angel."

He thinks for a minute, before saying, "Hey, you're right." Switching back to the others, he apologises, "Sorry about that. I thought it was a ghost story."

"Do you like films?" asks Jana, searching Tommy's face.

"You bet," he replies. "I love all the martial arts films. Lun said he might show me a few moves." Lun, standing slightly behind him, smiles at us, while raising his eyebrows to the sky. That tells me all I need to know about Tommy and his ambitions. "What's your favourite film?" he asks Jana.

"I don't have a favourite, Tommy. I like most of them; not because they're all good, but going to the cinema gives me a reason to dress up, not that anyone would see me, though."

"You must have a favourite," Tommy insists, but Jana shrugs and shakes her head, and then he looks at me. "What about you?"

"I don't know, really. The Odd Couple, I suppose, or Kelly's Heroes, perhaps."

"I've heard of Kelly's Heroes, but that was a war film. I don't like those."

"It was a comedy, Tommy. Yeah, it was supposed to be a war film but a funny one with Telly Savalas, Clint Eastwood and the funniest of the lot, Donald Sutherland. He was brilliant, standing there on his tank, shouting out and playing music as loud as he could. What was his name now? Er. ... Mmm. ... Jeez, I can't think."

"I once watched Love Story with my boyfriend and ... ." And Affiong stops speaking, a lump in her throat and a tear in her eye. She moves away, putting her hands to her face. Jana goes to her and they walk off together.

"What's up with her?"

"Never mind, Tommy. I think she's coming to terms with being among normal ghosts again, and she's thinking of her past."

"I don't have any sympathy for her. If I was Jana, I'd leave her alone. To tell you the truth, I'd have sent her packing."

"Don't be like that, Tommy. You have to learn to forgive and forget," says Lun, "and if you want me to teach you karate and kung fu, then you'll have to control your emotions."

"But she nearly killed Micky."

"Affiong did no such thing. You must make sure of your facts before opening your mouth."

Tommy glances at Lun and then at me, hoping for support, but I offer none. "Lun's telling the truth. Now, let's leave her alone." Tommy nods his head and goes on about films again.

When the two girls return, Affiong seems much happier. Whatever Jana has said to her has done the trick. She joins in the laughter when we change the subject to television comedies, and some of the ghosts try doing impersonations of famous characters.

A little while later, I leave the others and walk towards the big house. Realising that I can't get in, I consider going back for help. And I'm about to do exactly that, when another ghost, a Villager, is passing by, so I enlist her help instead. Taking my hand, she hoists me in the air and passes me through the window, her arm outstretched. When she releases me, I watch her arm fall back and out of sight. I shout my thanks and sit down with the bedroom book. The book keeps me occupied for some considerable time. It's only when my head starts dropping and my eyes start closing that I decide to strip off and go to bed. Laying my head back, I start thinking about my day.

I'm interrupted by Jana's voice. "What do you think you're doing?" she asks, sitting down beside me. "I thought you'd have waited for me."

"You've got your own room."

"That may be, but I haven't finished with you, yet." I give her a weird look, but she carries on, "I've been thinking about you and that Cathie."

"Give it a rest, Jana."

"No! Why should I?" She looks down my body and moves forward, her hand moving to my groin. I jump up and off the bed. "Micky! Don't be such a spoilsport. If you think I can just forget about you and her, in that field, then you must be off your trolley. You didn't hold back with the description, did you?" I grab my boxers and pull them on, trying to take her mind off sex.

"You're sex mad, Jana."

"No, I'm not, but if you must know, I've been having wet daydreams about you and her, and how I wish it had been me instead. Please, Micky, can we finish what she started?"

"Jana, that was years ago. I was a young man then."

"As far as I'm concerned, it was today, and you're still a young man. A very handsome and virile young man and I can't get your stiffy out of my mind."

"Tough!"

"I'll wait 'til you're asleep then."

"In that case, I'll stay awake."

"Please, Micky?"

"Forget it, Jana. If you want sex that desperately, then go and see Anna and Moira. I'm sure they'll be more accommodating."

"I'm not into women. Okay then, will you let me lie with you?"

"No!"

"Aw, go on ... just for an hour?"

"I don't trust you. As soon as I nod off, you'll be at me."

"I won't, Micky, I promise, and you know ghosts can't break their promises."

"I don't know anything about that."

"Well, they can't."

"On one condition."

"Go on."

"You get me a pair of pyjamas."

"That's impossible."

"Why?"

"Ghosts don't need pyjamas."

"We don't need underwear, either, but we have them."

"We do, actually. Lots of female ghosts wear short dresses and we don't want naughty men being tempted every five seconds."

"Men don't need any, though."

"That's true, so you might as well take them off," she suggests, nodding her head at my boxers. "Mmm, you look tempting, Micky, even in boxers – you know, well developed. Be a sport and let me hold you."

"Not in a million years."

"Listen, Micky. If we're still alive in a million years will you take them off for me then, so we can make love?"

"In a million years? ... Yes! It's a deal."

Then raising her voice, she shouts, "So you'd wait here for a million bloody years, hoping for some other gay to join you – if another gay has a ghost dream that is – rather than make love to me now?"

"That won't happen. Believe me, I'll find one I like."

"You never listen, Micky, do you? I've told you umpteen times that there aren't any gay ghosts."

What will I do? Shit! I'm not going to give in. I can't. "Okay. You can stay with me, but keep your hands to yourself. And I'm leaving my boxers on."

Jana stretches out on the covers and I'm about to join her when another voice asks, "What's all the noise?" Anna is in the doorway, with a black kimono wrapped around her body, and she seems very angry.

"Sorry, Anna," says Jana. "We were having a heated debate, but it's alright now."

"It better had be. And Jana … .?"

"Yes, Anna."

"If the pair of you are having sex, well, keep it quiet."

"We're not," I jump in.

"Yes, Anna," replies Jana, at practically the same time.

When Anna leaves, I glare at Jana, giving her a mistrustful look. Climbing up on the bed, I lie back, staring at the ceiling.

"I'm sorry, Micky. I'm so sorry."

"Stop fretting, and let me get some sleep. And don't forget, Jana … one hour."

"Okay, one hour. Listen, Micky, I've got an idea, and it's so easy. If you pretend that I'm a man, you'd enjoy sex with me then … wouldn't you?"

"You! A man? That'll be the day." Smiling at her, I pull my tongue, and she smacks me across the belly.

After a bit of slap and tickle, with me teasing her, she gives up on the sex angle. We talk for a while, with Jana telling me more about Affiong and her boyfriend. She thinks that Affiong will behave herself and wants to hang around with the two of us, at least until she's fully accepted. Jana coaxes me into letting her put her arms around my body and she kisses my nose. I don't respond.

CHAPTER SEVENTEEN

Moving my arms about the bed, as if still asleep, I can't feel Jana's body anywhere. She's gone ... or has she? Opening my eyes very slowly, I sneak a peek around the room, and true enough she kept her word. My boxers are still in place, constraining Jana's preferred start to the day.

She didn't half get me going last night – winding me up, just for her own satisfaction, and then making me look a pillock in front of Anna. Imagine Jana agreeing with her not to make noise during sex. Well, she didn't get any. Getting off the bed, I make my way to the window and stare out on another new day. Several ghosts are running about and they all seem excited. What the hell is going on? Picking my trousers from the chair, I'm about to pull them on when Jana floats through the door.

"Micky! Hurry up."

"Why? And why are all the ghosts running around like headless chickens?"

"Stan's here."

"Stan? You mean, as in Stan and Ollie?"

"Yes! I mean. ... No! Only Stan has come."

After pulling my pants up as fast as possible, I grab my top and throw it on. My socks and boots soon follow, and then, taking Jana's hand, I drag her through the window.

"Now who's a headless chicken?" she asks, making pecking noises with her lips. We float to the ground where Moira, Anne and Nancy are waiting. "Where is he?" asks Jana. "Micky's so excited, he nearly wet himself."

"He's around somewhere, talking to Anna," says Moira. "Sure, he'll be in to see the class afterwards, so you won't miss him." We stand around gossiping and asking questions of each other. When Tommy and Freda show up, Anne and Jana take us inside where we all sit down to wait. Jana moves to Anna's chair and relaxes, cracking jokes and impersonating our Tutor.

Minutes later, Anna enters, followed closely by Stan Laurel. He doesn't look a day over forty, and is wearing a grey, double-breasted pin-stripe suit and a black bowler hat. We can't take our eyes off him as he approaches the table, his side to side walk and serious, yet funny, expression trying to hold a smile at bay. He cocks his eyebrows several times at Nancy, his right hand reaching behind his head, tipping the bowler slightly forward.

"Are *we* taking class today?" asks Anna, looking directly at Jana.

"If you'd like me to."

Stopping where they are, near the head of the table, Anna says, "No Jana, I don't think so. Ladies and gents, I'd like to introduce a good friend to us all … Stan Laurel."

Stan offers his hand for us to shake but, being too far away, he pulls it back and lifts it to his bowler again, straightening it once more. He searches our faces, turns to Anna and then back again to us, saying, "You sure are a swell bunch. Yes sir." Stan moves his arms about, first to us, then to Jana and Anne, back to us and once again to Anna, now with a huge grin developing from one sticking out ear to the other. "Yes sir. It's nice meetin' ya all." In awe of him, we answer, murmuring our hellos and other greetings of welcome.

"Stop this carry-on," says Anna. "Stan's only a ghost, the same as you." Stan turns to her and pulls off his hat, scratches the top of his head, his fingers extended, and he appears to look puzzled. Both myself and Nancy can't help sniggering. Tommy looks bewildered. Maybe he's never seen Laurel and Hardy in action. Perhaps he's never seen a black and white film. "Stan is going to tell you how he became a ghost. It's not unusual for a famous actor, or actress, to die and return as we have, but in Stan's case the circumstances were somewhat different."

Leaving his bowler on the table, he stands up straight, folding his arms. "She's not kiddin'," he says. "I have my best buddy, Babe, to thank for me being here."

"Who's Babe?" interrupts Tommy.

"Shush," whispers Jana, still in Anna's seat.

"It's okay, Jana. The young man's right. He wouldn't know that I called Ollie … Babe. He'd be here with me 'cept for him fallin' in love with some dame in Ohio. Me and Ollie were together a long time and I cried when he died. I didn't know he was a ghost. It was only later that Ollie told me how he used to visit me when I was sick, but I didn't know. Ollie doesn't mind my tellin' ya all what he did for me … no sir, but it wasn't really him that brought me back." He scratches his head again, looking confused. "I was dying, and, up to the time I became ill, Ollie used me as his regular host. I didn't know, of course. How could I?

198

Anyway, when I became too weak to enter, he realised that he'd never see me again. Ollie started feeling sorry for me, and for himself – so much so that he couldn't be bothered to take the nectar or let the other ghosts help him. Some could see how badly he felt and they were trying to encourage Ollie to enjoy his life and go back to tellin' his funny stories, but he wouldn't. He became so depressed that his ghost life started dwindling away.

"Anna and Jana could tell you more, because they were two of the assisting ghosts, and it was Anna who thought of approaching a Mindbender for help. Anna's a swell dame … yes sir. She persuaded this Mindbender to enter my dying body and try forcing me to dream of becoming a ghost. Anna's idea was that if I came back as a ghost, then Ollie would cheer up and recover his strength. If I'd died without dreaming as I did, then Ollie would have probably died again." First smiling at Anna, he then turns to us again, looking serious, yet content. "You have to understand that I wasn't here when Ollie played jokes and made the ghosts happy. He told me later that he was happy being a ghost at first; that it gave him the chance to visit me, even though I was getting older and sicker by the minute. And I don't exactly know how the Mindbender did it, but, so I'm told, I had a dream of dying and coming back to talk to this white horse with a bowler hat on its head. I know where they got the idea of the dream from, but how the Mindbender managed to implant it in my head … well, it's a miracle. Yes sir … a miracle. Nowadays, me and Ollie are working on plans for a comeback in ghost films, but we're gonna have to get our ideas inside some director's head."

Stan drops his arms, swings them about, and says, "Well, it's been swell talkin' to ya all. Yes sir." He grins his half-moon grin again, puts his bowler on, and sits back in a seat which isn't there. We burst out laughing as he climbs to his feet, looking behind him. Although nothing there, he still dusts himself down, and then raising his face to us, he smiles. "As you can see, I'm not funny all of the time, especially when Ollie's not around, but if any of you would like to dance and sing some of our songs afterwards, then I'll meet you outside."

We nod our heads and talk to him about which songs he wants to sing. Stan asks Nancy about America and Virginia and which part she's from. I think she's taken his fancy, and even Freda, who appears a little jealous, wants to get in on the action.

Presently, Stan leaves on the arms of Jana and Anne, exiting through the door. Anna turns her attention to us, and, when not getting any firm response, tells us to take a break. She helps us through the window and we wait on the seats outside. Several ghosts have gathered, and when Stan and the two ladies come round the corner, we all start singing ... In the Blue Ridge Mountains of Virginia. Stan joins in, followed by the two girls. Tommy just laughs at everyone. We spend some time clowning around, with Stan recalling some of his old films and telling us about all the mistakes they made in their lives. "They weren't all fun times," he says.

Anna makes her presence felt shortly after, coming out to drag us back inside. We say cheerio to Stan, and then do as we're told.

Later in the evening, while lying in bed, I reflect on my day so far. The visit by Stan – the joy it seemed to bring to the other ghosts; his seriousness as well as his humour; and his mindbending story. When he mentioned both Anna and Jana, and the parts they played, especially with it being Anna's idea to use a Mindbender to save Ollie's ghost life, it makes me proud to know them. I'm proud that Anna is my Tutor and that Jana is my Ghost Monitor, and as I hum Blue Ridge Mountains again, I think of Anna and our lesson.

Already knowing most of the info' that she spouted during the day's teachings, I had time to sit back, watch and listen, as Freda, Nancy and Tommy took everything in. Anna went over the drowning aspect first, without once mentioning Plato and his Scribe. I thought she should have, so I told them the story when we finished. The lesson continued with Anna giving the details with regard to using hosts on a long term basis, about our choice of hosts, and the length of time we'd have to stay inside their bodies. I queried the purpose of using a host for a great length of time and, to be fair, she did say that we didn't need to use one if we didn't want to. The main reason is that we'll gain extra time in holding onto our strength and our flying time, plus other added benefits such as extending the abilities of our senses so we can see further and hear better for a longer time and a greater distance. Our senses of feeling will be heightened, and so, too, will our grip when holding things like quills, flowers, and other tools if necessary. We'll be able to hold objects far longer and not so clumsily, because we'll be able to adapt to real life situations while inside the host.

"How long is long term?" I asked her.

"It depends on how long you want to stay inside someone else's body," she replied. And then she went on, "If you stay inside for two years, then that's better than one year; three better than two; and so on. The longer you stay inside … the more time your body will retain its abilities." Tommy looked flustered and asked her to elaborate, so she did. "If you enter a long term host for one year, then you'll have to top up; by that I mean re-enter this or another long term host, every seven years to retain these additional abilities. If you stay in your host for two years, then your retention time is fifteen years; three years is twenty-five years; and it gets forever longer for each year you choose to stay inside your host. Do you get my drift?" she asked.

"What happens if this host is sick, gets sick, or gets injured in some way?" asked Nancy.

"If it's serious" she said, " … get out. Otherwise, you may stay inside. We have a ruling which only concerns the long term host. Once you make a decision to enter a host for this purpose, then you must let us know in advance so we can monitor the situation. When you take the plunge, you'll be given an allowance of sorts. By that I mean … if you are in a host for either one or two years, then you may leave that host once only, for sickness reasons perhaps. If you take a host for three or four years, then you may leave up to three times for similar reasons, and if in a five year host or upwards then your opportunities to leave increase accordingly. But let's be honest," she went on, "what ghost, in their right mind, would want to stay inside some other person, possibly some dipstick, for more than three or four years? You'd have to be loopy. There are other things to consider, and these are … you can go back inside your hosts after their health has restored, but you do have to make up for the lost time. And, also, you can't enter any other host while you are out, or you'll have to start all over again." Tommy's face dropped on hearing this. He'd been passing comments about sick leave, and he hinted that he wouldn't be able to stay inside someone for any length of time. Anna went on, "Anyway, by the time for a top-up, you might have become a Tutor or Gatherer, so you might not feel one is necessary anymore."

Anna warned us about the wrong type of hosts and advised us to use people we know, such as family or friends, particularly if we know them to be fit and not too old. I wondered about my choice of host, and when

Mary came to mind, I rejected her on account of the possibility of Ben manhandling me. I thought of Samantha and rejected her also. And, besides, with her being my niece and having already seen her wedding present, I'd better leave her alone. And what if she comes back as a ghost? She's had the dream, so she says. She'd kill me for having used her in this way. My thoughts went to Joyce and I considered her for quite some time. She has an interesting character but she *is* too flighty, and her liking for the brandy might keep me in a permanent stupor. I'm not sure who I'll choose, but I'll work on it when I'm out and about. I might ask Jana more about the benefits of using a host in this way or whether I should bother with one at all. I mean, it's not as if I'll need any extra time to retain these abilities when I acquire them. I can top up as I choose; wherever or whenever I like. What's the problem with that?

I asked Anna about the tingling sensation that Mary and Sam felt when I kissed them, and she told us that ghosts can affect the living in this way. She also said that nectar causes a stronger sensation within our bodies, and that we can transmit this more effectively to the tender and responsive parts of the living. You should have seen the faces on both Nancy and Freda. Freda was excited, while Nancy seemed to blush. Tommy, on the other hand, looked as if he wanted to play with himself again. I started thinking about Simon and the way he let his mouth cling to mine when he kissed me. One thing's for certain – when I'm topped to the gills with nectar, I'm going out and I'll enjoy giving these tingling sensations time and time again.

As it happened, Anna continued on the nectar theme, explaining its importance to our ghost lives. She told us that the best nectar for ghosts comes from fuchsia, especially the wild flowering type growing with abandon in Ireland. We could, of course, use other bell flowers which will do nearly as well, but the fuchsia, she said, lasted longer and was generally stronger than other flowers. She then gave us a list, with pictures of flowers including bluebells and tulips, and she advised us on other good flowers in different parts of the world – the honeysuckle from the trees of the same name in New Zealand, various flowering cacti in North America, and many of the tubular flowers in Asia and South America.

She went on to tell us that we gain our ability to fly by lying down in shamrock or clover, stressing that shamrock was far better. She also stressed that shamrock and clover give us the ability to pass through walls and other solids. She let it be known that as clover can be found in most countries, then, where necessary, we should use it. Anna explained how shamrock gives ghosts a longer flying time than clover, and that a trip to Ireland is a must.

This, in turn, led to a discussion about worms. "Worms," she said, "are a pain in the neck. We don't know why they are such pests to ghosts, but for some reason or other they can sense when we are lying in the grass. As far as we know, they're the only species that do, and when they come into contact with us they leave a mark on our skin. Admittedly, these marks disappear after a few months, but if you're careless and go lying in fields by yourself then the worms will sense you and slide along your body. They don't penetrate our skin, but they do rub against it. And while lying in shamrock or clover, we have to strip off completely. We must turn around giving the whole of our ghost skin the benefit. And the longer we lie down, the longer our flying time and the better our ability to pass through walls. Also, don't leave your ghost clothes lying on the grass because the worms can slide along these as well, and then, when you put them on, you'll still get the marks. Perhaps, it's due to them being a hermaphrodite species but that's only a guess, and while I might be wrong … I just might be right."

Tommy asked her how we could avoid them, and she said, "One ghost would have to act as a decoy, by luring the worms away to another corner of the field, while the other ghost waits. Then, when it's safe to do so, this second ghost can lie down while the worms are kept busy. Once their senses are activated by the first ghost, the worms will follow that particular ghost and his, or her, movements, and we've proved from experience that they don't fall back to the second ghost unless the first one stops acting as the decoy." We all looked worried by this revelation. "You'll enjoy the experience" she laughed, "of trying to keep the worms chasing you. You'll be hopping up and down, attracting them to one corner and then moving twenty feet to attract them again, and so on, keeping them busy while your friend gains flying time. Once you see them coming to the surface, you'll have to move fast, and I mean … fast," she added. "When you're out in the countryside, you should sit on stones, walls, or anything other than grass. The worms won't bother you then." Nancy and Freda looked aghast at the whole idea, while Tommy had changed his tune. He made it known that the excitement of being a decoy appealed to him. Well, think about it, he's still only a kid, isn't he?

It surprised the rest of us when Freda asked whether any people had come back as worms. We laughed at the idea and Anna then told us she assumed some people had. She went on to explain about the cycle of life, which Simon had mentioned to me. Famous names, both bad and good, cropped up, and at the mention of Hitler, Anna laughed again. "He's a dung beetle and, as far as I'm aware, he'll keep coming back as a dung beetle." This drew a round of applause. Anna went on to tell us that nasty people always get their comeuppances in the end. We asked her about warmongers and murderers, hard working people and the greedy, and her answer was that unless they had dreamt of being a ghost, they'd return in a form befitting their life. She gave an example, saying that those who acquired their wealth at the expense of others always seemed to return as worker ants. Other than that, she didn't say much else on the subject. Tommy wasn't about to let this drop, though, and mentioned Genghis Khan, to which she replied, "Dung beetle, despite his widespread DNA."

And it went on, with Tommy asking, "Richard the Third?"

"Dung beetle."

"Joan of Arc?"

"Jeanne d'Arc is among us. She's a ghost."

With the exception of Tommy, we showed our surprise, while he seemed intent on pursuing his own agenda. "Harry S. Truman?"

"Tommy," she said, "go and read your bedroom book. We could go on all year answering questions like this. Now, let's think about getting finished for the day."

Anna told us that our trip to the west of Ireland is imminent; either tomorrow or the day after. Some ghosts, she said, were going with us to top up their strength and bring back supplies. She even hinted that we should help once we've sampled the fuchsia.

Tommy queried this, thinking that his learning to be a ghost, the sucking of nectar from fuchsia, and the lying in shamrock, was all that he needed before going out on his own. Anna, however, informed us that we have to go through a test of some sort – writing the full requirements of a ghost and what has been learnt to date. Furthermore, she made us aware that we were still being monitored until this test is over. We have to prove our throwing and carrying abilities, our senses of seeing and hearing, and then prove that we can give life if required. Anna said that unless we fulfilled these obligations, then we'd only be of use to ourselves and not be in a position to help the ghost community as a whole. In the end, she said, the choice was our own.

Before we left, she told us that once we'd acquired all of our basic abilities, then we could, if we wanted, go on a haunting trip and then visit some of the Dreamers. This information was music to Tommy's ears, and any thoughts he had of doing a disappearing act soon vanished.

CHAPTER EIGHTEEN

"Hey, Micky, get your lazy backside out of bed."

"Give us a break, Jana. I haven't had a proper lie in since the day I met you."

"Oh, yes you have."

"When, may I ask?"

"Not long ago, and you had nearly a whole day's rest, as I recall, in some swish hotel in Munich."

"Uh?"

"Don't you remember the last time you let me have your body?"

"In that penthouse? You practically raped me."

"I seem to remember you enjoying the occasion, and you didn't try to stop me, did you? Now, shift. We're leaving today and we've got people to see and say goodbye to."

"What's the big deal? For goodness sake, we're coming back."

"Some of the ghosts might not be here when we return, and, anyway, it's good manners. Don't you realise that the ghosts have taken a liking to you, even if you do think you're gay. Those that know don't treat you any differently, do they?"

"I suppose not."

"And that's a far cry from the attitude adopted to gays in the living population. My god, Micky, most people don't accept gays, and when they do hear of them, like that gay bishop or vicar – whatever he is, there's an outcry, like it's some kind of mortal sin."

"Are you saying that you don't mind me being gay?"

"Sort of, but you're not really 'gay' … gay. You know what I mean?"

Pulling myself from the bed, I stretch my arms before sitting on the edge again. "You're a funny old girl."

"Watch it you … less of the old. Only I'm allowed to make those jokes."

"Ha! Ha! Just as if. You're convinced that if I had my time over again, and met the right girl, then I'd have been straight. Aren't you?"

"More than likely. I figure that it depends on whether she grew a moustache or not." Jana laughs, folds her arms and relaxes, deliberately flashing her eyes up and down.

"You seem happy this morning. What happened? Did you sleep with

Stan last night, by any chance?"

"Now that's something worth thinking about." Her hand goes to her chin, and her face takes on a look of concentration. "Hmm ... . No, I don't think so, although Stan and I have shared some moments."

"Did you ever sleep with him?"

"Of course not. I don't know who he shares his bed with, if anyone. And, even if I wanted to, it's too late this time round. He left last night."

"I thought you knew everything about all the ghosts, especially in this village."

"In this village, yes, I've a good idea, but Stan spends most of his time in America, and powerful as my senses are, they're not that good."

"But word gets round."

"Yes it does, but we didn't know anything about Affiong and her life, did we?"

"Affiong wasn't famous, though."

"That maybe so, but don't you think we'd have heard something, especially with her being one of the gang of nymphomaniacs that threatened our lives? We all have secrets of some kind, but if we keep our mouths shut, who'll find out? ... Nobody!"

"Yeah, you're right," I sigh. Jana crosses to the bed and sits beside me, wrapping one arm around the small of my back and placing her other hand on my lap.

Quietly, she says, "I've found a new pair of boxers for you. The latest fashion, Micky – you know, tight where it matters."

"That's nice. Now, what's on your mind?"

"Nothing, Micky. Nothing really."

"Is there anything else worth trying on?"

"Me," she smiles.

"I'll say this for you, Jana, you never give up. You're right, you know."

"About what?"

"If you'd been my girlfriend that last time, when I made my choice, I'd probably have chosen girls instead of boys, but would you have settled down with me?"

"Micky! What a beautiful thing to say?" Very quickly, she lifts her head and plants a smacker on my lips, her hand just as quickly moving to my crotch. I'm about to push it away, but she's quicker, taking my hand again and this time pulling me with her, up and off the bed. "It's a pity but we haven't got time for that. Anyway, we need to conserve our energy. And talking of energy, we have to get down to the flower shop this morning."

"But I thought we had some nectar in the village?"

"There's hardly any left. The ghosts transporting Dorothy and Helga made a feast of it. I hope to hell that the shop has enough fresh flowers, or we'll be searching the houses. It's a bad time of year, Micky. Now, if you lot had died a few months earlier we'd have had no problem. People were giving flowers for presents at Christmas. Not to worry, though. We'll stop on the way if we have to." I nod my head, and then she playfully smacks my bum. "Now get your arse in gear." Crossing the room to the chest of drawers, she slides her hands through the wood and pulls out a pair of boxers, specially shaped. She brings them over and drops them on the bed. Turning around, she grabs the ones I'm wearing and pulls them down. Well, that is, she tries to, but I've anticipated her move and am holding the waist band very tightly. Jana leans her head back. "You don't think, for one minute, that you can stop me?"

"You won't be seeing my tackle for a long time."

Jana, still gripping my underwear, says, "You mean sod. I searched everywhere for these and you won't give me the pleasure of putting them on."

"I didn't ask you to, did I? Now leave me alone and turn around ... and keep away from the mirror."

"Right," she says, and then, quick as a flash, she pulls violently, ripping my boxers to shreds. I'm left holding the waistband as Jana drops the torn bits on the floor, her face moving closer to my body, her hands reaching out, and I leg it across and behind the bed. Lifting my eyes just above the mattress, I notice her picking up the new pair and then rolling towards me. "Come on, Micky ... be a sport."

"No! I'll do without them."

"I'll tell the others."

"You wouldn't do that. You wouldn't risk our friendship."

With that, she lies back, tossing the boxers at my head. "You win, Micky, and, no, I wouldn't spoil what we have. You're like a breath of fresh air and the best thing to happen to me for a long time." Still hunched down behind the bed, I turn my back and slip the boxers up my legs. I have some difficulty trying to manoeuvre myself into them and only notice Jana at the last second, moving quickly above me and looking down. "I love it when you squeeze them like that," she says, just as I'm pushing my tackle into place. Her watching me, reminds me of me watching Simon, and I smile at the thought.

And her watching me reminds of something else. "Oddball!"

"They look fine from here," she says. "I'll check them out if you're worried."

"I don't mean me. Oddball was Donald Sutherland's nickname in that film I was on about."

"You *do* have a funny way of remembering things, don't you? Now, stop playing with yourself and get dressed, or I'll come over there and give you a ball or two to think about."

Shortly after, we head downstairs, and I'm newly kitted out in another blue top and a pair of black trousers. I've kept my boots – I like them, and Jana has found me a leather jacket. I still can't quite believe how well ghosts can dress. The choice seems limitless.

We spend the rest of the morning going from house to house saying our farewells. And after some playful warnings regarding leprechauns and some brief instruction from Anna in the correct manner to suck nectar, we take flight in a south-westerly direction. Stopping en route at a flower shop in Liptovský Mikuláš, for the first time as ghosts we newcomers start sucking from flowers. We're not alone, of course, as Jana and our other escorts top up their own strength.

Soon after, I'm flying along in the careful hands of Jana. I turn my head to the others. Anne Boleyn has Tommy in tow, Nancy and Moira seem to be joined at the hip, and Lucia is taking care of Freda. Affiong, who is in need of an energy boost, is tagging along with Petra, while Maggie flies alone. We fly for about an hour, over snowy hills and frozen streams, tiny villages and slow moving cars, eventually reaching the outskirts of Bratislava where we make another stop for nectar. We spend little time in the capital before heading off again, west across Austria. Jana explains that by heading towards France, we are likely to encounter warmer weather and greener pastures. The scenery, she implies, will give a lift to our spirits.

It seems to take forever, and I can't, for the life of me, understand why we didn't take an aeroplane. On we go, passing over Innsbruck, Liechtenstein, and then over the border into Switzerland. I think about the time and how dark it has become, and another thought crosses my mind. I don't know what date it is, or even the day of the week. Time has elapsed by the minute, the hour, and the day, and I haven't really considered it since the Friday I was buried.

Once over the mountains, Jana points out Lucerne and tells me that we're stopping for the night. She turns and signals with a shrill whistling noise for the others to follow. Minutes later, the rest of us are waiting outside a hotel while Lucia and Maggie go in search of some empty rooms. Their return, soon after, brings good news, so we make our way inside.

Maggie joins me and Jana in one room, while the other eight split up equally. At long last, she tells me of her plans to fly by Aer Lingus from Paris to Shannon. I was beginning to think we were flying to Ireland under our own steam. Thankfully, having Maggie in the room keeps Jana sexually inactive, both verbally and physically, and I'm more than happy to use the floor as my bed.

Early the next morning, we're up and outside and still waiting for Tommy and Lucia to make an appearance. When they *do* pass through the hotel wall, he's in a bedraggled state and still pushing his shirt into his jeans, while our ghostly friend Anne throws her head back laughing. "I haven't had so much fun in years," she says.

"Why? What happened?" asks Maggie.

Freda looks embarrassed, while Anne explains. "Think about it … three naked females, all gagging for it, and one naked young man with a horn that won't go down. What would you do?"

"You didn't?" whispers Maggie.

"We did. I'm surprised you didn't hear us."

"But he'll be too knackered to fly," Maggie suggests.

"It's me you should be worried about. He doesn't have to do the donkey work," says Anne.

Lucia bids us good day, Tommy just grunts, and, soon after, we soar into the sky and make our way over the Swiss-French border. As we cross the green fields of France, I notice only the odd hint of frosty white patches as the snow melts away. Eventually, we reach the outskirts of Paris, and the Eiffel Tower comes into view. Beneath us, I recognise the area known as Marne-la-Vallée Chessy, with Disneyland at its centre, and thoughts of Mary and Samantha enter my head. Jana smiles, lowers us down, and we do a couple of fly-overs, watching some of the morning's visitors enjoy themselves. Not for long though, as we're soon heading on towards the airport.

Once there, we find we have an hour to wait, so I take a walk around the place. My interest is taken by the fashion boutiques, the many passengers waiting for their flights, and, needless to say, the attractive appearance of the young men. It's only when Jana grabs me that I realise that I've overstayed my time exploring. Hastily, she takes my hand, flying me through the wall, above and across the tarmac, and onto our flight. Some of the others have a dig at me for going missing. However, we do take off on time and spend a couple of hours on board the fairly empty aeroplane.

Arriving in Shannon, we break off from the travel to take in the Irish air. And it's just as well, because the wind and rain seem to be blowing everything everywhere.

"Don't you feel the difference?" asks Moira.

"The difference in what?" asks Nancy.

"The atmosphere of the place. That feeling of being laid back. Most of the people, over here, are laid back. It's that kind of life. We Irish don't hurry unless it's to our advantage. Every country has its own pace, and we have ours."

"Yeah! Dead slow and stop, unless it's to the pub," chuckles Lucia.

"Now, we're not that bad, I'll have you know. We're damned hard workers. Who do you think built all the roads in the likes of England? The Irish, of course," says Moira, answering her own question.

"They weren't all Irish," I contradict. "If you must know, nowad ... ."

"Don't you be interrupting me, Micky. It mightn't be the same now, with all the new labour and all that, but we're still the same people."

"Shush!" orders Jana. "Let's just wind down for a while, at least until this storm is over."

Presently, we head off and race towards Achill. I say race, because Petra has laid down a challenge as to which of us will be the first to reach the megalithic tombs. I sail through the air with Jana. The other Monitors look after their charges while Maggie still flies alone. Jana is fast ... very fast, yet Anne Boleyn and Tommy still have us in their sights as we cross over hill and dale, mountain and stream, and several small towns. The trouble is that if I blink, I'll miss half a mile or so of land, and this misty weather isn't helping either.

We seem to have left the rest behind and I'm sure we're going to win, and, for me, it will be the first time that I've ever won anything, albeit with the aid of a partner. As we fly over a small town, Jana slows down and says, "Castlebar! Do you fancy a Big Mac?"

Laughing at her, while the wind flies through my face, I answer, "I didn't like them before and I don't need one now."

"Don't look so serious, Micky. It won't be much longer. Achill's only round the corner."

"Are you sure?"

"Of course I am. We've only about sixty kilometres to go."

"That's not round the corner, Jana. That's nearly forty miles."

"That's nothing compared to the distance we've just flown. Now, hold tight and watch me fly." And with that, Jana goes into overdrive and my arm is nearly pulled out of its socket. A few minutes later, she shouts, "Newport! ... Achill next stop."

Believe me, I'm shit scared. Actually, that says it all, and I'm only thinking this when the sky goes black. We drive ourselves into a heavy rain storm and, almost immediately, the wind picks up. Jana slows ... and slows, dropping gradually out of the sky.

"Are we there?" I shout.

"No! Not yet. The rain I can handle, but it's this bloody wind," she replies.

"Aw, don't stop me now, Jana. We've got to get there first."

"No, Micky. We're too near the coast and we might get blown over the water. I don't fancy being brought down in these conditions. Don't you remember our flight to London?"

"But we're winning," I plead.

"I'd rather stay alive than win a stupid race." I'm disappointed, yet I know that she's right. While the wind grows ever stronger, we get slower, and I become even more dejected when Petra and Affiong pass us by. Petra slows down to Jana's pace and after a few words between them, herself and Affiong are off again. About five minutes of slow flying leads us over a bridge, and then Jana forges on over some houses, fields and bog-land. In seconds we are floating down towards Petra and Affiong who are sitting among the megalithic tombs.

"Hi, Micky," says Petra. "Welcome to Achill Island and Slievemore Mountain."

"Oh, hi," I answer through the rain, still wishing we'd won.

"Snap out of it, Micky," urges Jana. "We'll beat them home, don't you worry."

"Fat chance of that," says Petra.

"Okay ... okay," I say. "This is ridiculous. Why the hell did you want to meet here, of all places? It's not exactly the most comfortable place to meet. And it's still pissing down."

"Rain doesn't bother us, though, does it? But, there again, the rain will bring the worms up," says Petra.

"Ugh! I hate worms." Affiong's face squirms while saying this. "I hate being the bait for them. They're so slimy, and having to jump around trying to avoid them gives me the creeps."

"Don't be such a wimp," says Petra, eyeing Affiong. "You've been a ghost far too long for them to bother you." Looking at me, she says, "They don't hurt us, Micky. They only leave marks."

"I know," says Affiong. "I had them all over my face once. It was horrible, and it took ages for the scars to disappear."

"Why your face?" asks Jana, looking surprised.

"It was Helga's fault. We'd had an argument about . .... Oh, it really doesn't matter, but she wanted to teach me a lesson. She and Dorothy held me down with my face on the grass. They got marks on their hands, but they didn't care. I couldn't face anyone for a long time after that, and those two just made fun of me."

"So, why didn't you leave them then?" I ask.

"I would have, but I didn't want to be on my own," replies a sorry sounding Affiong.

"What's with the tombs?" I ask.

"They're historical, Micky," Jana replies. "Some of the early ghosts were of pagan origin, and with this being a pagan burial site we make it a rendezvous point. Some of the pagan ghosts are still alive, but they're not from around here and we don't know whether this is a change-over place or not. We've never been attacked in Achill, but that means nothing. As I said before, bad ghosts tend to hang around the villages and they are far too lazy to travel." Jana takes a quick glance at Affiong, before adding, "I think Affiong has changed, though."

"Hello there, we've got company," Petra informs us. We turn and watch Tommy, Anne and Maggie swoop down. On landing, the girls greet each other with a bit of banter. Shortly after, the others arrive, and, now reunited, we make our way down the mountain, over a graveyard, and then pass over an old deserted village. We make a quick left turn, go up and over a hill, and then down to a row of new houses.

"Well, Micky, here we are. We'll be sharing a house with Lucia and Freda. They'll have one bedroom and we'll use the other."

"Why? There are enough houses for a room each, or a house each if it comes to that." I'm not trying to be funny, but I'd like some privacy.

"No can do, Micky. Other ghosts come and go, and some of the owners live here."

"You'd better leave me alone, then."

"Spoilsport."

"No, I'm not."

"Yes, you are. Hey?"

"What's up?" She can tell how disgruntled I am.

"Next time, Micky, you can go on top."

"Jana! That's enough."

"I'm only teasing."

We say no more until we're inside the house, and only then to organise which bedrooms we are using. Going to the window, I notice lights going on in some of the houses, and looking to the sky all I can see is darkness. Lucia comes up behind me, saying, "Are you ready for a night on the town, Micky?"

"What are you on about? Where's there to go around here ... dancing with the fish?"

"Don't be silly. They have a disco in one of the pubs. It's a gas, and there are usually plenty of young men." Suddenly, the idea appeals, so I nod my reply.

"It's not for me," says Jana. "You three go along. I'm going to bed."

"I be tired as Jana," says Freda. "Me want sleep."

"You're very wise, Freda," says Jana. "These two can flirt around as much as they want to. And Micky?"

"Uh-huh."

"Be careful, and don't lose sight of Lucia. She's apt to wander when someone takes her eye."

"Leave him alone. If I fancy a bit of the other, then someone else can bring him back."

"Just make sure he's safe."

"Of course, I will. You know I'm not irresponsible," snaps Lucia.

It's not long before Lucia and I venture forth to a disco unknown … at least for me. Instead of flying, Lucia grabs my hand, swinging me down past the row of houses, and then we turn right onto a main road which has ditches and grass for pavements. We reach a tiny village with only a couple of shops. Houses, through the dim light, are set back off the road, and as we come to the bottom of a hill, the lights and noise from one of the pubs seem to liven up the place.

We carry on, however, through the village and down towards the ocean. Sitting down on some rocks, we look towards the harbour and notice the fishermen sorting out their nets and cleaning their boats. Lucia suggests that it might be best for me to gain some flying time and I'm not about to argue. On her instructions, I sit where I am until she shouts. Lucia walks off, stamping her feet on the ground. Minutes later, her voice comes over, telling me to lie down, so I strip off my clothes and do as I'm told. It seems funny, watching her jump about while I spend the best part of an hour turning over and over in the grass. It must have shamrock in it or why bother, but, for the life of me I can't see a thing with the darkness closing in around me.

Presently, when Lucia makes her way in my direction, I jump up and pull my clothes back on. "Try flying, Micky." And I do. Very slowly, I float up in the air and hover for a few seconds. "Don't overdo it," she says. I'll be honest. I'm surprised that I can fly at all given the length of time I was lying down, and I thank her on my return to earth. She insists on me experimenting with the worms so I follow her around, hopping all over the place.

Shortly after, we leave the field and fly back to the village. We enter a pub called The Drunken Duck, which has a huge oil painting in the foyer of, would you believe, a duck. Lucia smiles as she pulls me on past the few locals inside. She points to a wall and encourages me to walk through it, unaided. I do so, and she's right behind me as we enter a disco. Huge banners advertising a leap year party are positioned over the bar and near the door. The coloured lights that are bouncing around to the music give the room a lively atmosphere, but the scarcity of customers has the opposite effect. Either, we're very early or they start dancing very late.

Lucia insists on dancing with me and won't take no for an answer, so I'm stuck in the middle with her while a few girls giggle in a corner. A couple of lads are drinking beer at the bar while four others sit round one of the few tables available. The only others present are the two staff – one, a girl serving behind the bar, and the other, a man in his late twenties who is waiting by the door to take the entrance money. All the while I'm looking, Lucia bounces me around, not giving me a chance to relax.

Eventually, I persuade her to let me sit down and she joins me, away from the bar area. Approximately ten minutes later, Petra, Affiong, Tommy, Nancy and Moira show up, with the latter talking to another person – a man, in his fifties, with a broad Irish accent. She introduces him, and this ghost, Séan, is full of himself and can't stop cracking jokes. His hands are everywhere. That is, he has them all over the women – on their knees; feeling their thighs; touching and rubbing their bums; and taking liberties with their boobs when he can. Lucia smacks him away, each and every time, telling him off and poking him in his chest with force enough to hurt. Moira, on the other hand, eggs him on. Petra couldn't care less, but Nancy seems nervous. Tommy has little to say and, like Affiong and myself, watches the carry on around us. Séan completely ignores Affiong, however, and I don't know whether it's because he knows about her nympho days or whether he's racist in any way. I doubt it's the latter, because I can't imagine that kind of behaviour being tolerated in the ghost world.

Later on, I mention this to Petra and she tells me that Séan isn't in the least bit racist, although he is wary of Affiong having heard about her recent exploits. Petra tells me more about him and how much of a womaniser he is, and she reckons that before long even Affiong will be catching his eye. Some of the girls go dancing and Séan joins them, trying to waltz Moira off her feet to rock music, and then falling all over himself while tangoing with the taller Petra. He doesn't seem to have a care in the world and has the rest of us in stitches.

The disco gets busier, yet still not crowded, and now and then I watch the door and the people coming in. One young man takes my attention. He looks heavenly, and when the flickering lights hit his face, I fall in love again. What the hell ... why am I dead? As this guy walks across the dance floor, with two of his mates by his side, he stops and looks straight at me. I stand up and lock my eyes on his body. "He's a ghost!"

I say, quietly, but Affiong has heard.

"He's not, Micky, and he's not looking at you. Now sit down before you make a fool of yourself." I don't want to sit, and I don't believe her. She grabs my arm, but I pull away and edge toward this handsome young man. He still has his eyes on mine, so I reach out, putting my hand, very gently, on his face … and my hand goes through his skin.

At that precise moment, the man walks straight through me and I turn to see him shaking like a leaf. His arm hits that of another man, knocking this guy's beer from his hand and over his clothes. The second, and now very wet, young chap lashes out, knocking my fellow down. On seeing this, several other lads join in – some saying it was all an accident while others steam in with their fists. Soon after, some girls get involved, while others try separating the brawling crowd.

I don't get the chance to move as they rush through me, but then I feel a pair of hands guiding me to the far wall, well away from the bedlam I caused. Looking back at the crowd, I see that Séan is still in the thick of it, swinging away to his heart's content, not hitting a thing or anybody, his fist and arm disappearing every time he lands a blow on someone, and all the time he is laughing and yelling, and in his element.

The next thing we see is … nothing. All the lights go out, and Lucia, who is my saviour once again, pushes me backwards through the wall. Once outside, we walk to the front of the building where the pub lights are still on. Slipping inside, past the picture of the duck once again, we both notice that the customers are fully aware of the commotion round the back. Some are laughing, while others are concerned that their Johnny, Anthony or Fiona are in trouble. We're soon joined by Nancy and Petra who tell us that the lights are back on and the fighting has stopped. Petra goes back for the others, but she soon returns with the news that everybody is happy and that if we don't hurry up then we'll miss the spectacle of our lives.

We're off in a flash, up in the air and through the wall, and once inside the disco I am taken by the scene in front of me. My handsome young man is standing at the end of a long arch of arms. All the young men on one side and girls on the other are standing with their arms aloft and the tips of their fingers touching those of the person opposite, while a young girl, no more than twenty, is walking under and through the human tunnel towards my man. She reaches him, blood on his lip, and

217

kneels down. She then asks, *"Martin, darling ... will you marry me?"*

Then it dawns on me. This same young girl was sitting in the corner behind us, and it was she he was staring at. I feel such a fool for causing all the mayhem, but I'm happy for them both, and then my ears hear the young man reply, *"I'd love to."*

All the women, including Jana, Petra, Lucia and Nancy start shouting, *"Ring! Ring! Ring! Ring!"* and they keep on shouting until the girl places a ring on the man's finger. I'd never heard of a man wearing an engagement ring, but I suppose there's always a first time for everything. When the girl stands up, both she and her Martin kiss, and the first person to congratulate him is the guy he had the fight with in the first place. When it's all over, we head back to the houses.

Lucia, not having copped off, tries her best to tempt my mind and body, pushing me back on the settee, but she's out of luck. She still manages to kiss me quick and pinch my bum before I make my way upstairs. It's so nice not needing anyone else to hold my hand. You know ... that feeling of independence. I can tell you that it's been a long and tiring day, and, once in bed, I relax, closing my eyes thinking about Martin ... and how unlucky for me that he's not a ghost.

CHAPTER NINETEEN

I can't get over the views from the top of this mountain. The rain has stopped. Well, to tell the truth, it hasn't started yet, so I'm taking advantage of the situation. Our new ghostly acquaintance, Séan, had forecast a fine day today and so far, although it's early, he's right. At least, now that I have the ability to pass through walls unaided, I can do a little exploring by myself. On the other hand, Séan did say that he often spends time up here when the sun is out and the thought of having someone new to speak to appeals to me. I can't imagine what the locals do to pass the day at this time of year. Being so used to towns and cities, I think it would bore me rigid after a while.

And speaking of the locals, I'm watching one this very minute, and I could swear he's watching me except that his binoculars keep moving slowly from side to side. Turning my head around, I cast a glance behind and see a few heavy-bellied sheep going through the motions of chewing on the grass. By the looks of it, it won't be long before these give birth, and on turning my eyes back to the man and his binoculars I realise that it's the sheep he's counting. Why the hell would anyone be bothered to count their sheep – unless, of course, it's for the EU subsidy? He drops his binoculars and starts counting on his fingers, occasionally scratching his head, and then he writes something down. He lifts his head once more and checks in another direction, pointing and counting again. How does he know which ones are his bloody sheep? He can't be the only farmer around here ... surely? That wouldn't make sense.

Standing up, I look immediately ahead of my body expecting to see my shadow, but I don't have one. Other than the day I went ski-jumping, sunshine has been in short supply, and on that particular day my mind was on other things as you well know. It's such a great feeling being able to fly by myself after only an hour in a field, and yet I know I'll have to spend a lot longer avoiding worms to increase my flying time. I'm so close to being a ghost in entirety and then I won't have to rely on others for assistance, and since sucking nectar from the flowers, my senses have sharpened considerably. Yes, I had noticed the difference, but being here, on my own, has given me the time to think.

Prior to taking the nectar, I couldn't see as far or as clearly as I can now. And looking up again, my eyes take in the picture of Keel Lake and, beyond it, the Atlantic Ocean stretching out on its way to America. Gazing out at this great blue sea, with the sunshine dancing on the water, a fishing boat comes into view from behind the cliffs of Minuan, and I follow its left to right path as it heads for the village of Keel and Purteen harbour. It was one thing to watch the fishermen emptying and cleaning their boats yesterday evening, but you wouldn't catch me in one. I didn't mind travelling on cross-channel ferries or cruise ships, but I couldn't spend time in a small boat, going ever so slowly up and down with the swell. I tried it a couple of times and threw up a couple of times. That is, I started throwing up from the time the boats left dock and didn't bloody stop until I was back on dry land. The first time was when I was a young boy and the second when in my early twenties, and I vowed after that second time ... never again. There has to be easier ways to make a living.

While looking down at the boat as it nears the harbour, two other movements catch my eye. The sheep farmer has put away his abacus ... I mean his fingers, and is climbing into his battered old red car, and two ghosts are flying in my direction. Seconds later, Jana and Moira glide down towards me.

Jana moves forward, first hugs and then kisses me on both cheeks, whispering, "Why did you sneak out without me, you naughty boy?" She smiles while slowly pulling away.

"And good morning to you, too," I reply. I then turn to Moira. "And a good morning to you, too, Moira. Did you sleep well?"

"Indeed I did, Micky. Indeed, I did. And what got you up so early, this fine morning?"

"Exactly that," I reply. "As soon as I opened my eyes, the sight of the sunshine pouring through the window seemed to give me a new lease of life. So, here I am, in such a perfect place on a perfect day."

"Well, looking at you from a distance, you cut a fine figure of a man standing here on top of the world."

"I wouldn't call it Mount Everest."

"Maybe not, Micky, but you're on top of Achill's little world." Turning to Jana, she says, "And if I were you, I wouldn't be letting this man out of your sight. There's many a ghost would like to get their hands on him, myself included. You're a mighty lucky woman, Jana. Mighty lucky!" – If I didn't know better, I'd say that Moira is a tad jealous of Jana, but why? Surely, she knows about me by now, and, even if she doesn't, I doubt that Jana has told anyone about our little fling.

Jana takes my hand and pulls me towards the huge stones where we sit down. Moira sits at my other side and we engage in small talk, discussing the scenery, last night's shenanigans at The Drunken Duck, and our plans for the rest of the day. Moira suggests a day in Westport and climb up Croagh Patrick, but Jana insists that we spend our time in Achill due to the weather and the likelihood of it changing back to its normal mist and rain.

"Besides," she says, "I'm sure Micky would like to strip off and take in the goodness of the shamrock while the sun is out."

"I'd like that," I answer, "and I might as well explore the island while I have the chance."

"Ar-agh, you'll have plenty of time for that, so you will. You'll be here for the next six to eight weeks, at least. That's more than enough time to be taking the green stuff, so what's the hurry?"

"Moira! If Micky wants to relax, then let him be," replies Jana, now glaring at Moira with a deliberate show of resistance and protection. "If you want to piss off to climb Croagh Patrick, well, go on then, but don't forget to take your bloody shoes off when you do."

"Okay! Don't get your knickers in a twist. I'm not going on my own, and, anyway, it was only a suggestion." Moira then adds, "You forget that I lived and died here, and I know the place like the back of my hand. Ah, you're right I suppose, and a tour of the island wouldn't be a bad thing."

"What was it like here, back then?" I ask her.

"Sure, a lot of the old stone houses are gone and new ones built; just like the ones we're staying in." Jana leans forward, plants her elbows on her knees and rests her head in her hands, staring out on the ocean, while Moira carries on. "I've watched people leave here in their droves; all looking for work. You know how life is. Micky, once you're trained and flying on your own you'll want to know how your family and friends are, and it was just the same with me. I come to Achill very often and it's not only for the fuchsia and shamrock." I nod my head in understanding. "I remember when the blasted potato crops failed and so many people died. Some were saved by changing their religion and … "

"Huh?" I interrupt, and Jana turns to her, also surprised by Moira's statement. "What's religion got to do with it?" I ask.

"Religion had nothing to do with the crops failing. It was only our complacency and ignorance in not doing crop rotation, and the soil became useless to us. We'd started getting lazy and became reliant on supplies from other parts of Ireland. Our fisherman, too, didn't work as hard as they once did, and what was caught was shared between their families and friends, and not much was left for anyone else. The British – sorry Micky, I don't mean you personally, but this was back then you understand – well, they didn't like the continual trouble from the Irish and they were determined to set an example. So, they drove the fighting Irish into the south and west of the country, and then decided to prevent the new food chain from getting through. It wasn't an attack against the ordinary working families, but more a way to prevent the fleeing Irish fighters from getting food. This was going on for quite some time between the late 1700's and through the 1800's, so farmers, like my family, were trying to get more from the land than we could, and, as I said, we farmed the land badly. Our problem lay in the fact that Achill is an island, and at that time there was no bridge between us and the mainland, so our suffering was obvious.

"However, when the Reverend Nangle showed up and started his soup kitchen in Dugort – just down there," she points at a small village to the left of us, "he insisted on the people joining his church and renouncing their Catholic faith, just so they could get a meal. Being a man of the cloth, so to speak, he managed to get supplies through, but we ordinary people couldn't. Well, anyway, quite a lot of us wouldn't give up our faith … and why should we? It was blackmail, and we were more afraid of not going to Heaven and the retribution from Our Lord than we ever were of dying from starvation. Some changed faith and, as I found out later, they changed back again afterwards. If I'd known then what I know now, I'd have done the same, and I'd have made sure everyone else knew. Those that could afford it sent a member, or two, of their families to America, England and other countries. Some even went to the Far East; to Singapore and places like that. Religion and politics have an awful lot to do with a person's suffering, let me tell you. Sure, there are families here, now, that are part one religion, part another, and some have no religion at all. Looking back, I can see what an awful bloody mess it all was … . What do *you* think?" she asks, staring at Jana.

"I never had religion. Well, perhaps I did, but I was too young to understand everything, and I was only just learning about Saints' Days when I went into service with you-know-who." Jana casts a glance at each of us. "When I was a child, my parents would tell me about Jesus and God, Heaven and Hell, and Satan. I enjoyed the stories about Jesus' life, but not his death, and I accept that he might have existed, but not in the way people have portrayed him. I don't believe in the so-called miracles he supposedly performed, although I did then. You know what? I don't believe in any of the others at all – not in God, Satan, nor Heaven or Hell. As far as I'm concerned, none of them exist, and I'm sure we're all agreed on that point."

Moira nods her head, but I don't. "I believe in heaven and hell, but not in the way you might think."

"Micky, you told me you didn't believe in God. So, have you changed your mind?"

"No, Jana, not at all. Don't get me wrong. I still don't believe in God, but I do accept the fact that an ordinary man called Jesus once lived. However, I also believe that heaven and hell exist."

"That's bloody stupid," says Moira, looking at me as if I'm stupid. "Wait a minute. Here comes Séan. He's still religious, so I'm sure he'd like to hear this crackpot idea of yours."

When Séan lands beside us, we say our hellos and then Moira fills him in on our discussion. He looks at me, scratches his head in much the same way as Stan Laurel, and then sits down, saying, "If ya must know, Micky, I do believe in God and everythin' else, and that we ghosts are just his way of creatin' an in-between life of some kind. I don't understand it but, to me, there has to be a creator of some kind. Now, will ya tell us how ya can believe in one damn thing and not the other? Ya can't separate them. Either God exists, and with him, Heaven, and so too does the blasted Devil and his fiery Hell. But ya can't be havin' these two places, as yourself says, without having God and that other rotten shite."

Jana lies back on the slab of rock, and turning to me, she smiles, winks, and says in Mrs Doyle fashion, "Ah, go'wan, go'wan. Will'ya not tell us where heaven is, Micky? Will'ya not?"

"I will if you give me half a chance. In the first place, heaven and hell aren't places that people can go to or come from. They're only words."

"My God! Will ya listen to the man? He's a mahogany gas pipe if ever I heard one. Sure, he must be. His head's full of ridiculous ideas."

I'm about to reply when he shouts off again. "Of course Heaven and Hell are places, Mick, whether ya believe in them or not. If ya don't believe, then ya still know where they're supposed to be in the eyes of those who do."

"I completely disagree, Séan. Now, if you'll listen and let me explain, then maybe you'll understand how they can exist, while your God, Allah, or whoever else you might think of … don't." I take a moment, before continuing. "My idea of heaven and hell is a very simple and logical one, and while I was alive I gave this a lot of thought, especially when some of my family and friends died. I'd go into church and pray for them out of respect for the memories they gave me and the good things they'd done in life, however trivial these things might have been. I wasn't praying to God. I was praying to them and my memories of them. When the priest or vicar used to say that these dead people are now in Heaven with God, I knew in my heart he was saying this just to humour the congregation. How would he know what kind of person the deceased really was? The more I thought about heaven and hell, the more I used to listen to the families and friends at the funerals." Turning my head and looking into the faces of Jana, Moira and Séan, I carry on. "Think about the funerals you've been to, both while you were alive and since you've become ghosts. How many times have you heard the mourners say how good a person the deceased was? How many times have they talked about all the good and happy times they had with the deceased? Did you ever hear anybody say anything bad about the person … perhaps once or twice, if ever?"

"Of course people remember the good things about their friends and relatives when they die. That's natural," answers Moira. "I've never heard anyone speak ill of the dead, unless he, or she, was a murderer, or evil in some other way, but the ones speaking badly about them aren't, usually, at their funerals."

"Quite right, too. Why would we want remember the bad in people?" asks Séan.

"But people do. Don't they, Jana?"

Jana nods her head. "Yes. That bitch! And I'll never forget her funeral, and how the people cheered and jeered, knowing she was dead, and if they could have torn her body to pieces … it wouldn't have been enough."

Turning their attention back to me, I add, "And then there was my funeral, and those two prats who couldn't keep their mouths shut. I wonder if they went to Evelyn's funeral, and if they did, did they speak ill of him as well?" I notice Moira and Séan looking confused, but I'm not going to elaborate. "You see ... that's my point. I believe that heaven and hell are the memories that the people, who are still alive, have for their dear departed loved ones, or hated ones. Heaven is the memory of all the good things that a person remembers about a dead person. They may be small memories or big ones, sad ones or happy ones, but whenever a person reflects, or talks to others in a good way about their deceased friend or relative, then in their own state of mind, their loved ones are in heaven.

"On the other hand, being in hell is being forgotten by everyone, or being remembered in a bad way at some time or other. Again this is a state of mind, so that when a person has these bad memories of someone, then that living person's mind is in turmoil and he or she becomes unhappy remembering the dead person, or is unhappy reliving the circumstance that caused the memory, and, in turn, this memory – in their mind – causes them to believe that the so-called bad or evil person is in hell. This bad memory is a state of mind, telling them that this person is now in hell, where he or she belongs. The strange thing with this is ... this same dead person will still be remembered by others, perhaps family and close friends, in a good way, and to them the dead person will be in heaven. To my way of thinking you should forget what you can about these people, try not to remember them, and then, to you, they'll be in hell. Being forgotten is being in hell. Being remembered in a bad light is being in hell. But why remember them when you don't have to, and so torment your mind with them. Forget them ... and leave them in hell."

"That's one hell of a philosophy. I'll have to give it some thought," says Séan, searching my face, while rubbing his chin.

"Hmm. I like that idea, Micky. So, when I don't think about the bitch, then she's in hell, and when I do, it's all bad anyway, so she's still in hell." Jana sits up, turns her face to mine, and plants a smacker on my lips.

"Jana! You didn't tell us we had a brainbox in the village," adds Moira. "Wait 'til the others hear this."

"He's not a brainbox, Moira. If you think about it logically, it's just common sense. Like me, neither you nor Micky believe in God, or the use of religion as a tool of strength, although we do believe that the use of these has created some moral values."

"Okay. We're getting in too deep now, so let's change the subject," replies Moira.

"I don't know about you guys, but I fancy sunbathing in shamrock," I suggest.

"Ah sure, that's a great idea. I know a nice little spot, just along the road there," says Séan, pointing towards a tiny cottage among some trees.

"I'll join you," says Jana. "Are you coming, Moira?"

"Later on, perhaps, but I want to find out what the others are up to."

With that, I once again take up my Superman stance and hoist myself up, and now that I'm flying wild and free, I feel so happy. I keep soaring upwards until my body becomes encircled in cloud, so I slow down and stop. Floating down again, until I have sight of land, I search the mountainside below and can only just make out the other three, still standing where I left them. Slowly I descend and as I approach them, they fly up to meet me.

Séan leads the way and seconds later we are gliding along the Slievemore Road, over a very small stone bridge, and past the tiny cottage with its wild fuchsia hedges. About forty yards further on, Moira stops us outside a private piece of land with a fixed mobile home sitting in the centre. Its gate is tied up and the fence in place, and an apple tree, without its apples, stands to the left of the mobile home. All the surrounding hedges are fuchsia, and the rest of the place, except for a small grassy area to the front, is growing wild.

"There used to be a house on this site. It was the first two-storey in Achill, built in the old stone tradition. Polly used to visit the house after she died. Her daughter and then her granddaughter, in turn, used to live here with their families. Her daughter used to own the cottage next door and the family kept the most beautiful garden you could ever wish to see. How I miss sitting in that cottage and its garden. It had the warmest atmosphere you could ever imagine." Moira's soft caring brogue has us in its spell, as she continues. "On a nice summer's day, I'd sit among those flowers with Polly, and we'd talk and watch and listen while her daughter took care of the rhododendrons, the different coloured roses, the bluebells, and others too many to name. Of course, Polly loved the cottage and the two-storey, both buildings covered in ivy. That's what they called the big one – Ivy House." In Moira's eyes, I can see tears, and they look like real tears, but my eyes must be deceiving me. "Séan, don't you remember the deliveries ... all the horse drawn carts with the meat, the veg', the sweets and biscuits, the tinned and jarred foods from Dublin, England and elsewhere?"

"Indeed, I do," he answers.

Moira carries on reminiscing. "And then there was the mobile library, when they first started bringing cars and vans to the island. Me and Polly watched when first her grandchildren, and then her great-grandchildren, were born in either one house or the other, sometimes in the night with the aid of the old oil lamps. Agnes, that's the daughter I'm talking about, would sit by the flickering light, reading or talking to her sisters when they were at home. She used to look after her grandchildren something beyond love, and it used to have Polly and me in tears of happiness. There were bad times, too, like the time that the two-storey was left to rot, but I won't go into that. Those things are better left alone unless Polly wants to tell you the story."

"Where is Polly?" asks Jana. "I haven't seen her for – my god, it must be thirty years."

"America. New Jersey, to be precise," replies Moira.

"She's been here once or twice in the past few years," says Séan. "I bumped into her near one of those houses by the graveyard. Polly had been in to visit one of her great-grandchildren, she said, but she didn't stay in case she upset the dogs. She told me she'd been to Merseyside and North Wales meetin' the newer generations of her family. She certainly gets around, our Polly, and it's amazin' to see her as an eighteen year old ghost, checkin' on her family as it grows forever bigger. Now look ye two," he says, staring at me and Jana, "are we goin' to stand here all day watchin' Moira shed tears, or are we doin' some sunbathin'?"

"I'd better go, anyway," says Moira. "Nancy will be wondering where the hell I am." And with that, she bids us adieu and flies off over Keel Lake. Séan turns us around and leads us straight through a hedge and into a nearby field, practically opposite the mobile home. As we hover over the field, I'm happy to see that there aren't any cows in sight and I feel safe, not that I'd have to worry about them anymore.

"I'll go to the far corner and attract the worms, while the two of ye hang around here, and whatever ya do, Mick, don't be puttin' your feet on the ground until Jana tells ya to. When ya see me jumpin' into the next field, give it about fifteen minutes and then ye'll both be safe to strip. I'll keep the slimy little buggers occupied for a couple of hours and then one of ye can tease them while I have a nap."

Jana pulls me close and drags me up and onto the hedge, where we sit and talk about this and that, while Séan clears the ground for us. About twenty minutes later, he shouts, attracting our attention, and we watch him fly into the next field. A similar time elapses before we see him fly up and even further away. At least he had the sense to let us see him. Jana pulls her clothes off, leaving them on the hedge, and I follow suit. Then, hand in hand, we float to the ground and lie down, letting the sun shine on our bodies.

"Séan seems to be a serious kind of person sometimes."

"He's not really, Mick. I don't get to see him very often, but when I do, he's always laughing and joking. He's a very happy ghost."

"So, how come you don't see much of him?"

"He's like Polly ... always here and there, and when he does visit our village, I'm usually away, monitoring someone or other."

Raising my head, I rest it in my hand and watch while she lies back. "Do you have any wishes, Jana?"

"Now and then I wish I could be a Mindbender, but I know it's not possible."

"Why?"

"Why what? Why do I wish this, or why's it not possible?" Jana turns on her side, facing me, and the sun sparkles off the gold and green colours of her eyes, making them dance. "And what are you looking at?"

"Your eyes. They're beautiful. They seem to tell a story of their own."

"Mmm ... thanks, Micky. Sometimes you say the nicest things." She lays her hand on my chest and strokes my ghost skin very gently, occasionally playing with my nipples, as she says, "So, which 'why' is it?"

"I understand why being a Mindbender isn't really possible because we know things have to happen as a natural circumstance, but something may come up in the future. Take Affiong, for instance. It happened very quickly for her, so don't lose heart. But why do you want to be one?"

Jana closes her eyes for a while, twitching her mouth and nose. Then she opens them again, saying, "Imagine all the things you'd like to do in the world; you know … to put it right." She uses the nail on her index finger to draw invisible patterns on my body. "Just think about getting inside the heads of all these powerful people – the good, the bad, and the downright obnoxious – and making them change their minds. And then we could stop the wars, and make them use the money spent on arms to feed the poor."

"Jana, you know that a Mindbender doesn't have that kind of will power."

"You heard what Stan Laurel had to say about how he had his dream. A Mindbender influenced his thought waves and made him dream a specific dream."

"That was different. He was in a weakened state at the time, and, anyway, the Mindbender only encouraged a dream to be dreamt, not an action that could change society. Influencing people when they're on their last legs and when their mind is nearly gone, is totally different from trying to persuade an obviously strong willed person in power to change their deep set thoughts and motives."

"I know you're right, Micky, but it could be fun trying. I can implant ideas in people's heads already, as you saw with Patricia in the pub, and you saw the affect that had. She knew she had to check on her children, so think how much power a Mindbender acquires. They never really talk about the strength of their abilities, and it makes me wonder."

"You have a point. I wonder what Affiong can tell us. Do you think she'll remember any of her life and some of the things she's done in that field, or will she have lost the memory of her mindbending days when she lost the ability?"

"You won't know unless you ask her, will you?"

"Why me?"

"She's got a soft spot for you. I don't know, but there's something about you, Micky, that gives people confidence and a belief in themselves. Besides that, you turn people on."

"What?"

"Don't act so surprised, but I'm only talking about the women, so don't get your hopes up."

"How do you work that out?"

"I'm sorry, Micky. I have a confession to make, but you must promise not to get angry."

"I'm all ears."

"Promise?"

"I promise. Cross my heart and hope to die." I trace a cross where my heart used to be.

"I don't want you dying on me, but what's with the cross? You don't believe in it."

"Jana, it's only an expression. Okay then, I promise to stay cool."

"Lucia and Luisella knew from the off that you were gay."

"You told me already. You said that Simon probably opened his mouth."

"No, Micky. He might, very well, have told some ghosts, but it was me who told the two girls, that first day at my change-over place."

"So that's where they got this inkling. Why the hell did you do that? I suppose that's what a somrov is … a gay?"

"No, Micky. I'm sorry, but you have to understand. When the girls flew down to greet us, we were only saying hello to each other, and asking what we'd been doing, where we'd been, and who with. And for us it was always the same answers – the usual everyday things, and the girls mentioned the donkeys they'd met, that type of thing."

"Donkeys?"

"Yes! Donkeys! … Somárov! That's what we call idiots in Slovakia."

"So, all this time, I've remembered the word for a donkey."

"Or idiot, depending on how you use it, but never mind, Micky. At least you've learnt something new, today. Now let me finish. I've been feeling guilty about this for far too long."

"Go on then. You told them I was gay."

"Yes, I'm sorry, but I did it for your own protection. When I was introducing you to Luisella, Lucia mentioned that you looked alright, and I could see from her face that she fancied you. So did Luisella, as it happens. Anyway, to cut a long story short, I told them you were a warm person, in a way – that's 'trochu prihriaty'." I'm confused and am about to interrupt when Jana raises her hand to shut me up. "In our language, to say a man is warm is to say he's gay, but this still didn't deter Lucia. She said that she still wouldn't mind having your body, gay or not, and I could see she was serious. After that, I joked with them about your tackle and how impressive it is. That's it, Micky. That's all there is."

"You're having me on," I laugh. "But why tell them then? It could have waited."

"I could see the way they were looking at you, and I'm sure you could see it yourself. Don't you remember?"

"Yes, I do now. I remember their faces and what they said. They were nearly fighting over me on the way to Pribylina."

"To be brutally honest, I wanted you for myself. So, telling them you were gay was my way of putting them off, but it didn't work. And think about Moira, this very morning, and her comments about you and me. If she had half a chance she'd be inside your pants, and she wouldn't think twice about it."

"She did seem to be jealous, and then you made a big demonstration of kissing me, not once but twice, the second time on the lips."

"I meant that."

"Why? Was it just because you liked what I said?"

"Yes and no, Micky. I did like what you had to say, but that's not the only reason." She gazes into my eyes and a couple of tiny tears creep into hers. "I love you, Micky. You're the first person I've ever loved, even if you are gay. I don't want to lose you to somebody else, but I think I might ... and I'm afraid."

Resting my hand on hers, I look into her beautiful eyes, and softly say, "Please listen, Jana. If the thought of falling in love ever enters my head, then you'll be the only female I choose, and if, as you say, there aren't any other gay ghosts, or only those I don't take a fancy to, then you should be happy. I don't want to go through life without love; both mental and physical ... it'd kill me. And, if you must know, I do love you and you mean a lot to me, but I have to find myself. I have to be me and explore this wonderful new world."

"Thanks, Micky. You've made me so happy, just to hear you say those lovely words, and I know, already, what you've yet to find out."

"Yet to find out?"

"Yes, but I can't tell you. You have to live your own life and find out for yourself."

"Fair enough," I answer, confused.

Lifting herself slightly, Jana kisses me on the lips very gently. I don't pull away, but she does, yet her face is still close to mine as she starts giggling. "Can I get married in white?" I feel but can't see the expression

231

on my face, but Jana can. "Micky, don't look so shocked. I know where you're going and I'll always be close by in case you need me. Only you can sort your life out, but I'll be there for you … always. And while I'm waiting, I promise not to play around with anyone else. I promise, and cross my heart and hope to die." And as she crosses herself, I burst out laughing, and then give her a cuddle.

"Thanks, Jana, and I'll be there for you if you ever need me."

"I know you will, Micky. I know you will." And as she gives me another kiss, her hand idles its way down my body and cups my tackle. "And this little stiffy will be all mine, and I'm so, so happy. I've never ever been so happy in my life. Come on, Micky, let's have sex among the shamrock."

"Hey! What do ya think the pair of ye are playin' at?" Jana pulls her hand away, and we both look up to see Séan closing in on us. "Ye can't be comin' here, fornicatin' on top of our beloved shamrock. Have ye no decency aboutcha, at all?"

"I'm sorry, Séan," I answer, embarrassed.

"Don't take any notice of him, Micky. His reputation is worse than Simon's, and when it comes to the ladies, Séan doesn't care where he does his fu … fu … fornicating."

Séan pulls his clothes off, leaving them beside ours. "Sure, I'm only coddin' ya, Mick. Jana knows me too well, but not intimately, unfortunately. However, we can make amends for that this very minute," he suggests, chuckling as he lies down by her, placing his hands on Jana's hips.

"Not bloody likely," she says, slapping his hands away and jumping up on the hedge. Pulling her clothes on as quickly as possible, she adds, "I'll look after the worms while you two get to know each other. At least I'll be out of harm's way … and Séan's."

As Jana flies off to do her job, Séan shouts after her. "Mind them worms don't bite yer arse. They leave a nasty mark."

Jana, still flying away, turns around and raises her middle finger, shouting back, "And up yours, too."

"Ar-agh, she's a fine figure of a woman, and there's plenty of the spirit in her. Let me tell ya, Mick, if I could get the chance for a roll in the hay with that one, it'd be with God's blessin'. And aren't ya the lucky bastard she's taken a likin' for?" With that, he lifts his head and looks at my body. "Well, I can't say you're any better in the hardware department than meself, but maybe it's your youth. I wouldn't mind knockin' twenty-five years off *my* age."

"I hear you don't do so badly."

"Now, don't be heedin' everythin' these women tell ya, Mick."

Turning on my belly, I ask, "When did you die, Séan?"

"It was a long time ago, Mick. A long time ago. I was workin' in London and had me a job buildin' the tunnels on the Underground. I was down in the Tootin' area, deep beneath the ground and whistlin' away to meself, when a slab of concrete fell and crushed my skull."

"Not very nice. I'm sorry to hear it."

"Sure, what the hell. I'm here now, and that's that. I was lucky in a way. I had no wife nor children to speak of, so I didn't leave behind all the worry about money and that kind of thing. And it was just as well, because in those days we didn't have all the insurances and pensions that they have now. Families struggled when the breadwinner died ... let me tell ya."

"What about brothers and sisters, and your parents?"

"I only had the one brother left, and he was a drinker. Sure, we all were, but that's the way we passed the time; either eatin', or drinkin', or sleepin'. Whatever we earned went on the booze and the board and lodgin's."

"So, Séan, you were working on the Northern Line."

"I was then and I am now."

"Come again."

"I'm a Haunter, Mick, and now and then I go down the tunnel to prowl around. I go to other places as well – castles and stately homes – but I like visitin' where I died. I travel on the trains sometimes, while other times I walk the track, and it's gettin' bloody worse down there. There are far too many trains. Once upon a time, I'd be able to walk the sleepers from Balham to Tootin' Broadway without a train tryin' to run me over, but now ... it's bloody chaos. Trains every five seconds – well, it seems like it – and when I hear the bloody things comin', I have to fly for my life. I feel like packin' it in and havin' an easy time."

"So, why don't you? Anyway, the trains can't kill you."

"Sure, I know that, but it's nice to be able to beat them. You know, as a matter of principle. And there's this one fella, Bony ... he's got me and Mabel hooked to the job."

"Mabel?"

"Aye, Mabel. She's another ghost. Ya might meet her one day, but I'll tell ya about her after. This Bony fella – well, to tell ya the truth, I didn't know his name until Mabel told me. Anyway, Bony is a driver on them new trains, and the first time I met him he was in the tunnel in Tootin' Broadway Sidin's. Sure it's amazin' how the mind sees things, Mick.

"There I am, floatin' around at the entrance to the sidin's, jumpin' out of the way of the trains as they're comin' in and out, and this particular day, after the driver changes ends, he opens his side door and looks at me, eyeball to eyeball. I'm singin' some Irish song at the time – The Town I Loved So Well, I think – when he starts shoutin' out ... *'Who's there? Who the bloody hell's there?'* Well, Mick, what can I do but answer him, but he can't hear me talkin'. So, I start singin' again, and then whistlin', and the silly bugger's head is goin' back and forth, him cussin' and panickin', and the next thing I hear is himself, Bony, talkin' to his controller and tellin' him about me bein' on the track. Now, I can't hear the controller's words, mind, but the next thing I see is Bony, standin' in the door space and tellin' his controller to listen. And what d'ya think he does next?"

"Go on," I encourage him.

"Well, I start singin' again, and this Bony just pushes the phone straight out the door and moves it up and down, and I, now bein' only a few feet away, float up in the air and sing down the phone to his boss. A few seconds later, Bony pulls the phone back, puts it to his mouth and says ... *'Didja hear him? Well, didja hear him?'*, and then he says ... *'I will. I will. I'll keep my eyes open'*, and with that, Bony closes the door. But before he pulls away, and with me bein' the inquisitive sort, I jump up beside him and keep my mouth shut. And just after he sits down, he says to himself ... *'Go bloody slow, he tells me! Like fuck I will'* ... and he drives off as if the Devil, himself, is chasin' him. I can't resist it. I have to stay with him, and I do; all the way to Burnt Oak where I meet up with Mabel and tell her about this fella."

"And what did she have to say?"

"Well, that's when she tells me about this other guy who gets spooked every time he passes near her. I tell her about my man, talkin' to himself all the way up the line, and how I won't open my mouth, just in case he has a heart attack or crashes the train. And him, sittin' there, crossin' himself somethin' fierce, then takin' the Lord's name in vain, and then apologisin' to God and crossin' himself again. It was a hoot, Mick … a hoot. He's a gas man, that Bony."

"He's a medium, then," I suggest.

"He's a medium, alright, and I'd say he's a first generation medium at that, and his kids'll be mediums as well."

"But, surely, he'd have been able to see you?"

"Not at all, Mick. Not at all. It's very rare that ya come across a medium that can see ya. Speak to ya … yes; sense ya … yes; but see ya … very, very rare. In fact, I've never met one, although a few of them Dreamers have made their acquaintances, but they don't let on who or where they are or if they're still alive."

"How come this Bony couldn't hear you when you were speaking to him?"

"Well, to tell ya the truth, he never shut up. He kept yellin' and talkin' to himself, and, after all, I'm not a loud speaker, am I? Now when I'm singin', I do put my heart into it."

"Are you from Achill, Séan?"

"No, Mick. I'm a Galway man meself, but, as I said, I've no family left, and because a lot of ghosts congregate here, both durin' and after the winter, I've made Achill my home. It's somewhere to meet and keep up with the craic."

"And what about this ghost, Mabel?"

"Well, let me tell ya. Mabel used to live in an old people's home in Burnt Oak – somewhere near the hospital – and she died there. She was single and had no family to speak of, so she'd hang around the home, visitin' her friends. The trouble was, they knocked the place down, but she didn't want to leave the area. It's alright now, though – she has a family."

"What do you mean? How can she have a family if she didn't have any relatives?"

Séan bursts out laughing and sits up, the fat on his belly shaking. "She's adopted Bony." And he laughs even louder, unable to control himself.

After a little while, Séan calms down. "Ya see, Mick, on many occasions she'd be waitin' near the site of her former old people's home and sometimes she'd go walkabout, and she was on one of her walkabouts when this tallish skinny man, with a shaven head, turned a corner and walked straight through her. He not only shook like a leaf on a windy day, but turned around, looked Mabel in the eye and crossed himself, sayin' a prayer as he did so. Mabel, as ya can imagine, was intrigued, because she'd never before had anyone cross themselves and pray to her after bein' inside them. All anyone had ever done was shake a little, and that's all. Mabel followed him to his house and went in to see how he lived. A lovely wife, he has, and two lovely daughters. I know – I've met them. Anyway, Mabel decided to wait around, keepin' herself quiet, and the very next day she followed him to work. She didn't enter him again for a while – she only watched, but not long after, she decided to take the plunge and went into him, and she stayed inside for a couple of weeks.

"Mabel won't mind me tellin' ya this. Sure, she's told so many ghosts that it's a wonder the whole world doesn't know, and she's always told me that she has no secrets. The thing is … Mabel was ninety-two when she died, but she returned as a sprightly young thirty year old. She played around with a few ghosts when she knew the score, but she was never satisfied with them. She did the usual hauntin' and the workin' in the village thing, and she still does some now and then, just to keep her hand in, but the thing is that she'd never had the fulfilment – ya know, an orgyism I think they call it – until the time she was inside Bony while he was humpin' away, havin' sex with his missus. Mabel said that she was so turned on by the whole thing that she couldn't leave him be. She told me that just bein' inside him gave her a thrill."

"So, why did she get out?"

"He had an accident of sorts … some kind of operation on his leg, and he was on the medication, so she had no choice. Instead of goin' to work with him, she'd go walkabout or take the bus somewhere else for a bit of variety, but sometimes she'd just stay at his house. Now, Mick, Mabel isn't a nosy person, and sometimes she gets mixed up with names and spellin's, and how to say the words and that – dyslexic, I think they call it. Quite a lot of ghosts have one affliction or the other, so be warned, Mick."

"I know, Séan. I can't say the word 'fu … .'."

"There are a lot of ghosts with that affliction, and if that's all ya have, ya don't have any worries. Besides, some of these afflictions pass away after a time. Anyway, as I was sayin', Mabel was on her way out the door one day, when this hand-written note was thrown through the letter box and it was addressed to someone called Bony, or that's the way she read it. Now she told me that Bony was not the name she'd heard him called by his family, but she liked the name Bony and she's called him that ever since. Maybe it was that orgyism thing she was thinkin' about."

"So, what's his real name?"

"I can't tell ya, Mick, as a promise to Mabel. I know who he is, but I keep my word."

"How did you meet him for the second time, then; you know, find out he was the same person from Tooting Broadway sidings?"

"When Mabel told me about this man, and her goin' to work with him, well naturally, I asked her what he did for a livin', and she said he drove the Tube. I was interested, and as she already knew about me and my medium, I asked her to let me meet her fella. Ya see, Mick, it was too much of a coincidence – two mediums on the same line, so she took me to his work one day and, sure enough, my fella was her Bony. I only went to his house the once and saw his wife and kids. He was workin' at the time and I didn't want to poke around. I've always believed that one ghost shouldn't interfere with another ghost's life, unless they're asked to do so. So, there ya have it, Mick ... the story of me, Mabel and Bony."

"You're a good talker, Séan. I hope my life as a ghost is as interesting as yours."

"Well look at ya, for God's sake. You've only just begun and ya have Jana eatin' out of the palm of your hand. If I should be so lucky, I'd be in Heaven. A nice tasty thing like her would set me off a treat. Now, don't go lettin' her escape from ya ... will ya?"

Turning on my back once more, I stare up at the small white clouds as they creep across the blue sky, and grin. Thank heaven he doesn't know about me as yet, and I hope to god he never does. I know he's not gay, but even if he was I couldn't fancy him, naked or not. Séan turns and flops onto his belly. After a while, he says he's going to sleep ... and he does. Jana returns and I get ready to take my turn at keeping the worms away. Before flying off, I notice that she's kept a fair distance between herself and Séan, and she blows me a kiss as I wave her bye-bye.

CHAPTER TWENTY

The past few days have been both exhilarating and tiring. Exhilarating, because being here has been like a breath of fresh air. I'm not really talking about the air, as it couldn't be much fresher than it is in Achill, but I am saying that this place has opened my eyes to the beauty, the humour and the naughtiness of the other ghosts, the local people, and the world as a whole. Being here, and in so short a time, my mind has started to clear and I can now sense the opportunity that lies before me.

And it's been tiring, because I've done the most stupid things like getting involved in flying races, having a go at one of Petra's who-shall-we-enter parties, and trying to ward off the persistent sexual advances from Lucia, Affiong and, of course, Jana. We've also been lucky in that it hasn't been cloudy and so nothing spoilt the views. The weather has been remarkably sunny and mild, and on the way here, this morning, I noticed that even some of the garden flowers had sprung into life. That doesn't make any difference to me, as you now know. I can suck nectar any time I feel like it. Watching and listening to the waves as they crash upon the sand, sending the sea water and its salty white froth further up the beach, gives me a feeling of not being alone. However, the solitude of this place makes me want to keep my thoughts to myself.

I'm sitting in front of a huge rock, on the beach, at Keem Bay. It's not the biggest beach on the island and I can't say that it's the cleanest, because they're all so clean and clear and full of pure golden sand. I've chosen Keem because of its isolation. People don't bring their children or dogs down here so early in the day because the other beaches are handier, and, at this time of year, there aren't many people on the island, anyway. The other day I saw some early morning surfers, but they were using the beach at Keel, not only because it's huge, but also because they can go out an awfully long way with their boards, and with the beach being so wide, from Minuan to Keel, there is a constant roll of waves to carry them in.

Dugort beach and the Golden Strand are on the back side of the island, looking towards the mainland of Ireland, and while I could have gone to either of them, I wanted to come here and strain my eyes, all points west, to see if I could see America. Of course I can't, but my imagination can run wild if I let it. It's sunny again this morning, but the omens aren't good for this afternoon, when heavy rain and strong winds are due in off the Atlantic. And do you blame me for trying to make the most of the few hours left of the sun?

I still don't know the date as yet, but we are in the first few days of March. Séan told me that. He'd been looking over someone's shoulder, in The Bog Trotter pub, and was reading the form on the horse racing page. I asked him why he bothered and he said that it was all part of the excitement. He told me that he'd bet against himself – no money mind you; but the idea was that where he'd visit next would be determined by the results of the races. He tried to explain how he arrived at his decisions and it gave him, he said, a reason to watch the racing on the television. I told him that he could go wherever he wanted and anytime he liked without all the messing about, but he said it was the challenge and the excitement in watching the races that drove him on.

He's funny … Séan. He'd brought up the subject of horse racing on the day we went sunbathing off the Slievemore Road. When I returned from my stint at worm attraction, both he and Jana were sitting up and, while he was talking, she couldn't stop laughing. Wanting to know what was tickling her fancy, I asked, and Jana made Séan start all over again.

And so he did. "Well, it's like this ya see. I was tellin' Jana about my trip to the Cheltenham Festival in a coupl'a weeks and she didn't bloody know it was the horses I was talkin' about. Big meetin' it is, Mick. Ya should come along with us."

I was surprised at the suggestion that she was going and asked her if it was true, and she nodded her head in response. Then I agreed to join them. On hearing this, Séan said, "Ar-agh we'll have a good time, but ya better watch out in case ya enter someone full of the Guinness. The place will be packed solid. Anyway, let me tell ya the bit of craic that I was tellin' Jana."

Before he could restart his story, Jana jumped on the hedge and picked up their clothes, throwing Séan's at him, and while she got dressed, he just sat there, telling his tale. "Ya know, Mick, I was never interested in the horses until the day I caused one of the biggest upsets in racin' history. I'd been here in Achill, and was on my way back to London when somethin' caught my eye. Unlike Jana, I've never had any fear of the water and it didn't bother me to be flappin' my arms while crossin' the Irish Sea. Normally, now, I'd be hittin' land over Anglesey, but on this occasion I decided to carry on over the water and the North Wales coastline. Ah sure, it made a change, Mick. We can't be goin' the same way all of the time. You'll find that out for yourself. Anyway, I was flyin' on and eventually reached the top of the River Dee and, soon after that, the Mersey estuary, and I knew I'd be hittin' Liverpool in a few seconds. Well, let me tell ya now. Just as I was crossin' the water, up comes an almighty blast of wind and it threw me sideways and northbound, and so when I reached Liverpool I dropped down lower. Carried on, I did, and soon after, I spied a pile of horses runnin' round a race track, and so, being inquisitive, I glided down to have a look. And would ya ever believe my luck, but no sooner am I near the ground and hoverin' over the crowd, than the bloody horses flashed past the winnin' post. So, straight away I flew off, but instead of leavin' the track, I waited for the next race to watch the horses. While waitin', and not wantin' to be mixed up in the crowd of people, I looked for somewhere to rest my head. Now, not wantin' to be attractin' the worms, I settled for a nice lookin' hedge on the course, and there it was that I lay meself down.

"Well, Mick, I shut my eyes thinkin' I'll get forty winks, but I was wrong, because a coupl'a minutes later I heard the poundin' of the horses hooves and they were gettin' louder by the second. I sat up, turned around, with my legs danglin' over the side of the hedge, and there was this pile of horses runnin' straight at me. I didn't even have time to think and the first horse was comin' at me somethin' fierce ... and, what's more, it didn't even have a bloody jockey on its back. Well the horse was so close and runnin' so fast, but instead of jumpin' over my hedge, it must have sensed me and it dived to its right, bringin' down one horse after the other. By this time, my mind had started to work, so I had the decency to lift meself up and watch the carry on from a sensible distance. Horses and jockeys were fallin' all over themselves. Some jockeys remounted to try the jump again, but while they were sortin' themselves out one horse sneaked right through the lot and made it. The rest were havin' none of it, but when they did get goin', the other horse, Foinavon, must've been nearly a furlong clear. I'll never forget the fear in the eyes of that poor horse, Popham Down, and I'm a might sorry about that. Now I know they call it Foinavon's Grand National, and that's fair enough, but they named the fence I thought was a hedge after Foinavon as well, and I think that's wrong, because they should be callin' it the Popham Down fence. I must admit that my interest in racin' started on that particular day, and while I like goin' to the races, Mick, I keep well away from the horses."

As Séan stood up to put his clothes on, I told him that it was all a cock and bull story, but he insisted he was telling the truth, and then Jana had another dig at me about ghosts not being able to lie. On hearing this, Séan looked at me, shrugged his shoulders, then said, quite seriously, "Mick, I don't lie."

Afterwards, we made our way back to the houses where we met up with Petra and Maggie. According to Petra, Moira had thrown up the Westport idea again and the others had gone with her. We spent the rest of the afternoon sight-seeing, with Séan giving us a guided tour of the island and telling us some of its history. The views from Atlantic Drive were superb as we watched the waves throwing themselves against the rocks. We had a look around Grace O'Malley's Castle and spent some time in Achill Sound, floating in and out of each building as we went along, and then we took a rest in the little restaurant near the bridge.

Pointing to the bridge, Séan told us, "Built in 1888 it was, and before that, the people'd have to risk their lives swimmin', or else they'd cross in a boat. And talkin' about boats, there was one that used to carry people from Ireland, over to America, and, one day, didn't the bloody thing sink … and not that far from where we're sittin'. Sure, and didn't some people from Achill lose their lives on board that ship." He went on to say that if we needed to know any more we should either ask Moira or read one of the local books. We sat and watched people coming in to eat, or else they'd just take a pot of tea and a scone or two. We talked and joked. I got to know more about Maggie and Petra, and the only occasion we had to move from our seats was when the waitress came to clear the table. This told us it was time to go and, anyway, it was already dark outside.

We flew back to our lodgings and I went for a short nap, but Jana wouldn't let me sleep. She was in an ultra sexy mood and I asked her to behave. She only laughed, saying that she didn't want to wait until our wedding night. You can imagine my reply. I tried sleeping, all the same, but she kept playing with my body, trying to undo my trousers and rubbing me up and down, and I must admit that I was getting horny, but I still wouldn't give in to her demands. I had the advantage you see, because I wasn't relying on her, anymore, to take me flying or for walking through walls. She gave up in the end, but by this time the others were back from their trip, and Moira had walked straight into our room, telling us to come to The Drunken Duck. And so we agreed, but not before Jana told Moira off for barging into the room without being asked. Moira seemed annoyed at first, but then backed off, apologising.

We met in the pub, but I had no intention of going into the disco. There were only ten of us – ghosts that is – because, according to Lucia, Séan and Freda were practising birth control methods. With it still being winter time, even though spring is just around the corner, the pub was less than half full and seats were readily available, but not all in the same area of the room. However, we found seven free seats at two of the tables, and the other three, Maggie, Tommy and Affiong, stayed close by.

We chatted a while, and that's when Petra, a firmly built girl of average height and mousy coloured hair, suggested having the who-shall-we-enter-party. She told us it was a game she often played when several ghosts were together. Not being squeamish – quite the opposite, in fact – I agreed, as did the others. Jana told me to be careful, as she'd played the game before, and Maggie, now wearing a well-fitting burgundy dress, was very excited by the whole thing. Affiong, with her hair now fashioned in a much cuter style, looked even more like Halle Berry than she had earlier, and I told her so. When she disagreed, in a shy yet happy way, I insisted it was true. She just smiled a wicked smile, but Jana had caught it and glared at me. I whispered to her that I was only complimenting the girl, but she still pulled a face.

The game started with Petra going around the pub's customers, sizing them up, and when she returned, she allocated each ghost a person to enter. The rules were simple in that we had to stay inside someone until he or she finished whatever drink they had, and then we were supposed to swap with the nearest available ghost. If there weren't any ghosts free, then we had to enter someone new. And this was where the problem lay, because we were only allowed thirty seconds to size someone up before taking the plunge. To tell the truth, it was a shambles. Some of the ghosts stayed inside their hosts for ages because they were very slow drinkers.

Occasionally, a couple of ghosts were carted off outside, their hosts with drinks in their hands, and after a few swaps I, too, joined Tommy and Jana out in the fresh air, while our hosts abided by the no smoking in the pub rules. While our hosts were talking, so too were we, and we weren't paying much attention to what our hosts were doing. Two of them were men in their early twenties and mine was a young woman. While talking about who we'd been inside, they smoked, and Tommy's host was smoking a roll-up. We stayed outside with the Irish trio while they stamped out and then started more fags. It wasn't long after this, though, when Tommy said he felt awful and that his head was starting to spin. Both Jana and I jumped out of our people, pushed our hands into Tommy's man and then dragged him out. Tommy raised his hands to his head and yelled. When he stopped the noise, we took him by the shoulders and were about to carry him inside, when Tommy's host turned to his friends, asking, *"Do you fancy a spliff?"*

Jana looked at him, saw what he was smoking, and laughed. "Spliff! So that's a spliff. Why didn't you just say it was a joint? And here's me wondering when you were going to tell me what the damn thing was. I'll get you for that, Micky … when you least expect it."

"It's no big deal," I replied, smiling.

"Perhaps not," she said, "but having me wondering all this time … is."

"I'm sorry, Jana. I'd forgotten about it," I answered, and I had.

We helped Tommy inside, and when the others saw that he wasn't feeling too clever, they left their hosts and joined us around our table. Maggie, too, was feeling groggy, and after asking who she'd been with, we checked out her host – a middle aged lady with a glass of coke. It didn't make sense until we saw the woman topping up her coke with some Bacardi from her bag. She must have been doing this all the time, and I suppose it was a pretty effective and cheap way to get drunk. And with Maggie being, somehow, unaware of what was going on, it's no wonder she was under the influence.

I took Maggie outside to liven her up, and soon after Jana reappeared with Tommy, to give him a boost. When we were satisfied with their recovery, Jana grabbed my hand and walked me along the road towards Purteen. But instead of turning up the hill to our accommodation, she carried on and on, not letting me go. Being tired, I needed to crash out, so I tried freeing my hand, but, despite her size, Jana had the better of me. I pleaded with her to let me go but she didn't take the slightest bit of notice. It confused me, especially as I feel my own strength increasing each time I suck on the fuchsia. Perhaps I'm not getting enough … fuchsia, I mean.

On reaching Keel, she asked me to go for a drink, and just to humour her, I agreed. Inside the pub, Jana looked around, studying the people, and then led me to a table where four people were sitting, drinking beer. "I'll have one of them," she said, pointing to a pint of lager. Quizzically eyeing her, she reminded me about the champagne. Now familiar with the art of moving things, I was about to try lifting a glass but Jana stopped me, saying, "Not yet, Micky. Let's make this haunting one to remember. We'll wait until they've refilled their glasses and settled down again."

"Why?" I asked.

"Listen to them," she replied. "They're all a bit old in the tooth, but they seem like people who'll tell a good story to whoever comes in here. So, let's give them a story they'll be telling for years. Now, we must be careful not to spill the drink on anyone." Jana then explained exactly what to do, while we laughed and listened to our party of four enjoying themselves. One of them called the barman, and presently a new pint was sitting in front of each of the men. I was about to start when Jana stopped me again. "Wait until they've had a sip. You know what drinkers are like. One swallow and then they'll talk for a while."

I agreed with her, and as soon as they'd taken a drink I moved forward cupping my hands around the glass of a fairly stout red-faced man. Meanwhile, Jana moved to the other side of the table and copied me, saying, "On the count of three. One! … Two! … Three!" And we pulled our glasses at exactly the same moment, and as they reached the edge of the table, we hooked our little fingers beneath the pints, hoisting them up and tilting them. We were so fast that the men didn't have time to react, and we simultaneously poured the drinks down our mouths. When the glasses were empty, we placed them back on the table.

You should have seen their faces, and Jana was nearly crying with laughter. I just stood there, open-mouthed, and it seemed like an eternity before the red-faced man bawled out, *"Didja see that? Well, didja ever see anythin' like that in your life?"*

A woman at a nearby table, obviously having watched the action, stood up and called to the barman.

"Patrick, you'd better have an exorcism done in here. The feckin'

pub is haunted." People around the room were very quickly gabbling on their mobile phones.

"I've never seen the like of it," said one of her friends.

Another man, broad shouldered and grey haired, shouted, *"Patrick, ya can forget the bloody exorcism. We want another two pints here ... and we want different feckin' glasses."*

Not long after, the place was packed, with everyone going on about the glasses and the beer. Several people from The Drunken Duck had shown up, including the other ghosts, and Jana was in fits telling them about our double whammy. Both Nancy and Tommy were desperate to have a go, but Jana said that it'd be too much too soon. Tommy was disappointed, naturally.

Jana and I soon left, going back to our house and then to bed. It wasn't sleep at first though, with her after my body and me keeping her at bay with the thoughts of Dorothy, Helga and a moustache going through my mind. Eventually, Jana gave up trying, turning away in a huff.

The following morning, however, she caught me off guard. I don't know whether she stayed awake all night to catch me out, or woke up early. All I know is that she was banging away on top of me and kept on going until we came together. I can't say I didn't enjoy it – I'd be lying if I did, but if I didn't have this hard-on problem every morning then I'd feel a lot safer. Jana lay by my side, smiled and made small talk, then kissed me again before flaking out. I didn't hang around. Downstairs, I found Lucia reading a magazine, and when she saw me she asked how I felt. I told her I was slightly jaded without saying why. Lucia said that Freda was still out with Séan and that we'd be lucky to see them for a week or two. Looking at me, she asked, "What are you up to?"

"I'm off to find a nice secluded spot to soak up the sun," I answered.

"You can't do that on your own. The worms will get you," she warned.

"Well, come with me," I suggested. I felt safe with Lucia, because she could have taken advantage of me in the chalet but didn't, and, besides, one of us had to keep the worms away.

"Of course, I will," she eagerly answered. We left the house and soon after entered a field she'd been using with Freda. Before starting, however, Lucia floated over the shamrock, inspecting it and sniffing.

"What are you looking for?" I asked, hovering along beside her.

"Cat's malacky," she answered, her eyes still searching the grass.

"Mal … what?" I asked.

"Malacky!" she exclaimed. "You know, cat's mess. That's what Moira calls it. The cats around here don't care where they shit." Once satisfied that the place was clear, she insisted on sunbathing first. I wasn't fussed, did my worming duty, and when it was my turn with the shamrock, I stripped off, lay back, and closed my eyes.

The next thing I remember, my eyelids were flickering, as if in a dream. I imagined a soothing and gentle rocking motion on my body and I liked this feeling. And then my eyes opened. Lucia was stretched out, her head on my chest, kissing my skin and pushing herself down on me. I tried pushing her away, but, just like Jana, she's deceptively strong, and she slowly kept pushing up and down. I was still knackered from the morning's carry on and couldn't help myself. And when the heat spread through my loins my natural instincts took over as I wrapped my arms around her body, rolling her over. A few thrusts later, I was filled with that beautiful burning sensation once again. I stopped moving, but she wound her legs about me. Soon after, her body stopped its rocking rhythm and I lay there on top for some considerable time, with Lucia kissing my neck and face until she was totally satisfied.

Only then did she ease me to one side, saying, "You're lovely, Micky. I know ghosts don't marry, but there's always a first time."

"Don't do this to me," I begged. "Jana told you who I'm looking for and what I am. I know she has."

"You're not gay. No man can make love to a woman like you just did and still be gay," she went on.

"What is it with you women? You're always take advantage of me, either when I'm sleeping or when I'm in a weakened state. That's immoral," I told her.

"It's just sex," she replied. "It's only a bit of fun, and you can't say you didn't enjoy me."

"No, I can't, but I enjoy being gay, and when I meet the man I like and he likes me, then I'll be happy. So, will you lot stop talking about marriage and sex, and let me get on with my life?" I asked.

"You'll be back, Micky. There aren't any gay ghosts. I know. I've travelled the world umpteen times and I've yet to either meet one or hear of one," Lucia said, leaning up beside me, her well developed breasts resting on my arm. She went on, "Lots of ghosts have heard about you being gay, but they think you're only winding them up."

"Well, it's not me who's doing the talking," I answered.

"Let's go," she said, adding, "I'd better fix your hair. We don't want you doing a Tommy. And you didn't tidy it after your fling with Jana this morning." I sat bolt upright, staring at her, as she went on, "Jana's very noisy, isn't she? I bet they heard her up and down the road."

Looking angrily, I challenged her. "You mean that you knew, all the time you were screwing me, that I'd had sex with Jana, and you still went ahead and fu ... fu .... Oh shit! You know what I mean. What kind of friends are you ... and after all these years together? It's disgusting what you lot get up to. You've got no sense of decency. At least gay people try sticking with their partners."

"You don't really believe that, do you? I bet you didn't stick with the same man in your other life and you won't find a man to stick to in this one. In fact, you're not going to meet another gay ghost, and I'm not joking. So, get a life, Micky. And as far as me and Jana are concerned, we're the best of friends. Me, Jana, Luisella and Petra ... we stick by each other; we look out for one and other; and we share everything, including men. Look! I'm sorry for taking advantage of you, but you shouldn't be showing off with that stick of rock of yours – standing to attention for all the world to see. What's a girl supposed to do ... ignore it? Not bloody likely, that's what I say. We females have a hard time finding men. Men that are halfway decent, that is. So when some sexy man comes along and offers it on a plate, do you think I'm going to turn it down? Get real, Micky." Her reply stunned me.

Lucia dressed and flew off. When I was ready, I didn't know what to do. I felt like pissing off and going to England. And if it took somewhat longer to gain my flying time, I didn't really care. I took to the air and headed towards Slievemore Mountain and the deserted village. I sat on the stones of one of the ruins, well away from the worms, and thought about my situation.

I talked to myself out loud: "I've just been fu ... 'd twice in one day and I'm angry with myself. I'm angry because I know that Jana loves me and I know that I love her in some silly way, but not in the way she'd like. Okay, I didn't mind the sex with her and, to be truthful, I didn't mind the sex with Lucia, but it was wrong. I know what I want, but if, as they keep telling me, I have no chance of finding a male ghost that takes my fancy or there aren't any gay ghosts at all ... what will I do? Jana shouldn't take advantage of me like that, and Lucia shouldn't have even contemplated sex with someone she knew to be with someone else ... her best friend. I'll have to tell Jana before she finds out from Lucia or anyone else. Perhaps she'll leave me alone, and that will be a blessing. Yes, that's the right thing to do, because this sex thing is getting out of hand. Look at Freda ... . She went off with Ivan. I don't know if they had sex but the implication was there. Then she was in that foursome with Tommy, Anne and Lucia. And now she's off with Séan. And then there's Moira, giving me the once over and lusting after my body, and before that she went off to bed with Anna, our Tutor. So how many others has Anna had – either men or women, and what about the way she makes innuendos about sex? Lucia took Tommy's virginity, albeit after he died. Maggie is going to make a home with Ivan and, by all accounts, it's to make them honest ... so what does that tell you? Hmm ... Luisella? I wonder why she didn't come here? Anyway, she was arguing with Lucia over me, so she must be into sex in the same way. Then there are the others – Helga, Dorothy and Affiong – raping endlessly until their victims nearly die. What is this ghost life except sex, sex, and more sex? But there again, would I be thinking like this if they were all men and gay, or would I be just like the women? Perhaps they are right after all. Nevertheless, I'll still have to tell Jana about today's events with Lucia."

You can see, now, how my days have panned out so far, and I still haven't told you about the Affiong incident, but that won't take long because nothing happened. What I mean is ... I didn't let anything happen.

I'd just finished talking to myself and was still sitting on the ruins, when a pack of dogs came running up the hill with a couple of young kids giving chase. These girls were throwing a ball and the dogs were racing after it when the ball ran up beside me. There was nothing I could do because the dogs were so fast and my mind was elsewhere. As you can imagine, when the first dog reached me it ignored the ball and let out the loudest howl you could ever hear, and it then ran off, its tail between its legs. This dog's howling was worse than Jana's banshee cry. The next dog approached but this time I managed to fly away before it sensed me.

By the time I got home, Jana was nowhere to be seen, so off I went to sleep. I don't know how long I was out, but I had a rude awakening. I was in that dreamlike state again ... just before coming to life, and I had this vision of Affiong climbing up beside me. I thought that I was just remembering the earlier bouts of sex with the other two girls and that her face came to me by mistake, but when I felt her hands working their way down my stomach, I realised that I was bloody stiff again. My eyes shot open, I sat up, dived off the bed and donned my clothes. Affiong was scared stiff when I started shouting. She covered her nakedness very quickly, begging me not to say anything. I asked her why she was attacking me. She said she wasn't – that she'd been watching me since I came back and that she could have had me any time. She explained that she was nervous about going near a man in case the wrong thing was said about her and that she might be sent away like Dorothy. Not satisfied, I asked her why me, and she said that I'd come on to her the night before in the pub. I couldn't believe she thought I wanted her, so I put her straight regarding the compliment I'd paid her, and then I told her to forget the incident. Once downstairs, I suggested that she leave before Jana returned. She did.

I went back to bed, leaving my clothes on this time. I thought some more about Affiong, wondering whether this little thing might drive her away again. I'll have to speak to her, if only to give comfort. Eventually, sleep came, and when I woke up it was daylight again. Jana was sleeping naked beside me, so I just lay there. Closing my eyes, I tried to dream, but dreams wouldn't come. When Jana awoke, about two hours later, she assumed I was still asleep. She closed her arms about me, nuzzling her nose against my ear, and pecking me birdlike on the side of my neck. She let her fingers play with the buttons of my shirt and then pressed her leg against mine. Thankfully, that's as far as she went, so I played dead for at least an hour. Jana rose first and was staring out the window when I spoke to her.

She came back to the bed, lay down beside me, and held me close. I told her about my thoughts and all the things I'd been telling myself, ending with my encounter with Lucia. She didn't like it, but I told her what Lucia had said – about their friendship and their usual ways with men and sex, and then I told her it wasn't entirely Lucia's fault because of the way she found me. Jana laughed on hearing this, saying she understood.

I'd already told her my thoughts on Anna, Freda, Ivan, and so on, and this, in turn, led to a discussion about the sex life of ghosts in general, and the enormous amount of sexual carrying on. Jana agreed that there were probably too many ghosts changing partners, but she said that there wasn't much else to do. She went on, saying that sex is a fantastic outlet for our energy. I have to agree with her on that point, because each time I've had sex, since being a ghost, I've been totally knackered and sleep does come easy. My problem is in the waking up with a stiffy each time, so I think I'll be wearing my clothes in bed from here on in.

Late, yesterday afternoon, we went racing. Séan and Freda were still missing, but the rest of us, Affiong included, had some flying races, up and down Keel beach. We started from the top of Minuan and had to fly to Keel and back, five times. Anne, Petra and Jana were level pegging all the way, with Lucia just behind them. Affiong dropped out about halfway through, and Tommy stopped on the lap after. The rest of us finished, but I tied for last place with Nancy – the pair of us crossing the line holding hands and laughing.

We spent some time in the pub in the evening, and the talk was still about the pints of beer and having an exorcism. We didn't stay there long before heading home. I jumped into bed, fully clothed, and went to sleep.

I was still in the same position when I woke up today. I kissed Jana on her forehead and the tiniest of smiles crept onto her face. I didn't hang around, though, because I wanted this time alone, to think and reflect.

Well, I've been doing my thinking and my reflecting, and now it's time to gather some fuchsia. I think I'll find a hidey hole to do that. Out of sight, out of mind, so they say.

CHAPTER TWENTY-ONE

Flying along without a care in the world and full of my daily ration of fuchsia, I turn to Jana and ask her if she's still going to Cheltenham with Séan.

"I'm not sure," she says. "The thing is, Micky, I've been having such a relaxing time having you near me, and everybody seems in such a good humour. I'd be afraid of missing something."

"I know what you mean, but if you're not going, then neither am I."

"You don't need me to hold your hand. If you want to keep Séan company, then, for goodness sake, go."

"It's not about keeping him company – he doesn't need any. Séan has his horses to think about and he'll be spending his time watching the races. Okay, I know he's funny and quick-witted, but I'd rather stay here with you. And, anyway, he wants to go for three days."

"Why, Micky, I do believe you care," she says, throwing me a kiss.

"It's not that, Jana. I don't like big crowds and, according to Séan, the place will be packed to the rafters. If I can't walk around safely or get close to the action – and I don't mean the horse racing, then there's no point. I'd like to go racing one day, perhaps to Royal Ascot or my own course, in Newmarket. At least, in the summertime, if the crowds are too big, I'd still be able to find some place to relax."

"We'd better tell him then. If I'd known, in the first place that it was for three days, I wouldn't have agreed to go. And Séan's one of these characters who won't stay in one place for any length of time. He might pick someone up at the races and go off with her or him, and he wouldn't tell you. He goes missing all the time."

"I agree. Freda looked totally shattered when they came back. Ten days, and nobody knew where they were. And then he went off by himself for another three, and he didn't tell her he was going. You saw what she was like ... edgy, not wanting to talk to anyone, and feeling used. And she was angry, thinking he'd gone off with another female, when, all the time, he was at another race meeting, here in Ireland."

"Yes, and now he's back she can't get enough of him."

"Come on, let's tell him now." I see she agrees, and then ask, "He's not bisexual, is he?"

"Of course not. Whatever gave you that idea? Has he been trying to chat you up?"

"No! It's just that you said he regularly picks people up and that sometimes it's a man."

"Oh, that! No! Séan meets people everywhere, and whether they're male or female it doesn't matter to him. He enjoys the company and having a laugh. It's certainly not for sex, unless it's with a woman. Séan always has a twinkle in his eye when he meets a female. He tried it on with me, didn't he? His philosophy is … hands on first and see where it leads, and it works for him sometimes but not with me. Freda, on the other hand, is vulnerable, being new and available, and it might be mean to say this but she's not the youngest or most striking woman you'll ever see."

"You're right, Jana."

Swinging around, we fly back across the Golden Strand, Dugort beach and its tiny village. We pass close to the top of the old bog road, down past our field of shamrock, the mobile, the lovely cottage, and on as far as Crumpuan. Seconds later we float down towards Séan's house. His is the next but one to ours, and once inside we call his name. His Irish brogue comes back with the message that he'll be down in a minute.

One minute turns into fifteen before he makes himself visible, tucking his shirt into his trousers on entering the room. "Sorry to keep ya waitin'," he says, pushing his hair back. Neither Jana nor I can stop smiling.

"That's okay," says Jana. He sits down on the lounge chair opposite, rubs his hands, and grins. "Séan," she says softly, "we have something to tell you."

"Don't tell me," he replies, an excited look on his face. "You're goin' to be the first ghosts to get married. So, when's the big day?"

"Séan, we're not getting married," I reply. "It's about Cheltenham."

"You're not goin'," he states.

"That's right," says Jana. "We don't want to go for the three days, and going for one is not on the cards. It's too far, too much messing about, and there will be far too many people."

Séan chuckles to himself. "Ar-agh, now don't be worryin' about it. I'll be all over the place, anyway. If ya must know, I'm goin' to be bringin' Freda with me. I promised her and I'm a man that keeps me promises. And with me and her havin' a bit of a thing together, well I wouldn't be havin' much time for ye two anyway. I was goin' to tell ya this evenin'. It's not that I don't want the pair of ye along, and you're still welcome if

252

ye change your minds, but I was worryin' about, maybe, leavin' ye on your own."

"It's worked out well for us all then," says Jana, smiling and placing her hand over mine.

"Ah sure, why don't the pair of ye get married, anyhow, and we can be havin' a great party. Just name the place and the day, and I'll be there, so I will."

"I've told you, Séan, we're not getting bloody married." Séan looks at Jana and winks.

I watch Jana as she winks back at him, and I don't think she sees me as she mouths the word 'soon'. Our conversation comes to a halt when Freda floats in through the window, says hello, and sits down on the other side of Jana. "What you three be doing?" she asks.

"Freda, my lovely, you're wastin' your time tryin' to cod these two," says Séan. "They know, full well, that we've been havin' sex. Sure, didn't they catch me puttin' my clothes on and then I forgot to do my hair."

Freda looks as if she's blushing, then asks, "Where did you two go today?"

"Nowhere really. We acted as worm bait for a while and then had a big feed of fuchsia juice."

"We should do that, Séan." Turning back to us, she says, "I hear you two be getting married. You have set date, no?"

I don't bother replying and instead look towards the ceiling. However, Jana answers, "We're not getting married, Freda. Micky doesn't want to and, after all, he's only been a ghost for five minutes." Unseen by the other two, Jana squeezes my hand, before continuing, "I'd love to marry and settle down, but I don't think I'm his type – not long term, anyway."

"Oh, Micky, I be surprised at you."

"I'm not one for marrying, Freda. I never have been," I answer, seriously, hoping to make them drop the subject.

"I think you two be perfect. You two be beautiful together. I wish Séan be like you, Micky. He be, how you say, flighty."

"That I am, Freda … that I am. Well, ya can't keep a good man down, now can ya?" says Séan. "Mind'ju, if Freda can put up with me goin' missin' every so often … well, we could be gettin' hitched ourselves." His eyes wander in my direction while nodding his head to the side, winking. "Ah, come on, Mick. Why don't ya marry the girl and stop

253

messin' us about? We know she's crazy about ya."

"We're ... ."

" ... .not gettin' married. I know," he interrupts, resignedly.

Changing the subject, I ask him, "When are you travelling to Cheltenham?"

"Tonight, Mick. There's a flight about seven o'clock to Birmingham, and from there we can fly by ourselves. There's a little house in the centre of town, not far from the night life. We'll spend the three nights there and come back on Thursday evenin'."

"Have you been working on your racing system?" I ask.

"Sure, as long as the Irish ones win I don't give a fig. The craic is great and the horses are the same, but we'll never see the likes of Arkle again, and that's a fact. But ya wouldn't be knowin' about him anyway, Mick, now would'ja?"

"Never mind you and your Arkle. You'd better leave soon. Look at the time," says Jana.

"Jeez! You're right." All our eyes glance at the clock. "Come on, Freda, and don't be botherin' with a spare pair of knickers. I'll get ya some over there." Freda blushes again. Jana and I get up, wish them luck, and then go home.

Lucia is relaxing on the couch when we walk in and the three of us spend the rest of the day chatting. It's about ten o'clock when the two women call it a night. I decide to stay downstairs in the darkness for a while, thinking things over once again.

The past fortnight has been fairly consistent. I spent a lot of the time getting to know the other ghosts, finding out how and when they died, what their characters were like, which ones were comical and which were serious.

Surprisingly, Anne Boleyn is a funny person. She was telling me about the times, years ago, when she used to hobnob with all the affluent people – at their parties and at the balls, and how she went with some of them on their holidays to the Seychelles, to Goa, and other exotic places.

She told me a story of the time she was in need of some emergency life, and how she jumped inside this extremely rich lady who was bedecked with jewellery and other fashion accessories. This lady, she said, was plump and middle-aged, and the only sober person in the mansion at the time. Anne, apparently, had made the mistake of entering a man not knowing that he'd been taking morphine. The effects from the drug were close to catastrophic, and so it was that the plump lady became Anne's saviour for the night. The problem was that this lady went to bed with her equally plump husband and poor Anne couldn't get a wink of sleep. Anne described the bout of sex before settling down for the night, but then the snoring started. But worse than the snoring were the horrible loud noises as the two aristocratic fatties were lying back to back and blowing scented kisses all night. When I looked at her kind of funny, she looked at me as if I was stupid, saying, "For god's sake, Micky, they were farting." Anne told me of other incidents in her ghost life, bad and good, and no doubt she'll tell me more before too long.

Petra, on the other hand, seems to be a more disciplined type of person. She tends to stick religiously to the rules in everything she does. She seems to know the rights and wrongs about everything, and I'm sure she could prove invaluable if I ever need some sound advice.

Both Lucia and Affiong have been behaving themselves. Having said that, I'm not sure whether they're up to mischief with some of the other ghosts, or, perhaps, entering people for anything other than a bit of fun. When I say they're behaving, they are leaving me alone now – sexually that is. In all other ways, we're getting along fine. Lucia is very funny and still teasing me by way of a joke, and the stunning Affiong and I have had some in depth discussions about her life in Nigeria and her after life as a ghost. I haven't asked her, as yet, about her mindbending recollections, but one of these days I'll get around to it.

Freda and Séan have been away most of the time, but I think we all know what he's like by now. Tommy talked a little about his childhood and his later problems with acne, and he said that the only two things he's liked about being a ghost are having an unblemished skin and losing his virginity. I didn't press him, anymore, about his ghost life and whether he was still having the occasional sex with Lucia. Unless he wants to tell me, then it's his business. Nancy seems to get on with everybody except Tommy. It's not that she doesn't like him; she talks to him and all that; but she thinks he's a bit wet behind the ears.

The only one I haven't really talked to is Maggie, but what she did tell me explains a lot. Over the years, she's learnt the art of scribing and helps Anna now and then, but she prefers life as a Villager because it doesn't cause her much pressure. She said that becoming a ghost had taught her so much about life and that her general knowledge had improved immensely. She was also looking forward to seeing Ivan again, and that most of her time is spent thinking about him. Now, Moira can talk the hind leg off a donkey and does so from one day to the next. Sometimes she can be very deep and sinister – not in a bad way, but with mournful feelings and some anger. She's also fairly intelligent and we have had some lively debates.

As for myself, I've spent lots of time soaking up the shamrock so I can fly even longer and faster, and I've been increasing my strength and senses from the wild fuchsia. I've enjoyed the many games we've played while also continuing my lifting and throwing practise.

The weather hasn't been too hot. By that, I mean it's been awful – raining nearly every day, sometimes with high winds. Other times it's been misty, with the clouds so low that you can't see in front of your face at times.

As for me, I'm tired, and I'm fed up wearing my clothes in bed, but what can I do? If I strip off, I stand a good chance of being attacked by Jana. I suppose I'd better leave them on, but, there again, maybe I won't. I'm going to bed.

CHAPTER TWENTY-TWO

I had no idea of the time, but it was still dark when Jana woke me up.

"It's like trying to wake the dead," she said. I asked her what was wrong, and she replied that she hadn't been resting very well and was still awake when she heard a disturbance downstairs. "Hurry," she ordered. "The owners will be up here any minute. Lucia's found another empty house, so get your skates on." I dressed quickly, grabbed my spare clothes, and followed Jana out of the window.

The second house was much the same as the first, except for the furnishings and colour schemes. Lucia had been waiting in the lounge and as we sat down she laughed, saying, "It would have been so funny if that couple had run upstairs for a bit of nookie while we were sleeping, or, better still, if you two were bang at it."

"It wouldn't have been a problem. We could have had a foursome, couldn't we, Micky?" Jana cheekily suggested. I shrugged my shoulders, not saying a thing. I was still tired and told them so before going up to bed. Sleep, though, wasn't easy to come by. Getting up again, I crossed to the window and stared out at the early dawn light as it crept through the dark shadowy clouds over Crumpuan. The past six weeks have seemed like an eternity, and it's not that we haven't enjoyed ourselves – we have, but the weather hasn't been too kind. Except for a smattering of sunshine on the odd dry day, the rest of the time it's been miserable, with the rain ever persistent and the mist so thick that you could cut it with a knife.

Taking advantage of one of the few dry days, we went on a tour of Newport, Westport and Castlebar, to visit the shops and look around, and we did go to the top of Croagh Patrick. We cheated, though, by flying up the mountain. The towns' shops were quiet and Moira pointed out that it was too early in the year for tourists; that the bulk of the visitors wouldn't be here until late spring and summer. Several shops were full of memorabilia, which sat alongside the sweets, the music, the fishing tackle, and the food, depending on which of the shops one was in at the time.

Even on this particular day out it wasn't completely dry, as a few dark clouds came over and threw a shower down through us. And although the rain never bothered us, as such, we still decided to follow a group of people into a pub where a man – an Elvis impersonator – was rehearsing for later in the evening. We sang along with this guy, Jerry, a tall young man with a quiff, as he sang ... Love Me Tender, Jailhouse Rock and Are You Lonesome Tonight, and I can tell you that both Séan and Moira have excellent singing voices. We three others were calling on them for an encore. So, when the man started again, both Moira and Séan burst into song. I must admit that they were more convincing with the lyrics than our friend, Jerry.

When the rain stopped, we exited the pub and soared up and down the coastline, and I took a chance by joining Séan in a flight over a fishing boat to see how they were getting on. When Séan suggested that we go down on the boat for a closer look, I told him no, but he insisted, saying that it's impossible for a ghost to get sea-sick. He was correct, and we spent about fifteen minutes on board before returning to Moira, Jana and Freda, who were sitting on a rock while dipping their feet in the water.

On another dry day, soon after, Séan took me to see the Seal's Caves at the back of Slievemore Mountain. I was still a little reluctant to cross the water, but he put me at ease. As we hovered over the water, we managed to see a few seals and, although fearful, I ventured inside one of their caves for a closer inspection. On our way back home, we sat on the pier in Dugort, watching children paddling and playing in the surf, while other people walked their dogs. Séan told me about his trip to the races, his lively nights out and in, and his time with Freda and the few tricks he taught her both in bed and out. I mentioned the visit to the pub and the playful haunting that Jana and I had accomplished. He laughed, giving me some more stories of a similar fashion.

On other days, we sat around talking, Moira telling us of the time, in recent years, when loads of people came to the island searching for gold.

"They were convinced" she said, "that gold had been found in one of the streams running down off the mountain. And, soon after, people were coming from all over to check the mountains both here in Achill and on the mainland. The inspectors, or whoever they were, all agreed that there is gold, but not enough to destroy Mayo's mountains by digging it out."

She told us about the, supposed, lost winning lottery ticket; that someone had mislaid it while going over Crumpuan. It turned out to be false, of course. It was then, she said, "I'm sure someone starts all these cock-and-bull stories just to get the people here, but why do they bother? Wouldn't anyone be happy to come to an island of dreams, such as this?"

The rest of the time, we took to the shamrock and the fuchsia as if there were no tomorrow. We'd lie down in the wind and rain for hours at a time. We sucked the nectar, going from flower to flower, racing each other and counting, to see which of us sucked the most. Needless to say, I still haven't won anything.

"Boo!"

"Jesus Christ!" Whipping my head around and seeing Jana smiling, I ask, "What the hell are you scaring me like that for?"

"My god, Micky, I'm sorry. You really are scared, but why?"

"You surprised me, that's all."

"Didn't you hear me? I've been watching you for ages."

"Why didn't you say something then, instead of creeping up and scaring me to death?"

"I did, but you'd gone deaf. Then I wanted to see how long you'd stand there thinking. You take everything so seriously."

"No, I don't."

"Yes, you do."

"I don't! I'm ... ."

"Yes, you do! Remember the last time?"

"What last time?"

"When you were shouting out the window at Oscar Wilde."

"Oh, that!"

"Yes, that! You told me then that you were a thinker, and, now, I walk in here and your mind is so far away that you didn't even answer when I asked why you weren't sleeping."

"I've been remembering what ... ."

" ... Lucia said," she interrupts. "You think that everybody on the island is talking about us having sex, each and every night. Don't you?"

"You know that's not true. I wasn't thinki ... ."

"Lucia doesn't tell a soul anything. She promised not to open her mouth about us or her little fling with you in the field, and she can't go back on her word."

"You're as bad as Ben. You never let me finish what I'm saying."

"Ben! You're sister's fella? What's he ... ."

"Never mind Ben, and let me finish," I shout, now frustrated. Jana folds her arms and frowns. "I wasn't thinking about sex or what others might be thinking. I've been reflecting on our time here in Achill and the fun we've had. We're leaving in a few days, and ... ."

"Tomorrow."

"Tomorrow! ... We're leaving tomorrow?"

"Yes, Micky."

"I thought that we ... . Oh, it doesn't matter." Moving past Jana, I sit on the side of the bed and reach my hand out towards her. I take her hand and pull her close, sitting her down beside me. "I like it here, despite the rain. I'm going to miss this place so much. I didn't think I'd like the peace and quiet, but I do."

"I like it too, but we have to go home."

"But Pribylina isn't home to me ... not really, and nor is Achill. Don't I get a choice?"

"Yes, Micky. We can't force you to do anything."

"There's a 'but', isn't there?"

"Yes."

"So, what is it?" I ask.

"Do you want to be alone, Micky? I mean ... really alone; no other ghosts to talk to; not making new friends; not having fun or arguments; and missing ghosts like Tommy hiding behind trees playing with themselves?"

"No. Not really, but ... ."

"No buts, Micky." Jana lies back, pulling me with her. "And you'll miss me, won't you?" She places my hand on her breast and I let it linger there.

"Yes, Jana ... I will." She kisses me softly on my lips and then pulls slightly away, and I whisper into her mouth, my eyes in hers, "But what about my life?"

"We are your life, Micky. I'm your life, and so are all the other ghosts, but when we leave here there won't be any ghosts left. Yes, there might be the odd stranger that you don't know and once every two or three years, perhaps some of us will return, but we don't come here every year. You might enjoy the scenery and the fun in the pubs, but if there aren't any ghosts around to share a joke with, then what's the point? And when the weather is miserable, who will you talk to?"

"I hadn't thought of it like that. I was thinking of staying here, then going back and forth to London like Séan. That way, I'd be getting on with my life, yet still have friends here to come back to."

"Micky," she says, so quietly that I can hardly hear her, "you know what Séan is like. The man can't be serious. You couldn't live his kind of life because you care about people. He doesn't, and I'm worried about Freda."

"Why?"

"Séan doesn't care tuppence about her. He'll tell her that she has to go back with us. I know he will. He'll say that she has to finish her training, and he'd be correct as far as that goes, but once she's gone he'll be off with someone else. He's a smashing ghost in a funny sort of way and he loves telling stories, but he never stays with one ghost for any length of time. If he was alive, he'd be out in the pubs and clubs, picking up new bits of stuff every single night. Deep down you know this, don't you?"

"Yes. I do like him, but you're right."

"And, anyway, you have to finish your training. You have to write an article about ghosts – what they have to do and the rules we have to abide by, and you have to prove you can do certain things like restoring life to other ghosts in an emergency; all that type of thing."

"I didn't know that. I thought it was just a simple test."

"Well, you do now."

"But what if I, or any of the others, don't want to go back and do it?"

"Then you won't accomplish your training, and if you don't earn some kind of working ability, then you'll end up like Dorothy and Helga. There are others like them, of course. I don't mean that you'll go sex mad and start raping men and women, but, eventually, you'll become miserable and other ghosts might shun you because you won't help out. It's not that you don't want to help, but you need to have the abilities."

"But I know how to fetch and carry, and I know how to restore life. You've done it to me and so has Lucia."

"It's not that easy. How will you know when a ghost needs your help? How will you hear another ghost telling you, from a distance, that something is wrong somewhere? Ghosts need each other, and when that particular Dreamer, who was looking out for you, knew that you'd arrived and where you were, messages were passed to Simon and me through a grapevine of ghosts. You know, that distance thing – the one hour hearing ability and the two hour sensing ability. How will you sense when another ghost is close by? Micky, can't you sense a ghost approaching Achill this very minute?"

"No, I don't. I thought that came with the nectar."

"It does, but you only acquire the ability to do things properly when you pass the test. That's what this article is all about. Anna has to be satisfied that I, and the others, have taught you as much as we can for the moment. Until you pass out, you'll never beat me at anything."

"I wouldn't be too sure about that." And pushing my body on top of hers, I use my newly earned strength to keep her pinned down.

"Micky," she squeals, "I didn't know you cared." I watch her smiling as she tries pushing against me. "Oh darling, you're so strong," – and a split second later, I'm thrown up in the air and flipped on my back, with Jana now on top of me, saying, "but not strong enough."

Her whole length, although shorter than mine, presses into my body, and in surprise I ask, "But what about the nectar? I took loads of it."

"And so did I, Micky. I haven't had nectar for ages and my body was in a weakened state before I came here, but I'm fully charged now, and, being a Monitor, I can use my strength in a more efficient way."

"This is crazy. It makes me feel like a complete novice."

"Micky! Oh, Micky! You're not a beginner at all. You've learnt so much about our rules, and you've learnt how to relate to other ghosts, but please come home with me and become the finished article. That's why you have to write one. You can put it in your own words because it's not an exam paper or anything like that. Have a go at the throwing and lifting things first and get them out of the way. Listen to Anna when she repeats the information about hearing and sensing other ghosts – that's so important. It's no good me telling you, because Anna does and says things in a different way. Anna likes perfection, or near perfection, and she likes order in everything. I admit, I know it all, but I've become so used to doing things in my own way that I've adopted some bad habits. We all do, including Anna, but she's still a stickler for the rules. Think, Micky, about when you learnt to drive a car and how correct you were in order to pass the test, and then tell me the truth. Afterwards, did you stick to the rules religiously, or did you acquire bad habits?"

"Of course I drive recklessly, occasionally, but I'm not that bad."

"You see, I'm right, but Micky, you don't drive anymore. Come with me, and don't become a cranky old ghost that might become prey to other unscrupulous ones."

"Okay! Okay! I'll come back."

She pushes her lips to mine again. "Micky, I know it's getting brighter outside but let's get some sleep."

"I'd love to Jana, but I can't while you're pressing down so bloody hard." With that, she relaxes her body and slides to my side, wrapping her arms around me. I turn my body into hers, holding her gently.

"Are you comfy?" she asks.

"Yes, really comfy." She snuggles into me, and I don't stop her as she pecks my neck with her lips time and time again, and she only stops when she conks out. I close my eyes, safe in the knowledge that we've kept our clothes on.

"Jana! Micky! Wake up! ... You've got a visitor." I've been awake for a while and I know I slept well, but I couldn't move or I'd have woken Jana.

"Who is it?" I ask.

"A surprise," answers Lucia.

"Okay. We'll be down soon." And then, shaking Jana with my free hand, I start repeating her name in her ear. A minute later, after some gentle encouragement, she starts making purring noises.

Opening her eyes, she smiles and kisses me. "What's the matter, you naughty boy? Do you want my body?" She puts her hand to my trousers ... and squeezes.

"If you really want me to go home with you, then please ... " I focus my eyes on her hand and then back to her face.

Still smiling, she releases her grip, but then squeezes again, very quickly. "Misery," she says, before jumping off the bed.

"We have a visitor," I tell her.

"Who?"

"I've no idea."

"Well, let's go and find out." We head through the door and float downstairs.

"My goodness! Look at the lovebirds," says Simon, casting a wicked grin my way. I can't believe my eyes and a lump comes to my throat. He's as beautiful as ever. His lovely blue eyes linger on mine ... and I want to kiss him again.

"Hi, Simon," says Jana. "How's it hanging?"

"Same as usual. Always ready, as they say."

I'm gobsmacked, not only at how sexy he is but also at his couldn't care less attitude in front of others. "H ... Hello Simon," I nervously say.

"You okay, Mick? Still mincing around?" he asks, smacking his lips with a kiss.

"Simon! Leave Micky alone," snaps Jana. "If you've only come here to tease people, then piss off."

"Can't a guy have any fun?" he responds. Lucia looks on with interest. To my knowledge, she's not aware of my obsession for Simon, nor how he led me on when he picked me up.

"Not with us," answers Jana, angrily. "Moira is here, as you probably know, so go and annoy her."

"I know she is. I've just left her," he says, chuckling to himself. "You won't see her for the rest of the day. She needs time to recover."

"In your dreams," Jana says. "By the way, are you still taking the Viagra?"

"You didn't tell him," says Simon, his smile disappearing fast.

"Simon, you haven't, exactly, kept it a secret. In fact, you're so damn proud of your permanent affliction that you've told every ghost we know, and then you turn up here for your yearly fuchsia rations and expect us to spread our legs. You never learn, do you?" The thought of Simon coming here expecting sex – and what I'd like to do to alleviate his problem – has caused a stir in my trousers. I don't care what he says ... I still love him.

"Oh, shut up, Jana. You've always had that bit of jealousy inside you."

"Me? ... Jealous? I wouldn't be seen dead with that stump of yours anywhere near me."

"Cool it, you two. You should know better. I don't know what you've been up to Simon but, whatever it is ... stop. Jana's right and you know it. Either tone it down and make the peace or we'll completely ignore you. And when the word gets round, you won't be able to show your face anywhere." Lucia stares at him, having made her point.

"What's got into you two?" he asks, looking at the girls.

"Nothing, Simon," answers Lucia. "We don't mind a bit of fun but you go too far."

"You're joking, aren't you?"

"Listen, Simon. If you want sex on a regular basis, I know just the place," offers Jana, quite seriously.

"I know ... go and see Moira," he says, cocking his nose.

"No, Simon, not Moira. There are these two islands in the South Seas where some female ghosts are waiting, and they're gagging for it all the time. They can't get enough."

"Yeah! As if I'd believe something as stupid as that, and even if there were don't you think that loads of other ghosts would be there by now?"

"On the contrary, Simon," replies Lucia, "they've only just gone ... prisoners of war so to speak, and only Relievers, like you, can get them free – if you want to, that is. On the other hand, you could drop in and see them, string them along – you're good at that – and then have your way with them."

"You're winding me up." Simon's face shows he believes them, despite his reluctance to admit it.

"We're not," says Jana, adamantly. "Lucia and I are telling the truth. You know we wouldn't lead you on."

"I'm not so sure," he wavers. He can't be that desperate, surely?

"Please yourself, then," says Jana. "If you think we're pulling your leg, go and ask Petra, Maggie or Anne."

"I'll think about it," he replies. "I'm shooting off. I've got to suck some nectar; you know, after all the exercise."

"Bye, Simon," shouts Lucia, as he flies through the door.

"Bye," I say, quietly, though slightly disappointed.

"Thank god, he's gone. Do you think he believes us?" asks Jana.

"Probably not, but he'll be interested. It'll keep him out of our hair for today, I hope."

"I agree," I say, somewhat shocked by the carry-on. I'd like to see him again, but I think the girls are right. He told me he wasn't gay and now I know it to be true. So why should I bother getting myself worked up over him? It's such a pity. What a waste of a lovely body?

"Come on, Micky," says Jana, "let's go and buy some new clothes." Her eyes wander up and down my body, and, smiling, she pats her fingers at the still erect shape inside my pants. "Down boy ... he's gone for now."

"Where?"

"I don't bloody know nor care where he's off to," she says, gruffly.

"I don't mean him. I meant, where will we get the clothes?"

Jana, not convinced by my question, cocks her head and tsks. "In Achill Sound. They have some newly knit jumpers and I know just the one I want."

"I'll have to find Freda," says Lucia, "to make sure that she's ready to travel."

"Okay," answers Jana, and then, hurrying me along, we fly out and over the road, on our way to spend my last afternoon in Achill.

We take our time going round the few shops available, but, eventually, Jana selects what she wants and I pick up a new top and trousers. On the way back, we stop at the beach in Keel, at my request, and sit down to talk. Jana and I discuss the conversation I had with Affiong about her mindbending abilities. Affiong had told me that she gets flashes, now and then, of deeds she had to perform, but the visions weren't very clear. She said that since she's been taking the stronger nectar from Ireland's wild fuchsia, her memory is improving and that she'll let me know when she has the answer. After half an hour or so, we head back to the house, only to find Lucia pacing up and down in a desperate state.

"She's not fit to fly," she says, waving her arms about.

"Who? What are you on about?" asks Jana, confused.

"Freda! She's so upset. Séan's told her the truth. You know, about himself and his way of life, and he told her to find someone else. The other problem is that since she's been with him, she hasn't taken much nectar, and, worse than that, she's only lain in shamrock for a few minutes at a time. Jana … Freda was afraid of the worms. Séan would be in one field attracting them, but she was too damn scared to lie down in case there were still some nearby. And, what's more, he's had her flying all over the place."

"That stupid, stupid man. Wait 'til I see him. He should have had more sense and made her do as she was supposed to. He knows why we're over here," says Jana.

"And that's not all," Lucia goes on. "We all know they've been having sex – that's obvious, but he's been at her all the time. I don't know where he gets his energy?"

"Lucia! I'm not worried about him. All in all, he's here for half the year nearly every year. Sometimes he's here for a week, and other times for two or three. He's bound to be topped up. Besides that, he's a Haunter and has more energy levels than a New Ghost."

"You're right, Jana. What will we do? She's so depressed."

"Leave it to me." Jana tells us that she'll be back soon and flies out through the wall, taking the quickest route to Séan's house. Lucia and I discuss the situation further, while awaiting her return.

About two hours later, Jana comes back with Freda in tow, but it is Jana who looks the worse for wear. "I'm knackered" she says, " ... totally knackered. I need an hour at the flowers and then a good night's sleep with a very happy person." Her eyes pass, first, over me and then Lucia, and then focusing on me again, she says, "You'll have to do, Micky. Lucia will keep Freda quiet and rested."

"Why?" I ask. "Jana! What have you done?"

Lucia answers for her. "She's given Freda some of her life. Can't you tell?"

"I don't get it. Are you saying that Jana has blown so much of her own life into Freda that she's done herself damage?"

"Basically, yes. From the state of her, Jana must have had a difficult time in making Freda accept her kisses." Glancing at Freda, I shake my head.

"Don't look at me like that," says Freda, now upset again. Shit, I think, on seeing the moisture in her eyes. I'm in trouble now.

Quickly, I get an idea. "Jana, listen to me. If Lucia goes with you to collect your nectar, I'll stay with Freda. It'll be all right, I promise."

"Why? What can you do to help? What if she needs emergency life again?" asks Jana.

"Don't worry. It won't come to that, and even if it does then I'll give her some of mine."

Lucia intervenes. "No, Micky, that's far too dangerous. I'm responsible for her. It's me that's in trouble. I should have kept a closer eye on Freda while she's been here."

"Please," I beg, "just this once. Trust me."

"I don't know." First questioning Lucia with her eyes, Jana then turns to Freda, studying her face. "I don't know what's on your mind, Micky, but I'm prepared to give it a try." Switching back to Lucia, once again, she suggests, "We can use our flying time wisely, Lucia, even if it is only a minute or two."

Lucia's mouth forms a cheeky grin. "You mean the old blow job while we fly trick?"

"That's right. Now let's go, and, Micky … take good care of Freda," she orders.

Seconds later, Freda sits down, with me beside her. I talk and talk, and Freda listens. She doesn't seem to improve any, but, there again, she doesn't worsen. So, in trying to cheer her up, I tell her how I died, about my car crash … and about Evelyn. Freda can't contain the smile, and when I tell her what Evelyn became she bursts into tears of laughter. I didn't want to tell her. God forbid, it was private, but when she settles down, I ask her to promise that she won't tell a soul. She does. I lift my fingers to her face. "Let me dry your eyes." She doesn't try to stop me.

I mention my sister and the funeral. I tell her about Joyce and what she did for me and my family. I also tell her what I did to Joyce, but in more detail than the last time, and then Freda really comes to life. She starts telling me about herself and all the funny things that happened to her in Finland. After a while, I suggest that she should lie down and I follow her upstairs. Lying with her, on the bed, I put my hands under my head and keep her amused, cracking jokes and telling her other funny stories. She chuckles and sighs, and when she stops responding to my softly softly approach and lullaby voice, I take a peek. She's resting, eyelids closed, but I remain there, just in case.

Presently, the girls return and join me in the bedroom. Getting up, I whisper that I, too, am going to bed. I pass through the wall and they both follow, quietly asking what we'd been up to. When I account for some of our conversation, they seem content, and then Lucia wanders off, leaving me and Jana together. Now that we're alone, I slip my clothes off … all bar my boxers, and jump into bed. Jana follows suit, except she's totally naked.

"There's no need to worry, Micky. I have to conserve my energy."

"It's just as well. By the way, why can't we delay our departure? At least that would give you and Freda more time to recover."

"That's what we're going to do. You'll have to help us, though."

"Help you? How?"

"Keep an eye on Freda when we're not around – that type of thing. We dropped in on Petra and the others on the way back, and they're going on without us. It's no big deal. The village isn't going to run away."

"And what about Séan?"

"We'll try to keep our distance, at least when Freda is with us. She'll never be out of our sight. Okay?"

"If he's nearby, I'll keep him amused, or let him amuse me. Will that help?"

"Thanks, Micky. I knew you'd understand. The only problem we have now is Simon."

"Why's he a problem?"

"He knows we were setting him up. Petra told me."

"But you didn't lie to him."

"Of course we didn't, but he'll remember the conversation and try it on, somehow. Perhaps with you, just to get his own back."

"It's okay, Jana. I know he was teasing and leading me on, but once bitten twice shy, eh?"

"If you say so, Micky. Now, what will we do tomorrow?"

"You have to build up your strength."

"Not for long. We have enough flying time, so we don't need the shamrock any more ... well, maybe an hour or so. I can suck like the devil on the fuchsia to regain my levels, so that will only take a few days. Freda needs the time though, so Lucia and I have devised a plan. We'll take turns in blowing life into her, on top of her fuchsia intake. The increased life will give her the strength to suck faster, so we could be out of here in less than the two weeks. It all depends on Freda ... on whether she's willing to go along with the idea."

"Why wouldn't she? It's to her benefit."

"She doesn't like the kissing. It reminds her of Séan."

"I wouldn't kiss Séan, either. He's not my type."

"Micky, do you prefer kissing me?"

"Given the choice, yes, I do."

Very softly, she says, "Kiss me now ... please." So, turning my head, I peck her on the lips. "Come on, Micky, kiss as if you mean it. And, when you do, please blow and give me some strength. I need to recover quickly." Realising that she means what she says, I push my body up against her and press gently, placing my lips on hers. As I start kissing and blowing, she starts sucking my tongue. We move around slowly, our hands changing position and our legs intertwined, and I start getting horny. Pretty soon, I push my hand between her legs but she stops me.

"No, Micky! Please don't. I can't afford to lose any energy. And we'd better stop in case I'm tempted. Okay?"

"Not really," I reply, disappointed. I keep my hands cuddled around her body until we sleep.

Less than two weeks later, after me spending some time having laughs with Séan, we left the island and were homeward bound to Pribylina. I'm full to the brim, with nectar coming out of my ears. Freda only saw her ex twice, and they were both fleeting glimpses. Lucia kept a very tight rein on her. Freda, however, is already talking about other ghosts she has an eye for. Watch out Lun, is all I can say about her preferences.

We've acquired several new outfits, and what we couldn't wear, we carried. Our trip home was by train from Castlebar to Dublin, and then by plane to Vienna. Once there, we relaxed for two days in some swish hotel. We explored the city, gazing at and wandering around the wonderful St. Stephen's Cathedral. We travelled about on trams, buses, and an exceptionally clean underground system. I liked the city and said so to Jana. She advised me to visit Salzburg if I liked music, quaint buildings, lively food markets, and a wonderful atmosphere. She mentioned Mozart's birthplace and the Fortress Hohensalzburg on the hill, and I agreed to let her take me there someday.

When our mini-break was over, we took to the sky for the short flight to Bratislava. And then, rather than waste energy, we travelled north to Liptovský Mikuláš by train, before flying the short hop home under our own steam. To say we were missed is an understatement. The other ghosts, Anna included, all but laid out a red carpet.

After a good chin-wag with them, I took to my bed … alone.

CHAPTER TWENTY-THREE

Lying in bed and thinking about what to do before our session with Anna, I contemplate turning over and going back to sleep. It doesn't take long for me to change my mind because I've had an idea. I climb off the bed, stretching and yawning, and cross to the wardrobe where my new top and trousers have been hanging. I casually put my clothes on, and my socks and boots soon follow. Pushing my fingers through my hair, I admire my reflection in the mirror. I feel so free and easy with no-one watching me, and so, once again, doing what I did on the first night I died, I take up the stance of Superman before hoisting myself in the air. Again, of course, I'm successful, flying through the roof and up into the sky.

I know it's early because the sun is only just poking its nose over the mountains in the east, and that's the direction I take. Scanning the countryside beneath, I can see that the snow has all but vanished and the pine trees running up and down the mountain seem to have a feeling of freedom and freshness. Their dark green colour shows how strong they are and this makes me feel more alive and even stronger in myself. Why didn't I visit this type of place when I was really alive? I always followed the sun to Spain and the Canaries, France, Italy or Portugal. I never found America and, thinking of The States, I wonder whether Amerigo Vespucci is a ghost.

Swooping down towards a stream, running its course between the trees, I spy a small waterfall and lower myself to a nearby rock. I listen to the sound of the running water as it hits the stones and pebbles in its way. The steady flow from the still melting mountain tops seems to speed up in some parts of the stream, while it only trickles in others.

I think about salmon and trout and wonder whether they will come this far up the mountain to spawn, or whether they come here at all. I wish I'd tried fishing more often. It seems silly now, wondering about what might have been, but when I think about Séan and his horse racing and how he was never interested until he spoilt a horse race as a ghost, it makes me want to go back to a time before my accident and replay that part of my life, without Evelyn and the car crash. I'd do things differently, that's for sure. I'd visit countries and places that others don't think of, and I'd experience their peoples' ways of life.

Jana has told me about her country's specialities – potatoes cooked with such simplicity and finished off with delicious butter sauces or tasty broths; the cabbages, freshly grown and put in the soups; and she mentioned the wonderful cheese and how they wrap it in breadcrumbs to cook and then serve it with crispy salads and other side dishes, and how it tastes so different from anywhere else. None of the fruit is wasted, she said, because the people pick it and then store it in the cold rooms. Flans and puddings are made with the fresh apricots, and jams and sauces with the berries, but the important thing is that everything has a unique flavour. I loved my food, and the thoughts of what I've missed annoy me. Of course, food isn't everything and I'm looking forward to visiting some of Slovakia's historical sites. Jana has told me so much about the ones she has seen for herself. Now can you see why I'd like to go back in time?

And sitting on this rock, staring into the stream, I also wonder about how cheap it is to live here. Okay, that might not be true for the locals, but for a visitor … this is heaven. It's no wonder the Swiss, Germans and Dutch travel here for their ski-jumping and mountain climbing. And thinking of skiing brings back the memory of the day I was attacked on the top of the mountain and the views I had of the snow covered lake at Štrbské pleso while being carried away by Dorothy, Helga and Affiong. I'll have to go up there again while I'm here and this time I'll see the water. I have this fascination for water – listening to it while it travels on its merry way, or watching the waves crash and then recede as they did in Achill. For one reason or another, water makes me relax and think about life – the past, the present and the future, and I can tell you something else I'm going to do. I'm going to learn to paint … ghost style. I might have missed out on a lot of things in life, but I'll make up for them somehow.

Taking to the air again, I head back to the village and it doesn't take long to get there. My flying speed is amazing, and the fact that I don't need anyone to help is a bonus. As I said in the beginning, doors will be no barrier anymore, and I'm nearly there. I just have to write this article and throw a few stones about. Both Jana and Lucia told me that they were confident in my ability and I do feel sure of myself. I fly straight into my room and lie down.

It's not very long before Jana makes an appearance as she floats across the floor and up on top of me. "Now, what are you doing, bright eyes? It's not like you to have all your clothes on at this time of day. What are you trying to do ... spoil my fun?"

"I've been out on the mountains, listening to the birds." Jana smiles, her fingers caressing my forehead, while I continue, "I've been sitting by a stream and dreaming of my mistakes, and thinking where to visit in the future. The water looks so inviting, running down ... ."

"Pull the other one," she interrupts. "What made you wake up so early? You're not worried about Anna and the article, are you?"

"On the contrary, I had a great sleep."

"So?"

"If you don't want to believe me about going out, then don't."

"You're serious, aren't you?"

"Ghosts can't lie, or so you keep telling me. Why should I be any different?"

"I'm sorry, Micky. I didn't think, but whatever possessed you to go mountain climbing?"

"Freedom, I suppose. I don't need you to hold my hand anymore, and, I don't know ... I just wanted to."

Jana rolls off my body, lying on her back beside me and, with a lump in her throat, says, "No, Micky, you don't need me anymore. Perhaps it's time for me to go."

I sit up and turning to her, reply, "I don't mean it like that. I do need you, but I have to do some things on my own, and finding somewhere secluded, to sit and think and dream, is part of me being me. In fact, that's the type of person I am, and you should know that by now. I've been like that since I was a small boy, and it's my way of coping with everything."

"But, Micky, you don't have anything to worry about. Why can't you just enjoy being a ghost? You don't have to plan things out."

"I realise that, Jana." Rising from the bed, I cross to the window. "If you must know, I've been thinking about my past and what I've missed out on, and how things could have been so different if I hadn't gone out with Evelyn that Monday night. I might have come here on a holiday and experienced all the things you told me about, and I'd have visited other countries and learnt about their history and way of life."

I feel Jana's hand as it takes mine. "But you wouldn't have. Don't you see, Micky, that people keep playing out their normal everyday lives? You'd never have visited Slovakia or Achill because you had no reason to. Your holidaying days would still be spent in Spain – somewhere like Sitges from what I've heard – and on your weekends off you'd go to Brighton or Scratchwood service station."

"What do you know about Scratchwood?"

"You talk in your sleep."

"Huh!"

"Yes. You talk in your sleep."

"That's impossible. I thought that when ghosts conk out, we don't actually sleep or dream, or, as you say, talk."

"Before you died, I suppose you thought it was impossible to be a ghost?"

"Well, yeah, but you know what I mean."

"Micky, you'll learn something new every day. I've told you that before."

"Why didn't you tell me this before?"

"I enjoy listening to you, and, anyway, what's this dogging thing?"

"Dogging?"

"Yes. You went on about this place, Scratchwood, and people dogging, or something like that. I know it's got something to do with sex because your hands wouldn't leave your little pecker alone. It's no wonder you wake up with a stiffy every morning."

"I can't tell you."

"Don't be such a spoilsport. Are you telling me that I'll have to go all the way to this Scratchwood place to find out, because, believe me, I will?"

"Don't trouble yourself. It's not worth it."

"You must be kidding. After the way you talked, it's well worth a look."

"For god's sake, Jana, it's only a service station on the motorway."

"I'll find it."

"You mean it, don't you?"

"I told you, already, that you're the most interesting ghost I've ever met, and maybe it's because you're gay – sometimes that is – but the thing is, you've given me so many things to think about and do. I'll find out what this dogging is all about, however much you put me off. In actual fact, the more you play it down, the more interested I become. Don't you get it?"

"I'll save you the trouble then. Scratchwood is a meeting place for gays – well it used to be. Sometimes, I'd go there for sex, get what I wanted, and then I'd go home again."

"You?"

"Once or twice. I never used to flash my headlights; I'd wait 'til another guy did and if I fancied him then I'd jump in his car and we'd, you know … play around."

"You didn't?" she smiles.

"Yes, but only when I was desperate."

"I can't imagine you being desperate, Micky. Hmm … blow jobs as well?" I nod my head. "So, in reality, you went there more than twice?"

"Well, I suppose so," I say, sheepishly. "Anyway, lots of people go there, and not just gays. Straight people go as well. It's a meeting place for sex, if you like, and now people come in their droves, and all because of this dogging."

I hesitate for a few moments, but she urges me on. "So, tell me. What's dogging?"

"They like to be watched."

"They what?"

"People don't care anymore. Some get turned on by other people watching them have sex, whether it's gay sex or straight. And sometimes there are threesomes or more, depending on the size of car."

"You're joking?"

"No … It's true. Loads of people like to watch and get turned on while another couple go about their business."

"You mean fu … . er, screwing themselves silly?"

"If you want to put it like that."

Jana moves in front of me. "So, these partners in sex spread their legs, exhibiting themselves, and go through the full act of intercourse while a pile of strangers ogle them. Is that correct?"

"In a way."

"What are you saying?"

"They aren't always partners to begin with. They might be total strangers having it off, and sometimes other people join in if they want them to."

"You're having me on."

"No, I'm not."

"I'm going to have a look for myself. Christ, this is hard to believe, but if you think I'd miss out on something like this then you've got another think coming. Well, I never. Dogging! Just wait 'til I tell the others."

"You wouldn't? Anyway, you can't, because I've told you in confidence."

"Don't be silly, Micky. This isn't about a personal experience that you've had."

"It is!"

"No, it's not. I don't have to tell them about you and your times there, but with all these other people – total strangers, to boot – having sex in the open and wanting others to watch ... it's just too good to miss. Micky, if more than half the village isn't interested, then I'll be surprised. This village will empty. And I'll tell you something else."

"What's that?"

"I bet you a pound to a piece of cat's malacky, that Anna Majerníková is one of the first to go."

"No?" I gasp.

"Oh, yes. She tries keeping quiet about her voyeurism, but some of us have seen her watching us, and she knows we have. She doesn't get much in the way of sex, except with one or two of the females, but when she wants the real thing, then either she gets lucky, and that's rare, or she has to go inside a host ... but that's not the same."

"But she's got to be nearly sixty."

"How forgetful you are. She's nearly four hundred, the same as me, and who says that sex is confined to younger ghosts, just as it's not for living people." – At the mention of her age, I look at Jana and realise that as long as I don't die, I'll be in the same boat as her in a few hundred years. Okay, that'll make Jana ... oh, never mind. I have to get this growing old business out of my head. I really do. I'm a ghost and, like Jana, I'll be forever young. And then another thought hits me. The chances that another gay will dream of being a ghost have increased, and over the years, perhaps, lots of gays might. And with this air of expectancy, I can't stop myself grinning. "And what are you smiling about?" she asks.

"Nothing important."

"Just as if. I know that smile, and sometime or other I'll find out what's on your mind. Now, let's get going. Anna will be ready for both you and Freda. So remember … it's up to you whether you want to prove your throwing and carrying abilities first, or write the article."

"How long will it take?"

"What?"

"The article."

"As long as you want. You can go into detail if you like, but it's what you put down that will determine your abilities. Just make sure that what you write is correct, has a lot of common sense about it, and is logical. Micky, you're far too intelligent to remain a Villager, doing the same chores day after day. Look at Tommy. He's become a Haunter, and we know he's a rather naïve young boy. You'll be okay … trust me."

"Yes, Jana, I know I will."

"Let's go then." And with that, we make our way downstairs.

However, when we see Anna, she calls Jana to one side while I talk to a very excited Tommy. Apparently, the order of events has changed and my article has been postponed until we've been to a Dream Factory. When the two ladies rejoin us, Anna explains about the change of plan. Jana can't go – she has something important to sort out with Petra – but several others are getting themselves ready.

We're only minutes in the air before dropping down to our destination, and some Dream Factory it is – a few empty rooms in a hotel at Štrbské pleso. Straight away, Anna introduces us to seven ghosts, five of whom are female. I think it odd that there always seems to be more women than men. Even in the village, female ghosts outnumber the males by at least two to one. I turn to Moira and ask her if all ghost communities have the same sort of female to male ratio. And I've certainly chosen the right ghost to ask – it doesn't half spur her on.

"What do you expect, Micky?" she responds. "Think back to when you were alive and you'll see that people haven't changed much over the centuries. You men were all the same. And you're still all the same, now – going off to work and then drinking with your pals; spending all the money. We poor women have all the worries about what to put on the table; how we will feed the kids; where's the housekeeping money. More women dream of a better life than men, so women are more likely to dream of fantasies."

"I disagree. Men always want to improve and they have more ambition," I quickly reply.

"Yes, Micky, you're correct, especially in bygone days, but that's my point. If and when men dream, it's nearly always about money or their ambitions. Very rarely does a man dream of ghosts. Men dream of cars, entertainment, women, sex and more sex, and if I'm wrong, why then do all the young men have wet dreams?" Moira can't help laughing.

Freda butts in. "Moira is telling the truth, Micky. In Finland, the men are just the same. All they want when they go to bed is sex, and when they dream it's always about other women. My husband used to dream, and he used to talk through his dreams. It was annoying and mostly stupid, but one night he did make sense, dreaming away with a huge grin on his face. My husband dreamed about a young girl in his office, calling her name, Ingrid, over and over again, and saying what he wanted to do to her. And he talked as if she was really there with him, saying that he adores her, that he's going to buy her a new car, and that he loves her firm young body. He started making kiss, kiss noises, turned towards me with his thing sticking out, grabbed my breasts and started kissing my nipples." Freda squeezes her boobs while saying this and then seems slightly embarrassed. Nevertheless, she carries on talking. "I gave him such a thump in his … how do you say, er, kisser, but this didn't wake him. The next morning, I interrogated him but he denied everything. He said it was only a dream about a film he'd once watched."

"Perhaps, it was," Moira sympathetically suggests.

"No! No, it wasn't. I phoned his workplace and asked to speak to Ingrid. This lady said – 'Yes … Ingrid speaking'. I slammed down the phone and waited for him. I was so angry."

"I'm sorry, Freda," says Moira.

"Don't feel sorry for me, dear. It was so long ago, and I found out that the nearest he came to getting her into bed was only in his dreams."

Moira looks at me smugly, saying, "My point, exactly. Thanks, Freda."

Anna and Sunita – one of the Ghosts Of Dreams, turn their attention to us. Sunita is about to speak when one of the two males present quickly moves alongside. Glancing first at him and then back at us, Sunita says, "As you can see, my Scribe, Tibor, follows me everywhere, even to my bedroom, just in case I hear a dream."

Sunita is an extremely beautiful young Indian lady – that is, she's originally from somewhere in the Indian sub-continent. She is exotically beautiful, with adoring almond shaped come-to-bed eyes, and long black hair which falls enticingly around her perfect face and down over her shoulders. She is so slim, yet still has bumps in all the right places. Okay, I might be gay, but I know real beauty when I see it. She watches me sizing her up. "So, Micky, it looks as though you'd like to be in Tibor's shoes?"

I'm lost for words, but manage to utter, "N ... No, it's just ... er, nothing."

"Hmm ... yes. I think I know what you mean," she replies, licking her lips. "These dreams ... it's not that I actually hear them, as such, but my brain can pick up a dream if there's any reference to the person being portrayed as a ghost, and so I read this dream. As I do so, I say it aloud so Tibor, or whichever Scribe is closest, can write it down immediately. But it's not often that people actually dream of being a ghost. Mind you, quite a few dream about ghosts coming to get them, or scaring them in other ways. We, Dreamers, aren't looking for dreams like that, so it is important to know when the dream is relevant or not."

"I'll second that. It's difficult to know the difference," says Tibor, speaking for the first time. "I can be in full flow with my quill, and then Sunita will stop me in my tracks, saying 'wrong dream'."

Sunita continues with the explanation. "Yes. We have to be ready for the faintest idea of someone being a ghost. A person won't deliberately say – 'I'm a ghost', so picking up the right dream can be confusing. If someone is dreaming of being a spirit in any way, we'll read the dream. Other times, as Tibor said, mistakes are made. One day, I picked up on this dream in which a girl had visions of a ghost taking over her body, and the poor girl was in turmoil. I kept reading the dream, assuming she was seeing herself as the ghost, but even before her dream had finished she'd managed to cast this ghost out. For the length of time this imaginary ghost was inside her, I related my reading to Tibor. Okay, she didn't dream of herself as being a ghost, but you can see how close it was to being so and how confusing it can be for us."

"What happened to her?" asks Freda.

Sunita places one hand in her jeans pocket, splaying the other one as she replies, "As a matter of fact, I stayed with this girl's dream until the end, and as in all dreams we read, we know the person's name and whereabouts, so I made a point of trying to read some of her later dreams. As yet, she hasn't dreamt of being a ghost and nor did she repeat this one, but, generally, people who dream of ghosts, witches, the occult, or other spiritual beings, tend to have more dreams on the same subject, and it wouldn't surprise me if some of them dream as we did."

"Have you read any other strange dreams?" I ask.

"I have, Micky, many times. Our brains are also tuned in to the world's leaders and trouble-makers, and some other famous and, supposedly, important people." My thoughts go to Pocahontas, remembering that she had said the same thing. Sunita continues, "You'd be surprised at what some of them really think of other people in the world ... and in their own countries, and their congregations, and, also, how they see themselves and where they think they're taking everybody. I can't give you all the details because there are too many sordid minds out there – there have been for centuries. I've been a Dreamer for over three hundred years, so you might be able to picture the faces of some of these people, and then try and imagine their minds. Some were, and others still are, completely mindless ... and that's the truth."

"Can you give us an example?" Freda urges her.

"There are too many to choose from. Why don't you read your bedroom book? The dreams we dream are there, or they're in some of the latest writings that haven't, as yet, been transcribed to the books."

"I haven't had time, with trying to learn English and all this training," answers Freda. – I've read some, as you well know, and interesting, they certainly are, so I think I know why Sunita is being tactfully reticent. I've enjoyed many of the ghosts' stories and some of the dreams from the Dreamers, but there are passages which shook me to the core, such as the wicked dreams of the Grand Inquisitor, Torquemada. At least, he and his cronies got their come-uppance, turning into dung-beetles long before Hitler joined them. Even I haven't had time to read everything, but I have browsed through the newly written works, and, although fascinating, some of the latest revelations in the bedroom book are simply evil.

Freda begs her, "Please, Sunita, can't you tell me whose mind you're likely to read – just one of them?"

"Let me try and explain. Now, without giving any names away, it is the type of people we monitor that's important. As ghosts, we're all aware that our new life exists purely because of dreams, but we have to concern ourselves about those who rule the living and the possibility of world destruction and people manipulation. Therefore, we must keep a check on those in power; people such as America's President and his associates in power, and the many Prime Ministers and Premiers in other countries, their Cabinets and the opposing parties, as well as some of the big business chiefs, leaders of industry, and those in charge of their religions. And it's not only these but also the dictators and warlords of other regimes.

"The problem is that we can't monitor everybody because there aren't enough Dreamers. I won't know about a coup somewhere until after the event unless a dream comes into my head beforehand. This has happened on a few occasions, but not to me. We are fortunate that there are ghosts in every country, such as Mindbenders who, at our request, can push their heads inside some of their brains to see what's behind the dreams. Mindbenders will also read the minds of their accomplices to try and gather more information. And then we have ordinary ghosts, like you, who, in time, will be able to do the same. Dreamers only read the dreams, while Mindbenders and other ghosts gather information. As far as *willing* people to do something different, we haven't accomplished this as yet, except on a few occasions, but these were only trivial matters and something particular to ghosts. That is, we can implant an idea in the mind, but if the will of the living person is stronger, then we'll achieve very little. Of course, any ghost is capable of making a person move their eyes, lips and hands if the will is strong enough. Quite honestly, it seems to be an endless chore, reading some of the boring dreams that these so-called leaders have, and I'm happy they don't dream all the time. I'd die of stress or boredom and Tibor's hands would never stop writing. I'd like to pack it in sometimes because, other than when I'm sleeping, my brain never shuts off – you know what I mean?"

"Yes," agrees Freda. "I not like your job. Can't you change it?"

"Not by choice, unfortunately. If I keep my mouth shut and don't tell Tibor an important dream, there's a chance I could lose my ability, but what would I become?"

"Would it matter?" I ask. "The worst you can be is a Villager and that seems okay to me."

"I've thought about it. In fact, I used to be a Villager and I wouldn't mind doing the job again. And, with this in mind, I tried it once – that is

... not telling a dream to my Scribe – and, since nothing happened to me, I've repeated this many times." Sunita sighs.

"What? You mean you've ignored the dreams of some potential ghosts?"

"No, Micky. I deliberately kept quiet when one of these leaders had a stupid dream – nothing important I might add. I'd been considering the idea of not telling my Scribe for quite a while, as long as the dream wasn't about a ghost or some disaster."

"What happened," asks Anna, now looking very interested.

"Nothing! Absolutely nothing, and since then I try to let my mind wander when the boring dreams enter my head. I never recite them. I don't see the point."

"What's the problem then?" asks Freda.

"I still can't help reading the dreams, and it'll drive me as crazy as Joanna The Mad."

"Who's she?"

"It doesn't matter, Micky. It really doesn't matter. Sometimes, I think everybody's mad."

"It gets that bad, huh?" Anna asks, seeming to console her.

"Yes, it does. I need a holiday from myself."

"I wish I could help you," says Moira. "I've always had the impression that you Dreamers can give your minds a rest without having to worry about your job."

"I wish that was true and I'm sure there has to be a way, but which ghost can we tell, or do we have to do something else; perhaps write something down somewhere?"

"Have you tried?" asks Anna.

"Of course we have. We can get away but our brains go with us. I don't know if we'll ever get a proper break. If only there was some other way."

"How do the other Dreamers feel about it?"

"Most of them feel as I do, and they skip dreams as well. We discuss our moods and some of the dreams, and while most of the others can accept the dreams running round their heads, I'm not like that. I don't have the ability to switch them off or ignore them. I shouldn't have become a Ghost Of Dreams."

"But you know very well, Sunita, that what we become isn't of our own choosing," states Anna.

"More's the pity," she replies. "Anyway, you have a fair idea of the work I do and I wouldn't wish it on anyone else. However, since you're here, I'd better introduce you to the missing couple." Sunita leads the way, while I stay close to Tibor, who is carrying a small bag. I ask him what it's for, so he opens it up and shows me a few small writing pads, three quills and two containers of ink. He brings out the ink, showing me how to open the container.

Nancy and Tommy join us as Sunita leads the way. She stops outside a bedroom and calls out, "Rebecca! Are you decent?" Seconds later, a female voice bids us entry. As soon as Sunita sees them, she says to Rebecca, "Can't you keep your hands off poor David? He'll be worn out." Neither I nor Tommy can suppress our smiles. David's hair is up in the air and his trousers are down by his knees. Freda and Nancy roar with laughter and I check out his form. Do you blame me? Going through my mind is the fact that, like Simon, he's not wearing any underwear, and my eyes are glued to his strongly muscled thighs and shapely behind. Rebecca doesn't respond to Sunita's question, and, instead, introduces herself. David finishes dressing and turns around, and any thoughts I had of wanting his body quickly diminish. He's an ugly devil with a long drooping nose, a mouth that makes him look as miserable as sin, and a chin that curls up to his bottom lip … and that's being nice. Even his gruff voice turns me off, as he crosses the room and says hello. David is Rebecca's Scribe and, by the looks of it, her lover.

Anna has been watching and when my eyes meet hers she smiles, accepting the situation as normal. And when I think back to her and Moira going off together I'm even more inclined to believe Jana when she said that ghosts don't have much else to do by way of enjoyment.

We make our way back to the others and sit for a while discussing other aspects of ghost life. After hearing what Sunita had to say about reading dreams, I'm not sure that I'd want to become a Dreamer. Being a Mindbender seems more appealing. At least there'd be some kind of excitement in going here and there, trying to make people do or say something they normally wouldn't. The thought of my mind having no rest doesn't appeal. Imagine having your brain switched on to loads of petty dreams from people in high places. It was bad enough listening to some of their politically stupid and self-righteous ideas while I was alive, and to think that if I became a Dreamer, I might have to hear that crap all over again. … No chance!

The more I think about this, though, other matters enter my head, and turning to Sunita, I ask, "As a matter of interest, when you read a dream, do other ghosts read the same dream at the same time?"

"No, Micky, of course not. Only one Dreamer picks up a dream. Imagine the confusion and the duplicity that would occur. If we had to read everything everyone dreams, all of the bloody time, I think I'd drown myself. May the saints preserve us from such a thought?"

I still have a bee in my bonnet, and continue, "Are you able to pick up dreams in all languages?" And, before she can answer, I add, "If not, how far away do you have to be before you can, or can't, read a dream?"

"To answer your first question, I can understand nine languages and several local dialects from my own country. Your second question is a little more complicated in that wherever I go in the world, someone will probably speak one of the languages I understand. So, there is no getting away from people's dreams."

"So you speak all the widely spoken languages?" I press her.

"No, I don't. I haven't the faintest idea how to speak Mandarin or any of the other Chinese languages, and I'm unfamiliar with Portuguese and Arabic. Why do you ask?"

"I was thinking about where you could go on holiday. If you don't understand Mandarin, then go to Hong Kong, China or one of the other far-eastern countries. Failing that, you could go to Brazil or Egypt. There might be people there that speak English, Spanish, German, and so on, but what are the chances of them dreaming of being a ghost while you are on holiday? And, anyway, I'm positive that you could handle one or two dreams while away. The other point I'd like to make is that unless there is a delegation of politicians or world business leaders visiting the country you choose, you wouldn't have to listen to their dreams either. If you do your homework, and check in advance where and when these meetings are, then you should be able to find somewhere to give your mind a rest."

"My god, Anna," Sunita exclaims, turning to my tutor. "Where did you find this man?" Then turning to the others, she spreads her hands, asking, "Why couldn't we think of this?"

"Mick is our thinker, or that's what Jana likes to call him," says Moira.

I'm not sure I like the idea of Jana telling everyone about me.

"Well, he can come and think for me anytime he likes." Sunita casts her eyes firmly on my face. "And, he's not a bad looking young man. What do you say, Micky? Would you like to live with me?" – What can I say? I don't want to appear rude. After all, she is a Ghost Of Dreams. "Don't you like me, Micky?"

"Yes, I do, but … ." I don't know how to answer. That's my problem. If I tell her I'm gay then everyone will know and I'll be made a laughing stock. If I refuse her, she'll think I'm offended by her and her question … which I'm not. And I can't accept … can I? If I was any normal straight guy, this beautiful sexy woman would be the answer to a prayer, but I'm not. And then there's Jana. At least I know Jana's temperament, her whims and fancies, and I know she wants me for me, but I don't know anything about Sunita except that she needs a holiday and would rather be a Villager. She may well be the perfect lady but she's not for me.

Anna saves my blushes. "Sunita … he's spoken for."

"I'm not surprised. With his good looks and thoughtful ways, whoever she is, she's one hell of a lucky woman. Next time, hey, Micky?" Sunita gets up. When bidding us farewell, the men shake our hands while the females peck our cheeks. Sunita kisses each and every one, leaving me until last. Her lips close on mine and start sucking gently, and then she pulls away. Still holding my hands, she says, "I had to take something from you, Micky, if only for luck, but when you're free, remember … I'm available."

We take our leave and fly back to Pribylina. On our return, some of the Villagers gather round. Maggie and Luisella sit close to both me and Tommy, Luisella deliberately letting her body touch mine. She asks me whether anything exciting happened on our travels, but it's Tommy who replies, telling them about David.

The girls laugh, with Luisella asking, "Is his body worth going back for, Micky?"

Trying to hide my embarrassment, I cough, before saying, "I don't know what you mean." And, in order to stop any more talk of him, I add, "He's an ugly looking brute and I can't see how anyone could fancy him. He makes Tommy seem positively appealing."

"Are you trying to be funny," he says, now rising and glowering at me.

"No, Tommy, I'm not. You saw how ugly he is. If you were a woman, would you take him to bed?"

"Of course not," he answers, stepping back and resuming his seat. He carries on, "I don't know what Rebecca sees in him. I like her."

"Is she sexier than Lucia?" asks Maggie.

"She's as cute, I think, but I've only just met her. I like Sunita as well. She's beautiful. If we were alive, she'd be the type of girl I'd like to marry, but I don't suppose we'd ever have met." Tommy seems dejected, peering down at the ground and twiddling his thumbs.

"I've met Sunita many times," says Maggie. "And, as far as I know, she doesn't fancy her Scribe or mess with any of the others, but if you were to meet her again don't you think Lucia would get upset?"

"I haven't seen her for days."

"Never mind, Tommy, you can spend the night with me," suggests Maggie.

And to everyone's surprise, Tommy stands up again, stretches out his hand, and, blow me, she takes it. Then, calm as you like, she wraps her arm about Tommy's waist before toddling off together. Luisella smiles, points to me and then back at herself, as if we should follow suit. How the hell do I get out of this? I haven't promised her anything; she can't know about my encounter with Lucia; and she is aware that Jana has the hots for my body.

That's it! … Jana! I look her in the eyes, softly saying, "I can't, Luisella. I do like you, but you know I'll never upset Jana. You know how she feels, and with you two being the best of friends, I don't think it's right."

"I understand, and, anyway, I'm only kidding," she replies; yet I can see the sadness behind her smile.

We make small talk for a while and then take a walk around the village, and we're nearing Luisella's home when Anna calls my name. I turn towards her and notice Freda alongside. This is it, I presume … question time.

286

CHAPTER TWENTY-FOUR

Freda and I accomplished our tasks and have both acquired scribing abilities. She found it difficult, at first, to get a grip on the throwing activities. If she'd spent less time with Séan and more on the beaches with the rest of us, she'd have been more proficient. I knew that, and so did she, but I couldn't blame her for wanting to get her leg over. After all, it was Séan who led her on and I wasn't about to remind her about him, or the only thing she'd have thrown was a fit. Anyway, I coaxed and cajoled her, picking things up and placing them in her hands. She'd then do the same for me, and all the time she became more familiar with the feel of each and every object. We laughed and joked and eventually her throwing improved dramatically. She fetched and carried cups and saucers, knives and forks, and glasses – sometimes three at a time, until Anna called time. Freda still wasn't sure whether she'd done enough until Anna told her that she'd done slightly better than Nancy. You should have seen Freda's face. She was ecstatic.

However, Freda had no trouble writing the article and was finished in no time. Occasionally, I just sat and watched but she was writing like the clappers – so fast that I couldn't see the feather move. She later told me that the copying of old manuscripts had been one of her hobbies. I, on the other hand, took the best part of a day to write mine. It's not that I wrote a lot; I was more concerned about the content. I read through the first paper and answered the few questions asked, namely my name, the date of my death and my age at the time. I'm sure this was just to confirm the facts they already knew about me. Then I had to list all my family, my friends, and their addresses in case I go missing in action. I suppose there's some logic in that. I explained about my life and death and the type of person I was, but I couldn't say what I was dreaming about when I had my ghost dream. To be honest, I didn't have the foggiest idea, and how's a person supposed to remember something like that, especially after twenty-odd years. Why else would I look the way I am? But there again I could have had this dream anytime after that, somehow remembering my past. I decided, anyway, to tell the truth and shame the devil. That is, as I had no way of finding out about this particular dream unless I spoke to the actual GOD who read my mind or the Ghost Scribe who wrote it down, I had to say that I couldn't remember. There was no point in racking my brains forever or trying to make something up. God knows who or what might have been in that dream anyway. There were so many people in my life. It might have been something compromising that I'd never want to disclose, so why try and recall something from my past ... dream or no dream. Perhaps it was a trick question, to see whether I'd invent a dream, but that would have been telling a lie and therefore impossible.

The rest of the article was quite straightforward. I found it easy to explain how a ghost comes about, and then listing the different class of ghost and the responsibility of each. I gave my thoughts on Affiong, Helga and Dorothy, regarding what they did to me and the aftermath of the incident. Initially, I wrote that haunting to scare people didn't seem fair, but after more thought I changed my mind. And why, you might well ask? Well let me tell you. If people weren't fearful of ghosts there wouldn't have been any ghost stories or films, and then ghosts like me wouldn't be here ... would we? In a way, I suppose, scaring people explains quite a lot about our existence. If people never had an inkling about us, I might have ended up as another egg. I made a point of writing this down as well.

Mind you, something else was, and still is, bothering me. I raised the question, in my article, as to why ghosts can't help the living in some way; you know, in trying to avoid disasters, illnesses, wars and the like. Having said that, I suppose we do in some small way. Jana helped Patricia, telling her to check on her kids, and Stan Laurel was encouraged to dream a specific dream. For these reasons alone, I had to ask why ghosts don't get involved in helping the world improve itself. Perhaps this wasn't required in my article, but for my own peace of mind I felt it a necessary inclusion.

My writing took me into the following day and perhaps it was a blessing to have slept on it. I woke up bright and early and started writing with a lot more gusto. The article grew forever longer, with my speed increasing, and, not content to stick to the basic questions, I restarted the whole damn thing, elaborating and giving more detailed descriptions for each ghost; citing examples of their achievements on occasion. I went on to say that Relievers needed a special ability to locate and care for their new found friends, but I added information regarding myself and how I felt when I was trapped, and how Simon could have helped more instead of leaving it all to Jana. I made the point that Simon should have told me about Jana and what I was likely to expect. And while writing this, I found that I was a shade too hard on him and seemed to have made it personal. I stopped and rewrote that passage, telling the same thing but phrasing it in such a way that other trapped ghosts might benefit from my conclusions.

The longer I wrote, the neater I became, so much so that it more resembled the writing in the bedroom book. I had this urge to keep on writing and writing. I'd never written with a quill, not even for a bit of fun, but it seemed to me that I was nearly as good as Freda. I carried on writing, mentioning the Dreamers and their Scribes, telling of their abilities to read and write in different languages. How, I asked, could they learn so many languages and dialects so well and so quickly? I needed to know. I had this urge to know, and I wrote this down.

Eventually, I put down my quill and gathered my papers, and I was about to take them to Anna when Jana floated into the room. She told me, immediately, that I'd become a Ghost Scribe and then she kissed me. Apparently, Anna has some sort of intuition about these things and she was spreading the news. Anyhow, when we went outside, all the ghosts seemed to be out and about and they offered me their congratulations. I know I shouldn't have felt embarrassed, but suddenly I was the centre of attention.

All the patting on the back and the happy atmosphere led to talk about the Bojnice Festival of Ghosts and Spirits. Several ghosts were leaving for Bojnice hrad that very day, and among the volunteers were Tommy, Nancy and Freda. It wasn't compulsory and I had to think hard. I was asking myself ... 'Should I go or should I stay?', but eventually I declined the invitation. I wasn't being rude or anything like that, but I didn't fancy playing tricks on people, instead preferring to wind down at home. Besides, Jana didn't go either; she had a monitoring job to do in Poland. This was the something she'd arranged with Petra on the day I met Sunita.

When they returned from the Ghost Festival, I was filled in on the action. Tommy, as usual, made a fool of himself, accidentally dropping a jug of punch on some of the visitors after crashing into another ghost. Anna and Luisella performed a double act, giving the appearance of a ghost carrying its own head, and, in the evening, they held a ghost dance in the castle's great hall. All in all, they had a good laugh and I might join them next year. Nancy brought back some news, though. After a chat with Anna, she's decided to stay on for a few weeks before heading off to see her mother in Massachusetts. I think that she'll stay there, but who knows?

With Jana being away, I had time to explore. Maggie showed me how to mix the ink and make the paint from the different coloured petals. She explained the storage system, and the tricks used in hiding materials from the living. We called in on Soňa, the village seamstress, who was sitting at the spinning wheel altering ghost clothes. Soňa and Lun are an item. I caught them at it once … accidentally, of course. To tell you the truth, they weren't very discreet. And it's more than likely that everyone, bar Freda, knows about them. I spent most of the next day reading the bedroom book, and I was so engrossed in the stories that I gave up and went to bed only when my eyes gave out.

In the middle of the night, I was awoken by tickling fingers and the quiet voice of Jana urging me to move over. She cuddled me close, explaining her disappearance, and then went on to say how much she missed me. I remember smiling to myself, thinking about all these women who want my body and want my mind – from ghosts in high places like Sunita to lazy articles like Helga and Dorothy. And while I was thinking, Jana was wrapping her arms around me and pressing her naked breasts and erect nipples into my skin. Here we go again, I thought, but I was mistaken. The poor girl was shattered; her slow and steady breathing making me glance at her face. She was dead to the world, poor thing.

The following day, Jana took me on the trip she'd promised. We travelled east over Východná where the music festival takes place, on past the busy town of Poprad, and then further east to Levoča – a walled town with loads of history. We stopped there to inspect St Jacob's Church. At first, I didn't know why we were bothering, but Jana is proud of her country's past, and when we went inside I couldn't miss the altar. It was huge and so intricately built. It's reputed to be the highest wooden altar in the world, and Jana kept going on about its designer and builder, Master Pavol. In the square, outside, I couldn't take my eyes off the cage of shame with its padlocked gate. In days gone by, people would be locked up inside while others threw stones or rotten fruit at them. While there, though, I noticed the restaurants and all the food being served inside. I so wanted to join the diners and eat some food. I wasn't hungry … I never feel hungry, but the food looked so inviting. Jana got me out of there, pronto.

I thought we'd be going back but she led me on, this time south-easterly over Spišský hrad, one of the largest castles in Central Europe, then on again to our final destination – Hrad Krásna Hôrka. I couldn't believe my eyes, and it's not the castle I'm talking about. Inside, there's a dead body in a glass-topped casket and although very small it is still well preserved. She was known as Žofia Bosniaková and her ghost still bears the name. In fact, it's this ghost of Žofia, who, by resting inside her remains, helps to preserve the body. Even the clothes were in good condition.

Jana woke her up by shouting through the glass, telling Žofia that she'd brought a lovely Englishman to attend to her desires. And this made Žofia move, alright. She was up in a flash and making eyes at me, and I thought it was me who was going cockeyed. I might be a ghost, but what I saw was frightening when this ghostly lady, dressed completely in white, sat herself up. And, yet, an identical body with an identical dress, still lay in its casket. When the ghost climbed out and stood beside us, I switched my eyes from her to the still intact body in the casket. The ghost was now so much taller than her dead body.

I must admit that she did make a play for me. Žofia introduced herself by both her name and then her nickname, Biela pani – the white lady. And it's no wonder; the body in the casket was as white as a sheet. When Žofia took my hands, pulling me closer and pressing into me, Jana came to the rescue. Jana told her I was spoken for … pointing to herself with a wry smile on her face. Jana told her all about the latest goings on; the capture of the nymphomaniacs and what's been done to them. Žofia seemed happy with the news, her reasoning being that Helga and her friends have been killing off men for years. She kissed me a kiss of thanks when Jana explained my part in Helga's and Dorothy's downfall.

Žofia said that she's been here for hundreds of years and if she didn't have to leave her body to find nectar, occasionally, then the body would be perfect. She made a point of saying that it won't last forever; that nothing lasts forever. Žofia seemed depressed for a while, knowing that her body will eventually crumble, albeit in the distant future.

Jana didn't hide her feelings, telling Žofia that she was concerned about her loneliness. At first she asked her to fly with us to Pribylina, but

Žofia refused. Jana kept at her, until she agreed to fly as far as Levoča. We said goodbye to the corpse and flew up country, presently coming to earth in the centre of the walled town. We chatted a while longer until the time to part arrived. Žofia came closer, insisting that I kiss her on the mouth. I was somewhat dubious, but gave in, knowing Jana was nearby. She pushed her lips on mine, grabbed me around my neck and kissed me softly. Then, without warning she sucked and sucked, and I was about to pull away when her hand slid to my bum, pulling me into her body. She ground her pelvis into mine and started panting. I could feel her getting warm but I didn't react. I think my lack of enthusiasm showed because she released her hold soon after. Jana moved forward, ordering Žofia to suck as much life as she needed ... and she did, clinging to Jana's lips for a good length of time. We said our goodbyes, wished her well, and then made tracks for Pribylina.

While flying home, the thought of Žofia living her life inside her body never left my mind. At least she has a casket in a well cared for tomb. Personally, I wouldn't fancy living in a corpse – not even my own. And to think of my poor body being attacked by all those bugs and micro-organisms ... Ugh!

By the time we got back, night had set in and the place was deathly quiet. Once in my room, Jana didn't give me the chance to catch my breath. She wrapped her arms around me, hugging my body close to hers, with her head resting on my neck. She had her lips against my skin, repeatedly pecking and sighing. She softly whispered, "Micky, make love to me tonight." What was I supposed to say? What was I supposed to do?

But the answer to both was taken out of my hands when Jana pushed me back on the bed. I knew she was tired; she had to be tired ... especially, after letting Žofia suck her lips for so long. My mind and body didn't argue, giving in to her fingers as she clawed at my clothes. She kissed me desperately on my mouth, my chest, my belly button, and everywhere else that she revealed. When she brought me to attention, I couldn't help but respond, pulling her up and ripping the blouse from her body. She never wears a bra', and when my mouth closed in on her breasts she hoisted her skirt to her waist, leaving it there, and pushed her panties down over her knees.

Jana was like a demon possessed, pushing herself down on me. She felt me responding to her rhythm and slid her body ever so slightly forward, her lips finding mine. The movement and the kissing seemed to go on forever and I didn't want it to stop. I whispered through the kisses, "I love you, Jana. Jana ... I love you."

"Oh, Micky, I love you too," she replied.

It was only later, I realised that I'd probably put my bloody big foot in it. You know, in telling her that I loved her. It's not that I didn't mean it in a way, but Jana has always known how to play with my mind and my body. I should have kept my big mouth shut. Okay – it was the sex that made me utter those words, and sex can bring out the worst and the best in what people might say; what they mean; and what they don't mean. But sex also causes the biggest cock-ups in life, and I could have said no to her advances, but I didn't. The problem was that, in my mind, Jana would think I was going to stay and that I'd be a fool to leave her, simply because our love-making was so gentle, so caring and so beautiful.

I turned my head, studying her sweet but not so innocent face, and the satisfied smile from her open lips where a few wisps of her silky blonde hair were trying to creep inside. She looked so peaceful with her eyes closed, her naked arm stretched across my neck, and her body, face down, on the bed. She had shut herself off to the world, at least until the next morning, and I didn't know whether to laugh or cry. I was worried, not for me, but for Jana. How was I supposed to tell her the words she wouldn't want to hear? I couldn't sleep. I just couldn't sleep.

When my eyes opened the following morning, I was fully aware that I must have conked out sometime during the night, despite the way my brain had been working my tongue – talking silently to myself; twisting sentences around to see whether I could come up with the gentlest way to tell her that I was still going home. I never came up with the right answer; or maybe I did, but sleep had made me forget. I've often done this – it's a problem of mine. And, I suppose, you have too; you know, gone to bed with something on your mind, turning it this way and that and thinking you've found the answer, but when you wake up it's gone and doesn't come back for a day or two ... and always when it's too bloody late. It must be a curse of sorts.

Jana was still flat out and there was no sign of her moving. I eased my way from the bed and searched for a change of clothes. I pulled them on and, once again, relaxed on the bed, wondering what she would say and do. From where I was resting, I could watch as the many shaped light and dark grey clouds passed rapidly over the village, the blue sky beyond barely visible. I could hear the trees, the clattering of hanging pots, and the wailing noises from the rafters as the wind forced its way up the mountain. As I listened, the howling brought thoughts of banshees to mind, and this, in turn, reminded me of Ireland, of Achill, of Séan and Freda, of Lucia in the shamrock … and sex, and I was right back where I started … with Jana. It was a long time coming, but when it did, Jana's first movement was with her arm as it crossed my body, pulling me close. "Morning," she squeaked, yawning at the same time. I moved my hand to her hips.

"Hi, lazybones," I replied, with a smile. I was still unsure how to handle the situation, so decided to wait for the right moment.

"You sound happy this morning," she said, "but what's with the clothes?" Jana picked at my shirt. I hesitated, hardly able to speak. "If you think for one minute that you're going back to England without making love to me again, then you're very much mistaken." – I couldn't believe what I was hearing and my relief was obvious. I gave her a huge grin, kissed her firmly on the lips, and she responded by smacking me and saying, "Not yet, Micky, but, in the meantime, take your clothes off. I'm the boss today and I'm going to screw you silly. You can leave tomorrow. I don't know when I'm likely to see you again; it could be months; and from the first time you set foot in Slovakia, we've never spent a day on our own." – The way she stressed 'on our own', told me she meant what she said. Don't get me wrong. I could have argued the toss and left and there might have been ructions, tears, or both, but she accepted the fact that I was leaving. I was quite prepared to give her my body for a day, or two if I had to, but at least I knew that I'd be able to get on with my life. She went on, "So, Micky, when you give up the search for your dream man, will you make an honest woman of me? And before you say anything, I know that ghosts don't get married, but I don't want you falling for someone else. I missed out on marriage and all the celebrations with my family and friends."

I told her that I understood and I really did. After all, it's what most girls dream about. Looking at me sheepishly, she suggested, "We can have a long love affair, Micky … life long, and we can celebrate it with the other ghosts. It will be just like a wedding."

"But what happens if you meet someone better, funnier, or sexier?" I asked.

She had the perfect answer ... perfect for her. "Oh, Micky, there'll never be anyone else but you for me, and you know that's the truth."

It was at that point I said something totally unrelated to our conversation. I asked, "What real benefit could I get from using a long term host, because I'm inclined not to bother?"

Jana pinched me in my side. "Ooh, Micky! And I thought you were going to ask about us and our future together."

I still needed the answer, so I persisted. "Isn't what I choose to do part of my future? Should I use a long term host? Will it do me any good, and, if I don't find what I'm looking for, will it do us any good?"

This brought the smile back to her face, and she replied, "I'll tell you the truth. I think it will be good for you. It was for me." I asked her how come and she said it taught her so much about people and the enjoyment of sex. I couldn't believe my ears and it showed. Jana went on about the sensations she felt. I queried this, naturally. Anyway, she carried on, "Once you make the decision to enter a long term host, you have to be naked." I knew that and told her so. As Jana talked, she started unbuttoning my shirt. "Well, if you know so much, did you also know that we have to be informed ... that is, both me and Anna?"

"I don't remember," I replied, and I didn't.

"Anyway, you have to. And did she tell you that once you're inside a long term host you take their shape, and that whatever thrill your host feels then you'll feel it too?" she asked.

"You're having me on," I said, yet in the back of my mind I was excited by the prospect.

"I'm not, Micky. I'm not," she argued. "I had the most wonderful time inside my Dominique." When I asked her about this Dominique, she happily gave me the details. "She was a beautiful French lady – sexy, imaginative, and so full of life. She taught me so much about sex, men, and the way people think. She was a fascinating person. And, to top that, when I left her body I'd gained a sense of smell."

I was shocked on hearing this, asking her, "What? Are you telling me that you can smell?"

"Of course I can, but I'm one of the lucky ghosts, so I keep it quiet – you know, jealousy ... that sort of thing." She carried on. "You see,

Micky, I don't know why, but perhaps it depends on the particular host I chose, or the amount of time I spent inside her body. I've heard it said that as long as you don't take a break from your host's body, then it works, and that might be true. I enjoyed being inside Dominique, but I couldn't stay in her forever."

Wanting to know more, I persisted, "Is it really worth it, though?" I *do* like the idea of being able to smell and it might be worth the sacrifice for a year or two.

"I think you should try," she said, "and if you don't like it then get out, but as to whether it's worth it, that depends on your needs. Micky, if I was in your position, I know what I'd do." Well, I'll be honest. When I asked her to elaborate, I was dumbstruck by her reply. "I'd go inside a female," she suggested.

"Yes, I suppose you would. You are a woman," I responded.

But Jana wasn't giving up on this. "Why state the obvious, Micky? I'm thinking about what you want in life and I'm putting myself in your position and in your mind, and I think you should choose a woman."

"Why, for heaven's sake, especially the way I am and what I want?" I asked.

"That's just it," she replied. "You'd get the benefit of both worlds, wouldn't you? Try and imagine this female's boyfriend or husband."

When I said that the host might be a lesbian, Jana thumped me, saying, "Micky, you're so stupid sometimes. Don't choose a lesbian." My mind wandered to visions of myself inside a woman and I liked the idea, but in the right gay I could achieve the same thing. I, however, didn't mention this to Jana.

Something else was bothering me, and that was the talk of sensations. It didn't seem to make any sense, so I tackled her about it. "Jana, Séan told me about a ghost called Mabel and how she has a regular host. This host is not long term, mind you, but she still gets sensations and sexual satisfaction whenever she goes inside this guy, Bony ... so how?"

Jana replied, "I know all about Mabel and Bony. We can all get sensations – small ones, but they're not totally fulfilling. It might not take much for Mabel to warm to someone and, for her, this might be enough. And then there are ghosts who have multiple sensations inside certain hosts and so they keep returning to them, but most ghosts find it difficult to find a host that turns them on. You've been inside a couple of people. Ask yourself whether you felt any sort of thrill or other odd feelings."

Thinking back to Mary, I remembered a mini-sensation, but not in a sexual way. And then there was the fat lady who was on medication, and after that, Andy, but he was drunk. I wasn't turned on by my sister but I did feel a bit weird, so I gave Jana my reply. "No, Jana, I haven't had any that made me feel good about myself."

"That's hardly surprising ... you're not long dead. So, what are you going to do?" she asked.

I said the first thing that came into my head. "I don't know as yet. I like the idea of being able to smell flowers and fields and after shave."

Jana prodded me in the ribs. "You and your blasted after shave. I'll teach you for that." She jumped on my body, pressed my arms down either side of my head, and leaned forward. "It might not work for you. You could be in someone for years and still not gain the sense of smell."

Playfully crinkling my nose, I replied, "But there again it might, and that, in itself, might be a problem. I don't know how I'd feel being able to smell the frying of bacon, eggs, mushrooms, onions ... ."

"Shut up, Micky," she interrupted. "You'll have me feeling hungry. I went through the same thing and it took ages to ignore food. It really did. I learned to ignore food – I had to, and you will in time, but you shouldn't talk about it. Why do you think I rushed you away from that restaurant?"

"So, being able to smell isn't all it's cracked up to be?" I laughed.

"I hate the smell of new ghosts," she replied, "and having to stick my tongue inside their mouths to clean them is disgusting. And I don't like sucking that smell of death from their bodies – it makes me gag." – Let me tell you, I'm so glad that I haven't become a Reliever or Monitor. It's not that I can smell, but it's the thought that counts, and if she hadn't mentioned it I wouldn't have thought about it. I had to ask her why she did it. After all, she could do something else. She smiled a cheeky smile, and said, "It has its benefits ... like you." She kissed me gently, and then more aggressively. Jana manoeuvred one hand between us, working at my trousers. And my immediate thought was ... here we go again.

The rest of the day was spent sleeping or having sex, with little time for talking. On a few occasions, either during or after our love-making, Jana tried influencing me to stay, but, after some sleep, she'd wake up accepting the fact that I'm going back to England. In the end, I challenged her on this wavering, and she reasoned that the sooner I left and found out the truth ... the sooner I'd be back in her arms. And, on one occasion, she said, "Go and get it out of your system, but don't go jumping into some feather-brained tosspot or a pervert." – As if I would.

Some time in the evening, I opened my eyes expecting to find the slumbering Jana beside me, but she'd vanished. I lay there for, what must have been, a good hour, before she came back to bed. She refused to say where she'd been, despite my tickling. I kept at her until she said that it was something personal, so I left it at that. She had her way with my body once more, pulling me on top, and afterwards I collapsed, completely exhausted.

It's been a funny sort of day, today. Jana went missing, but later returned while I was dressing. She brought with her a black leather jacket, and after helping me into it, she turned me about to face the mirror. I admired my reflection – black shoes, black trousers, a cream coloured shirt poking out from the neck of a dark green jumper, and then the jacket. I felt great and I looked great, except for my stupid spiky hair. I raised my hands to my head but Jana stopped me. I watched her shapely back in the mirror as she tidied my hair and then I lowered my eyes to hers. A few tears had formed in the corners of hers, so I bent forward, kissing them away. She held me tight, crying softly, her body shaking with the sobs. A few minutes later I felt her relax. She edged away, still holding my hands, and said, "Let's go before I change my mind."

We made our way downstairs and outside. All the ghosts were there to see me off – Maggie coming forward and kissing me on my lips. Nancy and Freda made such a fuss of my leaving, while Tommy tried making a joke of it. I messed his hair and reminded him of the first time we caught him like that. He laughed with the rest of us, no longer embarrassed. Luisella kissed me and cried, while Lucia, on the other hand, held me close, patted my bum, and whispered, "Keep away from the men." The mischief in her face came with her smile, and when she kissed me she stuck her tongue in my mouth. This brought a round of applause and another bout of laughter. Affiong approached and offered her thanks. Finally, Anna offered me some last minute reminders before we left.

CHAPTER TWENTY-FIVE

Settling down inside the co-pilot, I laugh at the idea of travelling like this. It wouldn't have entered my head if it wasn't for Jana.

The first flight to Stansted was two hours away, so Jana wanted me to spend the time in her arms. We talked while watching the passengers come and go. We commented on people as they passed us by and, now and then, she'd point at some bloke or other, asking, "Do you fancy that one?" We made a joke of it, with me asking her the same about other men. It all seemed such a happy way to pass the time, but I could sense that she was getting nervous. She was trying to keep a lid on her feelings, but you know as I do that this is practically impossible.

The time for my departure was drawing ever closer, so we made our way towards my flight. Two uniformed men, one of whom took my fancy, stood near the embarkation point, and they were talking to another member of staff in, what I thought was, Slovenský. Jana couldn't help but hear that these were our pilots, and she joked about having this young guy in bed with her. I, of course, said that he wouldn't be a patch on me. And then she dared me to enter him. What would you do? – I told her I would and, immediately, saw she was a bit miffed.

"Go on then," she said, "but don't get too attached to him or you'll never find out what you really want in life." Jana kissed me passionately, begging me to come back soon. The tears welled up in her eyes, but she still pushed me towards the aeroplane.

Being inside this fellow certainly improves the scenery, and my expectations, as I journey home for the first time since I died. And this young man is also giving me a different meaning to feeling good about myself. I can sense his hand and eye movement, but, as Jana said might happen, I can't feel a sense of belonging inside his body. As he moves my hand to his groin, scratching his balls now and then, I'd have thought that I'd get a sense of excitement … but I don't. Perhaps I should be naked, but what will I do with my clothes. I suppose I can take them off and then put them back on later, but for the sake of two hours at the most, is it worth it? When I hear the pilots talk, I recognise some of their words – they are most likely Czech' – and then I notice the wedding band on my host's finger. Yes, he's a nice boy, but Jana's right. I shouldn't get attached, and the idea of me being inside him while he makes love to his wife is the last thing I need. If he was gay and spoke my language, then that would be another matter entirely. If I knew that were so, I might even consider delaying my visit to Ely and, instead, enjoy some well earned hanky-panky. And after all this time, do you blame me? We head beyond the clouds and I switch off, reflecting on the past few hectic days.

Time passes away with my memories, and we're now approaching Stansted. And I'm getting excited. No, it's not him. It's just that it's been such a long time since I've seen Mary. I wonder if she's still upset. It would be just like her. And how's she getting on with Ben? She might be getting married, and the mere thought of this hurts. I don't want Ben as my brother-in-law even though I am a ghost – I'm still here. Perhaps I should creep inside her head and – no, that wouldn't be fair to her.

My thoughts are interrupted when the aeroplane starts dropping, because my co-pilot has been given charge of the landing. Now this is different, and I feel as though it's me that's guiding it down to the runway. I can tell you … it's better than those computer simulators I used to play with. When the wheels hit the ground, I am proud of myself, despite the slight vibration running through our arms. I can't quite believe that I've landed an aeroplane.

With the journey over, I'm about to leave my host when he decides to scratch his balls again … and still nothing. I wonder about people's habits; how some bite their nails and others grind their teeth, while yet others constantly pick their noses, but scratching your goolies every few minutes, and quite openly too, is a new one on me. At the end of the day, I don't think this chap is my cup of tea. I take my leave and head towards my old workplace. Once inside, I watch and listen to some of my former colleagues, and it doesn't surprise me that I'm well and truly forgotten. Susan seems happy as she warms to her new boss, John Ferneley, whose name is emblazoned on my office door. I don't know him and don't know where he came from, and I'm somewhat disappointed that my old friend, Stan, didn't get the job. I take another gander 'round before flying out of the building and north to my sister's.

Minutes later, I'm swooping down to Mary's house and I can't help but notice the lights on in Samantha's bedroom. Slowing my approach, I float through the glass and the partially closed curtains.

"Oh, my god!" I should have known, but why bother with the lights on and the curtains nearly closed when it's light outside? I can't say, exactly, what I've just seen, and I don't know that I should, but if I don't then you'll probably get pissed off. Well, if you can't guess that they were fu ... . fu ... , oh shit, screwing each other to death, then you'd have to be thick. As I float down the stairs, I can't forget the image of a sweating Sam squirming down on Jack and the look of sheer delight, or was it pain, on his face. I'll have to ask her one day – when she becomes a ghost.

There's no sign of Mary and that doesn't surprise me, so what will I do – what do I do? The obvious, that's what. I go to my corner in the lounge, sit down and relax, but I'm not long there before Sam joins me, stark naked and still sweating. She grabs her handbag, rummages through it and pulls out a packet of pills. Naturally, I have to have a gander and, as I thought, they are after-sex pills. That must be Jack's lot for the day, poor bugger. Sam pops a pill, throws the pack back in the bag, and goes to the kitchen. A moment later I can hear the kettle being filled. Now, if she had been Joyce, then I'd have played around with her, especially after what I've learnt about mediums, but she isn't Joyce so I stay cool, closing my eyes and trying to forget the recent images of my niece's love making.

I try forcing myself to sleep but I can't as my ears pick up even the tiniest noises from the kitchen – the biscuits being taken from their tin; the water being poured; the spoons stirring the drinks; and Sam tut-tutting about. I can't think why she'd be annoyed, unless it's something to do with Jack. Perhaps he can't satisfy her. No, that's not true; not from the sounds they were making. Why can't I stop thinking about this? I listen to Sam's footsteps treading softly up the stairs. Thank goodness ... peace at last.

Uh, oh! That didn't last long. Someone, and it has to be Mary, is opening the outside door and coming in.

"Hi, kids. I'm back." Not getting a reply, she shouts again. *"Sam! Jack! Are you in?"*

"Be down in a minute, Mum," answers Sam. *" ... Just taking a shower."* Mary walks into the room, plops down on the settee and chuckles to herself. My keen sense of hearing takes in the noise of the shower and movement in the bathroom, and then the odd giggle from upstairs. It also appears that Mary can hear them, lifting her eyes to the

ceiling and chuckling again. Picking herself up, she goes to the kitchen, shortly returning with a hot drink.

Samantha joins us soon after, now dressed in a primrose tee-shirt … no bra, and a pair of not-quite hipster jeans – so low around her middle that I'm not sure what's keeping them up. I'll have to tell Jana about these, but, knowing her, she probably has a pair.

"*I've put the lamb on and the veg' is washed and in the steamer,*" she tells her mum.

"*You are a love.*" And smiling at Sam, she asks, "*How's Jack? Is he coming down?*"

"*He's in bed. He says he's tired.*"

"*It must have been the journey,*" suggests Mary.

"*More than likely,*" fibs Sam, smiling cheekily.

"*But why does he want to get involved in Spanish property? There's enough here to be getting on with.*"

"*Oh, you know Jack, Mum. He's never one to miss the chance of spreading his wings, and he's thinking of taking a Spanish agent as a partner.*"

"*Why, on earth, would he do something like that?*"

"*It makes things easier to sell the villas, and, anyway, there are so many different by-laws and Jack's Spanish isn't good enough to understand all the clauses. Besides, Mum, this agency he's talking about will only be a subsidiary company. It won't affect his business here.*"

"*Is he buying one himself?*" Sam looks quizzically at Mary, and then Mary continues, "*A villa, Sam … somewhere near the beach, perhaps?*"

"*We haven't discussed it. I'd like one, but we'll have to talk about it.*"

"*It'd be so lovely to spend some time abroad, dipping my toes in the water.*" Mary's eyes wander in thought.

"*Don't get ahead of yourself, Mum. We're not married yet.*"

"*Sam! You're not having problems, are you?*"

"*No, Mum, of course not, but I can't go asking Jack to buy a place over there. It's got to be a joint effort … even financially.*"

"*I still have Mick's insurance money.*"

"Go on, Mary … buy one for yourself. I've no use for it anymore," I tell her.

"*I know Mum, but that's yours, and you might need it in an emergency.*"

"*I'm fine, Samantha. It's there if you want it … that's all I'm saying.*"

"Thanks, Mum, and I'll remember that, but me and Jack have to start doing things for ourselves. I have to finish my degree and find a job, and, right now, that's more important. If Jack wants to invest in properties abroad, then that's up to him. When, and if, we marry, then I'll get involved, unless he invites me to do so beforehand."

"I don't know, Sam. The way you're talking, I'm not sure if you're really happy. And Jack seems to be tired all the time. He's always sleeping when he's here. Anyone would think he didn't have a bed in his own house. Maybe he's not well. He doesn't have much time for you at all, does he? Has he seen a doctor?"

"Oh, Mum! Shush! Do you want another cup of tea?" Mary nods and Sam turns away, avoiding the question. Her face says it all, looking totally frustrated with Mary, as she makes her way to the kitchen. If only Mary knew the truth ... and why doesn't Sam tell her? Mary's no prude – she never has been and never will be. I could tell Sam a few stories about my sister. I remember the days when our parents were away, and Mary's sexual conquests in her late teens and early twenties ... and that was back then. This is now, for heaven's sake, and everybody's at it, quite openly.

'Ding-Dong'

"I'll get it," shouts Sam. A second later, I hear her again. "Hi, Joyce .... Come on in."

"You're looking well, Sam. Is Jack still treating you alright?"

"Yes, of course. Why's everyone aski ... "

"Hi, Joyce," shouts Mary. "I'm in here."

"Tea or coffee, Joyce?" asks Sam in an agitated manner, as Joyce approaches the lounge.

"Coffee please ... er, no sugar," Joyce answers.

As she steps into the lounge, she casually says, "Hi, Mary. Are we still going?"

"Just as soon as I've finished my tea." I wonder where they're off to.

And I'm still wondering when Joyce steps close to Mary, whispering, "Is Sam okay? She seems a bit flustered."

"It's probably her period. Thank God I'm over all that," Mary replies very quietly.

"I wish I was," says Joyce. "That's why I'm late. I had to go all the way to Tesco's, 'cause that useless corner shop didn't have any of my size left."

"Pads?" asks Mary.

"No, silly. Tampons!" Joyce lifts her eyebrows. "I only came on last night, and it didn't half piss Harry off. I don't care about him, but my periods seem to be getting heavier."

"You should see your doctor," Mary suggests.

"A fat lot of good that'll do. It's just one of them things."

"I suppose you're right."

Mary and Joyce then get into a conversation about the news and weather, until Sam returns with their drinks. She disappears again for a few seconds, returning once more with her own tea and a plate of biscuits. The small talk resumes and eventually they finish their drinks. Sam goes to wash up and the other two make their way to the door. I pick myself off the floor and follow. Wherever they're off to, they're going to have company.

"We'll see you later, Sam," says Mary.

"Say hello to Uncle Mick for me." Now, there's a thing. I'd promised myself that I'd go and see my grave, and to have two fine ladies alongside is a bonus. By myself, I suppose, I'd reminisce and wonder about what might have been, and whether they'd neglect my body in its decomposing coffin. It's just as well that I don't have to worry, anymore, about my body going back to nature. I'm safe in the knowledge that so long as I don't drown, or come across Helga and Dorothy or others like them, then I'll remain a ghost forever. I didn't like the bio-degradable idea, but now … who cares? Mary was right and I respect her for it.

Once outside, I head for Mary's car, but they pass it by and keep walking in the direction of the graveyard. I float alongside, listening to the banter about Harry, Ben and Mary's Brian. Apparently, the last named has conned Jack into getting him a small flat with a low mortgage repayment. If you're in the business, I suppose, you can pull a few strings. Mary doesn't appear too happy though; criticising Brian for manipulating Jack – him being part of the family, so to speak. And she's not too happy with Jack for being such a soft touch. Ben is still courting Mary, but Joyce thinks my sister could do a whole lot better if she made the effort. Mary, on the other hand, seems content with her life. Harry, meanwhile, is getting on Joyce's nerves; calling around for a bit of nookie as and when he likes – sometimes blind drunk and in the early hours of the morning. I can tell you … it's fascinating listening to women chatter about their love lives when they think nobody's around.

Joyce is still going on about Harry when we reach the graveyard, and as we approach my plot she says, *"If your Micky was still alive and not bloody gay, I'd have made a play for him. I loved that man, even though he was the other way."* Poor Joyce. I could have fancied her if I was straight, but, had we got together, would she have remained faithful or still been as flighty as ever? I'll never know, will I? And does it matter? I'd made my mind up – I was gay and I was happy.

"He wasn't always after the boys, Joyce, but you wouldn't have known about that. It was before your time." Come on, Mary, I'm not that old, and why are you telling her about my life?

"I'd never have thought of Micky as anything but gay," says Joyce, both surprise and a question creeping into her face.

My eyes take in a baby conifer, proudly standing directly above my buried head, as Mary says, *"Tell me, Joyce. I've never heard you call Mick … Micky before, but you've just said Micky twice."*

"I don't know, Mary. It feels right. It's as if something's telling me to call him Micky; as if he should have been a Micky, not a Mick. Micky seems so friendly, but Mick and Mike seem so businesslike." Mary starts laughing, softly at first, and then louder, drawing tears to her eyes. *"What's tickling you? I don't think me thinking Mick should be a Micky is so funny."*

"Oh, it is, Joyce. Believe me, it is," chuckles Mary.

"Well?"

"It was so long ago. Honestly, Joyce, it doesn't really matter."

"Yes, it does. You can't go laughing at something as silly as this, tell me it's funny, and then say forget it. And you said he wasn't always gay. So, come on, Mary, spill the beans." Joyce opens her arms, staring and waiting for an explanation.

Mary still laughs quietly as she tries to get the words out. *"Let's sit down before I fall down,"* she says. They make their way to a nearby park seat. Mary smiles at Joyce and then turns back, gazing at my grave, saying, *"As I said, it was a long time ago."*

"I don't care," says Joyce. – I take the spare place at the end of the long seat and sit down, lean back, resting my right arm on the armrest and the other on the backrest behind Joyce's head.

"When we were small, we all called him Micky. I used to call him

Mickey Mouse and so did most of my friends, but my mother used to get angry, so she insisted that we drop the 'Mouse' bit and just call him Micky, and at the same time she told us to spell his name differently from the Mickey in Mickey Mouse." Mary sighs and relaxes her body.

"That's not very funny."

"Do you want to hear this or not?"

"Sorry, Mary, I thought you had finished."

"No. I was just remembering. Anyway, I must have been about fifteen or sixteen, and I used to go out with my friends, messing around and that. Several times, a few of us would go to a local hill where we'd watch this pervert play with himself. We didn't go there deliberately to see him, but he always seemed to be hanging around. We were all virgins at the time, but you know what it's like."

"Yeah! I used to watch my older brother when I was fourteen, and he never found out."

"Now, I say this man was a pervert because he knew we were watching, and he didn't care if it was boys or girls who were looking. I think us watching turned the bastard on."

"I get the picture," says Joyce. "You have to watch out for people like that, especially nowadays."

"I couldn't agree more. That's why there were always at least three of us. One particular day, we were hiding down the hill while this old git was carrying on, and then a couple of big lads came along and started throwing stones and swearing at him. This Dave ... that was his name, got up and ran away with the lads chasing after him, and the next thing we see is Micky and his friends watching him, us, and the big lads ... and we all started laughing. The thing is, Micky said that he and his mates were spying on me and my friends, and how we got our kicks. I had no reason to disbelieve him. What he was saying was true, and he and his friends used to remind us all the time."

"That's to be expected. That's what brothers do, isn't it?"

"Yes, I suppose so, but nice as Micky was, he used to torment me something shocking."

"You did something, didn't you?"

"No, not really. In fact it was Micky who did it to himself."

Come on, Mary. You've told her enough. Show me some respect after all this time; and, besides, I'm dead.

"Did what?" asks Joyce.

"We didn't know, at the time, that Micky was a bit of both."

"Bit of both? You mean straight and gay – a bisexual?"

"Yes. He always had a girl on his arm when he wasn't with his mates. He'd bring girls home and I'd watch him kissing them and touching them up, and he didn't care if I saw him. I never saw him go all the way, but I knew some of the girls he'd had. I'll tell you something, Joyce. Micky had a steady girlfriend."

"He didn't?"

"He did! He had the hots for this one for quite some time. Now, what was her name ... er, Katie I think, or, no. ... Cathie! That's it. They'd been an item for a while, going to the flicks, the dances, and he'd bring her home now and then. Mum was very happy. Micky had just started this job at Stansted, a junior position, but it wasn't bad money. Anyway, one day Micky took this Cathie out on a trip somewhere, with a hamper full of food and wine ... and guess what else?" Don't tell her, Mary. Please don't tell her.

Joyce responds. *"A pack of three?"*

"No-oo!. He had an engagement ring. He was going to ask her to marry him."

"You're joking? Micky? Get Married?"

"Yes."

"So, what went wrong?"

"I don't know. Honestly, Joyce, I really don't know. She obviously turned him down but I don't know why. When he came home that night, his clothes were a mess, the hamper was missing, and he had the hump. He wouldn't speak to anyone. He went to his room and stayed there. A few days later, I heard him phone this Cathie and he was in such a temper with himself. Not with her, though. He was as nice as pie when he was speaking to her. He kept begging her to go out with him and all the time he kept apologising, but when he got off the phone he would talk to himself."

"What about?"

"He kept asking himself why he was saying sorry ... that it was the cow's fault, and he wasn't talking about Cathie. I don't know who this other girl was. He never mentioned her name. But the thing is, Joyce, I'd never heard Micky call a girl a cow, either before Cathie or after.

This cow, whoever she was, must have said something to Cathie to make him so angry."

"Poor Micky. To think he could have been married with a load of kids. Was it this that turned him off women?"

"Oh, no! Not at all. It took him a few months to get Cathie out of his system, but he went out with a few other girls; just the odd date, but nothing serious."

"You see, Mary. Even you're calling him Micky now."

"Yes, I know, and I think it's only right. I started calling him Mick when my friends did."

"I don't understand."

"Come on Mary, you've told her enough," I beg.

"All the time he was going out with girls, he was also playing around with other lads his own age. You know ... playing with each other, sexually."

"Hey! There's no harm in that. Lots of school kids experiment when they're young. I went to bed with a few girls, just to see what it was like to be touched. I bet you did the same."

"I must admit ... I did when I was much younger, but it wasn't like that with Micky. I'd no idea that he was gay, bisexual, or whatever. I thought he was the straightest guy you could ever meet. At this time though, Micky was twenty – not a school kid, and, I didn't know but, he was playing one guy against one girl. It came as such a shock to me, Mum and Dad. My friend, Marie, told me. You see, her brother is gay and was always gay, and one day Marie caught him in bed with our Micky. I thought Marie would have kept it between us, but she let the cat out of the bag and told some of our other friends. The next thing is, they're all calling Micky ... Mick."

"So, what's wrong with that?"

"The Mick had an addendum."

"An add ... what?"

"Addendum ... something added on."

"I still don't get it," says Joyce.

"Jesus, Joyce," I shout, "you can't be that thick. Don't make Mary say it."

"I can't tell you. I never called Micky ... Mick, but when everybody else did, the Mick name sort of stuck. That's how it is, I suppose. Once *the word went round, girls didn't want to know him, and maybe that's why he made the choice he did … you know, being gay. I'm so sorry now, when I look back, especially with him being here. If only I could apologise to him. If I'd kept calling him Micky back then, and all these years since, then I'd feel much happier within myself."*

I stand up and watch the pair of them, Joyce's mouth still silently forming the words *Mick* and *add*, and then she twigs, looking down between her legs, and her lips form the words that Mary won't say. Joyce turns to Mary, saying, *"The lousy bastards. Why did they pick on poor Micky like that?"* I must admit that I'd expected something else to come out of her mouth, other than support.

"It was a long time ago, Joyce, and while the flower power and free love days were still in people's memories, gay sex was still taboo. It still is present day in most quarters, but now it's legal, and more families accept how their children are. I loved Mick. And I still do, God rest his soul. Never mind, Joyce. Usually, I say a little prayer for him while I'm here. You can join me if you like and then we can go to the pub."

"Good idea, Mary, and I can give him another toast. To my friend Micky and the day he nearly married." She still has a way with words.

"And, Joyce!"

"What is it, Mary?"

"Please don't repeat this 'Mick' business to anyone … anyone at all. Samantha doesn't know and I'd like it to stay that way. And in the meantime, I suppose, I'll still call him Mick. I'm so used to it now and I wouldn't like any awkward questions."

"On my life, Mary, I'll never tell another soul." And I believe her. Mary offers a prayer for me, gives me a few messages, and then the two of them make their way back home, stopping off, on the way, for a couple of brandies.

Back at the house, Mary takes out the meat and starts slicing, all the while Joyce keeping her occupied, chatting about Harry, Ben and the subject of marriage. Joyce is having none of it, not putting any faith in her man, while Mary isn't sure. She tells Joyce that she doesn't want to grow into an old woman without some male contact. However, Joyce keeps harping on about how dry a man Ben is and that Mary could never be happy with him. She's dead right.

Sam and Jack soon arrive on the scene, helping themselves to coffee, and, presently, the four of them sit down to dinner. Talk eventually turns to property and it's my house that comes up in the conversation. Mary doesn't know what to do, so Sam and Jack suggest he advertise the place for her, but, while I listen, it transpires that Mary isn't in need of the sum that a sale might bring, so renting out becomes another option. This is what they plan to do and it makes sense – giving Mary an extra income and the choice of selling when she wants.

Jack brings up the topic of Mary's birthday, suggesting that she and a few of her friends should go to the races for the day. Joyce is game, mentioning Alice and the two Pats. The only one with doubts, however, is Mary, who, when asked what's on her mind, replies, *"I'd love to go, but what about Ben? I'm not sure he likes racing."*

"Screw Ben," says Joyce. *"It's your birthday, so you should do as you please, and if he doesn't like it, well, tell him to get lost. In the end, Mary, he either he cares about you or about himself. Tell him, and if he tries changing your mind, then you'll see the kind of man he really is."*

"I agree, Mum," says Sam, eagerly, *"and it will be great day out. I remember when we used to visit Uncle Mick's and he'd take us for walks near the course. We'd watch the horses for ages and ages, and you used to so love the place."*

"I still do, Sam, and it will give me an excuse to visit his house and see what needs doing. I can't rent it off until the place is spotless." That's so typical of Mary, isn't it?

"You don't have to fret about the house. I can look after any repair work."

"Of course you will, Jack, but I'm thinking of the curtains and new bedding if it's needed – that sort of thing. The furniture and everything else are still there, and our Mick was a tidy man. He didn't drink much; he didn't smoke; and he didn't go … ." And Joyce laughs her head off before Mary can finish. The other two smile, as Mary says, *"You naughty girl. I wasn't going to say that."*

"I know, Mary. It was just … oh, forget it." Joyce glances warily at Jack.

They carry on discussing arrangements for Mary's day at the races, and this reminds me of Séan. I wonder whether he's still in Ireland or doing some haunting down the tunnels, or, speaking of horses, perhaps he's sleeping on another fence at Aintree. My thoughts are rudely interrupted by a jingle from Jack's mobile, but when I hear him talking about some house in Barcelona, I lose interest.

What to do, that is the question? Do I hang around here for a few days or follow Joyce home. Now that might be interesting, but I don't fancy sharing a bed with her Harry. When I hear Joyce and Mary making arrangements for tomorrow, I decide to stay here, but when the conversation turns to one of their everyday mundane chores, I'm not prepared to listen. I'm about to make tracks upstairs, when Joyce announces that she's going. As she gets up and walks towards me, I back off, letting her pass. Joyce dons her coat and, turning to Sam and Jack, she cracks a joke about sex and bed, then bids them goodnight. Mary walks her to the door, and as Joyce leaves the house, she throws her head in the air, saying, *"See you, Mick, and behave yourself."* Until that moment, I thought she hadn't sussed me out. It shows how wrong a ghost can be. Mary waves her off, shuts the door and, seemingly bewildered, she walks back to the kitchen.

"What was that all about?" asks Sam.

"I haven't the faintest idea," answers Mary.

"She must be off her trolley," suggests Jack, scratching his head.

"Perhaps Joyce thinks Mick should still be with us. We talked about him today ... quite a lot, in fact."

"Of course, Mum. He must be on her mind after visiting the graveyard."

"Yes, Sam, you're probably right."

I'm in two minds now. Joyce has left, so it's highly likely that the rest of the evening will be spent either in front of the television or in bed. I can join them or get some much needed rest. Taking the sensible option, I climb the wooden hill. The door to the spare room is shut, but this is no longer a barrier. I strip off and jump on the bed, remembering Simon in this very room, and as I lay back with my hands beneath my head, I gaze at the wall, the cupboard, and the window, and wonder from where it was that Jana spied on me.

It's been a trying couple of days, with Jana draining my body, time after time, as her sexual demands took priority, and then my waking early, not fully recovered. Then there was the journey. Okay, I spent some of it inside a fit young man, but not long enough to regain all my strength. I've been worse – of course I have, but a solid night's sleep will do me the power of good.

CHAPTER TWENTY-SIX

A few days have passed by and nothing untoward has happened in Mary's household. I went on a shopping trip to Cambridge with Mary and Joyce, and, in fairness to Mary, she is a hell of a lot faster behind the wheel than Ben.

On reaching Cambridge, I stayed close by as they hadn't indicated how long they were likely to be, and I couldn't very well ask. However, while the two ladies tried on several outfits, I took a stroll around the men's department, keeping my eyes peeled for any unsuspecting young men. I needn't have bothered. Mary knows when the shops are at their quietest and the boredom was tempting me to fly back on my own.

The next couple of days brought visits from Alice and Ben. Alice, by now aware of the birthday bash later in the month, had spoken to a few more pals and everything was being organised properly. When Mary told Ben, he seemed more than happy, and even volunteered to pay for taxis, both to and from the course. You could have knocked me down with a ... on the other hand, you couldn't – not the state I'm in. It later transpired, in a conversation between Alice and Joyce, that the latter had phoned Ben earlier, on the quiet, and told him what to say about the party. Jack took Sam to Oxford, and I haven't seen hide nor hair of them since.

As for me, I need to do something exciting. I'm happy that Mary's reasonably happy, and, other than sit around watching my family getting old, I have to go and live my life. I wish my sister farewell and head off for London. Who knows, I might bump into one of my fellow ghosts. But where will I choose as a starting point? And while I consider this, the answer seems perfectly obvious. So, with an air of expectancy, I head straight to one of my old stamping grounds.

Approaching Hampstead Heath, I slow down and glide graciously to the top of Parliament Hill. Easing onto the pathway, I cast my eyes over the huge expanse of London. I can sense ghosts ... several of them, and if they can't hear me from here, then they're either busy or deaf, and, as yet, I haven't heard of any ghost being afflicted with a loss of hearing. Opening my mouth, I make a loud piercing noise and sustain this cry while turning slowly on the spot. Satisfied with my performance, I take the bench behind me and sit to watch the kite-flyers flying kites and dog-walkers walk on by, all enjoying the air and their surroundings.

I'm wondering, not if but, when I'll get some response. Of course, you might be thinking that I could've found these ghosts myself. I could but I didn't want to interrupt them, just in case they were in a sexual embrace or some other embarrassing situation. Yes, I realise that most ghosts get their kicks from sex and they don't care whether they butt in or hang around watching each other, but I'm not really like that unless it's by accident, like the time Tommy was hiding among the trees.

I'm not alone very long before a young female ghost comes into view, so I stand and wave at her. The moment she lands beside me, I introduce myself, offer my hand and ask her name.

"You may call me Betsy. Betsy from Borley. So, Mick, you're in need of some help. What is it that ails you?"

"Ails me? No! You've got me all wrong. I was only hoping to meet a ghost or two, to say hello and that."

"Then you shouldn't have blasted my ears with your call of distress."

"Distress?" I eye her quizzically.

"You *are* new, aren't you?" she asks, moving forward and taking the seat. Betsy crosses one leg over the other, her skirt riding up her shapely thighs. She isn't the world's most glamorous person, facially that is, and her short brown hair is rather lank in appearance.

"I suppose I am in a way. I've been around for a few months."

"Is that all? You must learn to control your vocal chords. It makes a change for me, though … being the first ghost here." She leans back, stretching her arms out and across the back of the seat, letting her boobs push themselves in my direction.

"Are you expecting more?"

"Unfortunately, yes."

"Why unfortunately?"

Betsy stares at me, licking her lips very slowly. "Two's company and … it's too bloody late." Her head points skywards, and turning around I notice three ghosts approaching. I can't contain my smile. The bushy hair and big flopping belly of Séan is a sight to behold. Flying alongside is a dark haired female and another much younger man.

They're no sooner on the ground than Séan grabs my hands, saying,

"Well, Mick, aren't ya a sight for sore eyes, and how are ya doin'?" Without waiting for an answer, he glances at Betsy and then turns to me again. "Now, ya wouldn't be finished with the lovely Jana since meetin' up with this woman?"

"I don't quite follow," I reply.

"Ar-agh, Mick, sure how long have ya been goin' out with the nun?" he asks, pointing and glowering at Betsy.

Immediately, Betsy jumps off the seat and starts shouting. "Don't you nun me, you braggart ... always shouting your mouth off. You're such a stupid idiot."

His hand raised, he moves towards her, saying, "Eejit am I? I'll give ya eejit, ya piece of ... ."

"Shut up ... the pair of you!" orders the new female, pulling Séan away.

Séan can't keep quiet and, turning to me, says, "She'll lead ya on, Mick, and then drop ya for the next ghost that takes her fancy. I'm warnin' ya."

"You talk through the seat of your pants, you no good ... ."

"Why, I'll beat the shite out'a ya, so I will," Séan retaliates, lunging at Betsy once again.

"Stop it, Séan. Stop it, now! And you too," says the other lady. Looking at me, she says, "If these two keep quiet for a moment, we might make some sense from all this. Mick, my name is Mabel and this is Dick." Mabel nods her head towards the new man, who seems very laid back, standing with his hands in his pockets. I extend my hand to each of them and, introductions over, I explain about Betsy and how this is the first time I'd ever clapped eyes on her. Betsy avoids Séan's stare while confirming my statement and her response to my call. Mabel agrees with her, telling me not to be so loud in the future. I want to know what's caused all the friction between the two of them, but I'm not likely to hear a thing unless one of them tells me ... but I'm afraid to ask.

Dick tells me about his life and why he hangs around London. Apparently, that's how he died ... you know, hanging around, or to be more precise, he was hanged as a highwayman at Tyburn, although he claimed his innocence back then and he still claims it now. He says it was a case of mistaken identity and a bit of skulduggery on the part of the real criminal – another Dick. To be honest, if I didn't know that

314

ghosts can't lie, I wouldn't believe him. I'm not being cruel in saying this, but he does look a mite shifty.

Mabel walks me away from the other three, telling me about her life. She doesn't mention Bony, but the odd hint about being happy with her man makes my imagination run loose. Mabel is quite an attractive ghost – tall, slim, and well-spoken. In a navy blue dress, down to her calves, she seems rather conservative. She dedicated her life to teaching, being devoted to children for years and years, while the rest of her life ... and men, passed her by.

I ask her about Betsy, but she doesn't seem to know very much, other than when, where and why she died. Naturally, I'm interested; not because I fancy her – heaven f orbid – but something about her is bothering Séan, and I'm keen to know what it is.

"If you must know," says Mabel, "Betsy used to be a nun. It was so long ago ... back in the late thirteen-hundreds, I think. She died in the vaults of a rectory at Borley in Essex. The elders bricked her up alive because she fell in love with one of the monks. The two of them were trying to escape ... to make a life with each other, but they were caught. Their coach-driver lost his head and the monk was hanged. They were cruel days and cruel people, and can you believe it, Mick, they were all members of the church."

"That's terrible, Mabel, and all because they were in love."

"Yes, it is. It beggars belief."

"But don't you know why Séan is so angry with her?"

"No, I don't. Perhaps they had an affair and she packed him in for someone else. It appears to be something like that, or it might be something to do with the church." I shake my head, not understanding. "Séan believes in God. So did I when I was alive and when I first returned as a ghost. I don't now ... not for years, but some ghosts still believe and that's up to them."

"I know he does, but what's that got to do with it?"

"Perhaps nothing, but he was a staunch Catholic. And Séan might have the idea that Betsy was responsible for the monk's death – that she led him on to leave the church."

"That sounds a bit iffy. Besides, she was probably a more religious person than Séan, with her being a nun. I think it might be as you first said – she blew him out."

"I agree, but he never talks about her. Séan has women everywhere. Oh dear, I shouldn't have told you that," says Mabel, looking flustered.

"Don't worry, Mabel. Séan's told me plenty about himself and I've seen him in action."

"Have you?"

"Well, not actually, but … ." Suddenly, our attention is drawn to a shouting match going on behind us. On turning round, we see Dick in the middle as Séan and Betsy yell and throw punches at each other. Flying back the fifty or so yards, we jump in between them – me pulling Séan while Mabel holds Betsy. Neither have a mark on them, but Dick looks the worse for wear.

"Séan! Behave yourself."

"Ya shameless hussy! Jezebel! Get your arse out'a here before I … ."

Dragging Séan away, I ask, "What's got into you? You're usually so relaxed with life."

"I don't like that bitch, Mick. I really don't."

"Why? What's she done to you?" I ask, keeping my voice down.

"Not now, Mick … please. Let's go somewhere else." I can see that he's agitated, but I can't leave him like this. And I can't leave the others without saying goodbye; and to walk away so soon after meeting them is downright rude, and I'm not that kind of person.

"Give it a few minutes, Séan. In a way I feel that this is all my fault. The next time I come to London, I won't call out, and that way you won't have to cross swords with Betsy again."

"Don't blame yourself, Mick. This is between me and her, and I should have had the sense to keep my trap shut." I persuade him to walk back with me, and for a while after, we all manage to talk of other matters.

It turns out that Betsy came to London for the day, purely on a shopping expedition, and it was a coincidence that we both hit town at near enough the same time. Dick, meanwhile, says he spends his days in and around Oxford Street, Marble Arch and Hyde Park. I ask about the ghosts in Hampstead and Mabel enlightens me to the truth about two of them, one at *The Spaniards Inn* and another that wanders the heath. During my times in Hampstead, I'd been led to believe that there were loads in the area, but this is not so according to my new friends. I make arrangements to visit Dick in Hyde Park, and to also meet Betsy so she can show me where the Borley Rectory used to be.

Not long after, we – that is Mabel, Séan and I – take our leave, and head north towards Burnt Oak. On the way, I tell them about my sister's coming birthday bash and Séan's demeanour changes instantly. All of a sudden he's bubbly and acting as if everything that's just happened was only a bad dream.

"When's this day out, Mick?"

"The twenty-first," I answer.

"Ya mean this month … May?" The excitement grows in his eyes.

"Yes."

"Mabel. I'm goin' to treat ya to a day at the races," he says, grabbing her arm and squeezing her bum as we fly over treetops, rooftops and railway lines.

"Keep your hands to yourself or I'll tell my man." I can't help but laugh when Séan ignores her, playfully tickling and caressing her body.

Once inside Bony's house, I see the man who is driving Mabel crazy, his wife, and their two girls – Matilda and Christine. Mabel goes on and on about them, happy to talk. Bony, though, keeps complaining of the cold, and Mabel explains about the man's sensitivity to ghosts. Séan and I decide to give him some peace. Before leaving, Mabel gives me a friendly warning regarding Séan and his shenanigans. I exit smiling.

We make our way to a pub in Cricklewood, where Séan brings up the topic of Mary's birthday. He carries on talking about the craic we'll have, and he seems very keen to meet my sister. When I get the chance, I tackle him about Betsy, and, although he's not too forthcoming, he eventually acquiesces to my request.

"The thing is, Mick," he says, "Betsy was my Ghost Monitor and at first she treated me as if there wasn't another male ghost in the world. She doted on me somethin' rotten. Now me, I thought the world of her. I thought the sun shone out of her arse, and that's the truth. While I was alive, Mick, I didn't have many women. Sure, I never had the money to take them anywhere, and, besides that, I liked the pint. Betsy, though, was a blessin', and she had the loveliest pair of melons a man could lay his hands on. And every time she went on a new job, I felt safe in the knowledge that she'd always come back." Séan squares up to me, eyeball to eyeball, as if I was the person he hated, and he then continues. "I forgave her the first time." He stops speaking for a minute, but I don't want to ask him anything, hoping he'll find his tongue again … and he

317

does. "The bitch was screwin' around with every new ghost she looked after – both male and female. I had my suspicions, so I followed her at a distance. Sure enough, she no sooner had a new charge in tow than she was at his body. I couldn't take it, Mick. I jumped through that skylight window and pounced on the pair of them. There was a battle royal, I can tell ya, and all three of us came out with a few scars. They healed, thank God, but from that day to this, I've no time for her at all. She made me what they call me, Mick … a womaniser. I like their attention and the laughs I can have, but I'll never make a pig's ear of my life again, by settlin' down with one."

I really don't know what to say. One thing is certain though, and it's the fact that I've made the right decision to search for what I want in life. The thought of not finding my dream man and then returning to Jana only to see her shacked up with someone else would drive me mad. I feel sorry for Séan, but, there again, I don't. He's changed the way he lives his ghost life and he's happy being a playboy of sorts, so long as he avoids Betsy.

"Séan? Are you okay? I mean, like, will you be alright … er, on your own?"

"Of course, Mick. I feel fine, and I've your sister's party to go to. I've all these nice thoughts of the horses racin', and the women winin' and dinin', so I'll soon be in the mood for enjoyin' meself." We take a gander around the pub and spot a few women, and this puts the smile back on Séan's face. Now happy that he's back to his old self, I take his hand and tell him I'm going. I don't know where he stays overnight and I'm not sure I want to know. I've got other fish to fry, so to speak, so I bid him adieu and fly back to Hampstead.

CHAPTER TWENTY-SEVEN

After leaving Séan to his own devices, I checked into an empty room in one of the huge houses near Hampstead Heath. When I say empty, I don't mean it was devoid of furniture and finery. In fact, whoever owns the place must be rich beyond normal means. I don't know how much they paid for their wallpaper and whether they used their own money to buy it, but luxury doesn't come cheap. Anyway, who am I to complain? I took advantage of the situation and spent the best part of a week relaxing in a fine bed and reading books to my hearts content. This was, of course, in between the times I spent visiting all the gay pubs and clubs from Hampstead to Camden.

A couple of days were taken up with visits to the city centre where, on one occasion, I indulged myself with my first ever ride on the London Eye. The weather was fine and the views were impressive but, all in all, I'm glad I didn't have to pay for the experience. Given a choice, I'd still choose looking over London from the top of Parliament Hill. Another sunny day was spent sucking nectar from flowers in a nearby park.

I bet you're waiting to hear what I got up to, sexually, and who I met. To tell you the truth, I tried out a few possibles, but neither fancied them nor got any enjoyment from their bodies. What I missed most were the sensations – you know, the real feelings of belonging in a body. I just couldn't get it up, if you know what I mean. There were others that appealed, but they were either Brahms and Liszt or I didn't like their partners. I don't know if it's me being too picky – perhaps I am – but these days I'm more cautious, checking the people out by following them to the toilet and making sure they're not snorting coke or popping pills. Why take the chance when I have all the time in the world? Actually, I'm a shade disappointed in not finding at least one young man to turn me on. You might think … 'what does it matter, he's gay and would probably go with anyone' … but I'm not like that; I have taste … just like everybody else.

Lying here, in Mary's spare room, reflecting and wishing, I know that my day will come, and, who knows, it might be tomorrow at the races. I've made arrangements to meet Séan on the roof of the main stand, and, I suppose, it's as sensible a place as any. Whether or not he brings Mabel along, we'll have to wait and see. Knowing Séan, though, he'll probably be canoodling with some other female ghost, leading her on and making his mark before the inevitable fall. For a man with a pot belly, he doesn't do so badly. Closing my eyes, I try to sleep, but the image of Séan and his pot belly lying naked in a field of shamrock doesn't let sleep come easy. I let my mind relax … relax … relax … . *'I have visions of Joyce in the same field and she's pressing her boobs into my chest … and then a herd of stomping cows take her place. I can't get this field out of my head … and now it's Lucia on top, and as she fades away her face is replaced by Jana's as she pushes my body into the ground, getting me excited. I touch myself and smile at her, but it's not her anymore. She's gone, and now it's Evelyn who's biting me, snapping his teeth, blood everywhere, killing me. … '* – My body jack-knifes into a sitting position, my eyes wide open. Brushing my arm across my brow, I wipe the non-existent sweat away, wondering what the hell is going on inside my head. Moments later I lie back down, turn on my side and close my eyes.

Morning comes and with it the noise of a new day: traffic, dogs barking, and Mary and Sam running up and down the stairs like mad women, readying themselves for their day at the races. I've decided to stay in bed as long as I can … and why not? I'm not travelling with them – I'll be a lot faster flying, and, besides, there's no room in the cars. All together, they've managed to gather a party of sixteen, and yesterday, when Alice told her who was going, Mary was thrilled to bits.

I lie still, listening to the commotion as the door bell rings over and over again. The male voices of Jack, Ben and Harry are outdone by the shrieks and laughter from the ladies. I feel comfortable and safe in bed, and as long as they leave me in peace, I'll be happy. Trying to shut them from mind, I stare at the ceiling and wonder about last night and the beauty of dreams, or was it a dream? And if it was, it wasn't that beautiful. Not in the end.

Time passes and morning drags on into afternoon. I can hear the tinkle of glasses every so often and it seems as though they're all going to be half-pissed before they hit the racecourse. At long last, the sounds of cars' horns cause a shift in the movement downstairs. This brings out the nosiness in me and heading to the top of the stairs I count the bodies as the gang make their way outside. I scoot back to my room and dress.

320

Seconds later, I'm on my way, and within twenty minutes I'm hovering over the racecourse and on the look out for Séan. From the looks of things, racing hasn't started yet, although the crowd is quietly gathering and some horses are parading. My sister and her entourage can't possibly be here, so I won't waste my time searching the bars, but I have an idea.

Dropping from the sky at a gentle pace, and avoiding the bar and restaurant area, I study the other buildings, taking care not to upset the horses. When I find the jockeys' changing room, I'm in my element. A few have already donned their silks, but others are in the process of stripping off. My attention is drawn to one of them as he walks out of the steam room. Either he's been touching himself up or he's naturally like Simon, but the most impressive feature is the size – not his height; he's only tiny, but – of his erection. Whereas Samantha's Jack is a well built man with a less than average cock, this skinny fellow's is delightfully big. I can't take my eyes off his glowing pink skin as the other jockeys throw him playful suggestions. He starts laughing, joining in and offering himself to anyone, but I can't stop twitching and growing inside my trousers as a delicious warmth spreads through my loins … and I don't want to. I can't resist it – honest, I can't, and I slide inside the jockey's body. He feels so wonderful. Perhaps I've found my ideal man.

When we bend down to pull on his jock-strap, his head turns and we smile while watching another jockey exiting the steam room. This little chap is not so well-endowed, but sizeable just the same. I'm impressed. Who'd have thought that such small men could be fully grown in the nicest possible of ways? This racing business is certainly worth following and I think I'll encourage Séan to take me round the courses. My man stands me up again, pulls on his breeches and readies himself for racing. After some more banter between the men, we head for the weighing room. Once checked in on the scales, I enjoy being carried out towards the parade ring.

Damn it! I can't go with him – you know, the horses – and I have to ease myself backwards from his lovely tight-fitting body. The jockey stops and makes the slightest of movements with his head and shoulders. Never mind. I'll catch up with him later. Watching from afar, I keep my eyes on my future partner as he gets a leg up on a huge chestnut colt. Well, it's huge compared to the jockey … in both departments. As they make their way to the track, I fly upwards to the stand's rooftop.

"Ah, sure, where have ya been?" asks Séan, as I settle down beside him and, to my surprise, Mabel.

"I was studying the form."

"And, sure, what would ya know about the horse racin'?"

"To be honest, Séan, not much. Hi, Mabel, and how are you?"

"I'm fine, Mick … and you?"

"I'm tickled pink, Mabel. Thrilled to bits, in fact."

"Aye, and lookin' at the lump in your pants, whichever filly you've been playin' with should have finished the job."

"Maybe it's for me," says Mabel, placing her hand on my knee. I don't know where to put myself, so try to ignore the comments.

"Séan, I've a question to ask you."

"Well, fire away man, but make it quick. The racin' will be startin' in a few minutes."

"Can ghosts have dreams?"

"Ya haven't been dreamin' about women, have ya?"

"I don't know."

"What d'ya mean, ya don't know?"

"If it was a dream, it was sort of queer … you know."

Séan bursts out laughing. "Talkin' about queer, when I first met Simon, I thought he was as bent as a nine-bob note – him lookin' at me with that thing in his pants. Sure, he's an awful lucky man; it'll never go down. Viagra! Now that's somethin' useful. What d'ya think, Mick?" Fortunately, my trousers are back to normal and I don't answer, trying to show my ignorance of Simon by giving Séan a questioning stare.

Mabel looks into my eyes and then smacks Séan on his arm. "Leave him alone." Turning to me, she says, "Let Séan watch his racing and I'll tell you what I know. Ghosts can dream, Mick. I dream quite often. Perhaps, this is because I have a fertile imagination and I was always a well read person. I do wish I could understand the words the way I used to. I have a slight problem, Mick – a punishment for something or other, but for what I don't know. When I was new to ghosting, some of my early dreams were very fitful, but nowadays I dream of Bony, Debs and the two girls, Matilda and Diana."

"Don't you mean, Christine?" I ask.

"Huh?"

"Bony's daughter … you called her Diana."

"Dearie me, yes, you're right. I keep thinking of her as my little princess. I forget myself sometimes."

"Ar-agh, it's the distemper ya have," interrupts Séan, his eyes still fixed on the horses.

"So, it's distemper this time. The only dog around here is you." Mabel clouts him good and hard, and then turns back to me. "He can be so nasty, Mick, but you pay no heed. Now, tell me, what's worrying you?"

"I think I had a dream last night. I woke up in a sweat, but I wasn't sweating, and then I went straight back to sleep."

Mabel pets my hand. "Don't worry, Mick, but if you tell me what's ailing you, I might be able to put your mind at rest."

"No, Mabel. It's nothing worth worrying about. I was just curious. I wasn't sure about ghosts dreaming ... that's all."

"Quiet, ye two! The race is goin' off." As we watch the race unfold, Séan jumps to his feet, shouting the horses home. When they flash past the post, he stamps one fist in his other hand, cursing and blaming the jockey riding the second.

He's still complaining when we go in search of Mary and Sam. Eventually we find our party sitting near one of the bars. Ben's dancing about, chuckling and offering to buy all the beers. Every now and then, he shouts, *"Silent Hawk"* and kisses the ticket in his hand. As he, Jack and Harry go inside with an order, Mary and Joyce start talking about Ben and his big tip.

"How much did he have on?" asks Joyce.

"I don't know. I think he said twenty pounds," answers Mary.

"Twenty pounds! Is that all?"

"That's a lot for Ben, Joyce."

"Didn't he see the price?"

"Price?" asks Mary, looking dim.

I point out my sister to both Mabel and Séan, and he can't help but pass a remark about Ben and his bet. "If he's only had a score on the horse, then he won't be gettin' much in the way of drink from his winnin's."

"Why," asks Mabel.

"At even money or thereabouts, he'll only double his stake."

"What? Forty quid back? Is that all?" I ask.

As Séan nods his head, Joyce explains exactly the same thing to Mary and Sam. Sam laughs her head off and Mary casts an unhappy glance in her direction. Sam quietens down, and says, *"Sorry, Mum. I didn't mean to laugh. Listen, if you tell Ben to let you collect his money, then I'll go with you."*

"Why would I want to do that? It's his winnings."

"I know, Mum, but he's been bragging about winning two hundred pounds."

"Oh, Sam, I don't understand."

Joyce butts in. *"Mary ... Ben told Jack and Harry about this horse. He said he'd been given the word that it was a certainty and that he should stick his life savings on it."*

"So!" Mary still looks bewildered.

Joyce continues, *"Harry stuck three hundred on, and Jack had even more."*

"Yeah, five," says Sam, *"and I put on two hundred."*

"Sam! You never?"

"I did, too. So, if you get his ticket, I'll give you some of my winnings and then add it to his. He won't know the difference – we'll get him blotto. And, after all, it is your birthday."

"And I'll give you some of mine," adds Joyce. *"I had sixty on the tote."*

"Sure, ya have a fine niece there, Mick, and fair play to ya. And who's the other sexy bit of stuff?" While listening to my family, I tell Séan and Mabel all about Joyce and warn them to keep away from her.

"I don't believe you girls."

"It's a day out, Mum, and we have to let the mothballs out sometime."

"But two hundred pounds, Sam ... that's a lot of money."

Sam shrugs her shoulders, lifts her glass and Joyce joins her, making Mary take hers. When the men come back, Sam puts her plan into action, urging Mary on. Ben doesn't mind and the three women hotfoot it to collect their money. Jack follows and I watch Sam explaining things until they're out of sight.

Whatever was said between them, I don't really know, but when they come back, Mary passes a wad of money to Ben, who promptly splits it, giving half back to my sister. Mabel points out how kind Ben is to Mary. Soon after, Séan is off for the next race so I join him, leaving Mabel to enjoy herself with my family and friends. We follow the same pattern for the next two races, Mabel each time happy to stay behind. When Séan and I return after the fourth race, however, Mabel is missing. Séan, feeling responsible, wants to find her and although we can sense her, we can't see her. Following our noses, we are guided to the weighing-in room where a host of jockeys are going about their business. She's here – we know it, and it's the more experienced Séan who closes in on a line of jockeys who are waiting to weigh in. I smile and get excited when I see my man amongst them.

"Hi, boys," says Mabel, gently easing her head – and only her head, sideways from the very jockey that's taken my heart. This can't be happening to me. Perhaps Mabel is only trying him out for a laugh.

"So there ya are," says Séan. "Will ya come out'a the poor man before ya do him some damage?"

"I will not," she replies, still pushing her head through the side of the jockey's neck. "I'm going to keep him company for a few days." – Are my ears deceiving me, or what?

"W ... What about Bony?" I ask, trying not to seem desperate.

Mabel answers, "I can't keep tormenting the young man, handsome as Bony is. He can sense me all the time I'm near him, and if he didn't keep getting the shivers and shakes then I'd reconsider. I'll pay him a visit sometime soon, but, for now, I think I'll stick with this little chap. Don't you think he's sweet?"

"Y ... Yes. Yes, I do," I answer, nervously. This isn't in the least bit fair, but what can I do? I can't tell her that he's mine. What would they think? I can't keep my eyes from his as he moves towards the scales.

"So, Mabel, when ya know where he lives, will ya come and tell us?"

"Of course I will, Séan. Only you and Mick know who I'm with, so keep it quiet. I don't want to get a bad reputation."

I nod my head in agreement, as Séan says, "Sure, ya know I'll never say a word, Mabel, but ya might want to be watchin' out in case he's gay."

Mabel doesn't hesitate before replying, "That would be nice – two men for the price of one."

"Sure, Mick, isn't she the randy little minx?" And before I can answer, he says, "Well, Mabel, make sure ya stop ridin' him when he's ridin' his bloody horses."

"Go on, you two ... get back to your party. I'll stay in touch. I promise." Mabel purses her lips with a kiss for us both, and then pops her head back inside my lovely jockey. We wave her goodbye and go back to the stands. What will I do now – I'm desperate?

"And what's wrong with your face? Ya look as though you've lost the love of your life." I keep my mouth shut and, although difficult, I force a tiny smile. "She'll be back, Mick, but I wouldn't want to be in your shoes when Jana finds out you've been fancyin' Mabel." I have to change the subject, and fast, or he'll get suspicious.

"Condoms!" I exclaim.

"Ya what?"

"Did you ever use a condom?"

"What, in Heaven's name, made ya think of condoms?"

"Nothing … well, yes, I was thinking about my dad."

"What's he got to do with condoms?"

"I was thinking of you. You know, being older than him – my dad that is. Did you use them when you were alive?"

"Well, Mick, I wouldn't be usin' them now I'm a ghost, would I? But, to answer your question … no, I didn't. There were some around, I think – big baggy things, from the insides of pigs I believe, but I'm a God fearin' Irishman and a Catholic, and I had no use for them. Anyway, what's all this to do with yer father?"

"I was remembering the first time I ever used one."

"A condom?"

"Yeah."

"How old were ya?"

"Eleven. It wasn't like … ."

"Eleven! You? Havin' sex at eleven years of age? Didja ever hear such bullshit in yer life?" he asks, looking at the sky.

"I wasn't having sex with anyone. Me and my friend sneaked some from my dad's bedroom. They were big ones back then. Not the type you were talking about, but compared to today's they were pathetic. When we were very young, we'd go to the seaside and sometimes saw them rolling through the water – really long manky things. They were so long that you'd think they'd been on one of those horses. But, at that time, we didn't know what they were for and we'd pull the filthy things from the sea, thinking they were some kind of seaweed. We didn't realise that they'd come out of the sewers."

"Ya dirty bastard."

"I told you, Séan, we didn't know. Like I was saying, when I was eleven, we nicked half a dozen new ones from my dad and used them for competitions."

"Competitions? What ... to do with sex?"

"No, Séan. We used to stick them on cars' exhausts, and when they drove off we'd watch the condoms get longer and longer until they burst. We'd time them to see whose johnny lasted the longest."

"So that was part of your glorious misspent youth, eh?"

"I guess you could call it that, and then there were the water bombs."

"Sure, I've heard about them, Mick. Now let's be havin' no more talk about feckin' condoms. The next race is about to start."

We watch the race before making our way back to Mary. By the time we reach her, some of the party are ready to leave, nearly all the worse for wear. However, Séan has taken a liking to Alice and is tempted to enter her body. Warning him that she's nearly legless, he backs off the idea. Séan's not one for wasting time though, and spots another group close by, mostly women, and they seem relatively sober.

"Now, her, I like," he says, nodding in the direction of a chesty blonde with an attractive face. "She reminds me of Marilyn Monroe, and a cracker she was. I'm tellin' ya, Mick, I wish Marilyn had come back as a ghost."

"So, you're tempted, then," I ask, as he still eyes the blonde.

"That I am, and I might as well find out if she's got the matchin' curtains."

"Got what?"

"Is it stupid ya are, Mick? How's a man expected to know if she's a real blonde without havin' a look?"

"You wouldn't?"

"Well, I'll know when we get into bed. I'll see ya later, Mick."

"Yeah, okay Séan." He floats over and, as he slips into her body, a silly grin develops across his face.

I turn my attention to Mary and Sam, still sitting among the nine people left. Ben is out of it; Jack seems to be in control of himself as he talks to Joyce and Harry; while Alice is singing to everyone and no-one. Seeing that they're happy, I float to my sister and niece, kiss them a tingly kiss, and then go in search of someone to comfort me.

Entering one of the other bars, I notice two attractive men talking to a lady dressed in high heels, fishnet stockings, and a close fitting split-down-the-leg red dress revealing a healthy expanse of thigh. She has a strong back, and a mop of red curls adorn her head. My thoughts go to Séan and what he's missing. I move slightly closer and listen in.

The sexier of the two men, a brown-haired, cute-faced, twenty-something, says, *"Not yet, dear. All the boys I like don't want a long term relationship."*

"I don't want one, at all. Anyone I bring back to my place ends up nicking something – my mascara, my eye-liner, or anything else she can get her hands on. It's so unfair. And the cost is prohibitive." I'm over the moon. Moving even closer, I observe the young woman – I mean man, and she's pretty.

"Ooh, I know what you mean, Shirl'. I went to Boots the other day looking for a new puff, but their selection wasn't to my taste. I have this shadow, you see." This other man, with black hair and shaped eyebrows, pushes his face forward, pointing out the faintest of bristles underneath his nose.

"You should try electrolysis. That'll get rid of it," suggests Shirl', in a sexy, yet camp, voice.

"Not on my face. Someone else told me to go to a specialist."

"You should, pet," agrees the sweet looking brown-haired man. *"I know just the place, in Camden. Call me tomorrow and I'll give you their number. But phone before I go to work."*

"I will, Pete. These specialists … they're not too dear, are they?"

Pete replies, *"What do you want from life, Bryn. If you stopped buying all that junk and shoving it up your nose, you'd have money in your pocket."* At least this Pete seems to have some sense … and a job. Moving away from the bar, he says, *"See you in a jiff'."* I follow him to the toilet and watch … and I want to hold him. "Stop, Micky, behave yourself," I tell myself. When he's finished, he puts himself away, washes his hands, and returns to the bar.

"It took you long enough," says Shirl'. *"Been sizing up your prospects?"*

Pete smiles at Shirl' and Bryn. *"I'm always on the look out for that something different. You know what I mean?"*

"I'm exactly the same," says Shirl', then glancing at Bryn, she adds, *"and as far as this fella goes, he's bloody useless."*

"Speak for yourself," says Bryn.

"Now, girls, behave, or you might not get any dessert tonight," laughs Pete, now looking at his watch. *"I have to be up in the morning, so ...."*

"We're getting it up, tonight ... aren't we Bryn?" interrupts Shirl', gripping him gently between his legs. *"Come with us, Pete."*

"I'd love to, but I can't. Honest."

"You and your work ... and to think what the three of us could have got up to."

Pete smiles cheekily. *"Maybe later. Right then, I'll be off."* When he picks up and drains a bottle of Perrier, I'm thinking ... 'And sober, to boot'. Come to think of it, the other pair were fairly sober, also. Which to choose? Who would you pick? But there again, you haven't seen what I've seen inside Pete's trousers, and, not being into threesomes, I take my pick. Pete pecks them both on their lips and we leave the bar and the racecourse. We head south, with me in the back of the car studying him and his taste in music. We haven't been on the road very long when Pete lifts one of his hands and starts working a finger up his nose. I pull my eyes away. I suppose we all get caught short sometimes – no tissues, so I let it drift from my mind. I'm happy listening to the car radio. It makes a change to hear a variety of tunes, as opposed to an individual's choice which might be less appealing.

An hour later, we're in Pete's flat, in the heart of Watford, and watching television. I'm in his armchair while he stretches on the couch. He clicks the remote for his DVD player, and presses play. It's bound to be a blue movie – it just has to be. I haven't watched one for such a long time. It's not! As the title rolls, I can see that Pete has a copy of The Passion Of The Christ. I check through some other DVDs, lying loose by the tele' ... Man On Fire, Van Helsing, Blood Work. My god! They're all pirates. While I sit brooding about him and his films, the film on the box gets more interesting. Now and then, Pete does what he hadn't done earlier, and smokes the occasional cigarette. I don't object to him smoking. I can't smell or taste it, and, as long as he's otherwise fit, it shouldn't pose a problem when I climb inside him. I'm going to ... I really am. I feel that I owe myself the pleasure of someone else's body, and he might do me a power of good. The only thing I need to do is check out his flat for something untoward, and if there's nothing there then he's my boy.

When the film is finished, Pete has a shower with me watching and getting excited. While he dries himself off, I inspect the bedroom and bathroom for medication. The items of interest are many. I find various packets of condoms with differing colours and flavours. There are boxes of old videos – all blue movies, and several gay DVDs. But the most obvious things on show are Pete's range of dresses, female tops and skirts, padded bras, knickers – mostly crotchless, stockings, suspenders, loads of ladies shoes, and an assortment of ladies wigs. Having met his friends, this doesn't surprise me.

I strip off and wait until he's ready for bed, and just before Pete slips inside the sheets, I slip into him. He leaves on the bedside lamp and starts reading a book on history. That's novel, I think. I'd expected a dirty mag' or a thriller of some kind. As he relaxes, so do I ... and I'm feeling more comfortable by the second. After a while, we lay the book aside and our hands slide down our bodies, touching and playing with ourselves. I feel the heat as he ejaculates, and I'm satisfied. I can feel the sense of his pleasure as he sighs a contented sigh. Shortly after, he falls asleep, and though I can't see through his closed eyelids, I stay awake thinking about my day with Mary, Sam, Séan, my jockey, and, now ... my new boyfriend.

A few days pass by, and, other than hanging around Pete's place, waiting for him to come home from work, I take in some of the sights, and I must admit that I'm not overly enamoured with Watford. It's not as though I haven't been to Watford before – I have, a few years ago, but at that time the town had a huge swimming pool; several pools, in fact, all inside the one complex, and they provided an entertaining few hours for me and my friends ... lolling about in the warm or the hot waters, depending which pool took our fancy.

At that time, Brendan – him of the huge hands and the even bigger mouth – was my partner, and we'd come to Watford just for the swim or a change of scenery. Brendan always seemed to choose where we'd go, and that was part of the problem. It's not that I minded, mind you, but sometimes we'd go swimming at Broxbourne where we could stay outside on the grass, checking out the other tackle on offer. While there, we would either lie down close to each other, passing comments on who we fancied and what we'd like to do to them, or we'd strut around in our skimpy trunks or thongs.

As regards Pete, well, I went with him to his workplace and, I'm sorry but, I wasn't impressed. I don't find answering the phone and telling cabbies where to go that appealing. He wasn't swearing at them ... no; he's a bloody taxi-controller, and, quite honestly, I'd been expecting more of him. The only excitement I got was from the tiny television by the phones. It was the cup final from Cardiff, and I couldn't take my eyes off the footballers ... especially that gorgeous Ronaldo, as both he and Van Nistelrooy scored the goals for Manchester United. Perhaps I should have gone there to watch them all undress. As for Pete, I'm having second thoughts about this young man, despite his delicious voice and lovely bum. I hate it when he picks his nose. It's such a disgusting habit and it's turning me off.

After some time spent browsing round the shops, I make my way back to the flat and inspect his wardrobe again. Not long after, he returns with a pizza, which he scoffs while watching Anne Robinson make fun of contestants on The Weakest Link. He licks his fingers, takes a drink of orange juice, and then lights up. As he pulls on his fag, I wonder about his lungs, and I'm tempted to stick my head inside – just for a look, but I know that's impossible. When his mobile plays it's merry tune, I'm all ears. I can't help it.

"Hello, Daphne here," Pete answers, now using a very effeminate voice.

"I thought it might be you," he goes on.

"She didn't."

"Tell me more." For the next couple of minutes, Pete ... I mean Daphne, listens as the caller is obviously relating something of an encounter between him, or herself, and somebody else. Pete interjects occasionally with a 'yes', a 'she never', or an 'ahem' – all the time his face changing. Sometimes he's excited and other times he shows disgust. Despite my more acute hearing ability, I still can't make out the conversation from the other end. Too late, I think of pushing my head into Pete's, but next time I will.

"Will you be seeing her again?"

"Maybe she'll bring someone else along, so's we can have a foursome."

"What? You have her number?"

"Give her a ring then, and if she knows any others, tell her we'll have a party."

"I'm not kinky, cheeky. I haven't had a foursome for quite a while, and with a dong like hers … . Guess what, Shirl, I'm coming over all flush just thinking about it."

"Okay, then. Phone me tomorrow and let me know. Ooh, and Shirl', I nearly forgot. Did you hear about that couple in the car park in East Finchley?"

"Er, last week I think."

"A man and woman? Don't be stupid, Shirl'. It was two City gents … all suited and booted except for their pants. They were round their ankles." – Aye, aye! What's this then?

"No, they didn't. Their jackets were on and their shirt tails were flapping all over the place."

"They did! And they couldn't care less who saw them. The way I heard it, one of them train drivers was walking on the track nearby, and he couldn't miss them. He watched for a while but didn't disturb them, letting them carry on playing with each other."

"Stop interrupting, Shirl', or I won't tell you. They were between the bins and the cars, and the first one was bent over, with his hands on the bonnet while the other was behind, giving him what for."

"He was! Honest to God! This driver must have gone to tell someone, because ten minutes later, the security bloke and driver came back, this time with one of those big lamps, and they shone it on these two pervs."

"They are pervs, Shirl'. Who'd want to do it in the open like that, especially while young kids are walking about? Lots of people get off the trains and walk through that car park. Anyway, are you listening? This driver and the other geezer came back, and the pair of them were still at it, but, by this time, the second bloke was doing the honours. Even though the light was shining on them, the prats didn't stop humping 'til they'd finished. And then, calm as you like, they pulled their pants up and went their separate ways. Nobody said a damn thing to them."

"No, that's just it. They must have wanted everyone to see them. Maybe that's how they get their kicks."

"Yeah! They could be married and just fancied a change. Some wives don't know when hubby's playing away, or who with."

"Tonight?"

"No, not tonight. I'm on a promise."

"Hampstead."

"Yes, dear. Actually, closing the pub hasn't made the slightest bit of difference. I never used the place anyway ... just the car park."

"No, not yet, but it's easy for you, living close by. The nearest place for me is Scratchwood. Anyway, Shirl', I've got to go and do my makeup."

"No. I haven't washed the stains off yet, so I'll wear that short black slinky number."

"That's right ... easy access."

"Okay. I'll tell you tomorrow. See ya' love. ... Kisses." And Pete throws a couple of kisses down the phone.

As night draws in, Pete goes upstairs and I join him. I watch him stripping off, but I don't follow him to the bathroom where I know he's doing the three esses. Once back in the bedroom, he tries on several outfits, but settles for his original choice. He puts on matching black stockings and high heels, pulls a wrap from his wardrobe and drops it on the bed. After searching through one of his drawers, he pulls out a couple of pairs of black and red crotchless panties. He slides one pair up his legs – leaving the other with the wrap, checks the mirror to see how everything fits, and then sits down and applies his make-up. The piéce de résistance is the wig, and when the jet black wavy hair is clipped into place, Daphne admires herself once more. It's taken an age – a typical woman if ever I saw one. When he, I mean she, is happy with herself, Daphne makes her way downstairs, opens another drawer and pulls out a fairly large handbag – also black. She stuffs her spare panties, cigarettes, lighter, keys, and her money inside the bag, grabs the wrap, and makes an exit, turning everything off as she goes.

I run after her and jump inside her body. We toddle off down the concrete steps and out to her green Mondeo. Pretty soon we're heading south on the M1, towards London. Daphne lights up again, giving me a buzz of nicotine, and we open the window ever so slightly. While the car motors steadily in the middle lane, we listen to Razorlight's album and I'm pleasantly surprised. She lights up another fag, giving me a second hit in the space of a few minutes. Eventually, we hit Staple's Corner where Daphne makes a bee-line past Brent Cross Shopping Centre, on through Golders Green, and up the hill to Jack Straw's car park. Once there, we leave the car while Daphne has me adjusting her dress.

We dive in her handbag, once again pulling out the fags. I've had enough – not of Daphne, but the cigarettes – so I jump from her body.

333

When she's finished puffing, Daphne re-enters the car and I join her, but I take the back seat. It's not long before a guy flashes his lights. Daphne does likewise … twice, and the man crosses to her car. They talk for a minute or two and then this guy, in a white sports coat, sits down in the passenger seat. He lifts Daphne's dress and starts playing with her, while she does an Evelyn … bending over his body and making things happen. I can't resist touching myself and I'm sorry that I didn't stay inside her. Okay, I can easily slide back in, but I'm enjoying this experience. When the guy shouts out and grabs Daphne's head, my memories of that ill-fated night start flooding back. Regardless, I carry on playing with myself because the man in front is now doing to Daphne what she did for him. It's not long until she's satisfied, and after a few words between them, the guy leaves her car, returns to his, then drives away. Daphne takes out a tissue and wipes herself down.

Daphne isn't finished yet – not by a long chalk, and she takes out her make-up and a small hand-mirror. She re-applies her lipstick, tinkers with her eyelashes, and then relaxes, admiring her long red-coloured finger nails. Out come the fags again and I wonder whether a ghost can be affected by passive smoking.

A few more punters – not in the sense of money, you understand, but others of the same ilk as Daphne and myself – pass in and out of the car park, and Daphne enjoys fulfilment on two more occasions. In one case, she had to recline the passenger seat as she obliged this other man from behind, and then he returned the compliment. This time, however, although the man didn't like the idea, Daphne insisted on using a condom.

Time presses on and the sun has come out. I can't believe that she hasn't had enough excitement for one night and I'm not sure I like this carry on; half the time spent smoking her head off, and the other half picking bogeys from her nose with those long nails – and what's more annoying is that she's got some bloody tissues with her. It's six-twenty by the car clock and Daphne is busying herself, painting on more nail-varnish and humming different tunes. She takes out her mobile and phones someone, telling him – it is a him this time – about the night's exploits, but she spots another man approaching, and says to her friend, *"Anyhow, here's another one. I'll call you later."*

She puts down the phone and climbs from the car. Daphne says, in her womanly voice, *"Oh, hello dear. What can I do for you?"* I follow her out, so's I can stretch my legs.

"I hope you can help me," he asks.

Daphne smiles in such a naughty way. *"Well, now, it depends on what you like, and I'm game for anything."* I look Daphne up and down, at the stains all over her short black mini-dress, and if it was me who was seeing Daphne through his eyes … I wouldn't be interested at all.

"The thing is," he says, *"I'm locked in."*

"You poor dear," she says. *"If you want to spend a little time with me, then …."*

"No! Oh, you know how it is. I came here and, well, I got what I wanted, but I have to get home. The problem is … the barrier is locked down."

"I know, dear. It always is at this time of the day – from six o'clock 'til ten."

"You're joking!"

"I'm not, sweetie. Are you sure you wouldn't like a ….?"

"No! I have to get home. I've just finished the night shift and …. Oh, hell! What will I do?"

"There's nothing you can do, but wait."

"I'll have to phone someone."

"Do you want to use my mobile?"

"It's alright. I have one in my car. I'd better go. Thanks anyway."

"Perhaps I'll see you some other time," says Daphne, looking slightly disappointed.

"Perhaps. Bye now." As the man minces away, I look at Daphne again as she waves. I can't put up with this, and while Daphne leans against her car, smoking, I watch and wonder what to do.

Looking around me, I realise that a week ago I was staying in one of these houses … and that's where I'm going back to. I take a farewell glance at Daphne … Pete, and I suppose I can always go and visit him. I'm not sure that I like the female side of his being – too many partners; too much smoking; and, anyway, she has a dirty nasal habit. Her dress is a mess. The trouble is that Pete's such an attractive man and a very sexy woman … and everything I thought I wanted, but he's not for me. I blow him a kiss and fly off to the house with the white-washed gable. That's where my empty room is – with all its luxurious furniture, fine wallpaper, excellent literature … and a huge relaxing bed.

CHAPTER TWENTY-EIGHT

It's been a few weeks since I left Daphne – I mean Pete, and I've spent most of the time in and around London. Of course, I've been back to the car park and have watched my former love picking his nose. No, that's not quite true, because I turned my eyes away. I was tempted, on one occasion, to spend the night with him, and so I did. At least he gave me some sort of sensation, and I was persuading myself to stay, but, first thing in the morning, he was at his nose again. I'm afraid that it was one bogey too many.

You'd never believe this. On the other hand, I think you would, because one night I flew to Scratchwood to see if any of my old buddies were up there, and I bumped into Pete's mate, Shirl' – all dolled up to the nines and plastered in make-up. She pulled a few times, and to think she had the hots for that other fella', Bryn. But get this – one of her conquests was big mouth Brendan and I so wished that she did to him what Evelyn did to me. I had to watch, even though I was tormenting myself, wondering how my life might have been if Brendan and I had remained partners. I wouldn't have crashed my car and … and … oh, it's too late now.

A few days ago, I was flying over Earl's Court, so I dropped down to visit one of my old haunts. Back in the early eighties, we – we, being me and like-minded people – used to visit a pub called Subway, and it had the most pleasurable bar you're ever likely to see. This bar had holes in the counter; to be more precise, the holes weren't on the bar itself, but cut into the framework. And while we enjoyed a pint or two, others would be crouched behind the counter, unseen, and they weren't giving us the kiss of life. Aah! Memories. Of course, the whole place has changed now. It was later, the same evening, that I went to a gay disco at Embankment. It was my third visit there in as many weeks. I saw a few familiar faces from the past, and, while there, I went into their dark rooms where all sorts of canoodling and other goings on were going on. That's just it, you see – you have to know where to go, but not once did I meet another ghost patronising the same place as me. Perhaps Jana's right and there aren't any gay ghosts.

I climb off the bed and pull on my trousers, thinking about where to go tonight. I finish dressing and head for the local.

My old mucker, Andy, is in the corner of the pub, getting plastered as usual, and, nearby, talking to him, is a good looking guy in his late twenties. As I move closer, Andy's new friend pulls some change from his pocket. He buys some drinks, and, after passing Andy a pint of lager, he picks up a bottle of mineral water and starts drinking.

I think I've found my long-term host, or have I? After Pete, and my original thoughts about him, I'm not so sure. I like the idea of this man being gay. Well, he must be or he wouldn't be here, would he? And, although appearances can be deceptive, this guy, like Pete, seems to be tee-total, or, at the least, a sensible drinker. I don't mind spending the next two to three years inside his lovely slim body, and longer if his lifestyle suits mine.

From their conversation it transpires that his name is Malcolm and he's recently been away to a health farm. The more I hear, the more I like, but Andy seems to like him too. That won't really matter to me because I'd expect this Malcolm to have plenty of suitors, and being with him will give me the opportunity to get up to some hanky panky. If I'd clapped my eyes on this lovely creature when I was alive I'd have tried to pull him, so I might as well get the benefit of his body and whoever he dates.

They make arrangements to meet later on, and when Malcolm drinks up he leaves, with me in hot pursuit. Outside the pub, he pauses, giving me the opportunity to hop inside his body. He feels so comfortable and I'm pleased with my choice. After a little thought, Malcolm walks up the cobbled alleyway to the main road, turns left, walks a little more, and then turns right at the Tube station. On we climb, up the hill, and I'm wondering whether he's going to Jack Straw's, but instead of crossing over he turns into Hampstead Heath.

He carries me down one path after another until we arrive at an old oak tree, all gnarled and weathered. Close by is the trunk of a fallen tree where Malcolm decides to park our backsides, and then he sets his eyes and mine on a couple of young children. They are climbing in and out of a huge hole that's developed in the tree. He starts humming a tune I've never heard of, as our eyes linger on the two kids. I can feel my mouth drawn into a smile as he grins, but our smiles soon vanish when a voice in the distance, shouts, *"Patrick! Sally! ... Where are you?"*

"Here, Mummy. By our tree," the little girl answers. Malcolm turns

his head, and a young lady, being pulled along by a collie, comes into sight.

"I've told you before," she says. *"Now, don't go off like that again."*

The dog takes a strong tug and she lets go of the lead. It bounds up to the children as they climb out of their oak tree hidey-hole, and their pet starts playfully barking at them. The little boy picks up a stick and throws it high in the air and over our heads. Our eyes are on the boy and not the dog as it chases the stick, but when the collie comes closer it rears up and starts to growl. Malcolm puts his hand out to say hello to the animal, but it backs away, baring its teeth. Malcolm, not leaving well alone, decides to stand up and, guess what ... the poor dog legs it. I knew this was going to happen but at least it's not my fault this time. I hope Malcolm doesn't have any pets.

"Shadow! Shadow!" the boy cries out, now giving chase, while Sally runs to her mother.

"He's never done that before," the lady says, looking flummoxed. *"I'm sorry. I truly am. He's normally such a friendly dog. I can't think why he'd act like that."*

"It's quite alright. I like dogs and they usually like me. Perhaps, it's my new aftershave," suggests Malcolm.

"I doubt it," she says before turning away to follow Patrick and Shadow.

"Bloody hell! That's weird," Malcolm tells himself. Sitting down again, he studies the tree. A few squirrels are now hopping in and out of the hole and jumping around on the path, but they never come near us. Sometimes Malcolm smiles and other times I feel him frown, and I wonder what he's thinking about.

A good hour later, we hear footsteps and Malcolm turns as another man approaches. My mouth joins Malcolm's, as he says, *"Hi, Sid. About time you got here. Where've you been?"*

"I got side-tracked."

"Why? What you been doin'?"

"I've been watchin' that porn movie you lent me. I watched it four times if you must know."

"That's what they're for, aren't they?"

"Come on. Let's go back to my place. I've got some new ones."

Malcolm is up in a flash and the three of us head off to his friends place. We leave the Heath, cross to Jack Straw's car park, and climb into Sid's old Honda. We drive through Highgate and on past Finchley Central, eventually stopping outside a block of flats in Friern Barnet. Sid leads the way up the stairs, saying, *"Bloody lift's not workin' again. You'd think those wankers would fix it properly, wouldn't you? The bloody rent is high enough and the council tax is scandalous."*

"What rent and tax? You haven't paid any for years."

"Neither have you. Your old man's so rich that he picks up your bills. Anyway, that's not the point. The damn council would rather waste our money diggin' up all the humps in the roads, rather than fix where we live. Talk about jobs for the boys. They don't care how many kids are killed on the streets each year 'cause of people speedin, and all for the sake of savin', maybe, one person's life in an ambulance ... and that's a big maybe."

"But you drive, so why complain?"

"My little nephew was knocked down and nearly killed because of some tosser, and he wasn't officially speedin'. The prat didn't even get done, but if there'd been humps in the road ... the chances are he'd 'ave been goin' slower, see, and he wouldn't have hit our Rodney. And it's not just poor kids that get hit. I knew this kid who went to Radlett, and he was killed ... ."

"Leave it out, Sid. I know what you're sayin', and, as it happens, I agree with you."

Once inside Sid's flat, Malcolm opens the fridge and takes out a can of cola, opens it and takes a swig. Sid takes a beer and we sit down talking and drinking. Sid asks, *"Will we pull out the bed-settee or watch it in the bedroom?"*

I'm getting excited when Malcolm points to the bedroom. He stands up and leads the way as Sid grabs a video. I haven't seen a porno' movie for such a long time, and I can't believe I'm getting in on the action. I thought it was going to be with Andy, tonight, but this is an added surprise. In the bedroom, Sid puts the television on. Malcolm closes the curtains, blotting out the sunlight, and he then turns on a bedside lamp which gives off a pinkish glow. I'm wondering which one's the dominant male. When Malcolm grabs the front of Sid's jean-jacket and pulls him to his lips ... I know. My eyes are open, looking straight into Sid's, and my lips seem locked onto his. I'm afraid that my lips will force their way out of Malcolm's and straight into Sid's mouth, so I concentrate on every movement I make. I can feel my arms move as Malcolm pulls Sid's jacket off. I seem to be ripping his shirt, and then our lips unlock as we move apart. I can't feel anything except my own movements, and, when Malcolm looks down at Sid's body, I watch them undoing each others jeans. Malcolm lifts his head and again searches his partner's face. I can see the excitement flowing from Sid when Malcolm pulls him backwards and onto the bed. They restart the kissing and canoodling and my hands go wherever Malcolm puts them. I know we're pushing down his jeans and then I sense him kicking them away. They release each other, and, a moment later, two pairs of underpants are flying through the air.

I'm in my ghost clothes, inside a naked Malcolm, and my erection is straining against my boxers. It feels strange and I curse myself for not stripping off. Having no other option, I back away from Malcolm's body and release myself. The second I'm free, a loud yell explodes from Malcolm and he pulls his body away from Sid's.

"What's up, Mal? What did I do?" asks Sid, looking shocked.

"Nothing! You did nothing, but I feel bloody awful." Malcolm is shaking all over and holding his head with both hands. I keep still while Malcolm goes to the loo. We can hear him being sick and then hear the water running. When he comes back, as white as a sheet, he looks down at Sid's body. I follow his line of vision as he moves towards his pal, and is reaching out to him again when the door opens. A huge man makes his way towards the couple. Rather than go back inside Malcolm's body, I stand back and watch.

"Who the hell is this, Sid?"

"You know Carl, don't you?"

"No, I bloody don't. Have you been sleepin' with him?"

"What's it got to do with you, mate, and whatcha doin' with my boyfriend?" says the newcomer.

"Your boyfriend? What's he talking about, Sid?"

Sid is going red and his hands drop down his body, covering himself. "I was goin' to tell you, Mal ... honest. Look, why don't we have ... ."

"Don't bullshit me, Sid. I want to know, now, when you started two-timing me."

"When you were away, Mal. I went to a few parties; some straight and some kinky; and, anyway, what do you expect? We're not exactly

340

steady, are we? You were missin' for years, and you've had other partners."

"Hey, you ... go fuck yourself." – I don't like this. Carl's gruff voice and threatening manner is .... . Oh, shit! Malcolm has spun around and given Carl a dig in the ribs. And as the punches start to fall, Carl grabs Malcolm's head. Sid is looking on, not knowing who to cheer for.

I can't see what Malcolm's done, but Carl has dropped to his knees in agony – holding onto his balls by the look of it. Malcolm hits Carl again and again, then turning to Sid, he says, *"You're a prat. You've been balling him all the time, haven't you?"*

Sid answers, sheepishly, *"Mal, I'm sorry. I am."* Carl starts to rise, and, as he does so, Malcolm grabs him by the scruff of the neck, throws him in the hallway, and warns him to stay away. Seconds later, Malcolm's back, dangling a set of keys from his fingers. He grabs his clothes and starts dressing. It looks like my excitement is over for the time being.

"Mal. Mal! I'll make it up to you. Honest, I will," pleads Sid, moving towards him. *"I'm your mate, Mal. We can start again .... . Please?"*

"Sid, I've known you a long time – since we were kids, and I like you, but if you've been screwing around with dicks like him, then you've probably got an infection. And to think you wanted to stick that thing inside me. I've a good mind to break your fuckin' neck, or chop your filthy prick off ... or maybe both. You're stupid, Sid. You just couldn't wait, could you? And you know perfectly well that I haven't been playin' around. That was a shit thing to say. I like you too much to lose your friendship, Sid, but if you think I'll sleep with you before you're checked out, then you've lost your marbles. You might have AIDS, gonorrhoea, crabs, or whatever." My god, he's really sticking it to him. *"And do you know whether that prat has any infections or not? I bet you don't. Doesn't it worry you, Sid?"*

Mal's finished dressing and is pulling on his trainers, as Sid replies, *"Okay, don't rub it in."* Sid, himself half dressed, finds his jeans and makes some small talk. The situation settles down and they take time to drink some coffee. The likelihood of my seeing the porno' movie is now out the window, unfortunately, but there's always a next time. At least I know where to come.

Now back on good terms, Malcolm brings up the topic of sex again, and the safety of it, saying, *"Listen, Sid, you should call in at the doctor's* now. I'll get a taxi from there. It's for the best. I mean, like, if you're all okay and that, then there's no harm in us gettin' back together ... you know, properly that is."

"Yeah, I'd like that, and I promise to keep myself for you. Honest!"

"Okay, Sid." And with that they shake hands.

"Hey, Mal, speaking of quacks ... when are you going to see your psycho?" – Huh! What's he talking about?

"Tomorrow afternoon. I haven't seen her since I came home."

"If she thinks you're okay then she might put you back to work. You won't like that. On the other hand, she might put you back inside." – Inside? Inside where?

"Don't be stupid, Sid. You know me better than that. I'll invent something, but nothing too outlandish."

"It's alright for you. They'll believe what you say because you've got rich parents, and these bloody doctors only care about the money – especially the shrinks." Having seen and heard this latest carry-on, I'll wait until tomorrow before deciding whether Malcolm becomes my permanent host or not. I'm a bit dubious, with all this talk of shrinks and that, and, although he seems sensible enough, it's better to be safe than sorry. When they're ready to go, I follow them out and down the six flights of steps to the car.

The drive is only a short hop, and when Sid stops, Malcolm says, "Now go and get that check-up. They'll probably give you a blood test and an injection or two in your cock. It won't hurt too much. After all, it's only a pinprick." Malcolm laughs, but Sid doesn't appreciate the joke.

The three of us jump out, and after making arrangements for the following evening, Malcolm and I wander off. We catch a cab to Southgate, and fifteen minutes later, we're walking up the drive of a large detached house. I can see why Sid referred to Malcolm's family as wealthy. If his father actually owns the place, which sounds likely, then they're sitting on a goldmine. In the present climate, the place must be worth at least a million.

Once inside, Malcolm runs upstairs, so I take a gander around the hallway, the open-plan lounge, and an adjoining room which is filled with books of all descriptions. On I walk into the dining room where a huge table and its matching chairs centre the room. All the sideboards are of the same expensive wood, and a huge candelabra dangles from the ceiling. I'm not much of a connoisseur on art and antiques, but somebody in the house is. Peering through the rear window, I spy a garden that goes on forever, and, from its appearance, it wouldn't be out of place in the Chelsea Flower Show.

Presently, Malcolm joins me in the kitchen and puts on the kettle. When I see him pull down a mug and throw in a teabag, I think of how so like the rest of us the rich actually are when it comes down to basics. Mind you, I'd never have guessed how Malcolm lives by his choice of friends, but who's to say we can't mix with who we like. Perhaps, it's because he can't find any gays in the upper echelons of society. Malcolm doesn't speak 'far back' though, so his family might have acquired its wealth by sheer hard work. It sounds like it from the way he speaks. I watch while he makes the tea and carries it to the garden.

Rather than join him, I'm happier to investigate the house further. My nosiness takes me through the ceiling where I find myself in a large airing cupboard. Turning about face, I slide through the door and go from one bedroom to the next to see who else lives here. Malcolm, it seems, has a sister, and, from all appearances, his parents are sleeping apart. It's not unusual these days, I suppose, and when I remember Mary and Brian and how they split up, I find it pleasing that some marriages can work in some ways, but not in between the sheets. Maybe they don't want to rock the boat if the money's still coming in. Perhaps, their problem is one of age, but if their photographs are anything to go by, age doesn't come into it. Malcolm has a family photo in which he looks seventeen or eighteen, and he's sitting with his sister, mother and father. The photo tells me that his mum and dad look no more than forty, and his sister ... thirteen or so, but given that this was taken a few years ago it's slightly misleading.

Searching around Malcolm's room and finding a letter holder, I have to have a shufti. Using my new ability to lift the letters and move them from hand to hand, I can read them very quickly. I'm about five letters in, when I stop and stare. It's from a Dr. K. Phillips – a psychiatrist, and it confirms Malcolm's appointment for tomorrow afternoon. So, my Malcolm *has* needed treatment for something or other, and I'm about to find out what. I glance at the remaining three letters and then place them back in their holder. Stretching on the bed, I relax, closing my eyes and thinking about how my life might fit into his and whether all his friends are the same as Sid. I now have my doubts as to his choice of pal, especially when my initial observations in the pub looked promising. He seems like such a nice boy, but, as we all know, looks can be deceiving.

A while later, I go downstairs and out to the garden expecting to find Malcolm, but there's no sign of him, whatsoever. The mug has gone and, with it, my future mate. Where the hell is he? I check the rooms again, one by one, and then the locks on the outside doors.

"Bloody hell! Where are you?" I shout. I go around the place again and, this time, notice a postcard from the rest of the family. How the rich live, eh? … St. Lucia! And, according to the message, they won't be back for another three weeks. I glance at the fancy clock and see that two hours have elapsed since I lay on his bed. It's no wonder he's missing. Do I follow him to Hampstead and his meeting with Andy, or wait here?

I decide to hang on, rather than go traipsing around, trying to locate him, and I find a book to pass the time of day. Still being sunny outside, I head for the garden. As I pass through the window, the book falls from my hand. Damn! I forgot about that. So, jumping back in, I pick it up and search for an open window. Luckily, I find a small one in the bathroom, so I squeeze the book through. I take a seat among the flowers and settle down to read. As the plot thickens, I don't notice the time slipping away. Eventually, the light starts to fade and reading becomes impossible. So, giving up the ghost, I go inside and replace the book on the bookshelf. I decide to wait up for him and pass the evening relaxing in the comfort of the lounge.

It grows darker and darker and when he doesn't show, I head upstairs to bed. This time, though, I use his sister's room. It's not that I wouldn't mind sleeping with Malcolm, but he might bring one of his friends back, and the thought of another like Sid has put me on my guard.

The following morning, I go straight away to check on my new friend. He's not in his room and, by the look of his bedding, he didn't return at all. The clock says ten-thirty, and I'm wondering whether Malcolm will come home before his appointment, but, just in case he doesn't, I re-read the letter. It confirms his two o'clock meeting at an address in Central London – Harley Street, no less. And he definitely told Sid that he's going. So am I … with him or without him.

Midday comes and goes and still he hasn't shown, so I pass through the door and fly off, heading towards the West End. In fact, it only takes a few minutes to reach my destination. I've become so adept at flying that, pretty soon, I'll be able to keep pace with Jana and the other Monitors. Entering the foyer, I scan the list of doctors and their respective departments, which tell me the required floor. I head on up to the psychiatry department and sit in the waiting room for Malcolm's arrival. It seems like ages but, eventually, he turns up – about ten minutes early, and the first thing he does is try to sit on my knee. I'm a much quicker ghost than I used to be, though, and jump to an adjacent seat.

Bang on time, the receptionist tells Malcolm to go in, and when he moves, I am right behind him. I'm so close to and practically inside his body when he knocks and then enters the room. I'd been expecting a woman, but I'm dumfounded when I see that his doctor is so attractive. Having been with Jana and Lucia, my thoughts on the female form have changed somewhat, and I look at females in a different light, nowadays. Maybe, it's that being a ghost thing – you know what I mean? I used to think that a psychiatrist was an old goat of a man, with specs on the end of his nose, but this one is a definite improvement.

"Good afternoon, Malcolm, and how are you today?" she asks. She appears to me to be very young for a psychiatrist – no more than thirty, give a day or two.

"I'm feeling great, Doctor. Haven't felt so good for a long time."

"Good. Please, take a seat," she offers, pointing to one directly in front of her desk. Malcolm obliges, while she continues, *"I haven't seen you for quite some time and I'd like to know how you coped in the hospital."*

"If that's what you want to call it," says Malcolm, with a couldn't care less attitude. *"We both know it was a nut house."* – Did he really say nut house?

"Malcolm, it's not a nut house, despite what you may think, and we both know your stay there has been a successful one. Don't you agree?" This lady has a real sexy and soothing voice, and from the letters after her name on Malcolm's letter, she's well educated.

"As I said, Doctor, I feel fine."

"As far as I'm concerned," she says, while picking up papers and glancing at them, *"it won't be long before you're free to do as you choose. Another few sessions and the answers to some questions, and then we*

can clear you for a return to work. What do you think of that?"

"You mean, you're not signing me off?" he asks, a sigh of relief spreading across his face.

"No, Malcolm, not just yet. Both we and the police want to know if you're prepared to undergo some hypnosis." Malcolm agrees, nodding his head without looking at her. *"Doctor Bryant has informed me of your willingness, and the helpful responses from your previous hypnotic encounters, but I'd like to ask you some other, more involved, questions. Is that okay?"*

"Is this about my memory of the case?"

"Yes, I'm afraid so. We have to try and make you remember the other two men involved. According to you, they were the main attackers and you were under the influence of drugs at the time." – What attack? What the hell has he been up to? … And drugs? I didn't see any sign of drugs in his house, other than migraine tablets in the bathroom.

"That's why I don't remember, and I don't see how going under again will do any good."

"But you just agreed to do so."

"Look, Doctor. I don't mind trying, but I don't see the point."

"Malcolm, the police aren't satisfied and I can understand why. After all, the family of that poor girl … and the girl, herself, deserve an end to the crime. You were caught in the act of raping this young girl because you were so high that you didn't hear your friends telling you to run. There are witnesses to this and you have confirmed most of the facts, but …." – My ears don't hear anything else as I wonder about Malcolm and what the hell he's done. Rape! Jesus Christ! … A young girl. That's pathetic and it's bloody vicious, drugs or no drugs. Words are going on around me and I can't take them in, as thoughts of what might have been with him will never be anymore. Never in my life have I met a rapist and I've never wanted to, and if he thinks that – well no, he doesn't think it but, what I mean is that I'm not spending another minute in this guy's company. Shit! And to think I was inside his body. I wish I'd known earlier.

I move towards the door and am about to pass through, when I hear the words *" … and good luck,"* come from the lips of Doctor Phillips. Malcolm heads towards me so I slip back inside the room, out of his way. I don't want to see him again … ever. Okay, he might have done his time, either in prison or a mental hospital, and he could very well be fit to live in the community, but I've no idea whether he might slip back to his old habits, sexually or drug-wise, and I'm not about to take the chance. Do you blame me? I give Malcolm a good head start and I'm about to exit the room when the good lady doctor walks my way. I move through the door, and as she approaches her receptionist, I stop to listen.

"*What do you reckon, Karen?*" the receptionist asks.

"*I'm not sure as yet,*" the doctor replies. "*If we could just get beneath the surface with him, then he should make a full recovery. Even Malcolm has to find out the truth ... for his own peace of mind.*"

Karen, eh? And she does seem concerned about her patient. I wonder if she's like this with everyone, because if ... . Hmm, now there's a thought. If she's always so caring then I should check her out. You know, perhaps use her as my long term partner. I didn't notice any wedding ring on her finger, but that doesn't mean she hasn't got a man waiting for her, does it? I don't bother listening anymore and, instead, size up my options.

Jana did say that young women were the best partners to use on a long term basis. Even Anna talked about their hormone value, and the more I think, the more I like. One thing's for sure, though, I'm not going inside her body until I get to know her. She might be a lesbian or one of these women into dominatrix. It takes all kinds, and nowadays it's hard to know what your next door neighbour gets up to. Somehow, though, I think this lady will be alright. I hang about the waiting room as the good Doctor Karen Phillips resumes her work.

Just before four o'clock, Karen, now in a deep-purple coat, walks up to her receptionist, gives her a bundle of folders and some mail, and then heads for the lift. I follow, so fast that I fly through the lift doors and out the other side. I'm back in a second and standing beside her as she presses the ground floor button. I stick as close as I can without touching her, while she leads me outside, up Harley Street, and then on towards Oxford Circus. We haven't walked far, when she stops, thinks for a moment, and then makes some deliberate strides towards the station.

I keep my distance, above her and away from the crowds, as we journey through London, via the Underground to Bank, and then on the Docklands Light Railway. Eventually, we arrive at, would you believe ... Docklands.

CHAPTER TWENTY-NINE

This is nice. I wish I could have afforded a place so plush when I was alive. Karen has a wonderful three bedroom apartment overlooking the Thames, and if it was her who chose the décor, then she has more talents than I'd have imagined.

Wandering from room to room, I take in the tasteful furniture, modern paintings, and beautiful displays of Waterford crystal glass. Her swish curtains and the harmonising colours make the place seem alive and wanting to be lived in. Even her bathroom is so relaxing that if you were to go for a number two, you wouldn't want to be in a hurry to leave the room, and it seems that she has the same idea, because a few reading books are sitting on a toilet shelf.

After my tour of the property, I take a rest on a sumptuous leather settee, as she lays back in a matching chair – a mug of Douwe Egberts cappuccino in her hand. I know the brand well, and, besides, I watched her make it. The position I've taken allows me to face her and study her mannerisms. Is she any different at home, I wonder. I know that I was. Half the time, I'd put on an act at work, but at home I'd let my hair down. I suppose everyone's the same really, and as I watch Karen, she seems both contemplative and at ease with herself.

Now and again, she slurps her drink ... sort of sucking it from the mug instead of swallowing properly, and other times she rolls the coffee round her mouth before letting it slide back her throat. Each time, she smiles, fiddling with the spoon and occasionally giving her drink a stir. Once or twice, she uses the spoon to feed the coffee into her mouth, and this takes me back to when I was a child and would do the same with my cup of tea. She hasn't, as yet, poured her drink in a saucer and slurped it that way, but she'd find it impossible – she doesn't have a saucer to go with her mug. When finished, she gives a contented sigh, places her mug on the mahogany side-table and, using a remote, turns on the television. Leaving it mute, she flicks on the Teletext and searches the menu. It doesn't take her long to find what she's been looking for and I join her in reading the arrival times of flights at Heathrow.

Whoever she's expecting has put a smile on her face. Karen jumps out of the chair and carries her mug to the kitchen. Naturally, I follow. As I reach the kitchen door, she's putting the mug down and turning towards me, slipping her blouse off at the same time.

What the hell! She's another Joyce. Karen has such a superb body, and when she pulls off her bra', I'm amazed at how wonderful and firm her breasts appear to be. To tell you the truth, Karen is one hell of a lady … intelligent; classy in her own way; to say she is merely attractive does her an injustice – she is strikingly beautiful; and she has everything going for her. If she was a he, I could spend the rest of my life inside her. Mind you, she won't be short of suitors, and I wouldn't mind betting that whoever's arriving is one of them. Perhaps he's the only one. Karen doesn't seem to be the type to play around, but these days, who knows?

Karen slips by me and heads for the bathroom. She runs the bath, adding bubble mixture to the water, and then rolls her panties down her legs. After dropping her soiled clothes in a nearby basket, she turns around and sits on the toilet. This is where I disappear, I'm afraid. I remember being with Pete and having the same problem. I draw the line at watching something so personal and private, so I head back to the lounge to relax. My ears pick up the flushing of the toilet and then the splashing of water from the bath, but I'm not tempted to go and watch. Instead, I mosey about the lounge, glancing through her books and am surprised that they're not all about psychiatry, psychology, and other work related topics. Most of the books tend to be fiction from a variety of authors, and there are only a few love stories amongst them. Karen's taste in books seems to stretch from early classics by Walter Scott and Charles Dickens to present day thrillers. Settling my eyes on Dickens' Great Expectations, I pick it up and, browsing through, recall how he gave the game away in the very beginning. I still enjoyed the story, but thinking about him and some of his other books, and how he told about life as it was in those bygone days, I also remember what Jana told me about me – about us, and how we ghosts are real … and that ghost stories are just fantasy. Believe me … I'd never have believed that I could come back and be able to read stories from the imagination of other people; what they think ghosts look like and what they think that ghosts might do. They were and are clueless. I'm here now, as live a ghost as you're ever likely to meet, and I'm going to stay. I replace the book on the shelf and look for a ghost story, just to prove my point, but I have to laugh when my eyes fall on The Republic, by Plato. Now that's a ghost's story, but it depends on the way you look at it. I wonder if Plato read it again before he went down with the ship.

Leaving the books aside, I turn to Karen's collection of DVDs, wondering about her choice in films. This, too, is varied, from comedy films to action adventures. Her taste in music is quite ranging, from classical to modern, and I'm getting more excited at the prospect of using her as my host. All I need to know, now, is whether she's on medication, and if so … what? Mind you, there's also that tiny matter of her love life to consider.

First things first, so I decide to check on pills and other medical problems she might have. I make my way to her bedroom to look around, but find nothing there, and I'm just off to the bathroom when Karen comes through the bedroom door. I back away, avoiding contact, and pass through the wall instead. Once in the bathroom, I search the cabinet. Other than some Night Nurse for colds and a few aspirin, I don't find anything else to worry about, and so long as she doesn't overdose on these two items, then I'll be alright. I wonder if she's on the pill; I didn't see any. Perhaps, they're in her bag. Maybe, her boyfriend – if that's who's coming – is a girlfriend. I wouldn't fancy that. It's not that I'm against the idea, but I need a man, and if being inside Karen is the only way I can get one then she has to have a boyfriend. Do you see where I'm coming from? With this in mind, I go back to the living room for a closer inspection. Beside her chair are a couple of envelopes. I rush to the bedroom, to make sure I'm safe, and find Karen sitting, totally naked, brushing her shoulder length hair. Some clothes are spread out on the bed waiting for her body to fill them. Then, flying back to the lounge, I inspect the envelopes and find that it's not so easy to extract their contents. I manage, however, and the first thing I see is a Thank You card from a Sandra and Bob, and the second is a birthday card to someone called Don Fernando. The card has a loving rhyme written in Karen's handwriting, and the words … *'Darling … I've missed you and your body so much …. All my love, Karen.'* – At least, now I know she's not a lesbian. I replace the cards in their respective envelopes, and leave them as found.

Time passes with me relaxing in her chair, while a sexily dressed Karen cooks dinner. I can hear that she's happy, humming to herself, so I close my eyes, imagining life with her and this Spanish or Italian guy – if he is Spanish or Italian. With a name like that, he sounds like a hit-man for the mafia. I'm just considering how her sex life will relate to mine, when the door-bell chimes. I pull myself from my seat as she dives for the door.

On first appearances, I'm not sure whether I like this man at all, but one can't account for another one's taste ... can one? Karen pulls him to her breasts, kissing and clasping his nearly hairless egg-shaped head. I say nearly hairless, because he has the funniest looking goatee beard, seemingly, stuck to his chin. At least she had the sense not to meet him at Heathrow. Personally, I wouldn't be seen dead with him. However, he looks well able to handle himself: not from his size – he's no bigger than me – but from his odd facial expressions. In fact, he looks a bit of an egghead, if you pardon the expression, and not, in the least, Spanish or Italian. He doesn't even look like a Don never mind the Fernando, and as for being a hit-man, he looks more like one of Séan's mahogany gas-pipes. There's got to be something going for him, or why would she bother. Perhaps, he has a good sense of humour or he's great in the sack. I suppose he must be, going by the birthday card.

When they come up for air, I notice his face properly and, while they whisper sweet nothings to each other, I can't help but notice an earring dangling from his left lobe. How can a beautiful and sexy woman, with bags of intelligence, fall for a bald coot like this? And he's got a stupid earring. I turn away, annoyed. It's not that I have anything against men who wear earrings, or dresses for that matter – that's up to them, but on this man it just doesn't suit.

Well, I don't know. What do you think? After seeing this guy, I'm wondering whether Karen can be my host, but maybe he's okay. Why else would she choose him? It's not as if I'll be entering *his* body, is it?

When Karen releases Don's head, he backs away, grabs his bags and pulls them inside the room. Obviously, Karen is excited as she makes another play for Don, grabbing and pulling him onto the leather couch. I can't help but watch as she manhandles – or is it womanhandles – the clothes from his body. He doesn't bother to undress her, letting her skirt ride up her legs before ripping off her panties. Karen, meanwhile, undoes the buttons on her pretty top and skies it over her head, leaving her braless breasts exposed to Don's eyes. I move behind the settee and have a close up view of Don's bald head as it nestles between her boobs. Then, moving it from side to side, he lets his goatee beard rub against each nipple in turn.

The action goes on, and I'm fascinated. All the time that he's humping her into the leather, she tries grabbing hold of his non-existent hair, and not finding any, she pulls on Don's ears. When Karen's orgasm overtakes her body, she pulls even harder, eventually drawing blood. She calls out his name and his backside moves faster. Karen orgasms again – a more relaxed orgasm – with one of her hands lying at her side while the other dangles to the floor. She's completely knackered. When Don stops, he just lies there on top of Karen, the cheeks of his bum now seemingly soft when moments earlier they'd been strong, forceful and tense. Karen lifts her hand from the floor, rubbing it over his perspiring head, panting, *"Oh, Don, I've missed you so much."*

"If I thought you'd greet me like this all the time, I'd fly over every week." I'm dumfounded. I hadn't heard him speak properly – they'd kept whispering and kissing, and Don is not only English, but a Cockney through and through. So much for him being a hit-man, a Spaniard, or an Italian. So where the hell did he get his name?

"But you wouldn't, would you?" she asks. *"You've settled over there. Oh, Don, I get so lonely sometimes. Why don't you get a transfer?"*

"I've told you …."

"I know – money, money, money. That's all you think about … money and your bloody job."

"Leave it out, Karen. It's not just the money and you know that," he replies, turning his mouth to one of her nipples and sucking gently.

I can't resist it and I smack him on the bum, my hand going through his groin and into hers. I quickly pull away, but she squeals and smacks him in the same place as me, saying, *"Cheeky. I'll talk you round eventually. Come on, let's go and shower."* –That's strange. He didn't react. Perhaps her slap had more effect. Don climbs from her body, and, as he pulls her up, she wraps her skirt between her legs and picks her panties off the floor. I follow.

Karen runs the shower and tests the water, and, once she's happy, she jumps in and pulls the curtain across. When Don joins her, soon after, I push my head in and watch them soaping, slapping, tickling, and kissing each others bodies. They both get aroused and start screwing again, and they go on and on until fully spent. He's big … believe me; not enormous, but big and strong, and now I know why she likes him.

Not bothering to watch them wash again, I go to the bedroom and lie down on her purple silk duvet. A few moments later, Don walks in, still naked, and fishes around in one of Karen's cupboards. He pulls out a dark blue pair of shorts and draws them on. He then leaves the room, returning soon after with his bags. I watch, while he rummages through his clothes, and after selecting a light blue casual shirt, he carries it out, leaving the bedroom door open.

I'm happy where I am as I can hear most of their conversation. I can tell from what they're saying that they are both from working class backgrounds, and it goes to show that a good brain will always get you somewhere if you really try. Karen has done herself proud. Don is doing something with computers, but I can't make out whether it's working with them or on them. Whatever it is, Karen seems to think he could do similar in England and she keeps badgering him to give up New York. After a while, I hear her tell him – not ask him – to put on the kettle. I listen to his grunt of annoyance, but he obeys her just the same. If he has a problem with her, maybe this is it – you know, being bossy. This show of authority might be a one off, but, there again, it might well be the reason that Don doesn't want to come to London.

I spend the next couple of days watching Karen and Don explore their bodies, and I, occasionally, tease him with the odd squeeze here and there. After all, I have to have some fun. I follow them around town, and, being the weekend, they have time to spare. I go wherever they lead me, and I know all the places, of course – Leicester Square, Piccadilly, and the West End in general, but by staying near at hand I can really get to know them and what they both enjoy in life. I've gone this far with them, and the more I hear, the more I like. Some of Don's favourite things, while dining out, are starting a meal with a double vodka, wine through the meal, and, afterwards, an Irish coffee. Other than that, he's a relatively light drinker. He likes a pint of lager when they go to a pub, while Karen keeps to fruit juices. Karen enjoys a glass of red wine with her food, regardless of the meal, and when waiters suggest otherwise she always sticks to her guns. Don is great at telling jokes and I can see why Karen likes him or maybe loves him. I'm not too sure about the latter, despite her loving words when snuggling down together.

To be honest with you, I've considered the possibility of using Don as my long term host, but the thought of traipsing all over the place, flying over to and living in New York, doesn't appeal to me. It's not that I wouldn't like to go, but it's a hell of a long haul to get back to Slovakia. I do have to keep Jana and the others informed of my whereabouts and my goings on. Don, despite his shaven head, goatee beard and silly earring, does have something going for him. I must confess to enjoying their company, and their choice of television and films. In fact, being with Karen makes me feel safe, and, yes, I've decided to take the plunge. If it doesn't work out then I'll leave her, but, for now, she's as good a choice as any.

Having made up my mind, I might as well tell you that I'm leaving for a few days. I'm off to notify Jana or Anna, or get them a message, somehow, about my prospective long term host. I'll have to tell them what I know about Karen's life and how long I intend staying inside her. I've decided on three years and hope that I'm not making a huge mistake. I don't think I am, but one never knows. Okay, it might seem a bit sudden and, perhaps, I should wait for another year or two, but I feel that, for me, it's the right thing to do. And there's another reason for going now. Don is staying in London for the next four weeks, so I should be over there and back within a few days, and the thought of being inside Karen while he's making love to her is giving me goose bumps. Well, I think it is. I want to enjoy his body as much as she does, and if it's the only way to get a man, then I'm all for it. After all, I've been good since I've met them. You must have guessed that I've been lusting after him, not that he's really my type, but he's all man where it matters. And, as I said, I've been having the odd bit of slap and tickle, smacking his butt and squeezing his balls and then watching his reactions. He thinks Karen is responsible and, in a way, she is, but not being able to really feel him or her is so annoying. I know that I'll have to be naked to reap the benefits of her movements, so maybe I will get the thrill I'm looking for. Thinking back to Malcolm and how I felt inside his body, it whets my appetite, because I still had my clothes on at the time.

Why are Monday mornings always the same, with everybody rushing about, hurrying into work. Karen's just the same as I follow both her and Don to Harley Street. When we get there, Don tells her that he's off to East London, to visit relatives. They spend a fair while with their goodbye kiss, and when they part, I, too, say a temporary farewell. Of course, I know they can't hear me, but they are my new friends. I fly up in the air and head south across Oxford Street, and then keep on towards Gatwick Airport. I suppose I could go via Eurostar again, but as my intention is to get to Slovakia and back as soon as possible, taking a plane is easier.

Once at the airport, I check the flights and I don't care whether it's one to Prague or Vienna, but I'm taking the first to leave. As it happens, I join a flight to Vienna and happily ensconce myself in the pilot's cockpit.

When the aeroplane comes in to land, I'm wondering whether to go straight to Karen's or to her place of work. You might well be thinking – 'What the hell is going on, or has something happened to the aeroplane, or has the pilot forgotten his sandwiches?' – but, to tell the truth, you didn't really expect me to bore you with the minor details of my trip and who I saw there. Okay, I'd have told you if something exciting had happened, but it didn't.

Suffice it to say, that I was greeted by Maggie as I floated to the ground in Pribylina, and soon after I was engaged in conversation with Anna, relating my intentions to enter Karen. I gave her Karen's address, occupation and where she works. I gave as full a description as I could about Karen's age, health and appearance, and said that I wanted to remain inside her for three years. As Jana wasn't there, I asked Anna to tell her of my whereabouts, to which she nodded. Jana, she told me, is, more than likely, to be my Monitor while I'm taking residence in Karen's body. I mentioned Don, saying who he is and what he does for a living, and when Anna looked at me kind of funny, she smiled and told me that I'm a naughty boy. Boy, I thought … I'm a grown man, but I knew exactly what she meant.

It's early evening and Karen is bound to be working, and not being in the mood to listen to tales of horror, like Malcolm's, or ones of woe from other people, I head for her apartment. What better place to rest and look forward to long nights of lust, love and other magic moments. Just the thought of stripping off and entering her and waiting for Don to take our bodies is making me stiff. And, to think, I won't be like this when I take her shape. Yes, of course we gays have a feminine side, but it won't be only my side that's feminine in an hour or two.

How time passes as more beautiful thoughts run through my head, carrying me back to her home – my home – as if I've lived there all my life. I fly straight through her window and … . "Stop! Stop! … Wait for me." – Damn! It's too late. Karen is whooping and laughing with pleasure as she squats down on her lover, both of their movements coming to a halt. What is she doing here so early, besides having sex on the carpet? They are breathing heavy and pouring with sweat – her body stretched the length of his. I might as well wait 'til they've showered.

When they, eventually, go to the bathroom, I move to the couch and lie down. Immediately, my eyes focus on the wall clock and I realise my mistake. I haven't really made a mistake, except to remember that the clocks over here are an hour behind and not the two that I'd presumed. In fact, I hadn't given much consideration to time itself. But, despite that, to come home from work and start banging away before the tea's on the table … well, what have I been missing all these years? And I can't stay here wondering what to do next – they might be at it again.

Up I get and strip off my clothes, and, carrying them neatly, I take them to the bedroom where an open wardrobe greets me. Very carefully, I hang the jacket, jumper, shirt and trousers. I stuff my socks and boxers inside my boots and place them on a lower shelf. I'm happy and now prepared to take one of the biggest leaps of my life, into the body of a beautiful young lady. As soon as she appears, towelling her hair – the drops of water running down her naked breasts, I move a little closer. She sits, once more, in front of the mirror, still drying herself off, and Don walks in. He moves towards her, looking at her reflection, and he's getting aroused.

"Oh, no you don't," I tell him, rushing past his body and slipping inside Karen's. Oh, my god, this is weird. I can feel myself changing, ever so slowly. Whereas my body used to change in size, now I'm … I'm – this is crazy. I'm growing boobs. What have I done? I've lost my balls, my … . Oh, no! I've got a vagina. What will I do? Should I stay or should I get out? I'll get out. I have to. I can't go through three minutes like this, never mind three years. I'm about to jump out when the most delightful feeling stops me in my tracks. Don's fingers are playing gently with my nipples, as he kisses and licks my ears very softly. It's so pleasurable … and he's turning me on. I'm getting warmer by the second and I want to take him. One of his hands moves lower, down my belly and into my pubic hair, caressing me with his golden touch.

"Please ... please, Karen, turn around and let me make love to him," I beg. How did I manage that? I can throw my voice when hers – I mean, ours – is slightly open. At least I can do one thing for myself. Perhaps it's a way of communication ... you know, between ghosts. As his fingers creep forever closer to the centre of my being, Karen moves me around so I can hold him. I'm in heave ... . No, I'm not.

Karen makes me push him away – not hard or far, but out of reach just the same, and my mouth comes out with, *"Not now, Don. I don't feel so good."*

"What's the matter, honey?" he asks.

"I don't know. I've come over all queer." – I can't believe she made me say that.

"You should lie down for a while. I'll make you a nice cup of coffee."

"I think I will. Pass me that nightie." Don heads off to the kitchen and we – that is, Karen and I, slip her nightie over our heads. In fact, I shouldn't be saying this because her head is now my head, her auburn hair is mine, I am her, and, yet ... I'm still me in mind, but not in body. I suppose I still am me, in body as well as mind and I feel everything she feels, but not as before. Back then, with Pete, Malcolm, and inside the fat lady, I could only see what their hands were doing. I could only imagine what they felt, although I did have some minor sensations, but they weren't as strong as these. I can't leave her. I can't deprive myself of Don's body – of being able to feel the thrill of him inside me. I don't mind sharing him, and what Karen doesn't know won't hurt her.

And to think that Jana experienced the same while inside her Dominique, but she was a woman. So, no, it wasn't the same at all. She didn't lose her sexual organs and gain new ones. And for the moment, as Don brings in a mug of coffee, I don't care. He leaves the drink on the night table and bends forward, kissing us gently on our lips. We smile at him, and say, *"Thank you, darling. Where's yours?"*

"In the other room. I thought I'd watch a bit of tele'."

"Go on, then. Leave me all alone." Uh-oh. I think she's upset, but as for being alone ... well?

"I'll stay if you want but I thought you should rest." I must admit, he's considerate, but I'd rather he came to bed.

"No, it's alright. You watch your tele'." I can see that Don's not sure what to do; standing near the foot of the bed, his mind saying stay and

his body ready to go. I suppose we all get like that in situations like this … and they seem such a loving couple.

"Stay, you plonker. Can't you see that she loves you?" I shout through Karen's mouth.

Picking up her coffee, Karen and I wave him away, saying, *"Go! If you have to think about it … just go."* As we lift the drink to our lips, I forget about Don, because I'm dying to taste the lovely hot coffee for the first time in ages. It's at my lips, and I'm sipping … and it's going down, but, not only don't I feel the heat of the liquid as it passes through my system, I don't feel anything wet, and nor can I smell the aroma. What a let down. And, as it hits her tummy, the only thing I feel is a spasm – her spasm. Okay, I half expected this. I wasn't sure and I hoped for the best, but at least I felt the swallow – the movement, and the effect of our muscles, so that in itself is a consolation.

Here we go again. Another mouthful hits the system. We take our time with the drink, fiddling about with the spoon, and I'd love to be able to tell you what Karen's mind is thinking, but I can't. I can't even say that she's snarling or pulling faces, because she isn't. We're just sitting here, at the top of the bed, resting on some pillows, looking at the remains of the coffee and the small amount of froth that's clinging to the sides of the mug. We don't finish it, and, instead, place the mug on the table. Getting off the bed, we go to the loo … and pee. More to the point, she does the peeing while I go through the motions. It's a small price to pay for a love life with our Don Fernando.

My pain now gone, we walk through the door, and I ask, "Now, Karen, are we going back to bed or can we go and tempt our man into giving us a good time?" … We're going back to bed.

"Are you okay, love?" we hear.

"Yes, I'm fine," we reply, and as we pass the lounge, we take a peek inside. *"Who's winning?"*

"Sharapova!"

"Hmm, she's only a young girl," we say.

"She's good. Very good, in fact. She might go all the way." I wish we could – right now! Don goes on, *"Come and watch."* And, to my surprise, Karen carries me in and we end up relaxing into Don's cuddly body and strong arms. We move very little, except for the odd peck and the teasing from his playful fingers. He tells us about the rain delayed match as we

watch the Russian girl's spring-like jumps and superb volleys that take her through to the next round. Afterwards, Karen and I go to the kitchen and check the fridge.

"Don! Do you want the beef or salmon?"

"I'm not fussy."

"Beef it is, then." Don joins us and helps with the chips and carrots. Karen and I put the pre-cooked pot roast in the microwave, and not long after we're sitting down to a hearty meal at the dinner table. I can't say that I enjoy the beef and veg' as they go down our throats, although all the feelings are there. When we're done, even I feel bloated, but we still drink more wine and relax until bedtime.

Don's the first to bed, while Karen and I sort out some washing, throwing wet towels and a couple of sheets into the machine. I have to sit through another session in the toilet before having a quick wash.

This is it! It's the moment I've been waiting for as Karen and I sneak under the duvet. We wrap our arms around Don and start smooching. As his hands roam about, exploring our curves, we move our hands to his hips and pull him closer. His lips move down, kissing and playing with our skin. Bald he might be, but he's a beautiful mover, and when he reaches our nipples, I'm really warming up. His fingers tease me – tease us, spreading joy at the same time, and eventually he moves them between our legs. We look into his sexy blue eyes that seem to laugh with love … and I want him so much. Karen moves my hand and we take hold of him. Is this all I ever wanted? … You bet it is. And it doesn't stop there. In no time at all, he's pounding us into the bed with a fury. Why wasn't I born a woman with looks like Karen? I could have had any man I fancied, any time I liked. Our sex seems to go on forever and I'm getting hotter and hotter, and … .

"Oh, my! Oh, God! Oh! Oh! Don't! … Aaaaah!"

As we stop moving … completely wrecked, I can't help wondering what I tried to shout through Karen's mouth at the same time as her. And as we lie here with Don still inside us, I'm aching down there, with pleasure and a beautiful warmth. When Karen and I get our breath back, we coax Don from our bodies.

He holds us close, asking, "What the hell was that?"

"Oh, Don, I don't know. I've never known anything like it in my life. I felt so hot, but it was deliciously lovely."

"I know, and I'm worried in case there's something wrong."

"What do you mean?" He keeps his mouth shut. *"Don?"* – Still no answer, so we slap him gently on his arm. *"Don! Are you thinking what I think you're thinking?"*

"I don't know, but, Karen, I don't understand why we both got so hot. It was brill', but it was such a strange feeling."

"Come on, you two … it was me. Karen! Are you in there? It was me. Listen for god's sake." Jeez! She can't hear a word I'm saying.

"Don, are you sore down there?"

"No, Karen, not at all." We watch while he touches himself … and I want him again.

"Well, neither am I, and I feel normal. It might have been the Burgundy," comes out of our mouths. Hmm, now that's a good one.

"I don't think so, love."

Don moves his head towards us and kisses our lips gently, wraps his arms around us, and we snuggle close, closing our eyes.

"I love you, Don. … 'Night." – I'll go along with that, but I wish I could see.

Not long after, Karen is fast asleep and Don is in the toilet, and he's been in there for a while – running the shower and washing and swearing. I know what he thinks, and if it was me in his shoes, I'd be worried. But, there again, I bet that if I could read Karen's mind, she might be thinking exactly the same about him. It's amazing, really. We had wonderful sex and now I know what women go through … and such control. All the feelings and sensations were like heaven powering through my body, and reaching zones I'd never thought existed in humans, ghosts … or anything. Wait 'til I tell Jana. Of course, she'll already know. I don't care. I'll still tell her. I do wish we could sleep with our eyes open. That's one of my problems, you see. The point is, I can't see. My eyes are as shut as Karen's and, although she's out of it, I'm still awake – mentally that is.

CHAPTER THIRTY

Come on, Karen ... open your eyes. Our arms are wrapped around Don's firm body and I want him again, despite the sharp pain in my abdomen. A few minutes pass by and I feel his hand gently taking our wrist and releasing our hold on him. He must be going to the loo. Hurry back, Don, and make me happy. The slight movement has stirred Karen and I see the faintest glimmer of light, and as we turn on our back, another pain – like a small cramp, hits my lower stomach.

We open our eyes properly, yawn, and, when Don returns, we pull the duvet over our heads. Karen ... this isn't fair. I want to see his body. Dear god, no! Make him stop. I can't stand my feet being tickled. We start thrashing our legs about the bed as he persists in annoying me, but I can't stop laughing with Karen. At last, he climbs up the bed and our eyes meet, and then our lips ... and another tiny cramp hits me. We peck at each other and then, when he lowers his head to our breasts, Karen pulls his goatee beard away, with a *"Not now, pet."* His smile changes to one of disappointment, but nature has beckoned and we hop off to the toilet. The release is like heaven, and as soon as we're finished on the loo my expectations, of diving back between the covers and riding Don all day, come to nothing when Karen turns on the shower. We wash ourselves and, with a towel tied around our body, we head for the kitchen. In the meantime, Don, knowing he's not getting his morning oats, appears in the kitchen doorway, toothbrush in his mouth, and nods his head towards the teabags.

Shortly after, the three of us are sitting down to breakfast over which I learn that Karen is off work both this afternoon and all of tomorrow. It's just as well, I suppose, because I didn't fancy listening to people and their problems. At the present time, I've enough of my own in trying to get used to my new environment, both inside Karen and in her life. We talk sweet nothings about last night and then the topic of the sudden heat crops up again. Don isn't happy and thinks there might be something wrong with Karen. When we insist that she's fine and that we shouldn't let it bother us, he drops the subject. The plans for the day are discussed and Don isn't pleased at the idea of going to the opera, and he tells her so. Karen, though, is adamant, bringing up several names from history and their importance to the country's culture. Don argues the toss, eventually bringing his true feelings to the fore.

"Byron and Shakespeare mean nothing to me, they're just famous names in a book."

"You can't mean that, Don. I know you're only interested in computers, but you must enjoy some sort of culture."

"How many times do I have to tell you? I'm not into your poetry, opera, or the theatre. If you want real music, let's go to a rock concert."

"You're winding me up." And this tit-for-tat goes on for ages, with Karen finally getting her way. Don has agreed to smarten up for the evening, just to keep her quiet. We get dressed for work and, soon after, we're kissing Don goodbye.

The morning passes with my eyes focused on heaps of paper work and not a sign of Malcolm or anyone like him. We phoned a few of Karen's friends, telling them about Don's arrival and his stamina sapping talents on the sofa, on the floor, and in the bed, and I had to listen as her friends described some their sexual antics over the weekend. This could be quite enjoyable. I hadn't thought of Karen being so open about herself and her body. On our way home, we stop to shop for an evening dress – one she had ordered specially for our visit to Sadler's Wells. Our shopping done, we head for the apartment, the pain gripping me every so often, and I'm wondering what's going on down there. If she's got something wrong, I'd better get out and start all over again. Though, when I think of Don and how he excites me, I'm reluctant.

Don greets us with another kiss and we relax in his arms for a while – the radio on in the background. Time comes for us to get dressed and, before heading out, Karen calls for a mini-cab. It shows up a few minutes late, but not enough to matter. My favourite parts of the evening are when Don's arms are holding us gently, when his strong hands are in ours, and the tiny smooching kisses he seems to enjoy giving Karen when she least expects them. As far as the opera is concerned, Don's rock concert was a better idea. Don keeps quiet, and when it's over a smile creeps across his face. He's honest enough to say that he hasn't been swayed, but he's happy to take us for a meal in Chinatown.

As we sit playing with our chopsticks, feasting ourselves on won-ton soup, duck and pancakes, and chicken noodles, I feel so left out. How I'd love to taste the food and drink, never mind smell it. Don pays the bill and out we go, jumping in a black cab on Shaftesbury Avenue.

About twenty minutes later, we're back in the apartment and Don is opening another bottle of wine. Our conversation is light and comical, with Don cracking jokes in between the odd bit of slap and tickle. As the wine takes effect, the atmosphere becomes more intimate, the clothes start to drop away, and, while our hands explore our nearly naked bodies, we kiss our way to the bedroom. I'm so excited as our bodies entwine, with Don rising to the occasion, and he doesn't disappoint either me or Karen. It's only when I start to boil over that Don tries pulling away, but our legs won't let him, gripping him like a vice until we're satisfied. Karen mentions the heat again and so, too, does Don, but this time he doesn't carp on about it. The only problem I have is this damn cramp that keeps coming back.

We lie and talk for a while, and, as Don plays with our boobs, we can feel him getting hard once again. We don't stop him as he makes love to us slowly and passionately, and we move him around ... our bodies now on top. This is like paradise – the pleasure and the being in control and the speed our bodies move as we push him into the bed. It's over all too soon and we collapse together, lying in each other's arms. Soon after, Karen and I join Don in the shower, us lathering him and he us before rinsing off ... our bodies glistening. It's not long before we're saying goodbye to another day. My mind reflects on what we've been up to, how I'm enjoying these moments of comfort with Don, and on how right Jana was about taking a female for my host.

The next few days passed with visits to the National Gallery, the British Museum, and lots of lazy eating in many different types of restaurant. And, yet, all this has been playing second fiddle to our beautiful love making. Positions? ... There are too many to tell you. Karen and Don are so well acquainted with each other's bodies preferences, that I've been turned inside out and back to front ... and I must admit to liking it back to front.

We've just had our dinner – some ham, cheese, and a potato salad, and, despite the gripping pain, I'm ready for another adventure in bed. But ... and it's a big but, Karen isn't. We're in the bathroom and she's searching through one of the cupboards. When I see the box of Tampax, my heart sinks. As my hands help hers, we push one of the tampons inside our body, and let me tell you ... it's such a weird feeling. I don't suppose it matters to her – she's used to it, but for me it not only feels strange but has spoilt my night.

Bed beckons, and we're no sooner under the cover than Don wants our body. After a – *"Sorry love, it's that time again,"* from Karen, he asks us to give him a Sherman. I'm all for it and anything else he might desire, but Karen lets us down. Don hmms-and-ha's for a while, before nestling down and cuddling us to sleep. He's been here before, but I haven't ... and I'm gutted.

I don't want to talk about the rest of the week without sex. I'm frustrated as hell, pulling out and disposing of the tampons every five minutes – well it seems like it. Just the sight of them makes me sick. And then we shove a new one back inside. It's downright horrible.

Our period ends with a surprise – a surprise for me. The pains have gone, the Tampax has been stashed away for another few weeks, and I'm looking through the eyes of Karen at my first true ghostly friend, Jana. That she should arrive when the blood stops flowing is a pleasing coincidence. Don is out and Karen has me soaking in a bath of soapy water. I'm so pleased to see Jana as she sits at the end of the bath, one leg over the other.

"You want to watch yourself in there. You might drown," she laughs.

"I haven't as yet, and I've been dunked a few times."

Karen pushes our hands to our mouth, saying to herself, *"Ugh! This stupid tongue."*

"Hey, Jana, I don't think she likes me talking."

"She'll get used to it, Micky. After a while, she won't even notice the movement."

"Do you think so?"

"I know so. Remember Dominique?"

"Oh, yeah."

"I can't believe it, Micky. You've such a lovely body and a very sexy new voice. Wait 'til I get you in bed."

"You can't. She's got a boyfriend."

The excitement in Jana's face is obvious, and she jumps off the bath, clenches her fists and shouts, "Yes! ... Yes! ... Yes!"

"What's up? Are you having an orgasm?"

"No, but I will be later. What's he like – this boyfriend of hers. Is he young? Is he ... .?"

"Jana! You can't," I interrupt.

"I can and I will. When I was inside my Dominique we had threesomes and foursomes, and words can't describe the sensations."

"You can't do this to me ... to Karen. It's not right."

"Don't be such a bore, Micky. This will be the thrill of your life. So tell me, is he handsome?"

"You must be joking."

"I don't believe you. Nobody this pretty is going to fall for some creepy looking guy."

"You'd be surprised."

"Micky, if he's as bad as you're making out, you'd have left her by now. He must have something going for him." It's just as well Jana can't see my face, as Karen takes me for another underwater exploration, coming up covered in bubbles.

I'm about to reply when the outside door opens and Don's voice reaches our ears.

"Hi, Kas! I'm home. Where are you?" Jana is off in a flash.

"In the bath. Er, Don?"

"Yeah!"

"Pass a clean towel." Karen makes me stand and wipe away the soapy water, just as Jana leads Don inside the bathroom. "Thank you, darling," we say, taking the towel.

"You sound happy this evening."

I can feel the smile draw across my face, as Karen suggests, "If you make the dinner, I'll treat you to some afters." Don's face lights up.

"You're on! Will a take-away do?"

"You're a lazybones, but I don't mind," answers Karen. "I'll get the wine glasses ready." Don hurries off.

"Is that supposed to mean something?" asks Jana, looking us up and down.

"Sex!" I reply. "In this house, wine equals a night of sex, but not for you."

"That's what you think. Don, eh? Nice name and a cute face … shame about the hair. I like his feet, though – nice and big."

"Jana, you've got a one-track mind."

"And so have you. If you think I've come all this way to watch, then forget it." We climb out of the bath and wrap ourselves in the huge towel. As usual we sit by the mirror drying and brushing our hair. Jana half-sits on the bed, resting back on her elbows and studying my new face. When we stand up, Karen still has us facing the mirror. We drop the towel and raise our hands, cupping our breasts to feel the firmness. We let our hands slide to our belly and over our pubic hair, and then, placing a hand on each hip, we sway gently from side to side. Happy with herself, Karen makes me smile. "I wish my body was as beautiful," adds Jana, watching our reflection.

"Yours is," I tell her.

"Don't be daft, Micky. Karen's body is perfection itself. She has what every woman craves for – a strong flat tummy, good tone, and all her bumps are … ooh, so lovely. You men will never understand."

We spend some time chit-chatting about Anna, Lucia, and the others, and I have to laugh when Jana tells me about Tommy being caught fidgeting amongst the trees again. This time, though, he forgot about the worms. In the winter he had the snow for protection, but, as Jana says, his habit overtook his senses. The worms slid all over his legs, buttocks and sides, and he only noticed them when they reached his arms. He ran from his hidey-hole out into the open, totally naked and yelling, and trying to push the slimy things away. Luisella and Maggie were the first on the scene and they couldn't help but call the others out to watch. According to Jana, Tommy had only called in for a few days to speak to Lucia and ask her advice. Personally, I think he did more than speak to her, but Jana won't tell me.

By the time Don returns with lamb madras, pilau rice and naan bread, Karen and I have opened the wine and started drinking. He looks at the half-empty bottle and grins. After helping himself to a glass, we all sit down, divide the food and tuck in. Jana is seated on the spare chair at the table, watching me eat and passing jealous comments. All the while, Karen has me either eating or answering Don's questions. After dinner, we snuggle on the couch in his arms, while Jana takes the seat in the corner. We continue talking through the television programmes, having the occasional coffee, until it's time for bed.

After a quick shower, Don joins us on the bed and then the petting starts. Jana is behind us taking her clothes off, and if I could talk I'd tell her to keep her distance, but my mouth is kept busy kissing his lips. It's only when Don's lips move to our nipples, that I beg her, "Don't, Jana … please."

She ignores me, saying, "I thought this big feet idea was a joke, but, my god, he's everything I ever wanted."

"Jana! … No-oo!"

"Shut up, Micky, and let's enjoy each other." And we do, her hands in his, crawling all over our body, and us pressing into both she and Don. I know she hasn't taken his shape, but I'm still excited. As we squeeze him, Jana gets a buzz. When he presses his chest into our boobs, Jana squeals with delight, and when he enters our body, I can also feel Jana's pelvis crushing mine. This feels so erotic and I'm getting hotter by the second. It's not long before we're all yelling and groaning, the heat from our bodies at its utmost. At last, we relax but I know it's not over. Jana is insatiable and won't let Don off with one bout of sex. I know her only too well. I can see the sweat dripping from both his and Karen's bodies and we wipe some away.

Shortly after, we're at each other again … and again. It's like a marathon, and, for a reason I don't understand, instead of discouraging them, the heat in our loins is turning Karen and Don into a couple of sex maniacs. Eventually, tiredness overcomes us and we're all resting peacefully. I'm thinking that this is it for the night, but Karen breaks the silence. She tries persuading him, again, to come to London, and when I get the chance – between Karen's words – I beg Jana to somehow convince him.

Don, though, prattles on about how important this computer job is.

"I've signed a contract, Kas. If they had someone else good enough to set their machines and sort out their router, then they might consider a release."

Karen responds, *"Stupid computers! I agree, they're useful and they save time, but think of all these extras you do, this router and all that … . What's so bloody important? A computer's a computer, and that's that. Anyone can work them."*

"I wish they'd shut up," says Jana.

"So do I," I reply.

"Karen! They can't do what I can do."

"Why not?"

"I know how to operate their system and fix up all the add-ons. This router, for instance ... well, I have to make sure it's all wired up properly and re-route one new system into another and then re-route it to the computer, and ...."

"For God's sake, Don, shut up and re-route this inside here."

And we're at it again, our hands gripping his erection as we pull him on top.

"Yippee!" cries Jana, pressing herself forward. "I thought they'd never stop talking rubbish." I can't answer – my teeth are biting into Don's shoulder. "Micky! For god's sake, Micky! Watch the teeth, you're hurting me. I have no choice, and try forcing Karen's mind to relax our mouth, but Karen takes no notice. The sex gets more frantic, but our orgasms bring a respite. This is short-lived, however, and then we start all over again. Jana comes up for air now and then, telling me how much she loves us all ... that she can't do without us. The 'oohs' and 'aahs', eventually give way to two people and two ghosts wrapped around each other and not letting go. Karen's and Don's small talk stops before ours. Jana keeps talking of love and devotion, her words becoming more infrequent to my ears as my mind slips away into dreamland.

The next three weeks are a routine of work, play and sex, Jana leaving Don to join me and Karen at her office. I've never had so much fun, with Jana telling me to force my mind on Karen's. She has been influencing Don, with great success. The reason, she tells me, is that Don doesn't have the strongest of wills. I, on the other hand, can only overcome Karen's mind when she is tired or asleep, encouraging her to open her mouth so I can speak. Jana's powers over Don have brought a new meaning to our sex lives, with him trying new techniques nearly every time we're in the bed, on the couch, or in the bath.

The good life doesn't last forever, unfortunately, and disappointment befalls us the day that Don flies back to New York. We don't make the trip to Heathrow, instead sending him off with a last morning of wild and passionate sex. My sight was impaired with Karen's tears as he slipped through the door. Jana, though, was less concerned, telling me that she'll keep us company for a while longer.

At bed time, Karen and I sit on the cover, looking at Don's photograph, Karen, first sighing, then asking, *"When will I see you again, my love?"* – It's driving me mad.

"You'd think she'd forget about him for a few minutes, at least," I say.

Jana, sitting at the foot of the bed, replies, "Leave it out, Micky. You don't understand women and that's the point. In fact, I've just been looking at that wonderful picture of you."

"Where? There aren't any pictures of me here."

"Yes there is ... on the wall in the lounge."

"Don't be stupid. That's Karen."

"At the moment, you are Karen, an extremely beautiful and sexy Karen, and I'm going to make love to you tonight as long as I can."

"Don't be crazy, Jana. You can't do this to us."

"Watch me, and see how it feels." When Karen gets up to go to the loo, Jana follows, watching our every move. She laughs at me while we sit and pee, and laughs even more when we use the tissue to wipe ourselves, and then she runs ahead of us back to the bedroom. When Karen and I lift the quilt, Jana slips in beside us. The minute we're settled, she moves her hand between our legs and starts rubbing me. Karen can't feel her, but I can ... and I can't stop her, because I don't have control over Karen's hands and arms. Jana climbs on top of us, pressing her pelvic bones into mine, kissing my mouth and gently rubbing my boobs. Her motions become quicker, pressing ever harder into my body and Jana's fingers start to explore. I can't help it as she pushes me on to orgasm, the heat welling up inside me, and then my hand – Karen's hand, moves down between us and she joins in our activity. Very soon, I'm yelling with joy, and Karen soon follows – her spasms sending me off again, and all the time Jana is pushing herself down until she, too, shouts a cry of fulfilment. She collapses on my body, kissing me and sending tingles through Karen. We all lick our lips, turn on our sides, and then Karen falls asleep. Jana sweet talks me for ages, going on about our life and what it will be like when we're eventually together. I don't argue – there's no point. Soon after, she falls silent. Peace at last, but only 'til tomorrow.

The days pass and our work continues – seeing patients; listening; making notes; and offering advice. Quite a few patients have family problems, while others go flying off the handle – causing harm to their relatives. And there are more, like Malcolm, who have been involved in violent crimes. I try shutting myself off to some of the discussions, but when Jana comes along, she's all ears. And then, in the evening, she'll go on and on about what she's heard – what the person looks like and what they've been up to; and then she forms her own opinion about what she'd like to do to them. Thinking back to how she died, it's no wonder she gets upset. I point out that the majority aren't deliberately malicious and only have problems adjusting to life, but Jana only ever focuses on the worst of them. I always have to change the subject.

Six days after Don's departure, Jana tells me she has to go home. She says that it's a case of checking in and telling Anna what I'm up to and how I'm being treated. Knowing Anna, she'll be more interested in our sex lives. Jana kisses me goodbye, promising a speedy return. When she leaves, I'm tempted to follow. I've so enjoyed her company.

CHAPTER THIRTY-ONE

This doesn't make sense, and I don't know whether to get out of Karen now, or not.

Let me tell you why. It's been well over a month since Jana went home, and the only reason I'm still inside Karen is because an important development has taken place. If I'd known what was going on, I'd have jumped out of her body a week ago. But, being a man, I didn't understand what Karen was doing, what I was looking at, or why she was smiling, until she started phoning her family and friends.

Let me go back even further. Two weeks ago, Karen called into Boots and picked up some shopping. Of course I was looking at what she bought, but, while Karen's brain was occupied with her eyeliner and other things, my mind was off in a young man's bedroom. I'd noticed this chap while we were walking in to Boots, and his face kept coming back to me. I've become so used to switching off from Karen, so I try not to concentrate on everything she's up to. Well, it makes sense and, anyway, what would you do in my position? I'm not a woman; I don't think like a woman; and I'm only using her body to my own advantage. And, even if you do disagree with me, I don't think this is selfish. After all, put yourself in my place and then think about it.

As I was saying, we picked up this stuff, packed it in a bag, and brought it to work. Other than taking out a tuna and mayonnaise sandwich, we didn't open the bag until later that evening, and even then I wasn't paying too much attention. The thing is, when we went to the toilet, she made me pee into a container. I asked her, "Hey, what do you think we're doing?" but she didn't answer. Of course, I didn't expect one, but you know what I mean. Well, the next thing is that we're dipping this little thingamajig – like a thermometer – into the pee, and when we looked at it, a pink dot appeared. When Karen started laughing, I knew she was alright, but I also knew that I was in trouble ... big trouble. I had decisions to make – get out or stay in. Who do I ask, and who can I tell?

You see, not knowing the affect I might have on her body in these particular circumstances, I was in two minds what to do. My mind was in turmoil wondering ... 'If I jump out, will she lose the baby, or if I stay in' – and I didn't want to – 'will she lose the baby?'

I considered my options as we ate our dinner, but, afterwards, when she phoned her friend, Eleanor, relaying the news, her friend's reply stunned me. At some time in her life, Karen has had a miscarriage, so any immediate thoughts of leaving her had just gone out the window. For her future's sake, I had to get some advice … and soon. I sat through the evening, worrying, and stayed awake late while she slept. Okay, my eyes were closed but my brain was alive and our mouth was open. I took the chance and called out for help.

All thoughts of Jana and Don, coming back to enjoy our bodies in the not too distant future, made me want to stay inside her, but I knew this was out of the question. It took less than an hour for my call to be answered, and, to my surprise, it was Séan's former lover, Betsy, who came to my assistance. She laughed when I told her about the pregnancy, but when I mentioned the miscarriage she insisted that I stay inside. I asked her why, so she told me that it might be dangerous. Betsy wasn't too sure, but promised to check with someone else. I asked her to get in touch with Jana or Anna and she said that she'd do what she could. Her promise to keep the news under her hat brought me some relief. After all, I didn't want the world to know of my situation. Betsy stayed the night, sharing our bed but not our bodies. I had to chase her out the next morning … she was getting too comfortable, and, anyway, I needed the information quickly.

The next five days were business as usual and then we called in to see the doctor. She confirmed that we are pregnant and gave us a form asking all sorts of silly questions. I was embarrassed as we filled them in, and I thought she'd have known Karen's medical history anyway. So did Karen, but, apparently, these were routine questions. I was so annoyed … I'm telling you. Imagine asking whether Karen or Don have had herpes, syphilis, or are HIV. We talked about Karen's previous pregnancy and what happened then, and her doctor insisted we get plenty of rest. There were other questions, naturally, but thank goodness all's okay. She told us that we are six weeks pregnant … and I started counting back. I couldn't help swearing when I remembered Don and Jana … Jana inside Don, or was it just before she came. I wasn't sure, and it was all too much for me … and it still is.

The day after our doctor's appointment, Betsy returned, telling me that I've no alternative other than to stay inside the mother. These, she said, were instructions from a friend of hers – a ghost in France who used to be a nurse. Betsy kept me company for the day, asking me who it was that Karen spoke to every time she used the phone. To tell you the truth, my ears never stopped as Karen's mother went on and on. Then her sister and cousin phoned ... the news going round so fast. Her friends phoned, and then another couple called in, in the evening, offering their congratulations and plenty of advice. And, in between it all, Betsy pestered me for answers. I'm not saying I minded Betsy's company, but I wanted some peace and quiet. When we went to bed that night, Karen had me reading baby books which had so much information on first time pregnancies that my head's full of it. When we closed our eyes, I went out like a light.

Two days have passed since Betsy left, and we've settled in for another night's sleep. My eyes are tired from all the reading of Karen's new pregnancy magazines. You'd think she'd know something about it, being a doctor – well, a psychiatrist – but, there again, maybe not. She gave them the news at work today and the word spread like wildfire, some telling her to take it easy, while others said enjoy it while you can. I'm not sure I can take anymore.

At long last, she's dropped off, leaving the bedside lamp on for the fourth night in a row. I don't know about her, but I can sense the light through her eyelids. I always hated the light on at night, and I don't know why she's forgetting to turn it off. Perhaps, she isn't, but this isn't one of Karen's usual habits. Still, I might as well try switching off my mind.

"So, there ya are. Well, Mick, if I didn't see it with my own eyes, I'd never have believed it." My god! It's Séan. What the hell's he doing here at this time of night? Come on, Karen, open your eyes.

"Hi, Séan. What brings you here?"

"Sure, it's yourself I came to see. The word's about as to what you're up to, and if I didn't know any better, Mick, I'd think you were a bloody eejit. I must admit, though, you're a fine lookin' woman. Do ya mind me havin' a feel?"

"Don't you dare." But he doesn't care, his rough Irish hands cupping my tits and squeezing them gently.

"Now, Mick, sure it's an awful hard thing for me to say, but you're gettin' me all worked up. Now if your woman hasn't the knickers on her, I might be in business."

"Get your hands off, Séan. ... Now! Or I'll tell every ghost I meet what you've been up to."

"Ar-agh, Mick, you'd be too embarrassed to say anythin'." In a way, I think he has me spot on, but I can't let him realise this.

"Do you really think so? Your name will be mud and no woman will come near you. You'll be playing with yourself so much that your hand will be in a permanent state of grip, and then we'll *all* laugh. Is that what you want?"

My boobs are instantly free from his touch. "Ah, Mick, sure it's only coddin' ya, I am."

"I sincerely hope so, Séan." My god! That was a close shave. I wonder if he'd have stopped if he could have seen between our legs. "And, Séan, I know you're going to tell others about me and Karen – that's expected, but don't tell Simon."

"Well, Mick, that might be difficult."

"Why? It's not as if you see him that often."

"Sure, it's not that at all. If ya must know, Mick, I never speak to him. I don't give a fig's fart for the man. And that's one of the reasons I'm not on the search." – If my eyes were open and my face could move, you can imagine what my expression might look like.

"A search! ... What's happened?"

"He's gone missin' ... about four weeks ago."

"Four weeks! That's not long in a ghost's life. What's all the fuss?"

"He was on a job of some kind, and was expected back within the fortnight, but, ya know, Mick, there hasn't been a sound from that stupid mouth of his."

"What sort of job?"

"Sure, I don't know the half of it, but it was somethin' to do with checkin' on someone or other. The rest, I don't know."

"Perhaps, it's just taking longer than usual."

"You're right, Mick, so ya are. I think exactly the same, meself. So, tell me, what's it like to be inside a woman?"

"You should know ... you've had enough."

"Sure, ya know what I mean." – And I do.

"Most days are good, others bad, and a few are downright ugly, and that's the truth."

"Isn't it the same for us all?"

"No, it's not, Séan, and you know that perfectly well."

"Well, what's the problem ... with the ugly days, I mean?"

"It's too embarrassing."

"Ar-agh, go on with ya. What fun will we ghosts ever have if we don't tell about ourselves and our experiences? Come on, Mick, dish the dirt, and I promise to keep it to meself. I know ya can't see me, Mick, but I crossed meself, and not a word will pass my lips."

"Did you ever take a long term host?"

Séan chuckles. "What kind of crackpot do ya take me for? I wouldn't be wastin' my time, just for the few extras. I don't need the speed, the better sight, or the longer flyin' time. And I don't need any of the extra responsibilities I might get."

"What responsibilities?"

"Well, Mick, there's always the possibility that ya might come out of your woman a changed man. Ya might become a Haunter, like me, or else a Reliever. On the other hand, ya might come out of her exactly as ya are now."

"What? ... As a woman?"

"Will ya listen to yourself? Sure, aren't ya a Scribe?"

"Yes."

"Well, then, isn't it a Scribe that I'd be meanin'?" – He had me worried for a minute. "Now, me ... I didn't want to take the chance of becomin' somethin' different. I'm happy as I am, doin' my bit of hauntin', visitin' Achill and havin' the craic with the women, and tellin' my stories to the likes of yourself. I can lay in the shamrock to my hearts content, and then suck on the fuchsia until my belly's full. And, Mick, as long as I do my job, nobody bothers me. So, what do ya think of that?"

"Perhaps, you're right." I can't tell him about Don and our sex life. He'd freak out.

"Well, Mick, get out'a there and stop makin' a bloody fool of yourself. Get out and we can go to the races again. Sure, that was a great day ... and a great night too. Do ya want to hear about my blonde?"

"Go on, then," I reply, sounding excited. Séan proceeds with the account of his exploits, describing the woman and her matching curtains.

I'm quite content to let him ramble on, hoping he'll forget about my ugly days.

When he's finished his story, I ask, "Will you come here again?"

"Don't be messin' us all about. Come with me, Mick, and let's have a bit of fun."

"No, Séan. I like this girl and, all in all, she's a host in a million."

"I'll give ya your due, Mick. She's a mighty good looker; I'll say that for her. Ya know, if ya were to shave the hair off her head, she'd be the spittin' image of that lovely singer, Sinead O'Connor."

"She wouldn't!"

"Well, see for yourself."

"I can't, can I?"

"Sorry, Mick, I was forgettin' meself for a minute. The thing is that I always size a woman up by lookin' at her face and head."

"We all do, Séan. It's only natural."

"Sure, ya don't get my meanin'. Ya see, I imagine her to be bald, and then try and visualise what she'd look like without all that muck they put on."

"Muck?" I interrupt.

"Aye ... that make-up. If ya were to scrape it off, lipstick and all, and then give her a skin-head haircut, just like Sinead, then you'll see how beautiful the woman is."

"You're messing about."

"I'm deadly serious, Mick. Now, your woman there ... when she, er, what's her name?"

"Karen."

"Well then, when Karen wakes up in the mornin' and looks at herself in the mirror, imagine her like I do. I'm tellin' ya, she's a dead-ringer for Sinead. And if Sinead ever becomes a ghost, I'll be after her like a shot. She can lie in the shamrock with me anytime she wants."

"So, do you fancy me, Séan?"

"I fancy your Karen, not yourself. What do ya think I am ... a bloody poof?"

"You were pawing my body and playing with my boobs."

"I told ya I was teasin' ya. And, besides, it's a woman's body ya have and not your own."

"Okay, keep your hair on. I'll have a look in the morning, just to

please you. When did you get the hots for Sinead? What I mean is …
you've been a ghost for donkey's years."

"On television, Mick … on that Sky channel when it first started. I
was in this snooker club – one of them new ones that stayed open twenty-
four hours – and Sinead was on the box practically every hour. I sat
there for days on end, waitin' and watchin' and listenin' to her lovely
voice. I don't mind tellin' ya, Mick … nothin' compares to her."

"Poor Séan."

"Poor me? You mean, poor Sinead. If she doesn't come back as a
ghost, think about me and what she'll be missin'. Now, if I was a
Mindbender, then I'd do a Stan Laurel on her."

"And what about all these other ghosts, hankering after your belly?"

"Well, until she comes here – if she does, I'll have to keep them
happy, I suppose."

"Sinead O'Connor? Hmm, I'll check Karen out. I will Séan … honest."

"Aye, Mick, I'm sure ya will. Anyhow, I'll be on my way and give
your ears a rest."

"What's the hurry?"

"I'm off to a party with the blonde."

"You and your women."

"Sure, ya wouldn't deprive me of that?"

"I couldn't if I wanted to. Anyway, Séan, thanks for coming. I'd shake
your hand if I could, but I can't, so I won't."

"Ar-agh, I'll give ya a kiss instead and I'll pretend that it's Karen I've
been talkin' to."

"Forget it, Séan. I've a long memory."

"I'll be off so. I'll see ya later."

"Cheers, Séan … see you." And silence reigns once more. Now there's
food for thought. Séan is besotted with Sinead; Simon has vanished off
the face of the earth; and I've been sexually titillated. Séan's a gas man,
really, and it's been good to talk to him. I hope we're both awake the
next time he calls.

CHAPTER THIRTY-TWO

Jana arrived a few minutes ago, but I had to shoo her out of the bathroom. Karen and I were going through the motions, so to speak, and we're now busy washing our hands. Jana does pick her moments, doesn't she?

In the past three weeks, things have gone downhill as far as I'm concerned. I'm fed up with hopping to the toilet at all manner of times. It's mostly in the evening, when we're preparing Karen's dinner that she starts to heave, and then it continues on and off. I always thought morning sickness was something women got at that time of day, but Karen has developed her own meaning to word. The past couple of days haven't been so bad – since she gave up the coffee and started drinking herbal teas and only eating toast for breakfast. Our diet has altered slightly, and we haven't been throwing up as such, but the retching can be a pain in the neck.

We walk back to the lounge and sit by the phone, our eyes on the evening paper. Don phones twice a week, like clockwork, and we're expecting his call at any minute. We haven't told him, as yet, about the baby, and I'm dying to hear his reaction.

"Hi, Jana . .... It's been a while," I say, my voice showing discontent.

"I'm sorry, Micky, but I've been very busy."

"Did you get the message?"

"Yes! Isn't it fantastic?"

"You must be joking. Look, Jana, I want to get out of here."

"You can't. I'm sorry, Micky, but that's not an option."

"Yes, it is. You can't expect me to go through a pregnancy. It's obscene!"

"Micky, if she hadn't had an earlier miscarriage, then you'd have had no problem, but you can't take the chance of causing her baby to die."

"It might not die. Karen seems strong enough to cope with having her own baby."

"It is too early, Micky. Don't you understand?"

"No, I don't … and I'm pissed off."

"You'll get over it."

"So, how long before I can leave her?"

"We're not sure. The baby has to develop properly and gain a fair bit of weight. To be honest, Micky, none of us are sure. Anna is going to check some manuals and let us know."

"More books! I'm fed up to the back teeth with books and magazines about babies, baby clothes, and articles on breast feeding. For god's sake, Jana, there's such a long time to go."

"You can't stop Karen dreaming about her and the baby's future. It's only natural."

"For her, yes, but not for me. I want out. ... Now!"

"No, Micky, and that's final."

"You can't decide what I can or can't do however much I trust you."

"Okay, but think about this. From what I've been told, and correct me if I'm wrong, this baby came about since you entered Karen and not before."

"It seems that way."

"The thing is that if Karen has a miscarriage or the baby dies from a deliberate action of yours, then, more than likely, you will be responsible and could also die."

"You're having me on."

"It's not guaranteed. No-one can be certain, but there's always the possibility."

"You're telling me, then, that I'm stuck, but only until it's developed a little more?"

"Yes, and maybe longer."

"Get lost! I can't do this. I can't and I won't!"

"You have to." – What can I do? I thought Jana would help and give me the news I wanted to hear. I'm so angry and I can't bloody show it. And I can't help but shout at her through the newspaper Karen's reading. "So, what kept you?"

"I was searching for Simon. He went missing and ... ."

"I know. Séan told me. Has he turned up?"

"Yes, he's been found. Ghosts from villages, far and wide, were searching. One of them found his body, but only just in time."

"Huh!"

"He's alive and on the mend, but he's so lucky, the stupid fool."

"Why? What do you mean by stupid?"

"He thought he could get an easy lay. I suppose we're to blame."

"Us? Why us?"

"Yes, us. He was on a job, finding out something for Anna, when he decided to make a detour to a certain deserted island. I think that our mention of such a place, when he came to Achill, set his brain in gear and he found out about Helga."

"He didn't?"

"He did!" I wish I could see Jana's face. This can't be right. "Micky! Helga left him for dead. From what he can remember and is prepared to tell us, he thought she would be weak from living there on her own, without help of any kind. He admits to initiating the sex with her and she was only too happy to oblige. He was at her for ages and getting tired when Helga turned the tables. She turned him over and started pounding away. She wouldn't stop, keeping at him and at him, until ... ." – Why's Jana stopped talking?

"Is that it? You mean, she screwed him until she thought he was dead?"

"Not quite, Micky. It's worse than that."

"What's worse than death?"

"She knew she couldn't kill him. Helga's not that stupid."

"So, what's the problem?"

"She screwed him so much, obviously enjoying his affliction but, in the end, his stiffy couldn't stand the strain ... going soft and getting her mad."

"You're joking?"

"I'm not! And he was embarrassed telling us the story."

"So, you've seen him."

"Of course, I have ... as soon as I heard. I had to have a look-see, just to make sure. In a way, I feel sorry for the man, but you should see him. He's gutted."

"I bet he is."

"He's very weak, though, and will be for some time. When Simon's fit enough to go to Achill, he'll recuperate over there. The trouble is that he's talking about revenge."

"What's the point? Can't he just leave her to rot, alone and neglected?"

"She's escaped."

"She's what?"

"She sucked him until he was as near to death as possible, and then she flew away."

"But how? That's impossible."

"I've no idea, unless there was some growth of plant that gave her

380

some flying time. I suppose there must have been, or how else … .?"

"She'll be looking for her mate," I interrupt.

"Dorothy? I don't think so. I was in the party sent to check on her, and Dorothy was still there, begging to come home."

"Is she sorry?"

"She says she is, but can we believe her? And, anyway, with Helga on the loose, it's better leaving Dorothy where she is, under closer scrutiny."

"I think that's for the best." Karen and I make a beeline for the bedroom with Jana hanging on to our coat-tails. We throw our clothes on the bed, sit down and start brushing our hair. "I think you should talk to Simon. You know, to get this revenge business out of his head. I wouldn't fancy my chances with that monster."

"That's one of the reasons I'm here." I can see Jana's reflection, looking so matter of fact. "I came to see you because I wanted to, and I'd have been here a lot sooner if all this hadn't happened, but there's a more pressing problem. Micky, Helga is after your blood."

"She, what?"

"Apparently, one of the last things that Simon remembers is Helga laughing and shouting that she was going to kill you, even if she dies in the attempt."

"Are you serious?"

"You bet your life and the life of your baby. As far as we're aware, Helga hasn't heard that you're up the spout, but she wouldn't care anyway."

"How many ghosts know about this pregnancy?"

"I don't know, but with your situation being so different, the ghosts are excited. The news of the baby has spread, and that's why I've brought the others."

"What others?"

"Listen, Micky. Please understand that I had to speak to you first; to explain the immediate dangers and what we're doing to protect you."

"Dangers! Protection! This is pathetic, Jana. … Pathetic! You're telling me that I can't get out of Karen's body because the baby might die, and, all the time, Helga is baying for my blood. As far as I'm concerned, Karen and the baby have a better chance without me. I can't jeopardise their lives."

"Leaving her might do exactly that. You're as safe as can be, believe me. Besides me, six other ghosts are outside – all here to help, and others are on the way. We'll take turns, both inside and outside the apartment, to and from work, and wherever else you visit. She won't get through, Micky. You've got to believe me." — What can I do? My thoughts are all askew as Karen slides me across the bed. A few moments later, we are pulling on a clean nightie. "I love your body, Micky." Jana's hand reaches for our leg.

"Forget it, Jana. If you want to do something useful, go and sort out your friends."

My tone of voice has the required effect, with Jana sticking her tongue in my face. "You miserable git. If only we didn't need men." She disappears from view for a few minutes, returning in the company of Lucia and Moira. They both approach the bed, kissing our lips and asking how I am. Our little chit-chat is precisely that as Jana intervenes, placing them in other rooms. Shortly after, the phone goes and Karen has me up and rushing to the lounge.

"Hi, Don, I thought you'd have called earlier."

"I'm sorry, honey. I've been very busy with …."

"I know, stupid computers. Listen, Don, do me a favour, and, if you're standing … sit. I've the most wonderful news to tell you."

"You're coming to America?"

"No, Don, not that. We're going to have a baby." – Stunned silence, obviously, because it's taking him an age to respond. Come on, Don, don't keep her waiting. *"Don? Don? Are you still there?"* we ask.

"Yeah, I'm here." His voice seems all cut up. *"Karen, I hope this is some kind of joke."*

"No, Don, it's not," we timidly reply. *"I'm nearly three months."*

"This can't be happening. I thought you were on the pill," he says, sounding sterner and much louder. Oh, shit! … We're crying, and the tears are pouring from our eyes.

"Micky, what's the matter?" asks Jana, both she and Lucia watching the rivers flow. How does she expect me to answer in my state – sobbing, slobbering, and not able to twist my tongue while Karen's otherwise engaged? They should be realistic about this.

"D …D.Don," we struggle to say, *"I th … thought you w … w.wanted a baby. We agreed."*

"No, I didn't! Not unless I was pissed at the time. Honestly, Karen, I can't conceive that you're pregnant." It's getting worse. The phone's on the floor and probably broken from the force of our throw … and I've lost sight of the girls. The river's turned into a flood. Dashing back to bed, we dive on the cover, bury our head in the pillow … and we're sobbing uncontrollably.

"Micky? … Micky? Answer, will you?" asks Jana, holding me around my shoulder for comfort. It takes a while for our heaving chest to slow and our crying to become a whimper.

"He doesn't want the baby," I say.

"The dirty wanker! It's so typical of men. All they want is sex, but never think about the consequences. What did he say? Is he coming over?"

"No chance. He's in shock, and blaming her for not taking precautions."

"See! That's what I mean. If he didn't want a kid, he should have used a rubber." Am I listening to Jana or Joyce, or do all women think the same? And, do all women do the same after crying their heart out? What I mean is that Karen has turned us about and is writing away with vigour at a new fitness regime for the two of us to try. This is stupid and I tell Jana so. She's laughing at the amount of time that I'll be spending on the bicycle and rowing machines. It's as if Karen wants to prove something to him … and to herself.

She's just about finished taking her anger out on the paper … and on my mind, when another ghost walks in – Betsy. Jana relays the danger and gives her instructions. Betsy leaves us alone, and it's not long after that we're curled up underneath the cover, my head barely visible to Jana's eyes.

"Micky," I hear, "you should get inside Karen's brain and help the poor girl."

"It's harder than you think."

"You'll have to try it sometime, and, I agree, it's not so easy to put your thoughts across, but you must persist for your own good as well as hers." A few more words pass our lips before we say goodnight.

CHAPTER THIRTY-THREE

"It's lazin' in the park, so ya are. I could smell your perfume a mile off."

"Just as if. The only thing you can smell is trouble."

"Well it's trouble you're in, Mick. That's what I'm hearin', and I see ya have the bodyguards." And he's correct. Ivan, Lun and Dick are on the lookout for Helga; each at a safe distance – giving me some privacy, and yet they're close enough to pounce should Helga show.

It's just been six weeks now, since my protection began and there's still no sign of her. The men stay outside the apartment, checking all angles, while the females live inside, one in each room, including the toilet. I'm beginning to wish I wasn't here but, as Jana pointed out, Helga would find me regardless. My point, though, is that if I was free, at least I'd be able to raise my own hands to ward her off. It's so damn frustrating. We can't even go for a pee in peace. Thank heavens Jana has stopped pestering me and Karen with her fingers. Yes, it was exciting, and no doubt she'll be at us again, but for now she's doing her job, monitoring the situation.

Don's been in touch; the first time to apologise for his behaviour, and the second to see if any other options were available. We didn't cry this time … just gave him a piece of her mind. At the time, I suppose, termination was a possibility, and I did do as Jana suggested by telling her brain something along the same lines as Don, but Karen didn't let me bat an eyelid. This woman is so strong willed. The next time he phoned she refused to talk to him. He's sent a couple of letters, which she let me read – begging letters, but Karen and I haven't replied. Nor have we thrown them away. I wish she'd change her mind, and, god knows, I've been trying to do exactly that. I want him and his body back here as soon as possible.

"They're doing a good job, Séan."

"Well, Mick, is it true what they're tellin' me … that you're up the duff?"

"Who told you?"

"And does it matter who told me?"

"I suppose not."

"I tell ya, Mick, it's the immaculate contraception. That's what it is."

"I think you mean conception. Well, Séan, it isn't … far from it. It's more like a balls-up."

"It's that, too, Mick, but I do mean contraception. ... Indeed, I do. To my way of thinkin', it was The Lord, himself, who intervened and caused the condom to burst, and that's why you're pregnant. Sure, he wanted ya to have a baby."

"Christ, Séan, leave it out. Your so-called God had nothing to do with this, and Karen's boyfriend has never used a condom ... not since I've been inside her."

Pointing his finger in my face, Séan says, "Now, don't you be takin' our Holy Father's name in vain, Mick. I know ya to be a fine man, but it doesn't be suitin' ya."

"I didn't swear or take anyone's name in vain. Your God doesn't exist as far as I'm concerned, but if you want to believe, that's your choice and I respect you for it. You know how I feel, and I don't try to persuade you in your beliefs, so don't come the God Almighty business with me."

"Ar-agh, Mick, your soul will be lost to the devil himself."

"What soul, Séan? We don't have a soul. It's just a word and a lie."

"Well, it's Satan that has your soul already, Mick."

"The only one around here is the sole of Karen's shoe, and if you don't shut up then I'll tell her to belt you with it."

"Okay, Mick, now don't be gettin' agitated. I'm only here for the good of your health. If ya must know, I was goin' to tell ya about Simon."

"I know about Simon."

"Ah, so ya heard. Well, didja ever hear about his manhood and the state it's in?"

"Yeah! A while ago."

"It must be an awful thing to be nearly killed like that, and to lose his prized possession. It's despicable, that's what it is."

I know, I've been there, but I can't tell him, can I? So, I say the next best thing. "He'll live, Séan. He's a good looking bloke and he won't be short of a female or two."

"You know, Mick, I wonder what he wanted with that woman in the first place. Why do ya think he bothered to go all that way for the leg over when so many women are chasin' us men?"

"I really don't know, Séan. I've asked myself the same question and all I can think of is that the females around here were fed up with him always showing off and teasing them."

"Sure, maybe your right."

"So, Séan, how long are you staying?"

"Well, with me not bein' a fightin' man, I don't know that I'd be any use to ya, but if any of the women fancy a good time, I might stay for a while."

"They're busy, so forget it."

"You're a hard man, Mick. Anyhow, what are ya … three months gone, is it?"

"I believe it's nearer five."

"Five, is it?" He counts his fingers, mumbling to himself. "So, ya were in the club the last time I was here and ya never opened your mouth. Now, Mick, if it was me, I'd have been out'a her the moment I knew. Why don't ya come to your senses, man? You're lookin' fit, though, and it'd be hard for a man to tell whether ya were pregnant or not, but in another month the pair of ye will have the belly showin'."

"You're right, Séan, and it'll be nearly as big as yours."

"Well, I'm happy with mine – the women like it, and I didn't get it from a bit of jiggery-pokery."

"The women like it? Pull the other one."

"It's true, Mick. It's perfectly true. I was only readin' in the newspaper, just the other day, that women like men with a bit of a paunch."

"Which newspaper … the Beano or the Dandy?"

"There's no need to be makin' me sound like a stupid eejit. I mightn't be the cleverest ghost around, but I keep meself up to date with the goin's on."

"Fair enough, Séan. I'm sorry."

"Tell me, what's the craic back at your place? I mean, is there any room for another fella?"

"You can come back if you don't mind sharing."

"You're jokin', aren't ya? So, how many of ye are there?"

"Eight, not counting myself and Jana."

"Now, that's a crowd, and all because of that silly cow, Helga, goin' about causin' fear and misery. And is it only the three men ya have?"

"Just the three."

Séan's eyes light up, his mind working overtime. "Ar-agh, I might as well come back and help ya out."

"You'll have to be a lookout. Jana is taking this seriously, and no-one shirks their work."

"Mick, it sounds as though you're tryin' to put me off. I can turn my hand to anythin' when needs must."

"I'm sure you can."

"Which of the women have ya got?"

"At the moment, we have Affiong, Lucia, Betsy … ."

"Betsy? … My Betsy?" he interrupts, surprise and anger in his voice.

"Yes, Séan. … Betsy! In fact, she's very observant and can't do enough to help."

"Well, I'm not comin', so. Ya wouldn't be havin' me on now, would'ja? No, Mick, don't answer that. I know ya wouldn't tease me." — By this time, we're nearly home, and Séan's hands are balled into fists. Karen has me stepping out, and at the rate we're going we'll be back home in ten minutes or less. "Look, Mick, I'm sorry to be leavin' ya in these circumstances, but I won't be seen dead near that woman."

"That's alright, Séan, we'll have to manage. Will you call on me again?"

"I will, Mick, but I'd have to know that she isn't around."

"I've no way of telling you. It all depends on the capture of Helga."

"I suppose so. Sure, that bitch is a pain in the arse." – I don't know which of the women he's on about … Betsy or Helga, and yet, for Séan, it could be either. The closer we get, the more nervous he becomes – sort of sensing Betsy's presence, and then he moves ahead but turning to face me. "Ah, Mick, it's been good to see ya, but I'd better be off or there'll be ructions at your place. Take care now, and keep doin' the exercises.

"Yeah, Séan … I'll see you." He takes to the air and flies south. A few minutes later, Karen carries me inside our building.

It seems such a shame that he can't face Betsy, so's they could talk things out properly rather than bickering every time they meet. After all, when you think about it, he's enjoying his life to the fullest and Betsy doesn't seem to have any problems pulling the blokes. You'd think that, by now, they'd have kissed and made up and co-existed in a friendlier way towards one and other. I must persuade them somehow, but I'm afraid it will have to wait until I'm back on my own two feet and not in someone else's.

CHAPTER THIRTY-FOUR

Séan settled himself down, well away from the edge of the stream, wondering whether to stay in the area and take in the sights, or head for the Northern Line. He stretched his legs and then lay back on the grass, his hands beneath his head. His lips moved slightly, making a puckering sound, and then they turned into a grin as thoughts of Mick and his pregnancy crossed his mind.

"The damn fool," he said to himself. "Now, what kind'a eejit would be so stupid as to get involved with a pregnant woman, host or no host? Yeah, sure Mick's alright, but hasn't he all his ghost life ahead of him? And instead of bein' out here enjoyin' himself, he's taken the bloody plunge already. I'd like to know what they're bloody well teachin' them these days, and why they're all so fired up into gettin' the likes of Mick inside these long term hosts at the outset. It's downright foolish they are. It's never been a bother to me in not botherin' to take a host for any length of time."

He looked up at the cloudy grey sky, not feeling the cold air around him. Séan lifted his head, glancing down between his feet at the running water. "Sure, it's grand to be free to live my life as I like, and not to be relyin' on others for the instruction or protection. And isn't Mick the stupid one, anyway? Why the hell didn't he get out of the blasted woman as soon as he knew she was in the club?" He lay back down again and closed his eyes. "And why don't those other eejits tell him to get out; stayin' here, keepin' him safe? Is it plonkers they are ... the lot of them? Now, he might be gettin' a bit of the old pokey from herself and yer man there, but what kind'a ghost would want to be in that position in the first place? Sure, I know she has a fella, unless they've split up, but ya can't tell me that there isn't somethin' weird about the whole business. Never in my life have I heard of a male ghost takin' residence inside a woman for any stretch of time, and then for him to be in the process of givin' birth; never mind the pokin' and the proddin' from the boyfriend. It's strange, so it is ... mighty strange. They must be usin' poor Mick for an experiment or somethin', and it's not fair on the lad. Now, if that Betsy wasn't there, I'd go right up and pull him out, so I would."

"I do wish you would," came a voice from above.

On hearing the voice, Séan opened his eyes and sat up. "Who the hell is that?" he asked, turning his head from side to side, searching for its owner.

"It's too late to worry for you my dear. Any friend of Mick's is an enemy of mine," said Helga, swiftly approaching from behind.

Séan spun round, just in time to see a huge pair of clodhoppers aimed at his face. "Noooo-aarrghh!" Helga's big feet were inside the heavy shoes that caught Séan a direct hit on his chin. Being only halfway up, he didn't have far to fall, and fall he did, now lying head down and towards the water. Not quite unconscious, he groaned and shook himself, but he was still lying prone.

"Not dead yet, eh? Well, you'll soon be wishing you were," Helga threatened. Séan reacted as best he could, lifting his aching head and emitting a loud groan. It was the last thing he knew about. Helga jumped on his neck, feet first. She stamped and stamped, leapt off, and then started kicking him in the ribs.

Séan didn't move. He couldn't move. Helga carried on relentlessly – minute by minute, laughing, kicking and cursing, over and over again. She didn't want to stop and she told him so, not that he could hear her. She was in her element, badgering him with her words of hate, all the time thinking he was listening, and then, as if that wasn't enough, she dropped down beside his body and started thumping him ferociously. Her head was close to his, screaming her rants of destruction against all of Micky's friends.

She stood up, reached out her arms, and pulled Séan towards the river. Even for Helga, Séan's heavy body was a nightmare as she tugged and tugged, then chided him for being so fat. Close to the water's edge, she stopped her pulling and, instead, pushed him from behind. She cursed again while turning his body, finding it harder to manoeuvre in that position, and yet she persisted, ignoring everything else around her. Helga was ready for that great final shove, and seemed happy with herself, when out of the blue her head was side-swiped. Helga, not expecting a threat from anyone, was taken completely by surprise. She released her grip on Séan and turned to see who or what had hit her. Séan's body settled back to its previous position, though his head still dangled over the water. Helga, meanwhile, was now searching the sky for her attacker. She knew that whoever it was was mighty fast and accurate, and, in her mind, she was going to claim her second victim of the day. "Where are you, you coward?"

From the sky, like a bullet, a ghost appeared. It closed in on Helga so fast that she didn't recognise the ghost until the last second. It was a second too late. Affiong had hit her again – this time in the side, causing Helga to unbalance. Affiong flew off again, making whooping noises; sending signals to the other ghosts. Helga, not fearing her former friend, waited for the next attack … and it was quicker this time.

Once again, Affiong came from a great height and at speed, but as she neared her target she saw Helga bobbing and weaving. Still she came and aimed right for Helga's midriff. Helga still moved her body from side to side but kept her feet rigid, letting Affiong attack. Too late, Affiong realised her mistake. She should have tormented Helga until others had arrived, but she was too close to change her mind. Helga stood up straight, taking the full brunt of Affiong's attack in her belly. This time, though, she relaxed slightly at the moment of contact, making Affiong follow through. Helga fell back deliberately, into the stream, this time clinging onto Affiong's body. There was no splash at all – just the movement of the two of them as they tossed about in the shallow water. Helga put her strength and cunning to good use. Having caused Affiong to lose control of the situation, she now had the upper hand. She turned Affiong around, pushing herself on top. She used her rock of a fist and smashed it into Affiong's face. Then, not relaxing her hold, Helga pressed Affiong's head beneath the surface of the water.

Meanwhile, a nearly dead ghost could be heard. "Geroff her," he managed to say.

"Hah! So the fat ghost still lives. Never mind, I'll polish you off in a second and there's nothing you can do to stop me," laughed Helga.

A battered and weary Séan pushed himself forward, into the stream, while Helga kept watching his movements.

"Now, stay back," she warned, her eyes on his as he crawled closer – the water no more than halfway over his body. And all the time, Helga was still pressing down on Affiong's head. Shouts from above could also be heard and Helga turned her eyes towards them. But still she kept Affiong beneath the surface.

Lun and Ivan approached from above while Séan closed in from the side, but then the three men seemed to stop in their tracks. Séan looked on, wide-eyed and bewildered. He couldn't comprehend what was going on. He was still dazed; still sore all over; still angry at Helga; but, now, he was also starting to cry. Lun and Ivan flew much closer, but more in the direction of Séan rather than Helga. They seemed as stunned as Séan – Affiong had vanished. Affiong, they all knew, was no more. Even Helga now knew that Affiong was dead – she couldn't feel her face beneath her hand.

"You bitch," shouted an angry Ivan. "You'll pay for this," he warned her.

And, as if by magic, the three men watched while Helga's body started disappearing from the bottom up. It started fading away very gradually. The last they heard from Helga was a weak shout .... "Noooo ... ."

And that was it for her. Ivan helped Lun pull Séan from the stream. They eased him to the ground and let him rest. Ivan then kissed some life back into his body, feeling him grow stronger by the minute. A good while later, Séan, still looking the worse for wear, was coming back to his former self – more active with his mouth, but not with any happy words.

"Sure, I'll never forgive meself. Never!" he said, going on and on repeating this. The others tried comforting him, although they too were distraught.

Time soon passed, and with it Séan's story of how it all came about; how he was lazing and thinking, and nearly asleep, when Helga first attacked him. He told them how he felt so close to death from her kicking and beating, and that it was only God Almighty who must have kept him alive and his brain still functioning. Lun and Ivan berated themselves for not coming earlier. They were afraid to leave their posts, thinking it was all a trick to attack Micky.

The three of them admitted that they'd never seen another ghost die. They couldn't get it out of their heads that they had just watched a ghost being murdered and the one responsible duly die for committing the murder. They didn't believe it possible.

Then Séan blamed himself again, saying, "If I hadn't approached Helga when I did, then she might have released Affiong and let her get up. Sure, Helga must have known the risk to herself and she wouldn't have let it go that far – not even when she was injurin' me. I'll never forgive meself ... as long as I live." Lun tried to help him with his thinking, yet even he and Ivan had similar thoughts about themselves. They admitted that they could and should have tried to warn Helga of the danger she was in, in what she was doing.

The three of them were sorry sights when Jana, Dick and Betsy found them sitting on the grass looking into Affiong's watery grave. Ivan approached the newcomers, his finger to his lips, and gave them a brief account of both Affiong's and Helga's deaths. Dick went back to the apartment with orders from Jana to keep his mouth shut about all he'd seen and heard.

Jana sat down next to Séan, placed an arm around his shoulders, and comforted him, saying, "I'm sorry, Séan. I really am, but I need to hear it from your own lips. All I want is the truth as you saw it, and I know this is very hard for you but I want to hear everything from the beginning."

And she did, from the moment that Séan left Micky to the present, and all the while Betsy stayed in the background, just listening. Séan had noticed her but he was in no mood for an argument. The other two told things as they had seen them, with Ivan expanding a little more with the details. They hadn't liked telling the story, especially Séan, but very slowly Jana gathered all the information she could. She cried and Betsy cried. Betsy approached Séan and took his hand. He didn't stop her. At the time, he couldn't stop anyone from doing anything.

The problem they then had was how they would explain all this to Anna, and, more importantly, to Micky. They all discussed this for an age, eventually agreeing that Jana should make the decision about what to say and do. It wasn't that she wanted the responsibility – she'd suggested that Séan go back and talk to him, man to man, because they got on so well together, but Séan flatly refused. His reasoning – besides being upset, heartbroken, and still blaming himself – was that Affiong wouldn't have been where she was, in trying to save him, if Micky hadn't helped her become a decent ghost. He was ashamed that he'd been partly responsible for Affiong's death, and with her being a close friend of Micky's, he couldn't look the man in the eye to tell him. Séan wanted to take Affiong's place. He said that if he had died by Helga's hands, then everyone else would have been safe.

Betsy started talking to him, whispering in his ear. She still clung to his hand and he even responded by placing his free one over hers. She kissed his cheek and he turned and nodded, and, with a tear in his eye, he sighed, shaking his head. With that, Séan climbed to his feet, held Betsy close and kissed her goodbye. He slowly walked off without saying where he was going. Jana, being worried about him, urged Lun to follow in his footsteps, just in case. Betsy offered to help with this, but Jana said no. Then, crying once more, Jana headed back with Betsy and Ivan, all the time thinking what to do and say.

On the way, she made a decision to talk to all the ghosts privately. She made the choice of keeping them there, guarding Micky. She explained to the other two that if she were to tell Micky everything right away, then he just might flip and jump out of Karen, so endangering her life; that Micky would blame himself for saving Affiong in the first place. Jana didn't want to take the chance on his well being or that of Karen and her baby. She said that, somehow, Séan had to be told of this decision in case he eventually plucked up the courage to visit Micky.

Betsy and Ivan wholeheartedly agreed.

CHAPTER THIRTY-FIVE

The heavier we get, the faster everything seems to happen. Anna paid a visit, albeit a brief one ... took one look at me and decided to up the guard. There have been so many ghosts coming and going that I've lost track of half the faces. Roger – a sweet young man from Devon, and the finely toned Helmut, from Cologne, are two that I'll remember. You can imagine the dreams I had, thinking about their bodies and what I could do to them. If I wasn't where I am, and they thought as I do, I'd have no problem with this pregnancy whatsoever. So long as I knew that one, or maybe both, of them would be waiting for my body, I think I could give birth to twins.

Unfortunately, I was made aware of their sexual prowess when I overheard a discussion between Lucia and Luisella. It hasn't made me think any worse of them, but I'm a wee bit disappointed.

We wrote a Dear John letter to Don – not that Karen has found someone new, but more by way of an ultimatum. He kept phoning, though, sounding more disgruntled, but later on he softened his stance. Since then, we haven't broken the phone. In fact, everything's looking much rosier. The letter was her way of explaining that, with or without him, this child is coming into the world and that he has to accept some of the responsibility even if she decides to go with someone else. Karen doesn't have anyone else in mind, though, and only wants him to be involved, from near or afar, but she is adamant that his name will be on the birth certificate. We later told him that we still loved him a little, despite him not wanting to be a father, and that, barring accidents, he'll now be a daddy earlier rather than later. He's coming over to see us and I can't wait to have his body next to mine.

And talking about bodies ... what about my own and all the changes taking place? Why have I put myself through all this? Karen is so proud of the baby that I was forced to watch as the skin on our belly kept moving around. Was I happy? ... No! But I still had a huge smile on my face and kept talking softly while our baby changed position. And, worse than that – if it can get much worse, our nipples have started to leak.

Séan was right. I should have got out at the start, but both Jana and Anna have insisted that I stay the distance. How do they know so much? How could my leaving Karen's body cause problems for the child? I know that the baby is healthy. Karen has us checked as regular as clockwork – dragging me to the antenatal clinic with our pee in a jar; having our blood pressure taken while answering questions about headaches; or whether there's any pain beneath our ribs. Of course I have pain beneath my ribs – there's a baby inside me trying to get out. Perhaps, not yet, but I wish it would hurry up.

The midwife keeps going on about something called pre-eclampsia, asking Karen if we can see spots before our eyes and whether we have blurred vision or can see flashing lights. Is she stupid, or what? I have blurred vision every time Karen closes her eyes. One minute I'm having a conversation with Jana, watching her expressions and so on, and the next second she's gone. Not gone ... gone, but disappeared from view. It's so annoying. As for spots before my eyes, both Betsy and Lucia have no sense of fashion, turning up in polka-dot mini-skirts that don't leave much to the imagination. It's like the sixties revisited. Minis can't be coming back, surely? And after that, what next ... winkle-pickers?

I'm also fed up with Karen's exercise regime. Day in, day out, stretches here, stretches there ... I'm whacked. It's just as well I have her body to benefit me, gaining strength from her hormones. This morning was the worst, though, when I felt a funny tightening sensation in my lower tummy. I didn't know what was going on. I thought ... here we go, off to the loo again, but I was wrong. Karen was on the phone, telling her friend, Eleanor, that she seemed to be losing control of her mind and body and that she can't stop crying. Well, it's nothing to do with me. I've tried umpteen times to influence her thinking, but her will is too great. Yes, I joined her with the crying action and the wiping of the tears, but if her brain is messed up, then that's her problem. I've got enough on my plate. I'll give Karen her due, though. She's making sure I'll leave her body in decent shape, because, lately, we've been slapping on stretch-mark cream by the bucketful.

We've just had our regular check-up and we're now on the way to the swimming pool. I'm happily smiling – I don't have a choice – and Karen is happy that our little baby's finger nails have reached its finger tips; that it's about four and a half pounds in weight; and the head is in the correct position. I'm happy that I won't be giving birth to a little monster. I didn't know what they were talking about before – they'd called it lanugo, but, apparently, it's a soft covering of hair all over the baby's body, but now it's starting to disappear. At least, that's what the others in her antenatal class have told us. And who am I to argue?

While crossing the road, our eyes glance about and I notice Luisella and Dick floating ahead of us. They are our escorts for the day, while the rest keep watch at home. We toddle along with our belly pushed out proudly, and shortly after reach the pool. We get changed and then spend some time doing the breast stroke. I'd been worrying myself unnecessarily, thinking that I might be completely submerged for more than a few seconds. Karen, though, is a sensible swimmer, and any thoughts of losing my life in water soon disappear. Ten lengths later, we crawl out and dry off. Not long after, we're in a taxi and relaxing for a change.

Once back in the apartment, we make another drink of camomile tea, and, feet up on the couch, watch some tele'. We're halfway through The Paul O'Grady Show, when Karen drops off, leaving me blind to the programme and everyone else. "She always does this ... just before the news," I say, irritably.

"Stop fretting, Micky. You can still hear everything," says Betsy.

"There is that," I answer, still slightly annoyed.

The programme ends, replaced by adverts and then the news at six. In the background, Betsy and Lucia are having a chat about the men they fancy and who they've had. It doesn't surprise me anymore. I've heard so many conversations between these and other ghosts that nothing seems to shock me. I've found that it's only Jana who doesn't elaborate about her conquests because she doesn't want to upset me. And then there's Affiong – I haven't seen her for ages. She wouldn't boast, poor girl. She'd be too upset because of her past. The rest don't care. To them, sex is a part of our everyday life, and they're happy to relive their actions.

The news, I hear, is much the same – stealth taxes to fund the health services and schools; problems in the Middle East; another major company going bust putting loads on the dole; transport problems; and the congestion charge. It's getting worse not better. Karen, yanks my arm to the side, and the next thing I hear is a loud crash of smashing glass close by. My eyes open with hers and we can't miss the broken vase, scattered flowers, and lots of water on the floor beside us.

"Oh, God! What have I done?" asks Karen. Immediately, Karen and I dive to the kitchen and fetch back a cloth, a brush, and a plastic bin. As

we squat down by the couch, my eyes are focused on the upset vase.

"What are you doing down there?" asks Jana, just entering the room. I'm about to reply, when Karen, being extremely careful not to cut us, makes me say, *"How? What did I do?"* Tears enter our eyes, preventing me from seeing properly.

From my side, I can hear Betsy answering for me. "Karen's had an accident. She knocked the vase on the floor." Karen takes me to the kitchen again, where we replace the bin and pick up another cloth.

When we're finished clearing up, Karen rests our bodies on the couch again. Our eyes seem to be staring ahead, not concentrating on anything specific, and, all the while, I focus my mind on Jana's and Betsy's conversation. Jana is now sitting comfortably in the corner chair, while Betsy sits on the carpet.

Our conversation takes on a more interesting tone when Jana asks Betsy about Séan. She's reluctant, at first, to discuss their relationship, but Jana is a very persuasive and tactical ghost. She eggs her on and, after a while, Betsy is letting the whole story roll off her tongue. Betsy openly admits that she had a great time with him, but also admits that she had such a wayward life when she first became a ghost. Her faithlessness and lack of trust stems from the time she fell in love with another young ghost. But this young man had too many females to choose from, and so deserted her for another.

To think that she's been a ghost centuries longer than Jana, and that she came back as a ghost in a time when the Church seemed to be ruling the roost. I can't help but feel sorry while she relates her tale of life and death. To her, the Church was the law and order, having been brought up to be a nun as a consequence of the Black Death. Her parents had died when the curse hit the country, but, somehow, Betsy survived and was tended to by older nuns. They nursed her and taught her their beliefs, but in her heart she didn't belong. Betsy tells us about her longing, back then, to see the outside world, away from the convent at Bures. It was a visiting monk that took her eye … and she, his. And that was the day she started dreaming dreams of love and freedom. Her fantasies had started in Bures, but ended in such tragic circumstances beneath the rectory up the road.

Séan, she tells us, fell for her as soon as he saw her. It wasn't she who made a play for his body, but it was more a mutual occurrence that happened beneath the sheets. She tells us about his mouth that never stopped bragging about himself. They became an item of sorts, until Séan's roving eye and big mouth drove her into another man's arms. Betsy also tells us how she and Dick have it off every so often. It doesn't surprise me.

I wonder about ghosts. Why have so many had such terrible deaths? It's quite extraordinary. Karen eases our bodies from the sofa and off we go to the bedroom. Jana and Betsy follow, them talking and me listening. They've known each other for a long time, and it makes me feel like a novice to hear them ramble on about former boyfriends – men lost at war; from a Spanish sailor who sailed in the Armada, to a couple of soldiers who died in Napoleonic times. There were others, too many to name, but for two women who'd died so young, they have certainly lived their ghost lives to the full.

Not long after, Karen takes me and the baby to bed, and I close my eyes. Jana comes close, letting her nose nuzzle against ours. When she and Betsy leave the room, my mind switches off.

CHAPTER THIRTY-SIX

A week has passed, and Jana and the other ghosts have left, sadness written all over their faces. Mine would have been just the same if I wasn't where I am. The first I knew of the bad news was yesterday morning when Ivan dropped in. He told us about Séan trying to take his own life. Betsy nearly fell in front of me, shocked to the core. I was trying to watch The Wright Stuff at the time, but I had to switch myself off from Karen's choice of programme because I couldn't understand why Séan, of all people, would do something so unreal.

I think I know Séan well enough to say that he's not the sort of ghost to do himself harm for any reason at all. And I'm sure you'd agree with me on that point. Jana, who was sitting close by, got up and took Ivan to the kitchen, leaving me and Karen with Betsy for company. Naturally, I wanted to know what happened, and I wasn't too happy about being left out of the conversation. Betsy, sitting in the corner, tried to reassure me, saying it was probably all a mistake – that he might have had an accident or something, but there was more in Ivan's voice, when he said what he did, to raise my doubts. Five minutes later, they rejoined us.

Jana approached and knelt down before me, confirming the news about Séan. Looking pensive, she started giving the reason why, but I stopped her. Knowing that Jana can twist things to suit the occasion, I had to hear this from Ivan. They looked at each other, curling their lips, and then nodded.

With a mournful tone, Ivan told his story. "Micky, words don't come easy for me. I realise you've been kept in the dark for some time, but events have happened that might upset you greatly. I don't have it in me to explain the whole incident again and I'm not going to. It's too hurtful for me." I could feel a pair of hands resting gently on my shoulders. Being the only other ghost in the apartment, these had to belong to Luisella. Ivan went on, "Séan has been in a terrible state in recent weeks. He can't live with himself." I wanted to say something but I didn't. "Not long ago, we lost two ghosts and Séan feels somehow responsible for their deaths. He reckons that if it wasn't for him, they'd both be alive today. In some way, I feel the same, but I can live with my mistake. The upshot, however, is that Séan is not himself. He's been going around talking to fresh air, stopping everywhere there's water and just staring.

We've had Lun following him everywhere he goes, and Séan knows it. And we've had assistance from other ghosts, just in case he tried something stupid.

"Anyhow, the day before last, he was in Achill, sitting on some rocks near the ocean. Lun and Moira were nearby, watching his every move. Séan, though, couldn't care less. He'd obviously made a decision of sorts because he got up, turned around, and flew to the top of Slievemore Mountain. Moira caught up with him, trying to cajole the poor man, while Lun followed closely. But, for Séan, he'd had enough. He threw himself off the edge, straight into the sea, and Moira went after him immediately. Séan hit the water at a tremendous rate and went down. Moira stopped herself. She knew he'd come back up for a while, and he did – drowning isn't that easy. She hovered above the water, and, likewise, so did Lun, but he was further back to get a better view. About fifteen seconds elapsed before Séan's head popped up, and, quick as a flash, Lun and Moira were on him. They had great difficulty trying to keep a firm grip, hanging onto his arms and legs. With Séan being on the heavy side for a ghost, tiredness was creeping into their own arms, but they managed to pull him to safety. He knew then that he'd never be able to kill himself – not while he was being watched – so he went with the two of them, crying his eyes out. He said that the only way he could forgive himself was to tell you, Micky, the truth. He realised, he said, that he had to unburden his soul. Under the circumstances, with you being as you are at the moment, we advised him against this, but Séan was having none of it. Either he told you everything or he'd go to Hell.

"Séan's outside, Micky. He needs to speak to you."

I was speechless. My mind was asking who they were that died. And I wondered why I hadn't been told anything about this earlier.

Jana started speaking, rather nervously. "Micky, I'm going to tell you what happened as explained to me, and then Séan can come in and say his piece. But for the sake of Karen and the baby, you have to stay inside her body, regardless of what's happened. You must promise me that." — At that moment, I was ready to crawl out, but I knew she was right. I gave her my promise, knowing I'd have to keep it.

Jana then went on to tell me about the loss of Affiong and Helga, and Séan's part in it all. I couldn't believe what I was hearing, yet I knew it was true. Ivan interrupted occasionally, explaining how both he and Lun felt somehow responsible, but I couldn't take it all in at the time. When Séan came in, looking as glum as can be, he shook my hand, and in the most downbeat voice for him, he told me the events as he remembered them. Jana and Betsy quietly cried, while Ivan stood, head bowed, yet in control.

A day has passed and I still can't believe that Affiong's dead. But as far as Helga is concerned, I just don't care. To the others, the loss of any ghost is a tragedy. And I feel the loss of Affiong, and remember the time when she wanted my body. She knew I was gay, and yet she still loved me. I think about her life in Nigeria and how she was treated; then her time as a ghost ... reborn happy and full of herself. I'll never forget the day she confided in me. She'd lost her boyfriend and everybody else, and she'd given up on men until the day she met Dorothy. Yes, she attacked me, but I understand why and what led her to that way of life. I'll miss her all the same and wish she was here. We never did find out what happens in the minds of Mindbenders, and, with Affiong now gone, I wonder if we'll ever get an answer to our question. As far as Helga is concerned, I've no sympathy whatsoever.

When Don takes me and Karen in his arms, we push our baby into his midriff, letting him feel our roundness. We lay back while his goatee beard tickles our erect wet nipples. He's so funny, and I'm so happy despite the bad news. We haven't made love in the natural sense of the word, but we've toyed with each other's bodies, reaching peaks of ecstasy that others can only dream about. Karen and I were knackered, but a five-knuckle-shuffle put a smile on Don's face.

I feel so content, my head resting in the crook of his arm, as Karen closes our eyes. Don whispers the words we want to hear ... his love; his promise to watch over us and our baby; his promise to phone more often; and the faintest hint of the word 'marriage'. This seems to do the trick as Karen smiles herself to sleep, while my mind keeps ticking over.

Marriage? I'd never thought it possible. And if so, when? There's no way that Karen will let us walk down the aisle in our condition. And I can't see Don giving up his position, just to prove his love for Karen ... nice as he is. Not unless something's in the offing – job wise that is, and there's no way that I'll be able to sleep a wink until I work this out.

And I don't, as my mind goes round in circles, wondering whether I should stay with Karen for a good deal longer, just to satisfy my cravings for his body. This could be the best thing to happen to me, and the more I think, the more I get ideas. I concentrate on Karen's brain, urging her to marry him soon. I force a mental picture of a baby in Karen's arms with Don alongside – a picture of happiness. Suddenly, my mind goes blank.

And then it happens … and it's weird: *'Don is pushing a buggy through Hyde Park, arm in arm with a devoted Karen, and they're both smiling at their pride and joy … a tiny child with wrinkles all over its body and tufts of hair growing on its face. They seem deliriously happy and proud to show off their three year old son. The passers-by stop to touch the wrinkles and playfully stroke his head. Karen loves the attention, her belly sticking out with baby number two, and … .'* – my dream ends.

While we're spreading marmalade on our toast, Karen twists my mouth, saying, *"I had a dream last night and it was horrible."*

"So what," replies Don. *"You're always having dreams."*

"Shut up and listen," we tell him. He does and we describe the same dream that I'd had. I'm confused. Either I had the dream, or we both did, but I don't remember forcing this dream on her brain unless I did so by accident. I *was* concentrating my thoughts for a while, and, perhaps they did cross over, but I'd never deliberately put something like this in her head. We carry on talking, bringing up his promises for our future. And then my mouth utters the words I don't want to hear. *"Don, I love you so much and do want us to marry, but not until you're back here for good."*

"Why not, Kas? We can work it out. I know we can."

"I don't want a long distance marriage. They don't last and you know it. If you're happy to support us financially, that's fine, but I'm quite content to have this baby and hire a nanny or an au-pair. And when our baby's older, I'll find a nursery somewhere." Why's she doing this to me? She's joking – she's got to be.

"Please, Karen?" The pain in Don's eyes is obvious and I feel for him. I know exactly what he's going through as we give him a that's-the-situ'-now-take-it-or-leave-it look. *"Okay, then. I'm not supposed to say dick to anyone, Karen … not even you, because if the word gets out and they find out it's from this side of the pond, it could be me who gets the sack."*

We stare in expectation. *"Well, tell me,"* we demand.

"Will you promise not to say ... .?"

"Don! Don't insult my intelligence. If you can't trust me – the woman you love, to keep my mouth shut, then you'd better find somebody else."

You know, I get the distinct impression that women can, sometimes, be so cruel.

"I'm sorry, Kas, and I would have told you, but nothing definite has gone through, and I couldn't talk over the phone or send you an email in case they're checking on us."

"Will you get to the bloody point, Don? Who are they, and why would they be checking on the two of us?"

"I don't mean us two, Karen. I'm talking about the staff. The company have had some hotshot New York solicitor in, representing a client from London. There's talk of a take-over, but I don't know whether it's our company that's doing the buying or the other way 'round. If it's us, and the deal goes through, there's a possibility of me coming back to London to set up here."

"Why didn't you say so, earlier?"

"How could I? This deal might collapse, or it could be the other firm that buys out ours, and if that happens then half of us might lose our jobs. It all depends on what the new firm wants. Karen, I didn't want to disappoint you, and, besides, how could I promise you something that might go tits up?"

"Okay. I get the picture. So, when are you likely to hear?"

"Next week or the week after ... I'm not sure. Our attorney is working round the clock."

"Oh, Don. Wouldn't it be nice to hold each other every day and watch our little baby grow up into a beautiful girl or boy?" It sounds like heaven to me, even though I helped to say it. Christ, I need a pee. Doesn't she feel the pressure? It's like carrying a baby elephant, never mind a girl or boy.

Once again on good terms, we talk among ourselves about decorating the spare room for the baby. Don reckons blue, but Karen won't hear of it, insisting on a neutral colour. Of course, she gets her way. We tell him that it's our flat, not his, and, until he comes up with a definite answer about our future, he can help but can't decide. It's not hard to see who the boss is in this relationship. At long last, using the table to help, we push ourselves up and go to the loo. After draining our bladder, I'm so relieved and want to show it, but Karen keeps her mouth shut.

When he's ready, Don heads off to one of the DIY shops under strict instructions from the pair of us. Karen takes me back to the lounge where we sit, legs akimbo, on the seat by the phone. After a brief glimpse through one of the baby books, Karen has me ringing up for a new cot and bedclothes. After another trip to the loo, we get dressed for going out. We're about to leave when the phone rings.

"Oh, hi Mum. You just caught me."

"Hello love, and how's our little bundle of joy?" – Bundle of joy! For god's sake, our baby's not born yet.

"Coming along fine, Mum. Can I phone you when I get back? I'm off to see the midwife."

"Actually, Karen, I only rang to let you know that I'll be there this afternoon."

"Okay, Mum. I'll be home about two."

"Okay, pet. I'll see you later. By-ee!"

"Bye, Mum."

Karen is more than happy to tell her mother everything about our baby, and her mum loves every second. My tongue is in torment as Karen goes on non-stop, telling her that the baby is in the correct position and hasn't dropped down as yet; that the toenails are fully grown; that our baby has a firm grip; and the news that I'm happy to tell you … we have to prepare a hospital bag.

This, in turn, leads to Mum telling us a story about the time of her own pregnancy with Karen. I'm so fed up and try switching off, but let me tell you … it's very difficult. Fortunately, the topic of food comes up and her mum decides to do the dinner. Except for the chop-chop-chop of the vegetables being sliced and a quiet humming from Mum, my ears are given a rest. Don has only been seen twice since he started painting our soon-to-be nursery, and these were, as he put it, during his tea-breaks. Over a light dinner, Karen agrees to her mother staying over during the final week of pregnancy. This pleases her mum, of course, but not me. If there were such a thing as ear-plugs for ghosts, then I'd make Jana bring me a pair. The evening comes to a close when Don takes Karen's mum home in a taxi. He's going for a pint or three with his family and friends, so I don't think I'll be getting much in the way of fulfilment tonight.

Quite honestly, though, I don't think I could handle him – not the way I'm feeling.

Later on, we get a call from Don. He's decided to stay at his brother's for the night, and, to my surprise, Karen seems happy for him to enjoy himself. She takes me to bed where, after a quick browse through another baby book, we go to sleep.

It's not long before I'm in the middle of another dream … .

'Women, everywhere, are giving birth to babies with alien features. Maternity wards all over the world are in a state of panic, all wondering what's gone wrong; asking questions as to whether there's something in the water or thinking of other possibilities. The powers that be are quarantining every mother and new born child while they make their inquiries; and Karen and I are devastated as we look at our strange little girl with her long pointy ears, small round mouth and two tiny slits where the nose should be. We reach out to pick her up and … .' And the dream ends.

The next morning, Karen has me on the phone again, telling Eleanor all about our latest trip into fantasyland. Eleanor eases our minds, explaining that lots of soon-to-be mothers experience weird thoughts and nightmares. What has *me* bugged is the thought that either I'm having these dreams and transferring them to Karen, or vice versa, and if it is the latter, then, what's happening to my brain? It's one thing to be able to hear someone, or try and force something into a person's mind, but to read theirs is something else altogether. My most immediate thought is one of Jana and my wish that she was here so I could tell her about this new event in my life. Or is what's going through my mind all just a pipe dream?

When Don shows up, we spend the day talking and bandying names around for the baby. Karen refuses to show him the list that we've compiled and he starts throwing out names at random, each one more stupid than the last. We give up eventually, deciding to eat and then relax in each other's arms. Don's leaving tomorrow and I so want to enjoy him while I have him near. Not so Karen, who won't even let me play with him when we go to bed. Other than a gentle cuddle and a goodnight kiss, that's it.

CHAPTER THIRTY-SEVEN

Since the day Don left, we've been kept busy with visits from Karen's fellow doctors – Eleanor pretty regularly, as well as some of her other friends, all offering help and advice. We've also had other visitors, and they're still here. Jana and Luisella arrived a week ago, and they were soon followed, to my ghostly surprise, by Anna.

As soon as my eyes fell on Jana, I brought up this dream business, but she seems to think that they are mine and that I'm passing them on in my sleep. When I stressed that I was awake with my eyes closed during the first one, she told me that I must have been asleep but didn't realise it at the time. I argued the fact, but Jana went on about how crazy my imagination can be – reminding me of the times when she caught me in deep thoughtful trances. I knew what she was getting at and perhaps it was me after all. Jana went on to explain how it's easier for a ghost to transfer thoughts to a strong willed person, like Karen, when she is asleep.

Sometimes, Luisella joined Jana in the bathroom, enjoying themselves watching me and Karen bathe. The pair of them would strip off and jump in the bath, pushing their hands and heads on our stomach so they could feel the baby's movements through me. And they wouldn't leave us alone in bed ... feeling our swollen boobs and running their hands up and down our legs, and they deliberately had sex right in front of our eyes. You can imagine what I felt like, but Karen didn't know nor care. What, for her, was a dreamlike open-eyed state of wonder, as she made me talk to myself about the future, was an eyeful for me ... watching two beautiful and very fit young females pushing their bodies on to orgasmic delight, time after time. These women showed no sense of fairness, and, when I got the chance, I told them so. It didn't make the slightest bit of difference because the following night they were at it again. When Anna turned up, though, everything changed. The pair of them behaved and slept in the lounge. At least Anna brought a modicum of decency to the place, albeit temporarily.

Other than that, our routine has been much the same – up in the morning; off to the toilet; a relaxing bath; off to the toilet; a cup of camomile tea and a rice cake; off to the toilet ... and so on. We should have had a tube inserted and piped it straight to the loo. But in the past few days I've also had to put up with the incessant yakety-yak from

Cynthia. I'd only thought of her as Mum until this morning when one of her friends phoned and we answered. She doesn't look like a Cynthia – more an Olive if you were to imagine people by a fruit or suchlike. I'd hate to think of Karen growing into a lady so plump, but, I suppose, we'll have to see what effect this baby has on her body.

And talking of plump … well that's me, and I'm fit to burst. Our baby has dropped and the pressure is more than I can take … and I think we've started our contractions. I can't be too sure, not having been here before, but that's what Cynthia is telling us as we explain what's going on inside our bodies. While we wait for a lift, Jana is panicking. Luisella is naturally excited, and Anna is Anna – cool as a cucumber. Mum is happily gathering Karen's bags and helping with our clothes. Minutes later, our taxi arrives and we're on our way.

Don't talk to me about labour pains. A few moments ago, our waters broke and I'm fed up to the back teeth as one contraction soon follows another. In fact, they're so close together that we've been positioned on this bed in such an open-to-the-world fashion that I feel violated. Karen has refused gas, or any other aid, to help with the birth, and I'm looking straight into the eyes of my fellow ghosts as they peer between my outstretched legs. I can't put them down, either, because they are up in the air and held in stirrups. To tell the truth, Karen has my body at such an awkward angle that I'm pushing down while half-sitting up.

The urging noises from the midwife, two other nurses and Karen's mum, along with the cries from Jana, Anna and Luisella, all seem to help as Karen and I start taking deep breaths and pushing as hard as we can. We close our eyes, but I can't mistake the sound of Jana's voice encouraging me. "Come on, Micky … push, push, push … breathe, breathe, breathe … push, push … ." And then I only hear a confusion of voices as my concentration shuts them out. Now and again, our eyes open for a second or two, blurred with tears from the pain, and it seems like a punishment for something I might have done in my former life.

"Phh! Phh! Phh! Phh!" … Oh, shit! I feel as if I've been split in two, and … and. … *"Oh, fu … .! Don! You bastard! … Aaah!"* Karen yells. Believe me, if you're not a woman, then don't wish it on yourself. This child-bearing lark is not for the faint-hearted. The movement between

our legs is both strong and strange as I feel our baby slide slowly at first, and then pretty quickly, from our bodies. It's as if my bowels have opened as well as everything else, and when Luisella laughingly exclaims that we have pooed a little, I feel so embarrassed. Nobody says anything to Karen, as if it is expected ... but I feel dirty.

The cry from our baby can be heard almost immediately and this is followed by the happy voices around us. I'm still extremely sore and we're trying to get our breath back, but Karen doesn't give a fig. She has me both laughing and crying while the midwife tells us about our beautiful little baby boy. Anna is close by, whispering her congratulations in my ear and kissing our cheeks. She's soon joined by Jana and Luisella, who both have moistness in their eyes. Jana whispers words of her affection for me and my baby, and she cries because she always wanted what I now have. I don't know what to say, and, anyway, I can't because Karen has me looking, talking and laughing with Cynthia. Our eyes are on the baby while a nurse wipes him down, and then she covers him in a small sheet. Jana and Luisella stay nearby, and I feel the pressure and excitement from their fingers as the baby is passed to me and Karen for the first time. Straight away, it homes in on the nipple of my left breast.

My eyes never stray from the sight of our little boy as he sucks the living daylights from my body. And then my tongue moves, as Karen has me saying, *"My beautiful Johnny. Oh, Johnny ... I love you to bits."* And, while our lips kiss the damp fair hair on the baby's head, I wonder why – why Johnny of all names. Karen hasn't mentioned the name once; not in conversation with her mum, her friends, and, more importantly, not even with Don. Where did it come from, or will she change her mind? Somehow, I think Johnny will remain Johnny whatever Don thinks.

It's not long before we're moved and settled into another bed. Johnny is close by, fast asleep. It's good news week as far as we're all concerned. Our baby is healthy; Karen and I will be okay again soon – we didn't need stitches; and, best of all, if nothing untoward happens ... we'll be going home in three or four days. My three friends are still here watching everything that's going on, including a few more births. They are back and forward, from baby to baby, and they can't stop talking. Every so often, Jana pushes her hands to her head, always smiling and obviously pleased, and then she disappears for a while. Karen's mum has stayed behind, cuddling a new toy dog while sitting, smiling, and chatting away to her unaware grandson. Before she leaves, we pass her Don's phone number and a loving message.

Daytime turns into evening and more visitors arrive. Eleanor and some of her other friends pop in with cards and kisses, all peeking at Johnny and savouring the moment when he takes to my boobs again. For a bit of a laugh, Luisella pulls up her top and offers one of hers ... and laugh we do – the four of us. Anna is as happy and playful as the other two. It's as if she's been waiting for something really exciting to happen to one of her students. When night draws in, Jana decides to keep me company and I'm grateful for someone to speak to. Anna leaves with Luisella, heading back to our apartment for a rest. It's only when they've gone and everything is quiet that Jana confides in me.

"Micky, I've changed." She raises a hand to her head, giving it a tap. "Up here," she says.

"How do you mean?" I ask.

"I keep getting the urge to climb into someone's head. I want to get inside your Karen and give her piece of my mind, but you're already in her so I can't."

"I'll get out if you like. The baby's born, so what's the problem?"

"You can't, Micky. You know the deal and Anna would go bloody mad."

"I'm entitled to a break, Jana. After all I've been through, don't you think I deserve one?"

"I do, Micky, but if you hang in there, just think of all the benefits you might get."

"Like what, a sense of smell? I like the idea and in some ways it's appealing, but, Jana, you said yourself that it might not work."

"It's a chance you take, Micky, so don't blow it now. You've been through the worst and the best, depending on which way you look at it. I wish I'd been inside her getting all those lovely feelings from Don." Her mention of Don brings me back to reality and I know what I want to do.

"I'm going to stay, but only so long as Don and Karen don't break up."

"A wise decision if I say so myself. I'll be back soon, Micky. I have to go experimenting."

"What are you on about ... experimenting?"

"I've been in and out of people all afternoon, trying to persuade them to do things they shouldn't."

"Has it worked?"

"No."

"Perhaps you should be encouraging them to do what's best."

"I'll give it a go. See you soon." Jana slopes off, looking for a likely target. On her return, she has news of a minor success, but I don't know why she's so fussed. After all, it's nothing new for her. The day she told Patricia about her child being unwell is firmly rooted in my mind. Jana helps me pass the time away, gossiping about some of the ghosts and what they might have to say about me and my child-bearing experience. So's not to leave us alone, Jana sleeps upside down in our bed, giving me an occasional sighting of her feet, until we, too, nod off.

Babies have no sense of timing and we're no sooner in a deep sleep than we're wide awake again and nursing, so they call it. Karen dotes on our baby, whispering tender loving words in his ear. I can understand the necessity to breast feed while our baby is newborn, but I hope we have an early move to the bottle. When Johnny has had enough of our milk and is once again sleeping, we place him back in his hospital cot. Suddenly, the quietest buzz can be heard from close by. Karen has me up again and is reaching out for her mobile. For the next fifteen minutes, Karen, me, and Don go on about the baby and who he looks like. Karen gives him the 'Johnny' news and I'm pleased that he accepts it immediately. Their relationship is looking warmer with every word we speak. He plans to pay a flying visit to see us and his newborn son. I look forward to the day.

In all the time we've been talking, Jana hasn't flinched, and I had the feeling that she must be shattered. But as soon as our phone call is over, she is squirming around the bed and talking to me, face to face. While Karen has me smiling at her conversation with Don, Jana is begging me to give her his reaction. At news of his forthcoming visit, Jana throws herself from the bed and starts whooping it up in anticipation. Finally, she comes down to earth and back to bed.

The following couple of days brought more visits, congratulatory messages, and news of presents arriving at our apartment. We've been up and about, gradually getting into a familiar routine regarding changing Johnny, bathing him, and how often he feeds. Anna and Luisella have popped in and out, sometimes taking Jana with them when they leave. On one of her visits, Anna – with Jana's consent, let's me know what's going on inside the latter's head. Anna has watched her very closely, asking questions and testing her out on individuals, and the upshot of it all is that Jana has acquired an unstable mind. I'm not happy.

Jana is with me now, while Karen and I sit reading the newspaper. While Karen's mind is taken up, Jana probes mine. Jana can't understand why she's like she is, so she asks me to recall the exact day that Karen got pregnant. What does she think I am … a woman? And what's that got to do with her brain? To appease her, I start counting back the nine months, telling her about the different events and when they happened – the visits from Séan and herself, and, of course, my beloved Don. When Jana and I link the times of Don's stays in London with the times that she was here, she crouches in front of us, letting me see that the penny has dropped.

"It was our foursomes," she suggests.

"I don't remember." I do. Of course, I do. How could I ever forget? But I'm not prepared to admit it.

"It was you, me, and our two living lovebirds – all together, back in June. Micky, I'm positive."

"What are you trying to tell me?" I think I know what's coming, but I need to hear this.

"Don got Karen pregnant while we were all having sex together, and, somehow, my being in him at the time has caused me to go a bit batty. No, Micky, that can't be right. I believe we – me and Don I mean – caused this pregnancy, but the child being born as a result of this has caused my problem. Perhaps there's something wrong with Johnny."

"I had a funny feeling you'd say something like this. So, what can we do?"

"Nothing, Micky. It might be something to do with Don – his genes and all that."

"But, Jana, they weren't and aren't your genes."

"I agree, but stranger things have happened. Tell me, do you feel any different?"

"Not really. A bit lighter, of course, and my nipples are sore, but other than that, no. You're getting me worried, though. Not just for me, but also for you. I hope you sort yourself out." Jana's face, looking up at me from between the paper and Karen, asks all it has to without speaking. "It's me who's suffered, Jana. I'm the one who's gone through this nightmare and carried the baby full term, but you're the one that's been affected."

"It's not your fault, Micky. I'm still strong, and it's not as though I've lost my abilities."

Eventually, we bed down for another restless night. I think for quite a while about Jana and her complications. I think about Karen and Johnny, and Don and his body, and then my thoughts come back to me and the present situation.

CHAPTER THIRTY-EIGHT

Time presses on. And I mean time.

Since the day we left hospital with Johnny close to our breast, we've been on the go from morning 'til night. Karen has this idea that our baby is better off in the nursery and he's been sleeping there from the first day we came home. My thoughts were to let him share our bedroom so he'll be close at hand, but, as Karen told Don and whoever else asked, Johnny will grow accustomed to his surroundings and won't be so attached to us. Of course, she's quite right. After all, we have our work to go to, so, after Cynthia's stint at helping out, we've acquired the aid of an au pair for two years.

Don, when he first came, was as happy as Larry to meet his son. He had never looked the fatherly type, but he has gentle hands and a soft mind. Maybe this is why Jana is still being tormented. And time, they say, waits for no man, and, let me tell you, no woman or ghost, either. According to Anna, I've only two days left before I'm freed from my female environment, and it can't come soon enough. You might well be wondering why I haven't said anything before now, but what was there to tell? Yes, I could have given you a daily account of the past two and a bit years, but do you really want to hear my tales of getting out of bed and going to the loo six or seven times a day. I wouldn't in your shoes. And as far as Karen's patients are concerned, it wouldn't be fair on her to divulge that information for ethical reasons. However, if Malcolm had paid a visit, then I'd feel obliged to say something, but he didn't. Apparently, he was passed fit and left to his own devices while we were on maternity leave. Oh, and talking of maternity, we've just been to Boots to pick up another pregnancy testing kit. If you think I'm waiting around this time, though, forget it.

Don hasn't kept his word, not that he officially proposed to Karen, but it came a shade close. He's still in New York with the same company, but it's now under a new name and new ownership. Karen's happy because he's definitely coming back to London in two months time, and, this time, for good. I've been hearing whispers – if that's what you'd call secretive calls to Eleanor – that Karen is going to make an honest man out of him when he returns.

Being with Karen has had other benefits. We holidayed with Eleanor in Majorca last summer, and we were joined by, of all ghosts, Séan. He's been back to see me a few times and we've had the craic. He still goes on about Affiong, but now he doesn't blame himself so much. As far as the holiday was concerned, it was so relaxing as we lazed in the sun, and the only time I worried was the night we drank too much Tequila. Eleanor was pissed out of her head while my fellow ghost was inside her body. He only went in for a joke, thinking he'd benefit from a drink or two, but he got more than he bargained for and had to crawl out. Karen wasn't as bad, being a little more reserved with the alcohol.

Regarding the dangers to my wellbeing, I had another near miss not long after Johnny's birth. Karen went for a check up to the dentist. The spoils of war, or something like that, the dentist called it. Having a baby can cause all sorts of problems with the system, so he said, and I feared the worst … gas or cocaine. I didn't want to take the chance and was prepared to jump for my life, but fortunately we required very little anaesthetic.

Johnny has developed his mother's features – no wrinkles or beard, and our little baby is growing into a handsome young boy. Our au pair reminds me of Joyce in some ways, being a bit flighty but, other than that, she's as good as gold; handling Johnny very well and teaching him to talk. She's not a bad looker, either, and our mate, Séan, has taken a shine to her. The last time he showed up was in the middle of the night while Don was screwing us silly. Talk about voyeurism – Séan couldn't resist passing on the benefits of his experience, urging Don on. You'd think he was watching a horse race. I gave him some stick after that. Perhaps I gave him too much stick, because I haven't seen him for the past seven months.

Jana's been around, of course, in between her jobs. She played with our bodies, turning us on every so often, and on a few occasions Don's been there. And did Jana take advantage of the situation? You bet she did.

Something she said had me thinking. For one reason or another, there aren't many ghosts coming through – as in coming back as I have. I guessed that with kids, these days, spending their time playing on computers instead of reading books, then thoughts of ghosts don't enter their heads. It's a bit of a worry, really. With less young men dreaming,

I might be the only gay ghost for some time yet.

And speaking of dreams ... they've started again. Perhaps Karen is pregnant because I remember the last time. I don't mean ordinary dreams – I've had several about Jana, and others of Pete and Malcolm. In dreams of Karen's, though – and I know they're hers – pictures of Don, Johnny and another baby keep popping into my head. How do I know, you might well ask? I've been wide awake with my eyes shut while concentrating on hers. I think I'm changing, and the moment I see Jana, I'm going to tell her what's going on. She had me wrong before, with her thoughts that Karen's dreams were really mine. I can't prove this, of course, unless the pregnancy test proves positive.

At this particular moment, we're off to bed after tucking in our smiling Johnny. We admire ourselves in the mirror and I can't help thinking how lovely I am – and Karen, of course. Our face is so pretty, and strong looking too. It's as if our pregnancy has done even more for our features. The reflection of our boobs shows them to be in perfect shape and it's not surprising. We're still doing the keep-fit and Karen has had me toning up my muscles every morning. There's a lot to be said for spending time inside a clever and beautiful woman. And, of course, we have a man who knows how to treat us whenever he comes to stay. I do envy Karen, having Don to hold and love. I'm going to miss him.

We pull on our nightie and slide in between the sheets. Karen pushes my hand out to turn on the bedside radio, picks up a novel, and we relax listening to the voice of Mick Hynds singing his song ... *Dealers And Pimps*. I like it.

I can't believe that my time is nearly up. When I awoke this morning, Karen had me in the bathroom giving Johnny a shower. It was so different to hear him laugh as the water cascaded down his body. Usually it was a small bath, but he'd been watching the pair of us while we had our shower, and he kept on and on in his loveable little voice, wanting to be lifted in for a taste of the same. You should have seen him trying to cock his little leg over the side of the bath, and, eventually, Karen helped him. We had great fun watching as he slithered all over the place, sometimes standing and other times sitting and pushing himself between our legs.

We spent our usual day at the office, leaving early to do some shopping, and we then came home to a call from Don and the arrival of Jana. When Karen and I had finished our intimate conversation with her hoped for husband to be, Jana brought me up to date with the news. As the evening wore on, Jana was counting down the hours. She amused me by telling tales about her recent travels and the time she spent inside other people.

Talk turns to ourselves and how we feel. "Jana, are you still having these weird mind-hopping experiences?" I ask, still concerned about her state of mind.

"I am, Micky, and the urges to dive into strangers are getting stronger all the time."

"You should see a psychiatrist. In fact, we should find a way to ask Karen."

"Don't *you* start. I've been taking so much lip from Lucia and the rest that it's driving me mad. In fact, Micky, this is the closest thing to crazy I have ever been, and it's all because they won't leave me alone."

"I'm deadly serious, Jana. I'm in the perfect position to ask Karen about you. I'll wait until she's ready to drop off and then try. You never know, she might give some sort of answer. Karen often talks to herself when she has something to worry about."

"Leave it alone, Micky. I'm warning you. Anna says that I'm developing new abilities. So tell me, do you feel any different?"

"I've been having those stupid dreams again. They're not so stupid now, though."

"Have you been dreaming about me?"

"Of course, I have," I reply, "and also about Karen and a new baby."

"Is she pregnant?"

"Maybe. We bought a kit but we haven't done the test. But, Jana, these dreams – they weren't mine. I've been reading Karen's mind."

"That's not possible, Micky. Not unless … ." Jana stops mid-sentence.

"Unless what?" I ask.

"Wait a sec'. Listen, will you do me that favour, after all? Try and ask Karen about me. Influence her brain and suggest something … as if I'm one of her patients."

"I'll try." Shortly after, Karen starts nodding off, my eyes closing with hers, and I let my thought-waves sink into her brain. I give her every little tit-bit I know about Jana and what's bothering her, but nothing comes back. Jana tells me to think harder, forcing the information into Karen's mind ... and I do. It doesn't work.

It's early morning and I'm woken by the touch of Jana's fingers between our legs. I'm soon turned on, and Karen, who's still in a light state of sleep, pushes our hands down to join Jana's. It's not long before I'm dreaming of Don between my legs as Jana slides on top of us, and all the time our hands busy themselves. My eyes open as the throes of orgasm and the heat grip the three of us. Any thoughts of a nice long lie in vanish when Karen takes me to the loo.

"Thanks, Micky. You don't know how much it means to have loved you ... woman to woman." Jana has her head around the door frame, watching us take a leak.

"I enjoyed it too," I reply, "but I'll never take a chance like this again."

"Don't be like that. We've had a great time."

"You did, but it hasn't been straightforward for me. By the way, I've just had two more dreams and they definitely weren't mine."

"Maybe Johnny's birth has done something to both of us. Sometimes, Micky, I get the feeling his eyes keep watching me, everywhere I go."

"You can't be sure, can you?"

"No, but looking back, I might have been wrong about the other dreams you had, and you *might* have read something from Karen. We shouldn't worry too much about it. This might be simply because you're inside a long term host and you feel all of her sensations. I can't remember all the dreams I had inside Dominique, but I wasn't thinking of dreams at the time. I was enjoying her body, just as you've been enjoying Karen's."

We finish in the bathroom and slope off to the kitchen to put the kettle on. After a mug of coffee, we get ready for work.

"Shit! I forgot about her job," cries Jana. "What time are you back?" she asks.

"Five-thirty or six. It depends how much we have to do and whether we go shopping."

"Damn it! In that case, where are your clothes?"

"In the wardrobe … down the bottom, I think." Jana turns and goes in search of my long forgotten ghost-wear.

Another day at the office is over and we're on our way down Oxford Street, following our noses until we take a left into Debenhams. As we check out a new range of perfumes, Jana says, "Micky, it's time." I knew it was coming, but I didn't realise that we ghosts have some sort of in-built clock.

I hesitate about coming out, and ask Jana, "Why can't I wait until we're home?"

"Don't be stupid, Micky. If she's pregnant, then every minute you stay inside might cause you to stay even longer."

"Another hour or so won't make any difference."

"It could if Anna finds out."

"I'll take that chance. If you think that I'm going to walk out of Karen, stark naked, in front of all these shoppers, then you must be off your trolley."

"They can't see you."

"I don't care. I'm waiting." We carry on shopping for about half-an-hour, and then jump on the Tube. It doesn't take us long to reach the apartment, and, once inside, Jana's at me again. At the first opportunity, and under very strict orders from Jana, I push myself free – moving backwards very slowly. Karen still yells and shakes for quite a while. Our au pair comes running, asking what she can do to help, and, although still naked and worried, I watch as my Karen slowly comes back to herself. She washes her hands and throws water over her face, dries herself off and then leaves us behind and alone.

"Put them on, Micky … quickly."

I know something's wrong. My body still has Karen's shape. I still have her boobs; her tummy; her whole being … just as if I'd never left her. "What's happened to me?" I ask, with Karen's sexy voice.

"It takes a little time. Not very long, but you have to help yourself. Dress in your clothes and that will help. I reach across, grab them, and start pulling them on. Once dressed, we enter the bedroom and I see Karen's face in the mirror. I'm still her, despite my clothes and boots.

"Stop fretting and get a hold of yourself. This happens to all ghosts when they've been in long term. You're no different from anyone else."

"I am. I'm a bloody woman and I have this weird feeling in my head."

"So have I, Micky, ever since you left her body."

"I knew something was wrong." I move away from the mirror, go to the window and stare outside. I have funny feelings while my body starts changing. I'm worried. What if something goes wrong? I turn around and pace across the room. I wish the place was larger.

"For god's sake, Micky, walk like a man. Put the effort in or you'll be telling every ghost in the world about yourself and your former life."

"What are you on about, Jana?"

"You don't want to live your ghost life mincing about everywhere you go. Get used to your old walk as fast as you can. The sooner you do, the sooner your bum will take a man's shape and your legs will lose that feminine structure."

"I can't. There's no room in here."

"Very well, then." Jana moves to the wall, passes through, and calls me. "Micky, come outside. Let's try the pavement." And I follow her. I try flying, but, instead, I drop like a stone. Jana grabs my hand and eases me to the ground.

"My god! What happened? I can't fly anymore."

"No, Micky, you can't. You have to learn to walk first and then lie in clover or shamrock. You know the score. For now, though, keep walking. An hour's practise, going up and down the street, brings my body back to normal. I can feel my sexual organs develop and grow, my chest falling back into place, and, all in all, I feel like a new man. "You look terrific, Micky … the man I've always dreamt about."

"Give it up, Jana, you had me this morning." My voice is now back to its usual manly tone, as hand in hand, we float upwards and back into Karen's bedroom. I move to the door and, casual as you like, walk into the lounge as if I belong here. Karen is sitting with a jug and spoon, stirring some concoction for Johnny to drink. Jana follows closely and joins me on the couch, passing comments on how sweet and intelligent our Johnny seems to be. I watch his face as he tries feeding himself a small plate of spaghetti hoops. Acting the goat, I raise my thumb to him, saying, "Right on, Johnny … nice food?"

I nearly fall through the floor when Johnny smiles, looks me straight in the eye, points his spoon, and mumbles, *"Mummy ... Micky."* Jana grabs my elbow, pulls me up, and pushes me into the bedroom.

"Micky! He's a medium. Our little Johnny is a medium. We've produced a medium."

"You mean ... I have." I stare, surprise in my voice.

"Okay then, you have, but I helped. Micky, I want to bend minds. I have to. Jesus, Micky, I'm a fu ... fu ... a bloody Mindbender."

"And I think I'm a Ghost Of Dreams."

"You're not?"

"I am, honest. I've got one popping into my head this instant."

"Oh, my god!" Jana grabs a pen and a piece of paper and starts writing down everything I say. I tell her about a lost dog that's being chased by a cat, and a small boy on a tricycle following the cat ... and, soon after, the dream ends. "Micky, it wasn't a dream about ghosts. You'll have to learn to differentiate between them."

"How am I supposed to know?"

"Try switching your brain off. Concentrate on anything else but dreams. We're not prepared for reading them. Okay, I'm a fast writer but not that fast, and you don't know what your brain is looking for."

"I'll try, Jana ... . I'll try."

We stay where we are until late at night. Jana has been out through the bedroom wall, making noises to attract attention. When the first ghost arrives – someone called Daisy, Jana tells her the story and then urges her to pass the message on. I can't resist having another peek at Johnny, though, and wait until he's in bed. He looks so sweet, lying there with his little eyes closed and a cherubic smile on his happy face. Bending close, I kiss his forehead, and, knowing I won't see him or Karen for some time, I whisper, "Bye-bye, Johnny. Remember me to your mummy."

Once back in Karen's room, I sit down with Jana. We decide that it's better for them both that we keep our distance for a while. It's not that we don't want to see them, but we don't want any conclusions drawn by Karen should Johnny start acting strangely. He might talk to me again, and Karen might end up treating him, or, being the psychiatrist she is, having herself looked at. We can't risk it, for the sake of the child and his mother.

When Karen comes to bed, she treats us to more music from the radio, and Mick Hynds is on again, this time singing … *I miss you*, and as his voice is heard over the airwaves, Jana turns to me, saying, "I missed you, Micky, the real you, and I'll be with you forever." – I'm not so sure about that.

A few days later, we arrive back in Pribylina. Everyone greets us, congratulating me on my achievements in giving birth to a baby boy and on becoming a Dreamer. Jana, too, is given a huge reception. It all feels so wonderful.

Night falls, and I make my way to my room – still the same one, I'll have you know. I'm not there long before Jana joins me, standing just inside the door with a shocked yet pleasant expression on her face.

"Micky, you're not going to believe this, but you've got a visitor."

"So what, everyone wants to see us. But what's wrong with you? You look kind of weird."

"You'll see, Micky. I'll bring her in."

And I can't believe what I'm seeing. Jana has come back in holding the hand of a lady, in her mid-forties, with honey brown skin, and black hair which has the cutest curls of white to the side. Even the slight plumpness to her face suits her perfectly.

All dressed up in colourful Nigerian finery, Affiong says, "Hello, Micky, long time no see."

I rush towards her, reaching out and taking her hands. We hold each other close and I cry with happiness. It takes a while before words escape my lips. "But how? It's impossible. No. No, it can't be. You're here, but how come, and why the change?"

"Micky, slow down and let's sit. I've such a lot to tell you." Jana takes the seat by the desk, flipping the pages in the bedroom book, while Affiong explains herself. "The thing is, Micky, that when I was alive I had many dreams, and, fortunately for me, I saw myself as a ghost on more than one occasion. Of course, while Helga was drowning me, my only thoughts were that I was dying. Try as I might, I couldn't stop her. I knew it was the end for me and your face was the last one I recalled. I had so much to tell you, Micky. You were on my mind all the time. If it wasn't for you, then Helga wouldn't have been doing what she did."

"You were angry with me, then?"

"No! Of course not. How could anyone be angry with you? Anyway, the top and bottom of it is that instead of coming back as a snail, or some other such thing, I returned once more as a ghost in Nigeria. I came back as I saw myself in another of my dreams. I'm not the first ghost that this has happened to and I won't be the last. For all we know, Helga might be here, perhaps as a very young girl, but, if so, I think we'd have heard by now."

"Oh, Affiong. It's magic. I'm so happy for you ... for all of us, but what about Séan? He'll have to be told. You don't know how much he's been suffering. He blames himself for your death."

"Micky, you do go on. Séan knows. He's known for some months now."

"He what? Then why didn't he come and tell me?"

"I wouldn't let him. I felt it only right to see you myself, but I didn't want you getting too excited while you were inside Karen. Anyway, I've spent most of the time in Africa, going round the country with my fellow Mindbenders."

"What do you mean?"

"I've come back as a Mindbender. Straight up! I didn't have to do any training or anything. My ghosting abilities had never left me. From the moment I died, I was a ghost ... walking about in the centre of Lagos. I was met by a former acquaintance and she took me to our old Nigerian ghost village. It was unbelievable, Micky. As for the mindbending, I've regained this ability for saving Séan's life." I'm dumbfounded and I wrap my arms around her.

Shortly after, Séan walks in and takes one long look at me. "Well, Mick, is that yourself? I tell ya now, you're not half as pretty as the last time I saw ya. And there was me thinkin' of gettin' the leg over." We carry on joking, Séan full of the joys of spring once again, but it gets to a point where we can't keep him quiet. Eventually, we all go downstairs to rejoin the other ghosts.

Well, here I am, lying in my old bed, thinking about what I'll be up to in a few weeks time. Sunita, the first Dreamer I'd met, has been in to see me and explained how we can switch our thoughts to other matters for a few hours at a time. I'm so grateful, because other than when I'm sleeping, my head has been full of dreams. I haven't been able to differentiate a ghost dream from any other and my brain needs a rest. I've been advised to take a holiday to a far off country where I don't understand the language. I see that they've taken my advice. And true to her word, Jana has stayed close by, playing with my little stiffy until she's satisfied.

Thankfully, I'm on my own at present, happily smiling about Affiong and Séan. What a wonderful day this has been? I'm so happy for them, for us, for everyone. It makes being a ghost a delight. And while I reflect on the past, I remember how I laughed the day I died. I remember, all too well, my body on that operating table … and I remember Evelyn as if it was only yesterday. I wonder what he is at this very minute. Does he come back every time as an egg, or is he a puff adder or something like that?

As I close my eyes, for what I hope will be a peaceful and restful night, I can only wish you all … sweet dreams.